The Wind of Change

The Wind of Change is the Wind of Chance

EUDORA ALETTA

Suite 300 - 990 Fort St
Victoria, BC, Canada, V8V 3K2
www.friesenpress.com

Copyright © 2015 by Eudora Aletta
First Edition — 2015

Some scriptures from the Holy Bible, and quotes from world leaders are used. Words in this book can be used for references and self development. If desired, please contact the publisher or the author of this book.

All rights reserved.

No part of this publication may be reproduced in any form, or by any means, electronic or mechanical, including photocopying, recording, or any information browsing, storage, or retrieval system, without permission in writing from the publisher.

ISBN
978-1-4602-6583-3 (Hardcover)
978-1-4602-6584-0 (Paperback)
978-1-4602-6585-7 (eBook)

1. Fiction, Romance, Historical, 20th Century

Distributed to the trade by The Ingram Book Company

"...an intense story of love and friendship..."

—ROBERT QUEHL

"You deserve respect, dignity and love; young or old. With love, you can overcome the wind. Let us work and pray together that there is true freedom of respect and caring, and that the wind of change can sweep away the need for a life of jail." The Wind of Change recounts the fascinating journey of Zola, a beautiful young black woman, who is destined to become the queen of Pan-Africa. It is an intense story of love and friendship as told by a young Frenchman, Jacque François, who adores Zola above all else. The story is unique in its educational value, beautifully outlining the historical trials and victories of Africans worldwide, and speaking to the exciting future of a free and prosperous United States of Africa.

—ROBERT QUEHL

"Eudora Aletta's novel is breathtakingly intricate and critically creative. Through the story of Zola, Aletta places us at the crossroads of history, where we must confront the legacy of colonialism in the 'here and now' from the 'here and there'. No place on the map is exempt from this anti-colonial project that has important implications for both pan African unity and a relentless scrutiny of the West. Zola's story is not just an urgent plea for a return to humanity, but a different telling of what we MUST refuse about the future. The Wind of Change reminds us that a critical imagination is key to mobilizing against the vulnerabilities that proliferate within and condition the historical present!"

—DR. AMAR WAHAB, PHD
York University

Acknowledgements

I thank God for giving me the knowledge and ability to accomplish this task, The Wind of Change is dedicated to the father of democracy, Nelson Madiba Mandela (July 18, 1918 - December 5, 2014). 27 years, you did it. You proved to us that it is all worth it. Now you are the father of democracy. The world will never, never forget your worth.

Sweet Madiba, we love and we'll miss you; thank you.

No apartheid; we are moving forward. 'No segregation' was your watch word. You led a war without a sword, you survived the prison conditions.

You led South Africa to freedom; you will always be Africa's number one son. And you will always be an inspiration for me, as an author and as a human.

As well, I dedicate this to all the world leaders who died fighting for equality and freedom, those who are still pressing on to end the bloodshed in Africa, and other parts of the world, and the relief workers who go beyond fighting to put smiles on faces amidst bloodshed. Our heroes.

I also give loving thanks to my mother and god-mothers, my late father who last word to me was to be a part of change, not a part of chance, my beautiful children, family members, Logos Christian Family Church, Mount Zion International Church, East Mississauga Community Health Centre, and friends for their support. And a special thanks to Mrs. Elaine Quon for the endless love she gave to me. And, my editors, Robert Quehl thank you for being patient with me, and Winnie Czulinski, you are a darling, thank you.

Chapter One

Zola was not the first woman I ever loved. The first one liked to speak in images and riddles.

Ms. Yan Whun, says that love is like a plant that needs constant attention to bring forth its fresh green leaves. Without water and sunshine, it will wither, and soon perish.

Ms. Yan had a gorgeous face with long black hair always in a single braid touching her waist. She had beautiful dark eyes and her skin was whiter than most Chinese people. When we asked her why she was different from the rest of the Chinese people, she would smile and tell us to look around the classroom. We were all Canadian, but we were different in colour. "We are still people, aren't we?" she would say.

We kept quiet after her response, but we asked the same question as often as possible. She taught us to compare a healthy and fruitful relationship to an oak tree; because its stem is deep under the ground. If you are not around to nurture it, based on its solid roots it will keep flourishing like the tree planted by streams of water. Its branches might wither and shrivel a little, but it will not falter or die.

"Do not neglect it," Ms. Yan said. "Someone might cut it down." She was so small, she seemed somehow accessible to me. I often prayed that when I grew older, she would be my wife. My feelings for her got deeper and deeper.

On the first day of school, I met her going into the red-brick building. Her arms were full of books and papers, and things piled up in an uncovered box. She dropped a pen but didn't notice. I picked it up and followed her.

"Hello, miss," I said, thinking she was a student, because she looked so preposterously young.

"You dropped your pen."

"Thank you! You are very polite. What is your name?" she asked me.

"I am Jacque François; could you please help me find my class room?"

"Sure, François. You don't mind if I call you François, right? I love your name."

"And I think that you are very pretty, too," I dared to say.

"Let… me…see this, oh! You are with me," she said, and together we stepped into the class.

But everyone turned to us and I heard one or two of them snicker that I was the new teacher's pet.

And then I met Zola Frances. I still remember what was said.

"My name is Jacque, Jacque François."

She answered instantly, "Oh of course, nice to meet you Jacque, I like François better."

"Oh by all means, please do call me François," I responded joyfully."

I am Zola Elizabeth-Ngonloma, but you can call me whatever you like."

"That's many names for one person," I told her.

How can I describe her? There weren't enough words, or the right words, to tell people who she was and how much I loved her. She was my queen before she became the people's queen. "Nobody is born a noble, but nobility is earned," is a saying I like. That's what she did for herself, and if I learned anything from her, I learned this much.

I prayed that all her fathers, as she called them, would continue to stand by their words and support her in her "No more war, end the bloodshed. You too can make a difference." mission. I dared to think she needed me, but I also knew she was not going to be alone. Always surrounded by good people as she was, I knew she was a strong woman, and I knew she would survive.

Zola, the most courageous and strongest girl I have ever met, could also be stubborn when she was right. "Stand up for your rights and let no man put you down!" she would often tell her friends. As for her beauty, part of it came from her deep interest in the people around her, just like an angel always fighting for the human race. Whenever she bowed her head and looked up, you could see the deep gold in her hazel-brown eyes – with a piercing effect, when she was concerned, or impassioned or totally lost.

Zola's family did not have much, but like a lot of poor folks, they learned to share the little they had. It took me a while to understand why sharing was the importance of life itself. Zola was taught to share even if there was not enough for her. On the other hand, I was taught to save for the future; there wasn't going to be anyone to help me if needed. Besides, I grew up as an only child; I didn't have to share my toys, or anything. At school, when I saw something with any of the kids in the class, I ran and took it from them by force. It was just hard for me to let go of my belongings.

The Book of Proverbs says, "Teach children the way in which you want them to go, so when they grow up, they will not depart from it." Now that I have kids of my own, I am teaching them the necessary things in life, especially their moral reasoning. What is the meaning of life if one lived like an island or like a lonely bird sitting upon the roof? It is unfortunate that things are the way they are between us. It don't have to be this way, but that's just the way it is between us. Even though my Aunt May did not see my girls afterwards to be a part of their lives, but my little girls would grow up just fine even though my heart is longing for her. With all that I have learned over the years, I can say that I am a good father.

Even as I lay here, eyes closed to this sterile room, my body wasted by cancer, and a soft shuffle of nurses' feet outside my door, I can see only one person. My Zola. She was not an easy person to love.

Meeting Zola changed everything I believed in. Because of her, I learned that giving to someone who is in need has to do with the heart. When you give from your heart, you feel happy about it. I have been going to church since I was a little boy, and whenever the pastor preached, he would end the message with "Give a helping hand, share with the needy and love the broken-hearted."

On the other hand, I learned a different mindset about giving. Aunt May told me that the needed will always be around, and if I did not save for the future, I would become a person in need myself. I never really understood that part of her. If I was to turn back time, I wish that I grew up with the habit of giving. Up to the present, my children have not been able to see Aunt May based on the decision she made not to see me or have anything to do with Zola.

I missed her, it is still my dying wish to see my aunty. I loved to hear her imitate people. Her friends often told her that she sounded more like a black woman who was telling her experience of racism back in the days when the black man was judged by the colour of his skin.

"I'll agree more if you tell me that I sound like Ms. Daisy, but I like myself, and Ms. Daisy didn't like herself."

She argued with her friends around the coffee table about judgment. "May the good Lord be the judge between us. This is not my home; I'm not going to study this word no more. Every treasure I've got. I'm saving it in heaven where there are no mice and rats."

"You are wrong, May," her friends told her.

Aunt May was my father's only sister; in fact, she was the only living relative I have left from both sides of the family. I knew nothing about my mother, and I had to practically force her to tell me more about my parents' death. "Your parents died in an accident, that's all you need to know," she would say. I later got to the bottom of it and learned everything I desired to know. I can't speak for her, but I know this much: she was angry at my parents, but again, she never told me her frustration, but I know that she loved me.

Aunt May had a soft heart and she could be very pleasant when she wanted to be. She could also pretend and do the opposite. I never knew when she was genuinely tired because of her hollow eyes that made her cheeks seem weak. She always looked like someone who was just ready to go to sleep.

Regarding Zola, there was a particular incident that left me with questions about her, and for this reason I stayed around to find out more about her. It was like embarking on an adventure.

Her lunch was stolen on several occasions and she refused to complain about it. She even deliberately began leaving her lunch behind to be taken, without her showing any curiosity about who was taking it. She believed that whoever took the lunch was hungry, and the last thing that our school needed was more angry people. The hungrier a man was, the angrier he would be, she believed.

"Whoever it is needs to know that they are not alone," Zola said. I watched her leave her lunch behind for her invisible friend for nearly a year, until one day she found a note of gratitude from him.

"When you feed me, you touch me. You give me strength to think clearly and know that the world is not against me and I should not be against the world. I am not alone, because you've got my back. I know who I am, because of you.

Thanks, Peace."

I never got to meet Peace and neither did Zola. I went looking, trying to be a kind of detective, but it was a dead-end search.

I exaggerated Zola's beauty for some time, comparing her to the rose of Sharon and the lily-of-the-valley like the Bible describes. When something is good, you tell people how good it is.

I was generally a shy person with a big heart, but when I met her, all of that soon changed. She was the treasure I found who stole my heart from Ms. Yan, and Zola left our high school with an honourable reputation. Up to this present moment, everyone who attended Mandela High was motivated by her story. I will tell you one more thing; she was and is a true charismatic figure with a great appeal to the public. As the story goes on, you will get to know who she is and was, and why I could not stop praising her. For now, I would rather have you listen to how it all started, with all I have to say about Queen Zola.

I saw Zola for the first time in 1988 when we were in Grade 9. She was in Grade 9A and I was in Grade 9C. She was younger than most students in our class, but she was ahead of everyone. Every year she skipped a class due to her great knowledge and understanding. We shared Grade 10, but she was in Grade 11, since we did not have many high-school students. They advised her to leave the school, but she refused. When I was in Grade 11, she was in Grade 13, but she waited to graduate before leaving for university.

I do remember an incident from the very beginning, before I became friends with Zola. At that time, Ms. Davies never left her class once she entered the school; she was afraid of being hurt because of the many gang activities that had our school in bondage. She asked me to deliver a math-test book to the next Grade 9 class. I felt I understood her better than the other students did, and why she was so scared. Ms. Davies was actually a happy woman, but once she entered the school area, she became like a lonely child.

She and my Grade 6 teacher Ms. Yan looked like sisters. I often told Ms. Davies that the only difference between Ms. Yan and her was the hair — one short, one very long.

On my way to see the math teacher I noticed a commotion outside the window. A group of students were screaming and shouting over Zola's head. But that was a usual thing at Mandela High. I was curious so after delivering the math book, I made my way outside. It was a very cold day with a temperature of -30 Celsius with a wind chill of -62 Celsius. Most folks walking on the street had their faces and entire bodies covered. People were advised to stay off the street, but some of us just had to come to school.

And on this day, one of Toronto's coldest in history, Zola was like a paper doll outside in the wind blowing from north to south. One of the students had thrown her backpack outside, and she had dashed out to get it. One of them ran out with his hockey stick; as she tried to bend and pick up her pack, he would jab his stick to pull it away from her hands. Over and over and again he did it, spitting with laughter.

Everyone watched as if numb and dumb. Zola's lips were dry and deep blue; her teeth were chattering. I saw the whole thing happening and its outcome, but I just walked away and went back to Ms. Davies' class.

"The world is cold," I told Ms. Davies.

"Hmmm hmm, yea, my child, and it can also be very hot," she replied.

Then I explained to her what was going on.

"De heck!" she said and called the vice-principal.

By the time they got there, Zola had fallen on the ground unconscious.

"She needs some sun," the boy with the hockey stick said.

Zola's whole body and fingers had shut down like a computer, and her fingers looked frozen, like sticks of ice. I thought wildly that she looked like a city bear that was forced to visit a polar bear at the North Pole. It was just a 911 call away and she was at the hospital. I don't remember saying anything, but I was there; I just looked at them, the "hockey-stick students", and walked away. I was afraid they might call me names and come after me as well, but I wished that I had stopped them, rather than allowing her to go through the agony of freezing fingers and falling to the ground. It tore at my heart afterwards.

But fortunately, when she returned from hospital, we still became friends. She didn't seem to bear any ill will that there was anything I could have done to defend her.

After a year of remembering that horrible day, and trying to remove the dark cloud of guilt from my heart, I began to think of her as a star. I still didn't have the courage to walk up to her and introduce myself. But luckily for me, she became my classmate the following year.

In fact, Zola was my best friend from high school and up to the present; we spent most of our youthful days together, and every day was like some kind of rough treasure, taking this life journey with her. Even in her own struggling, she was the strength that upheld me when my strength had gone. And she made school a kind of learning experience, not to be found in any curriculum book.

After six months of sharing the same class with her, I realized that I was fond of her. Not just that, but I became very attracted to her. She did not talk much, but she would always end a conversation with a giggle and a glance or smile. Even when she was teased or bullied by "gang girls", she wasn't hurt by it. No – I said that wrong! Of course she was hurt, but she did not allow those mean antagonists to take away her joy. And she kept her studies a priority, because it was her future.

The majority of my fellow students were involved in gangs, as a defence weapon, and they had serious discipline problems as well. Bullying was an issue that separated our school from the public, and the Ministry of Education knew it. Our teachers were told that if they got hurt by any student, it was at their own risk, because they refused to have the school closed.

In fact, one student was killed by the girls in my school, but before they killed her she wrote a suicide letter to her parents telling them that she could not handle the pressure at Mandela High. The Fever Girls, as they called themselves, had denied her freedom and threatened her, and she wasn't able to concentrate. According to her mother, she did not take her daughter's words seriously.

"Whenever Ama talked to me about the pressure at school, I told her to get along with her friends. You need to get yourself more involved with school. I can't babysit you, Ama," Mrs. Hutton said as she stood in front of the press lonely and broken, with her sunshine no more. It was as if a whirlwind had simply turned in to a tornado and buried Ama in a flash.

"I was so busy working and keeping up with the pace of life that I did not pay attention to my baby. I am sorry, Ama, I am very sorry, Sweetheart. It is my fault that you are dead. I should have listened to you. My baby girl had no peace of mind," Mrs. Hutton said.

At the funeral, the vice-principal asked Zola to talk about the students' behaviour, since she was also a victim herself. Before Ama's death, there were school rumours about her going around that she was dating a teacher; of course it was a lie. She was seated alone, even in the cafeteria, and we later learned that she was a new immigrant and she barely spoke English. I remember once she shared a table with the Fevers, and as soon as she sat down they immediately left holding their noses – which I thought was very rude and immature. Ama had tears in her eyes. Though she tried to fight back those tears, she could not do it.

She was one of the sweetest girls on campus and it seemed so unfair she was a victim. She did not deserve to die. A beautiful girl, slim, with dark brown hair she always wore in a ponytail. Ama, who was about average in height, also had a great understanding of humanity, according to her mother. I never really talked to her, but Zola explained her thoughts on bullying and how it was destroying lives in general. She said:

"Bullying destroys your whole being, leaving you emotionally wounded while mentally damaged. In fact one can feel like disappearing at the time of the act, or living as an invisible creature. When that terrible thought gets in your head, it can make you feel like you are better off dead than alive. You just can't help yourself, only by grace. It is hard to overcome your emotional state of mind when it is being controlled by others. It is my prayer that everyone involved in bullying will soon come to their senses, and stop destroying their lives and the lives of others as well. On that cold winter afternoon, death was better than life, but I thank God that I was able to stand; it sure felt like hell.

"Hopefully this is the last time Mandela High is burying someone, they will realize that it is not a joke and they can put an end to this madness. Bullying is escalating in the world, and it is killing us softly. My family wants me to leave the school effectively tomorrow," Zola said.

"No, you can't leave," the vice-principal said. She almost sounded as if she was up to something and needed Zola's help. Zola smiled at me as I listened to them talk.

The Fever Girls thought of themselves as the most beautiful, and rich and famous, in school. But they were mean, and selfish, and their behaviour led them to murder. The mother of one of the Fever Girls told the press: "I give my child the right to develop on her own and learn how to think morally. But I don't believe in punishing my child."

It is impossible to discipline without punishment. It would have been better if she had not had a child at all. These girls were destroying as many lives as possible, and their parents did not take it seriously. How can you have children and not have the time to discipline them? But since she was not a caring mother, she could not possibly have been a loving mother.

Zola would say this, "As a parent, you don't relax; your responsibility begins when you hold the photo of the ultrasound in your hand and when you come out of the hospital holding that baby. As you get ready to hold the baby monitor, you control, and patrol the house.

"Mother controls and patrols,
She sees the pain and sees the rain,
She uncovers the scams and discovers her child
She does not spare the wrong to cover her shame
She directs to correct her child
She looks beyond and sees the pain
She listens to the sound of the rain."

The girls were going far and fast, it did not matter how far, but they were going somewhere. The Fever Girls, they called themselves. The leader of the Fevers took Ama into a deserted house and beat her, leaving her there to suffer and die. Their leader believed that Ama was more beautiful than she herself was, she told the police. "I saw her with my boyfriend three months earlier and I did not want her stealing him from me." She was standing in cuffs and with reporters; she had a rugged appearance, a short girl with a big mouth. I liked to see her wear heels and a miniskirt. She had fiery orange hair and a lighter complexion. I knew that she coloured her hair and had all the girls in her group do the same to unify themselves and distinguish themselves from the others.

She had a heart-shaped face with a wide forehead and a pointed chin, but square with a jaw-line that could chisel granite. I didn't even like to think about her and what she put her friends through. I was hurt when her mother talked about not punishing her. This girl also always thought people were out to get her. "What was her name again? I can't remember now." Ama died because of some teenage selfish satisfaction fantasy of control, the kind of control and power that is destroying the world.

Since the incident in 1988 with Zola, no one bothered her until after Ama's death. Since her comments with the principal and speech at the funeral, Zola opened a brand-new case against herself. Zola often stayed away from evil when she saw it coming, but she definitely did not fear evil. I saw all kinds of evil done in my school back in the days. In fact there was a street next to my school where prostitutes hung around at night. Most of those women did not work for themselves; they were being monitored by some big guy always in a white car, and others worked to take care of their family. The man in the white would follow them when the ladies landed customers. Ben, who attended my school, was often seen there with some of the Fever Girls.

There were also many homeless Aboriginal people who hung out on the street near the school. Most of them were separated from their families during the residential-school process. After many years of separation they returned home to an empty home; some of the fathers became drunks and their mothers vanished. With such a history, it is almost impossible to move forward alone.

The wind hit the Native Canadians in such a way that it blew everything away from their hands, leaving them naked and frustrated, with some of them hitting the very air they breathe. They were born with everything, but today they lived with nothing. The men were called drunks, and their daughters and wives were often raped and killed. It was the "power of control". What the child sees, the child will demonstrate. "No, it is wrong, Zola said. This reminds me of a song from long ago.

I was given everything in the beginning;
Still I was left with nothing at the beginning.
Ignorance of the truth had me in prison.
I was told that I am free, but I was only free when you were free with me.
I am my brother's keeper, and freedom is my right.
So freedom is the right of all mankind.

I will survive, I will survive.
Greatness is in me, and I am a survivor.
I might be denied and I will be hit, but I will not be
stopped. I will survive, as long as I have you.

No matter what they say about us, no matter what they do to us, together we can survive, because unity is power. Actually, I often heard my history teacher singing it.

Zola did not wear fancy clothes to look pretty, so the Fever Girls did not feel threatened by her. She was provoked, because she did not keep quiet speaking the truth. I did judge her myself, but once. Of course everyone did; what would you have done if you saw a girl wearing the same pair of jeans every day? Besides, Mandela High was the place for bullying. Zola was among the less fortunate students in the school, but that was no issue for her; she never really worried about what anyone thought of her. Though she wore one pair of jeans for almost a week, she smelled of one of the sweetest perfumes. A very organized person and neat in every way, she looked happy every day she went to school. And she didn't bow down to the Fevers. I later learned that she was from "The Hope Shelter," which was just across the street from our school.

Zola purposely left her lunch at home and had her grandmother Huan Yue bring it to the school. Her grandmother would often cross the street out of breath saying, "Hey…What's cooking? You…young lady, here is your lunch. I enjoy running up and down the street now, but sooner or later I will not have the strength to do it."

"Yes Maa, I will be at the university far from home. Xie, xie Maa! (Thank you Maa.)

"Ahh, buyong."(You're welcome.)

"God bless Maa," she would reply.

"You're welcome, my child, God laid it on my heart to take care of you," Huan Yue would say. "I am going to do this, until my strength fails."

Huan Yue had five children of her own and one of her daughters was supervising the shelter. As she and her children managed the shelter, she paid special attention to Zola, making sure that Zola grew in good health. Huan Yue was a very kind woman, and always joyful. She worried much about their welfare and would drive them around the city. Very strong and courageous, she looked more Filipino than Chinese.

Over the years, she kept cutting her hair until she barely had any left. But her blue eyes were beautiful, and "popped", which brought out the soft sand colour of her skin. It was amazing how people could change over the years; she went from a size 4 to a size 8. She did not miss church or the women's prayer group, so when her friends did not see her, they worried. "What's wrong with Huan Yue, did any one hear from her?" With her around, her senior friends had nothing to worry about.

She had so many clothes, but she chose a few favourites that included her beautiful cream-caramel dress edged with dark brown. With her average height, her skirt would hang over her shoes making her look extra tall. She always looked sweet and lovely. From her, Zola learned how to wear perfume. Whenever I saw her crossing the street, I would quickly run towards Zola, so I could eavesdrop on their conversation.

The fact that Zola was a black girl with a Chinese family was enough for the Fevers to use as a weapon to try to destroy her life. She was referred to as "the homeless girl". But instead of being ashamed of who she was, she considered herself very blessed to live in the shelter.

"I am privileged and it is a beautiful, life-changing experience for me," she told Ms. Lavender who was one of the teachers in Mandela High. That was one tough woman I can't ever forget. One thing I really liked about her was that she was bold, very bold, and full with excitement. Ms. Lavender was forty years old when we graduated from Mandela High, but even ten years later, she still claimed she was just forty. She was a beautiful-looking Jamaican woman with a cheerful heart who later became our good friend. Zola often said: "If I get a little older, I want to be like you, feel like you, and definitely look forever young like you."

Zola also managed to find a way to defend herself. She would often tell the girls that she would never trade her life for a million dollars. "I am not poor; greater is He that is in me than he that is in the world," Zola said to them. Not that they had a clue what she was talking about. I once heard her telling a group of guys who were kicking her backpack back and forth like a football, "All these things are vanity, but life is more precious and valuable.

"A helping hand is a leading hand; if you want to be a leader, start helping. I hope you realize this soon," she told them. Then, I thought that it was very strange for a girl in her condition to speak such powerful words. Those are words politicians used during elections. She should have cried for help rather than playing Franklin Roosevelt, or Abraham Lincoln. But I kept that statement in mind, and as time went by, I got to learn more and more marvellous things about her, which continued to attract me to her.

I prayed for an opportunity to be alone with her, yet had to wait for the right time, since I was still shy. I kept my eyes open as we passed by each other in the corridor, classroom, and outside, without saying a word to each other. I was even getting ready to challenge anyone who dared put their hands on her again. I prayed for the right moment, right place and time. But lucky me, it was nearer than I was prepared for.

It was time for me to meet my Black Diamond, shining like a marble and her teeth as white as sparkling snow. We had our first oral presentation and she presented, "A Wife of a Noble Character" and she later ended it with, "While she is called the African Queen." It took everyone's breath away, and it left me with butterflies in my belly for her. The presentation changed my entire state of mind and it was a life-changing experience for the whole school. According to Zola's explanations, the beauty of a woman was not physical, but internal. "When the inside is beautiful, automatically it will reflect on the outside."

"Nevertheless, physical appearance does matter, but going to extremes to stay forever young destroys lives much too early. Women nowadays have to look a certain way for the media to consider them beautiful," Zola explained. I didn't know where she was heading, but we were attentive with full interest. As I heard her speaking about beauty, I remembered a woman who had died a couple of weeks earlier from a botched breast-implant operation. Plastic surgery and removing wrinkles was becoming a hot business around the globe. Then she continued: "Like the multiple colours of a precious stone, so is the beauty of a woman with numerous characteristics. A 'super-woman'."

It was springtime, the flowers had begun to bloom, and it started raining that afternoon, as we all sat and listened. She continued the presentation: "Her husband has complete assurance in her and she is everything a woman is destined to be. Nevertheless, her husband is the head of the home, but not the head of the heads. All five fingers are not equal, but they support each other. Together they are called a hand. Tighter, a husband and wife are call partners. The woman has her own place, which makes her the captain of her ship."

Zola closed her book as if that was the end of her presentation. She handed everyone a piece of paper. She read from her copy: "A beautiful woman builds her home with patience and honesty as the pillar and foundation of her life; when there is a flood or stormy wind, she is secure. She is given wisdom to escape, so the flood will not destroy her. She has strength like a samba and the ability to enhance the master key. She is never weary, but always energetic and captivated. When she wakes up in the morning, she makes sure that her family doesn't go to bed wondering about the future, so she prepares ahead of time. They lack nothing. She honours the lives that she has been entrusted with. She is happy with everyone, and everyone is always delighted to see her. She makes delicious meals for her household, even for her employees.

"She opens her heart to those who need it, and she extends her hands to whomever needs it. She has made herself available and she becomes the window to many doors. Because of her, her husband is known and respected everywhere he goes, and she becomes his blue eyes. He loves her and gives her his undivided attention. She is the light that shines in many homes and a Band-Aid for many wounds. As a result, whatever she touches is profitable."

Zola stood with the paper in her hands, but barely looked at it. For the first time I saw my school principal looking with hope on her face, and her body standing proud as she looked at the day ahead of her. Only God knew what was running through her mind. She was probably thinking about who this girl was, standing before the class. It was still raining, so there was no chance of us leaving the classroom. In fact, it felt like we were watching a movie, because of the rain and the dark classroom.

My thoughts could not comprehend my feelings; I pretended to have been the lucky husband who was living in glory. "The beauty of a woman is worth more than a ruby with many colours." We were speechless as we listened with our mouths open. "A woman who is covered in strength and standing in wisdom is beautiful. She fears God and allows His will into her life. Every woman is a woman of noble character; it is the inheritance of women; she is the mother of the earth specially created with love from the rib of her husband. This woman is no different from you and she is found in every woman."

We all sat still, staring. Then she continued the second part of the presentation: "Now, the African Queen. The women are each called Super-Woman, and are like the Hebrew women of Biblical times. The woman gives birth and helps her husband weed the farm in just a few days. The woman works hard to help provide for her home. She does not sit and wait for her husband to sell the cocoa or coffee before she takes care of the family, or shares the bills. Even though her husband is the provider, and his duty as a man is not performed, there will still be meals on the table for the family. He acknowledges her and admires her strength, because she is his only helper.

"Her husband knows his responsibility; he does not take advantage of her. She uses her talents to feather her home. In her, he finds complete joy and they both put their hope in the Lord. Respect and love is the colour of her home, and those around her. Because of his love for her, she allows him to be honoured and dignified among royals. She looks up to him with delight and calls him 'Papa.' Her husband sits under the cotton tree with the chiefs while they sing a new song of freedom. On the soccer field with his friends, he sees her walking with a calabash of water on her head with the baby on her back, he says to the elders, 'There comes Mama, my African Queen.'

"Unfortunately, the woman's husband dies and leaves her with the kids. He was her heart's desire and her soul mate. He had a hold on her heart. In him she was complete, but now without him, she is incomplete. The certain death of her husband left her speechless; the thought of her husband disappearing like the wind left her hopeless. But she remembered the children, then she knew that she had to keep hope alive. 'My children,' the woman said. She is not lettered, but she is very intelligent. He covered her with love and showered her with care. With him gone, she knew that she had to stand, not sit. Then she begins weeding her father's farm to sow a seed in her children's lives. She pays their tuition telling them that it is the last they shall receive and it should not be wasted."

Then Zola looked down with wet eyes fighting back the tears. I could not believe what I was hearing, but I was right there. How can I not believe?

"I am exchanging my money for four zeros. I do not expect any higher marks from you my sons as you go to school. I am unable to tutor you and you know that, but I expect you to bring me those zeros; the four zeros represent 88%."

Her children grew up and all travelled abroad for better education, they got married, leaving their mother's home. Later, they returned home to where they first saw love, and where love ended for their mother. Her kids crowned her with pride and dignity like they saw their father do. They thought about their father and said to her:

"Mama, you are my African Queen,
Your love has no beginning and no end,
You are my good luck charm.
You are the hand that turns my light on when it is off.
Your voice reminds me to remember when I forget.
Your voice helps me to realize when I remember.
Your love gives me life, and lifts me up.
Your love is unquenchable, and unquestionable.
It is unconditional and compared to none.
It gives me strength and completes me.
It gives me hope and makes me whole.
In you, I find corrections and directions.
My faith is increased when I see you,
Mama, I see God in you, you are the apple of His eye.
You represent heaven which increases
My faith, and decreases my fears.
Heaven was made for a mother like you.
You made me what I am and I love you.
You're worth more than rubies,
The wind could not blow you away,
The wind could not hold you anyway,
But the wind made you stronger.
Mama, you are my African Queen.

"Ladies and gentlemen," she concluded, "Whether an African, American, Asian, Australian, or European woman, or the Aboriginal woman who was told she had to abandon herself and become who she is not, you are the mother of the earth. You are the queen of your nation. You deserve respect, dignity and love; young or old. With love, you can overcome the wind. It is love that will bring out the royalty and beauty in you. We have to live in love; we all can make a difference. We are all nobles, created for greatness. With this, I am done."

By the time she concluded, the Fevers did not feel any beauty or value in themselves. The classroom became very quiet as if there were no one in it, and if a pin dropped, it would echo. This was the first time in ten years to see our school this interested in something positive, our principal later told our head teacher. It was the evidence of change; it was on the way to our school. Change was coming like a rain to soak Mandela High, a fresh rain with a kind of morning sunshine that my principal had been waiting for all along. We witnessed the arrival of The Wind changing slowly, softly and sweetly. We saw it with our very eyes; it was just hard to believe that a gentle wind would blow in that direction.

After two hours of our listening to the rain, it finally stopped and the sun began shining, it reflected on us in the classroom.

"Right on time," I said to her but she did not hear me.

Our teacher Mr. Sibonakaliso Mudiwa Kamazulu, it is my first time calling out his name; "Don't worry about the rest, call me Kamazulu" he told us. He came from South Africa to give us a history lesson, but he could not help his emotion. Mr. Kamazulu is a member of the ANC movement who strongly believes in education and discipline. I saw him turning his face to the other side and weeping as he got ready to approach Zola. He stood up over me and said, "Mandela believes that education is the most powerful weapon that one can use to change the world. Today, you have contributed to the world. You've just made him proud. I will give you excellent. Boys and girls, remember to always do better than your best. Today, you have done better, my dear lady," he said. I felt that, if nothing had ever happened in our school, something was about to happen. It was the spirit of hope and change that visited us.

The wind blew that day and I imagined it as attracting everyone to pay close attention to it. It was cool and calm, fresh and soft, in complete control…and the atmosphere felt great. We all learned something new whether we admitted it or not. I looked with amazement at the shy girl who seemed to be on a mission, and very sure of what she wanted. She smiled with her beautiful white even teeth. Her brain was just as sharp. She was brilliant, intelligent, and outspoken for her age. I was carried away by her presentation.

She got an A-plus, and was the only one who got an A for that assignment. Out of forty-five students, only ten were able to do the project. When the principal and Mr. Kamazulu got through talking with her, I walked up to her and gave her a handshake. "Congratulations," I told her, and she smiled at me. I looked out the window and saw the wind blowing. It was the sign that the wind of change was coming to blow on Mandela High.

Chapter Two

My entire life had changed since the presentation. Zola was all I talked about and thought about. I would feel my body shaking when I saw her coming towards me. There was a time I saw her approaching me and I actually turned to run because I could not face her. But then I felt embarrassed walking in front of her, so I pretended to have dropped something so she would pass by me. Because of her, I realized that great butterflies could suddenly appear due to anxiousness or nervousness.

I had told my Aunt May about Zola's wise presentation. My Aunt May was never interested in much that happened in school; in fact, she felt the school should be closed based on its negative reputation. But her beliefs changed when I told her about Zola:

"Aunt May, you will not believe what happened at school today."

"I…don't want to know," she said.

"A girl presented the characters of a noble wife today, it was so wonderful, Aunt May, and you should have seen her."

"Did you say wife of noble characters, Son?"

"Yes, Aunt May. She is the most beautiful girl I have ever seen in my life. And she is full of wisdom," I said. As I got through talking, Aunt May got on her knees and began praying, thanking God that the girl was going to be my wife.

"Thank…thee, oh my God for answering…every prayer."

"Every prayer, Aunt May?"

"That girl…is special…and… preserved; she has the fear of God in her. Such people built on solid rock are created, created to do great things. It has been my prayer that you meet someone like her. A school like that where evil is established should be eliminated, but here is a God who knows His timetable."

I had no idea what she was talking about. One thing I knew for sure was that Zola was an amazing girl and I was not going to let her get away from me.

A few weeks after the brilliant and wise speech, I saw Zola standing by her locker trying to open it. It looked as if she had forgotten her combination. So I walked over to her with confidence and offered to help: "Hello, wise woman, may I?" I said in a low voice, hoping she wouldn't send me away. "It seems that you need some help; you have been standing here for a little while now trying to open this…thing…this…"

"Lock," she helped me end the sentence.

"Yes, that's the name I was looking for." I smiled as I took hold of the lock.

My heart was beating faster than church drums and I felt nervous like a rabbit twitching my ears trying to hear her better. I wanted to walk away, but it was too late. She looked right into my eyes as if hoping to have found something there. "Your eyes are blue," she said.

No one has done that before, looked right into me and told me the colour of my eyes. Soon she was going to be telling me I was six feet tall! Anyway, she allowed me to help her, and we tried for a little while, but it didn't open.

"I opened it this morning," she said with frustration.

I could see her hands were sweating, and she was nervous as well! I tried helping her one last time, then I realized, "This lock is new; it should not be hard to open."

"It is not; I used this lock last year," she said.

When she bent her head, her hair, in long black braids, fell straight into my face. "What a great smell," I said.

"What smell?" she asked me as she lifted her head and looked at me again.

"This hallway smells great; have they just cleaned it?" I asked, but she was looking at me like I didn't know what I was talking about. The corridor had always smelled funny with bad odours. But I had to say something to make her take her eyes off me. Our school was a gangster camp, smoking was in fashion: both boys and girl smoked. As a result, we all smelled of cigarettes. And there I was, telling her that the hall smelled great. I was confused; I did not know what I was feeling. It felt awkward, but great at the same time. For that moment, I began to daydream and hope that she would be my wife in the future…since my Aunt May was already praying for me.

I quickly snapped out of it and we laughed; her lock had been changed, and she had no idea. "Why was my lock changed without my knowledge?"

"Well! Why don't we go to the office and find out?" I said.

They had not changed it. We later found out that one of the Fever Girls had switched the lock, and put the old one in her backpack. The girls had felt humiliated by Zola's presentation, so it was payback time for her, or at least a warning to stay away.

Since Zola was full of wisdom, she should use some wisdom to open the locker, the girl who'd taken the lock later told her. "So what will you do to me? Bring it on? Let me see, one month of suspension will be fine," she said happily.

The girl gave her the numbers of the new lock and it opened. The girls were suspended for a week, but Zola interceded on their behalf and opposed the suspension. "Suspension is not a solution," she said, but the girls were happy for the suspension.

I was angry that Zola didn't want them punished after all the trouble they had caused her. "I want them punished, but not sent away from school," she said with a smile, not even looking at me. "Can't you see? If you keep them away from school, you keep them away from everything. You can't do that to them; they will miss out on their school activities. You can't use education as a punishment. Find another punishment for them."

"They need to learn from their mistakes, Zola," I told her.

"No," she said. "You are simply telling them that education is not important." Zola asked our vice-principal if she would punish her son by keeping him away from church on Sunday morning because he pushed his little sister down the stairs. "You know that he would rather watch TV than go to church, right? I would have these girls do community service," she replied.

Zola was right about one thing; I would love staying home on a Sunday morning rather than go to church, so my Aunt May would never suspend me from church. Zola told the vice-principal to use the incident as an opportunity to reach out to the girls. "Think outside the box," she said. "They are sorry for what they did."

"No, we're not," said one of the girls.

Zola pleaded for the girls as if she was their mother.

"It is lawful that they get suspensions, said the principal and the vice-principal. "We can't change the school rules and regulations; I am sorry, Zola."

School had ended and most of the students had left. As the suspension letters were prepared, Zola said: "It was a gift. Their intentions were not to hurt me, it was to wish me well. I blew it out of proportion. I am sorry for getting you involved in this."

"Zola, no! What?" I exclaimed.

"It was their way of apologizing for all their negative behaviours towards me. My lock was very old, so they decided to get me a new one."

Obviously, I did not understand what was going on with her, so I called her out into the hallway privately and begged her to let the girls receive their punishment, but it seemed she could not be convinced.

"Look, Sweetie, these girls have been digging into your flesh ever since you got into this school. Just last week your grandmother was at the principal's office. They treat everyone here like trash including the teachers. Well, except for Mr. Kamazulu, who is the 'African Power.' Frankly speaking, I would not have mercy on them."

"That makes us two different individuals, doesn't it?"

"Look, my dear, I understand that you want to play Mother Teresa or Muammar Muhammad Gaddafi, but these girls are bad news. Many of us would be happy if they disappeared without a trace."

"Then, you are no better than them," she said, obviously categorizing me with them, which I certainly disagreed with. She was the one left with the decision, but I was not giving up either.

"Doesn't it bother you that they are the reason your friends are committing suicide? You can't let them go flying in the wind like a butterfly that had just smelled a spring flower after the winter."

"I know," she said.

"Let me remind you about one last thing before you make your decision." My hand was over her shoulder, and I was feeling very special as I talked to her. "Do you remember Ama's funeral? That charming and beautiful girl was dragged into that old house and killed. They beat her up before killing her, and only one person was convicted of the murder."

I tried to convince her to let the girls be punished; the girls did not belong in our midst, and I smelled danger in the air. "Don't allow the wind to blow on you, it will destroy who you are. Now, my lady, are you willing to sacrifice your freedom, and security for them to destroy more lives?"

"No," she said.

Just around that time, the Ministry of Education was debating about closing Mandela High permanently. There were other things happening in the school area as well that we knew nothing about.

I asked her again: "Do you want this school permanently closed?"

"No! They can't close Mandela High," she insisted. "If they close the school, they close our hearts. The debate will be declined. It is very important that this school stays open. Okay, I will consider all of the victims when making my decision including myself. May those that died, their souls rest in peace," Zola said as she walked back into the principal's office. But as soon as she turned her head, she again had a change of mind. She looked right in my eyes and said that the girls were helping her. So, they did not get in trouble.

"Why did you do it? I can't believe you did that," I said to her.

"I did it for me, for you and everyone at Mandela High, especially the lives that have been destroyed. You don't understand right now but I hope you will someday." She tapped my back and walked away and said, "If you repay evil with good, the world will bow down to you, and the world will be a better place for all mankind. Unfortunately, we all struggle with that." She went outside and sat under a tree.

I followed her. "You seem to surprise me every time we meet. First, you played the Franklin Roosevelt speech about greatness, second, the wise woman speech, and now you are a peacemaker. What should I expect from you the next time we meet? Please inform me so it won't take me by surprise."

"Life is full of surprises and challenges. If I was to tell you now, then it will no longer be a surprise. Just get ready for the next adventure. We all need education, and this is something that should never be taken away from us, or compromised with anything. It is the child's necessary development," she concluded.

"My grandmother always told me that education is development, and it will bring you a moral sense of reasoning," I told her. I did not know where she was going with the education speech, but I knew I had to make a statement to be at the same level of knowledge with her – and it felt good lying even though I had no grandmother to begin with. The statement quickly came out of my mouth, and if it did not make sense to her, at lease she knew those words were powerful. I was about to be a friend to a resourceful girl, so I had to think of a way to be equivalent to her standard. I was soon to compare her with great and extraordinary people who were created to accomplish special tasks.

"The girls were not born this way; they made themselves this way," she said.

"Wow! It was fun spending my afternoon with you, quite an adventure." I did not want to keep talking about the girls, so I had to find a way to change the topic.

"Life without adventure is like breathing without a heart. It kills life," said Zola.

I'm sorry but I couldn't help seeing you fighting with the lock."

"Do you mean, the lock fighting with me? Did you keep the score?" she said, smiling and looking up at the blue sky. "I am delighted, you came through for me. I am very grateful. I really appreciate you helping me today.

I can't believe that we did not suspect the problem earlier, and you are the brain," Zola said.

I laughed as she talked; it felt great just listening to her. "How do you know that I am a brain, wise lady?"

"Well François, the lady has the ears and eyes, you know. Besides, we are classmates, aren't we?"

She was laughing as she talked so I was more confident with her. "Are you following me, wise woman?"

"Why would I follow you? Funny, very funny!"

How tall are you – six feet?"

"Are you always that quick in measurement?"

She smiled at me and responded: "I am five foot eight and still growing. I like your golden-brown hair, but why do you cover your face?"

"To hide my small ears and heart-shaped forehead."

"Since you dislike your ears, why don't you cut them off and create yourself a new face?"

"Thanks, Zola, I appreciate it." I didn't know what she was hinting at with the question.

"Covering your face is like hiding from yourself, my dear. You are as handsome as a baby cheetah, and with those blue eyes, you will be getting married after graduation."

"Amen!" I responded quickly. It was like she was reading my heart, reminding me of what I wished for.

At that moment, I remembered my pastor preaching to the church: write down your vision and make it a plan. She asked me if I was a Christian, and how Christian I was. How Christian can someone be? I asked myself. "I guess this is it," I said. "We are done for the day."

She looked at me as she took her backpack to leave. She had that Aunt May look when she was concerned about something. I took a little pause, then suggested walking her home, but she declined. Then I gave her a handshake, and she smiled at me. I had her small hand in my big hand and could not let go of it. "Wow! Your hand is soft," I told her.

"You are very impressive, but I have to go. My grandma's waiting for me. Another minute standing here and she will be coming to get me even though she is looking at us as we speak."

We said our good-byes and both headed home. "Hey…François? Would you give me a French lesson?" she called.

"I will have to pass. But I can take you to Montréal where you will meet many French people. I will see you tomorrow Zola."

"Good day, François."

I got home that day, filled with joy. Her voice was soft and calm, but when she wanted her voice to be heard, she put in extra power. On my way home, I became conscious of myself. I decided to study harder, dress a certain way, and change the way I walked to impress her, but Aunt May later told me to be myself.

"Aunt May, are you home?"

"Yes my love, why are you so excited? What is the big smile about?"

"I will only tell you if you promise me that there isn't going to be any Holy Ghost Hallelujah dance."

"Well, Son…you just said it! I am not promising you, but I will surely try.

"Your prayers are working, Aunt May. Keep on praying day and night, and don't stop. Do you remember the girl I told you about? The 'wise woman'."

"Yes."

"Well, I was a real gentleman. I came to her aid at school. I am so proud of myself, and you should be too. You know how you always want me to give a helping hand to people in need?"

"Yes, Son!"

"Well that's exactly what I did. Those mean girls did something very terrible to the wise girl again and I went to her rescue. This time, it was something funny. I spent the afternoon with her trying to help her out, so we later put the pieces of the puzzle together. I think she is going to like me."

"God, I love to see him like this, please keep him in this spirit."

"Aunt May, are you praying again? Please stop the imitation, you are not Ms. Daisy and you are not sounding like her. Just be yourself. Where is my food?"

I later told Aunt May that Zola was a peacemaker. After those negotiations at school, I thought Zola would make an excellent diplomat at the United Nations. I got the feeling she was going to help our school and bring serious changes.

"And one more thing. She waves like a queen, only with a genuine and sweet smile."

Our friendship grew stronger every day. Six months later, Huan Yue brought her lunch as usual, and met us lying on the grass.

"You are old enough now, young lady. You should cross the street and pick up your own food. You can't have the old lady running after you. Hi, Fat Boy, what's cooking?" she said as she walked passed me and gave Zola the food. "So...you keep her here after school every day, right? You keep her from doing her work. Why don't you come with her to the house? In that case, you talk...and she works. You lazy Canadian boy, don't you have work at home to do? Besides, you need to drink some ginseng and green tea to lose some weight; it's good for you."

My Aunt May does all the work at home," I said with a smile, but she did not look pleased with my response.

"You eat, and Aunty cleans after you, is that right? True Canadian," she said as she gave Zola and me a cup of warm soup.

"Your grandmother is very nice; she does not look Chinese at all. Usually, the Chinese people are slimmer and don't speak fluent English," I told her,"

"Yes she is nice. And you've not seen anything yet, wait until you get sick. Then you will see how nice and important it is that she lives for one hundred years plus."

I just stared.

She spoke with a happy smile." Oh, François, she is a Canadian. She came to Canada since she was ten and she is now in her seventies, and she speaks poor Chinese, actually."

But Huan Yue looked great, like fifty rather than seventy. How did she do it I wondered on my way home.

Since that day I walked along with Zola after school, and my Aunt May had no problem with it. Zola was the kind of person she wanted me to be around. Even though she had not met Zola, Aunt May loved her.

I had a big problem, though. If Zola was not a Christian, she was never going to allow me to be with her. She wanted me to stay away from non-Christian kids, but how were they going to know the Bible if I stay away from them?

"2nd Corinthians 6:14 says this: 'Do not be unequally yoked together with unbelievers.' God said so Himself and you can't argue that," Aunt May would often say.

Zola stayed present in my life, helping me to accept everyone as they were. And just like Huan Yue suggested, I drank green tea, and healthy ginseng to help regulate my body fat.

Later on that year, I asked Zola about her parents, but she quickly changed the subject. I did not really pay much attention since I thought it was pretty cool for a black girl to have a Chinese family.

"How do you call your mother at home?" she asked me.

"Well, Aunt May, she is my dad's sister."

"Why don't you call her Maa or Nainai. To show respect for your elders," she said and tapped my shoulder.

"I will go with Nainai, or Maa."

"Great."

Meanwhile at school, she got herself involved with many things including gathering supplies for our anthropology teacher. Mr. Teah was very conscious of his subject and he would do anything to see the students taking their education seriously. Even though most of the students did not come for days or weeks, and most of them were troublemakers, he didn't give up. Zola's presence helped quite a bit. He saw that Zola had the capacity to teach as well. Zola became a teacher's assistant in our school in a flash. Her passion for education drove her into teaching, and she became a role model for us.

She showed great interest in anthropology, and she loved discovering ancient things, but she was even more involved with history. The students thought that she understood it better than Mr. Teah, who got over-excited explaining the human mind. It did not take much time; change arrived. "To be a teacher, you have to be a lover of the subject, and the people you are teaching," Mr. Teah said.

Zola encouraged me to join the student council committee, and she was elected that year and the year after, in grade eleven, and grade twelve, as the school president. This changed our lives. Mandela High School that had been about to become "history" began rising again. We were now becoming the most talked-about school in Ontario.

Chapter Three

"We like what is happening, but we don't know how it happened," the custodian said. "Our school was awarded best school in Ontario and Canada for its improvement in academics. Our school became an inspiration overnight. The timing was right for Mandela High, based on all the peace talks and negotiation around the world about 'Free Mandela'. The man spends 26 years in prison, because he became noble, standing up for his rights."

Our school was funded again by the Ministry, and our teachers got full salaries as well. Our vice-principal said in one of her interviews that she saw a vision and believed that only love could bring it to light. Rather than dropping out, students were now returning. We got more volunteers than we needed and people wanted to associate with our school. All of our teachers before the makeover were all volunteers, including Mr. Kamazulu who had left his country to come and help Mandela High to gain a better reputation.

Many students had trouble with school because they came from broken homes. I often thought that a broken home is one in which one parent had walked away, but Mr. Kamazulu explained that a home can have two parents and still be broken. Home begins with your heart and when your property and all that you are worth are taken away from you in a flash you will be heartbroken.

"Dignity is what makes a man. What profit a man when he is not worthy of honour?" Mr. Kamazulu would say during a lecture. I often thought that he was more than just a classroom teacher. With his help, we all walked together and our school became number one. It is what you are that will make people run after you, not who you are. It was what we became that made us important. We made a quality and worthwhile decision which brought the school from zero to hero. We were neglected and rejected, but all of that changed now that we were working to reach the greatness within us.

Every time, I thought about the struggles the teachers had to undergo to save Mandela High, I saluted them. Our school was left alone to stand alone, in need, or waiting for a permanent shutdown. But here we were, everyone wanting to be a part of us, and for us. I guess that's part of the description of the world we live in. You are wanted when you are not in need. Here we were, we had more teachers than we needed. How ironic. My Aunt May would often say, "It is God, nothing else, and nobody but God. When it is all good, it is all God." My heart was filled with joy, and I owed it all to my best friend Zola who helped to locate and guide the way. She told one of the former members of the gang that he did not need power to become powerful, or to be accepted.

Most of our students believed in themselves again. Love, kindness and respect was our bylaw. Our school received appreciative cards and gifts for its tremendous transformation. I remember in one television interview, the principal said that love brings the best out of a child, and love was definitely in the air at Mandela High. It was ready to draw the best out of us.

Mr. Kamazulu told us to listen to an interview that became a message for us, and we fought hard to bring this message to live in our school and our hearts. "I have carried the idea of a democratic, free society in which people live together in harmony and with equal opportunities. I hope to live and see that achieved. If need be, it is an idea which I would die for." These were words from President Mandela and it became a wakeup call for the entire school and for the rest of my life. How can anyone listen to a message like that and choose to be cruel or prejudiced?"

Mr. Kamazulu and Zola had been sent to revive Mandela High. Mr. Kamazulu really helped us learn more about African history and world events. He would explain the significance of these quotes and even demonstrate a little skit for us. "Boys and girls, this is called geography. You need to learn about what is going on in the world. Africa is not a country; Africa is a beautiful continent with beautiful people," Mr. Kamazulu would often remind us.

We were to choose a famous quote for our essay that year. I didn't know much about African history. Until then, I thought that Africa was a country, not a continent. I felt like he was talking directly to me. I was very heartbroken by the many quotes I was considering.

Even after many years in prison, Mandela was willing to die for his people's freedom and liberation. Here, we were at Mandela High had been doing all in our power to destroy ourselves. My emotions could not comprehend the fact that Mr. Mandela was offered freedom, and he chose to spend his life in jail for freedom in his own country. He did not expect to be comforted, because the other prisoners had no comfort. The twenty-seven years that he spent in jail was not about what he did, it was about what he was going to do. He was going to protect the earth and heal what was wounded in the world, making it a peaceful place and giving hope to generations to come.

Zola stood outside talking and staring at the sky. "There is no greater love than what Mr. Mandela demonstrated for mankind. It is the great Agape love that we were created with, but man became selfish, loving himself rather than loving others."

"Are you talking to me?"

"No François, just a little thought in my little head."

"Your little head has the knowledge of fifty people, and it is as beautiful as the bright morning star."

"Okay François, thank you, you just made my day. I needed to hear that. I just want you to know that I could not have done all of this without you, and that you deserve credit as well, French Man."

"Well, my darling Black Beauty, the pleasure is all mine. I was created for this reason. To be your helper," I told her.

"No, François, I was created to be the helper," Zola corrected me. "Yes, 'Mother Ducky', besides, we are in this together; anything to save Mandela High.

"Zola, by the way, Mr Kamazulu thinks that he might know you from somewhere, but he can't remember."

"Yes, my dear, everybody knows somebody from somewhere," she replied. "I like him; he is very smart and committed to the ANC."

I turned to her to hold her book. "He is from the ANC and a godson of Madiba," I said? "Where do you think he learns to be humble? He learns his loyalty from the man of integrity himself," Zola said as she smiled at me. There was always a special smile on her face when she talked about Mr. Mandela.

"Hey, Canadian girls and boys! After graduation, I will take you all to South Africa to see Mandela the Black Power," Zola said as she imitated Mr. Kamazulu.

"I will tell him that you are always imitating him," I said, but when we saw him coming towards us playing with his moustache, we laughed and he probably figured we were teasing him. "Oh, there he comes now... Ooh! Mr. Kamazulu, Zola said – "

"Shhhh, don't let him hear you, French Man. He might give us detention."

"Sooo, boys and girls, what did I do this time?" asked Mr. Kamazulu. "Are you laughing at my belly that is growing! In Africa, this is called success." He rubbed his belly. "Teah is here, I teach you now, he teaches later. My dear lady, Zola, no escape."

We had another hour with him that afternoon. The time for him to return home was getting near, but he wanted to stay until graduation. He would tell us all kinds of stories about the African people's endless fight for freedom. There was a story he explained about a young man, from the Gbadi tribe, who sacrificed his life for his people to be free. Apparently, there was an argument among the two neighbouring kingdoms, and the peacemakers gave them guns to fight. The winner was going to receive more of the land. But a traditional priest said that war was not the answer, the solution for complete peace was burying someone alive. As they searched for a volunteer in the little village, this young man went to the king and gave himself as ransom for his people. He said "I am ready to die for the land." They buried him alive. For seven days, they heard him cry as he died.

At night, he would cry out, saying that the earth was as big as the sky, there was enough space for all humanity. War was not the answer. The soil needed water, not blood.

They still honoured him up to the present date. Mr. Kamazulu did not finish the story. "I will continue later," he said.

These stories were all based on truth, and quotes based on real life experience. He had a very heavy African accent as he talked to us, which we enjoyed and teased him about, but Mr. Kamazulu could also speak in a way that you never knew where he came from. There was sorrow in his face as he stopped talking; it was almost as if he was absent for a while. But it was a silent message of hope and faith according to Zola.

"Love is the key, and the only way to freedom. Whatever the circumstances surrounding the sacrificial burial of the man, he did it for love, peace and unity," Zola said. "Mr. Madiba spent twenty-seven years on the cool dark prison floor. He decided that he was not going to sit and watch his people be separated from the rest of the world; he could not stand by and do nothing. He did not keep quiet even in the prison cell; he spoke against apartheid: 'I will die fighting for equal rights, it is the right of all men!'" Zola sat on the bench as she talked and imagined the jail cell on that lonely island, and if any man could do what Mr. Mandela did. "God created him for this purpose and he was given the special grace to carry on the task just like Joseph in Egypt."

She continued to speak her mind: "Look François, we need not to fear man. We need more people like him to follow his example, and more light to shine in our lives. But unfortunately, if Madiba would die tomorrow, people will talk about what he did, but they will not act on it. This is bad, because life is about being proactive. He said that courage was not the absence of fear, but the triumph over it. The brave man is not he who does not feel afraid, but he who conquers that fear.

"You have conquered and overcome fear, Papa Madiba. You wrote the new exodus of our time. Someone needed to sit and write down the twenty-seven years in the jail cell without a place to call home. Moses saw the suffering of the people and pleaded for mercy upon them, but Madiba heard the cries of his people, and he could not come to their rescue," He had to give away his life. Madiba would say: 'If I can't help my people, to live for me is to die.'"

When she got through talking, then Mr. Kamazulu stood over her with a wet face as well, saying. "With this heart, you will go far. You have very big assignments in this world. Stay focused, stay very focused. If you called Madiba your uncle, put your faith into action."

He hugged her and we all headed to the Free Nelson Mandela protest that day. It was amazing how much affection he had from the students. He used these inspirational stories to soften our hearts, and to help us realize that there were people who struggled for others to survive.

That year, the black people in Canada began standing up to face their fears and many challenges. One important topic on the table was the all-black-focus school in the Greater Toronto Area, and Zola told me that it was totally wrong. I thought that it was a good idea, but when she explained to me her thoughts, I fully agreed with her.

"This will open a whole new chapter of discrimination; it is segregation. We should be moving forward, not back to the days when the black people were told that the white race is better than them. A separate school for the black youth is not the answer. Working on a strategy to get those who are less involved with education is what the Toronto School Board should worry about. I will tell you what the school board should be doing to promote academic achievement: they should get in to the minds of those youth and help them understand the importance of education. If the Canadians really are helping to free Nelson Mandela, the all-black school will not be on the discussion table.

"Here we are protesting that they should free Madiba; it is segregation that took him into prison. So if Canada agreed to open an all-black school, then they should stand with the segregators and keep on embracing segregation. What are they proving to the world, anyway? Is the white youth smarter than the black, are the black youth going to learn a special language or skill? If they allow this to happen, very soon the rest of the world will copy the Canadians.

"They sat down and witnessed Mandela High going down. The school board didn't have a solution for us, but they were ready to shut it down. Even up to now, they have not responded to our letter of petition that Mandela High stay open. Whoever wants to replace our school with a mall or a high-rise building, they will not succeed.

"Mandela High is a place of education, it is our future, and this is where we come to interact with our schoolmates. They will not take it away from us. The world has forgotten its meaning of life: it has all come down to money. The rich are getting richer and the poor are getting poorer each day," Zola said with conviction, and her facial expression had changed.

"Zola, are you angry?"

"No, I am not." She smiled and looked up at me.

I never really thought about replacing our school with a mall. Mr. Kamazulu told us that it was politics, but he did not explain the politics behind Mandela High. I don't know how she came up with all of those explanations.

Earlier in February of 1990, Mr. Kamazulu left the principal's office sweating as if he was under 35-degree Celsius heat and his face was shining as if a flash light was pointing in his face. As we found out, he had received a call from South Africa that sent him into the washroom singing. He entered the washroom but he did not use it, he simply looked at himself in the mirror as he sang. I ran into the washroom and saw him looking at himself trying to clean his face. He seemed anxious and overjoyed at the same time, but somehow, tears were rolling down his face.

"I can smell the ocean breeze, and see Robin Island from here, surrounded with hearts of laughter, I can feel, my...my..." He could not finish the sentence; it was stuck in his throat. I was standing next to him and I could see his shirt shaking, because his heart was beating very fast. We were beginning to worry, because he was still not speaking.

"Mr. Kamazulu, what is the matter?" Zola asked him, but he was still shocked from whatever it was that had given him this reaction.

After a moment of silence, he spoke out. "I...have prayed for this, I... have prayed...for all my life...for this, asking God for a miracle, but I did not believe that he was going to give my heart's desire... God is real, boys and girls.

"Yes, we know that, but you must share the news!" I told him. "We are all excited for you, but tell us what is so unbelievable, but seems true," one of the boys said, but he told us that it was top secret. "This is the day that I wish to have been home, walking on the streets of Cape Town with my head up." He said sadly as he was loosening his tie a little.

Zola seemed to know what he was talking about! She jumped from her seat and ran to him, giving him a long hug as they wept bitterly. Saying nothing to him, she walked away and went back to her seat.

"Patience, boys and girls, be patient," Mr. Kamazulu said. The class was dismissed and we went home.

Zola was very calm, I tried to push her as to what the excitement was, but she was just quiet and filled with emotion. A few days later, it was all clear and out in the open. It was the breaking news in the world. "The men who were denied twenty-seven good years of their lives are finally coming out of the dark to the light. They are going to have access to the blue sky and the free air without someone monitoring them." Zola said this after it was announced that Mr. Mandela was to be free on the 11th of February. 1990.

Mr. Kamazulu told us to sit by the television, because history was in the making. He could not stop wiping away his tears. "Mr. Kamazulu, does this mean that the Europeans are finally accepting the black man in South Africa as part of mankind?" Ben asked. "The black man has always been a part of mankind, whether he is accepted or not," Zola quickly answered Ben.

"Thanks, Ben, that was a very silly question to ask," I told him.

Mr. Kamazulu always told us that his parents died protesting against apartheid, but now it was time for the silent stone to split open. Even though the stone was still up in the air, it was ready to come down.

The man who took the burden of millions of people and placed it on his shoulder for 27 years, was forgotten. His accuser had forgotten him, but God did not forget his struggles, and wrangles. The man's love for equality and humanity revived their souls as they waited on his release. His pain became the rain that kept his people alive. Every tear that dropped from his eyes fell on them and gave them strength and hope as they prayed not to bury him on Robin Island. The people prayed that he would be free so he could lead them to freedom. He was in prison and powerless, but he was the future leader. It was really a long walk to freedom, and he surely led a war for justice without using a sword.

The TV was loud and I was sitting in front of it, very happy for Mr. Kamazulu and Zola, because it meant a great deal to them. He, Mandela, came second in their lives and God first. The two of them went downtown, in Toronto, to join the others in the African community to watch it together. I saw Mr. Mandela come down from the balcony waving, with a big smile, as the people danced and cried for joy.

My Aunt May tried to turn the TV off but I quickly agreed to wash the dishes for a week if she left it on. Mr. Mandela was a free man, just like butterflies that had been captured by cave bears. They smelled the air, and smelled the flower, but they could not get out of the cave. But, I said to myself, he was not quite free if he was not given justice. Equality for all men on earth was his theme song, so going to jail did not stop him. As soon as he got out, the struggle continued.

The Wind of Change

It was horrible, what the Europeans did to the African people, even the church that is supposed to demonstrate love, denied the black people love. "If the black man is a stranger and a slave on earth, what part of the planet did they come from? Where is their God?" It was my question, but I could not answer. I wanted to know for sure if the black man was a human, based on things that I heard about them.

But with Zola right by my side now, my questions were answered. Morality lost its grip on earth, those that read the Bible sometimes missed an important part that says, "Do unto others as you will have them do unto you, or "Love your neighbour as you love yourself."

These words were in my head as I was sitting in front of the television with mixed emotions. These Bible passages began popping into my head and, my Aunt May turned the TV off saying. "Son, all the fingers are not equal."

"These are not fingers Aunt May, they are human beings, they are people, for crying out loud," I said, but my Aunt May was sometimes stubborn.

When Mr. Mandela was released from jail a month later, he called to congratulate our school for its participation in his release. Saving Mandela High was a great political achievement, we later discovered. He asked to have a word with Zola; she took the phone and called him "Papa" and started to cry.

I later asked her if he, Mandela, was her father, but she said that he was the father of all the African people. She almost sounded like Mr. Kamazulu with his accent, but we all learned to talk like him, imitating him each day. In no time, all the students were talking like him. However, Zola was filled with emotion and tears as she talked to Mr. Mandela. They spent at least ten minutes in private conversation. I remember her saying something about West Africa, and then she closed the door behind her.

In June 1990, Mr. Mandela travelled to thank the Canadian government for its contribution and effort to end segregation in South Africa. There was one big meeting arranged at our school; people travelled from all over Canada to see him. Mandela High was not just a school after all; it was a school of history, a school that inspired many students around the world. Later on after our graduation, the principal wrote Zola telling her that someone from the ministry suggested that Mandela High become a private school. She had to fight to keep it a public school as it has always been. The school that was once a place for gangs and drug dealers had become an honourable school that they wanted to make an international school.

The academic development in the school was very necessary. If the school had been closed, or things were as it was in the beginning, this opportunity was going to pass us by: Mr. Mandela standing in front of our school and giving a speech that Zola built her whole life on, encouraging students to study, and study hard. Education is the only key that is able to open every door and change every life. Our school ground was used for many things that destroyed the lives of the students, but we soon forgot our failures and focused on hope. According to reliable sources, there was much conspiracy using Mandela High as a gate to carry on their business.

Canada played a big role in ending the apartheid, but why all the rules and regulations against the Aboriginals? They still lived on reserves and they are being pushed further up the mountain area. I tried to understand why a small school like Mandela High had such power, but then it was just hard to put the pieces together. It is politics, and I am not a politician.

Chapter Four

I hesitated asking Zola about her country of origin, but when I did, she told me not to be silly. "François, that is a very silly question to ask. Everyone in Canada came from somewhere, except the Aboriginal people. The time we spend asking people where they are from! When we spend the same amount of time asking people how they are doing, the world will not be as bad as it is. We should find a way to unite, not a way to separate. You came from Montreal and I came from Chinatown." We both laughed our cheeks out.

Mr. Kamazulu was very glad that President Mandela was acknowledging our school and they were able to connect. Our school was very important to him and many others, including Zola.

"Mandela reminds me of a great man who led Africa to her freedom during the 1950's black movement; it was all about 'Africa Unite now or Perish tomorrow.' Those were his words, and for sure, the Africans did perish. We have now risen up in unity and justice for all." Mr. Kamazulu said. "Mr. Mandela had to finish the work that that man started. His short life was all about uniting the African continent. If I could change a dictionary definition, I would create a new meaning for Mandela or create my own meaning for his name."

We asked him to give us some of the meanings he had in mind, and he went on: "The name 'Mandela' means 'power, hope, love, peace maker, light, and the voice for the people, change, courage, freedom, integrity,' and many more. Mandela is a very important man for the Africans and the whole world and an example that great change is possible," he explained. "When my office saw your school on the TV and how undisciplined you rats were, we had to come and help turn your hearts around. I had to come and put some African discipline in you all, and Mandela came to start his campaign right here. Of course saving you from yourself was the biggest campaign for us."

Mr. Kamazulu turned to Ben, an ex-gang member, and finished his sentence. "Look, I am very proud of you, Boy. If you change your thoughts, your actions will change as well. Mandela wrote that educational quote for you and you have proven him right."

Our school staff were very satisfied with the improvements to our school. Zola and I stayed late as usual, helping with hospitality, and often we heard Mr. Kamazulu walking in the hallway singing songs of love and freedom in one of the African languages. He spoke over ten African languages, which made him a typical traditional African Man who loves his people. He talked with great passion and power. He was very proud of his African heritage: "Africa is the most beautiful and blessed continent in the world. It is unfortunate that poverty is seeking our interest every day." Now, he was in Canada learning French. One particular song that I sang with him was the song of possibility in one of his native languages:

How can you deprive me of freedom?
When I was given the right to explore the land?
How can you say that I can't be loved?
When love is who created me?
How can you say that I will have no peace?
When I was born to be a peace maker?
How can you say that I am poor?
Yet, I am the heir of my Father's worth?
How can you prosecute me for my colour?
When I was created in His image?
How can you determine that I died before my first birthday?
When I was giving seventy years to live an extra ten as reward?
How can you use a machine gun to kill me?
I am just a human with a red blood cell.
How can you harden your heart toward me?
When the heart is where love begins.
My heart is as soft as yours, and we are one people, one earth, one nation, with one ocean, and one love under one sky.

My name is freedom and possibility, please let me live in freedom.
And accomplish the purpose for which I was created.
Please let me live my life.

As we sat down to do our class work, Zola walked over to Amanda, to discourage her from bullying her friends. Amanda was the girl of the 'key' incident, and who had attacked Zola in the hallway with a group of her friends on that cold winter day.

"Bullying is not a joke, Love," Zola said. "You are leading your friends astray. Do you want to see another suicide before you stop? I see that you are a good leader. Why don't you use your talent wisely? They usually say, 'To every good leader, there are good followers.' You have many followers, so just say it to the world, and they will listen. Why don't you lead them on a road that is marked with light and success for their future, or up the mountain where you can clearly see the rain falling, instead of taking them down the dark hold where there is destruction?

Then Zola asked her, "Would you come and be a part of the new transition student council?"

However, after all of this, Amanda refused and put on an arrogant attitude. Zola went back to her a few days later and whispered in her ear, saying. "You know, Hon…I know the people you are associating with. I even saw you yesterday, and I have pictures to show the police… It might end up on the evening news. The worst thing that could happen is that you could end up in prison. That will be the end of your father's political career. No one will believe that your father is not a drug dealer."

Before leaving, Zola turned around and added these words: "Maybe you don't know this, but the man who named this school board does not believe in hurting people. There was a time when he hated the white people who took over his land and treated them less than a pig. He lived in bitterness and anguish for many years. But one day he woke up and he remembered the suffering of his people, and then he realized that it was time to put his bitter hatred behind him for the sake of his beloved nation. If he had put pride before him, he would still be in prison and the people he was fighting for would continue to suffer while many perished. Nobody was born to hate, hate is learned, then practiced.

"There was always a mass grave ready to swallow up young protestors; thousands of them would be buried in a day. Many times, children went to school and never returned home. Like Mr. Kamazulu's father who did not make it to the evening meal, the great Steve Biko died trying. They fought for freedom. Today we can only remember them and continue the struggle of unity.

"Mr. Mandela's haters had the power to do with him whatever they desired. Their desire was to execute him, but they gave him a life sentence instead. Killing him was not a question, just a treacle, and hundreds of people would die with Mandela. They put him in prison for twenty-seven years, for his rights of wanting to live in a free and equal society. Today, he swallowed his pride and thought about the future of his followers, the whole human race. He did not want the world to receive his dead body from prison. Even though he was going to die trying, he also knew that there was a way if he tried. For the sake of all those people who died, the new generations of South Africa, his motherland, his haters became his best friends for a change.

"Listen to this one quote and go home, watch a movie called '*Sarafina*', then make your decision if you are ready for a change or you are ready to go down with your father."

As Zola was saying all of this, Amanda was sitting speechless, listening. I was sitting behind her watching Zola speaking words of encouragement, using life events to try to save Amanda from herself.

"If the pasture leads the sheep to the clean water, they will all drink from it. Bullying will create more problems for you and lead you into destruction, harming others on the way. You see how much trouble this school has been in.

"Did you see the documentary series this morning? He did not go to war to make himself famous, he became a negotiator. Yes! There was violence of demonstration along the way, but when it was time, he put himself and his people under control and walked in peace for love. Today, he is the father of many including myself, and godfather to the same people who destroyed him for twenty-seven years. A man once said that 'If you hold onto a rope, you need to hold it strongly, or you may fall on whatever is under you.' I see you falling into the river, and the only way out is if you hold my hand."

Zola then invited her to the self-control class that had just started. "Why don't you come and join us? It will be fun and there is plenty of room."

Amanda did not say anything, but her face was red, and in the next while, she broke three pencils. After that day, she was not seen in any cliques, and with her help, we were able to reach the rest of the group members. And soon after that, all of the groups were scattered. She was a completely-transformed girl. Zola used this strategy to abolish all the gang groups and cliques on campus.

As time went by, our school got, better, and better. All of the godfathers who were using our students to deal drugs or commit prostitution and child pornography, were gone. Some were behind bars, serving serious jail time, and some managed to escape. The Canadian agency of Interpol did a magnificent job, without causing any alarm. The students were given hundred-percent protection and they cooperated well. We were often on the breakfast news TV program because of our improvements. Ms. Lavender, our art teacher, really liked the attention; she dressed up every day hoping to be on TV.

The week that Amanda decided to give up bullying, a decision was made for Mandela High to be permanently closed. I remember that day when the observers entered the school to make their final decision. The students who usually hang around the school were all in class participating in discussions. The school was unique and still that morning – so much so that when the observers entered – they thought they were in the wrong school! One of them told the press that morning: "It is impossible. The school could not have changed overnight."

I could see the disappointment on their faces. King Solomon the great wise man said "There is time for everything under the sun," and it was time for Mandela High to shine in the community with flying colours. The school was not closed down.

Almost the entire teaching staff had something nice to say about Zola. Some said that she was a light that brought our school from darkness. Others would say she was an angel. "We need more of Zola among the youth in the world to make this world a better place. But this is what happens; when love appeared, hate disappeared." Our school had a complete makeover, "from serious cliques and gangs, to an inspirational institution." Now we were included in all of the provincial sports activities including track-and-field, my favourite. In fact, we won the spelling and math competitions twice in a row.

Some of the things that attracted me to Zola were her good leadership skills, and her sassy sense of humour. She had excellent moral reasoning skills—more than most girls her age. When her mates were busy looking for the newest novels or listening to the latest music, she was busy reading about Mahatma Gandhi. Or trying to figure out why Mother Teresa went out of her comfort zone to help make an impact on someone's life. At the end of Grade 12, I wanted to be more close to her than just a schoolmate, but every time I got close I did not feel right. I wanted to kiss her several times, but I did not have the guts to do it.

A year came and went with this mixed feeling inside of me; I did not want to distract her from school since she was doing so much already for the vice-principal. We went on an academic forum in Alberta, and on our way back, she asked me about what I was going to do after graduation. I could not answer that question because I had not made a career choice.

All I heard at home was about the prom night. Aunt May was waiting to see Zola for the first time. We were in grade 13 now and we definitely did not have much time. Zola was no longer a student; she was waiting to graduate with the others. She asked me in a certain way that showed concern about me. She was very calm and relaxed. It was almost like she was waiting to give a response to a question that I had not yet asked, or she knew what was on my mind.

As I watched her sleep on my lap, I had all kinds of thoughts running through my head. Maybe it was time for her to know how much I felt about her. We were both in our last year, and neither of us was involved with anyone, I mean relationship-wise.

"What is stopping us?" I asked myself in a very low voice, "I love you so much, If only you knew." Kissing her was not an option, but it was what I longed for. I could go right ahead and do it – but I could not! It was a long trip away from home, and she was resting on my shoulder, as I sat there with thoughts in my head. "I am eighteen," I said to myself. "It isn't real, but I'm just eighteen; why am I feeling this way? It is awful, but it feels great." I began talking to God, asking for help.

How could I fight an emotion as high as a mountain and as sweet as honey? Even though I had no opposition, I was still afraid to climb it and claim it. I was only eighteen and she was sixteen. My future was what I should have been thinking about, not a distraction. For our age, distraction was going to lead us to destruction and I could not allow that to happen. She had much ahead of her. I couldn't interfere with that but I also did not want to lose her either. "I can't lose her," I said out loud.

"Hmmm! You said something, François?" she said, waking.

"No, Love, go right back to sleep. It was just a thought, a crazy thought in my head. We are almost in Toronto…"

A few weeks later, it was Valentine's Day and everyone around us was planning for a party. The guys started calling me names: "Hey mama's boy, are you gay?" and another told me to turn her over to him, since I did not have eyes to see.

"Patience, guys, patience, these things take time," I told them.

"Says who?" one of them asked as they all started to coach me on what to say or how to walk. They did not understand what I was going through. My love for Zola was like a crystal glass or a young tree which could not easily be uprooted. I had to be gentle and careful with her. I wanted to be able to express my feelings and thoughts to her, but it was not the right time. If ever the time was seemed right, I did not have the right words. I didn't want a one-night time with her; I thought about spending my whole life with her. She was my "turtle", and it was my responsibility to make sure that no one put hot water in her shell.

On Valentine's Day of that year, I decided that it was time to tell her how much I was dying for her love. As much as I wanted her to be my lady, she was my best friend so I had to consider that as well. She was the one that prayed over our lunch every day. I started looking up to her more like a family member, but she was totally different in reality. She was nothing like Aunt May. Zola was very flexible, so I had to handle her with special care. I was protecting a long-lasting relationship – my friends had to know that. Facing Zola was an issue, so I decided to write her a letter.

"Dear Zola, I sit sometimes and wonder about us, and ask myself questions, questions that I cannot answer…but one thing I have come to realize is that I love you. I feel love for you; I see love when I look at you. I feel something much stronger and powerful in me. I think about you all day and night, and hope to be rescued by my own thoughts and feelings. Please give me a chance to love you. I do not know about tomorrow, because it cannot promise to anyone, but today, I know that I love you. You are the closest thing to my heart, and the best thing that ever happened to me; though of course, there is Aunt May! Will you be my Valentine? With love, François."

I wrote it with red ink. I read that letter at least a hundred times and I still remember all of the different positions I stood in as I practised expressing my love for her. I did not know what came over me; Zola had been my friend for so long, and I was not ready to jeopardize it for some crazy thoughts in my head. I did not want any foolish thoughts to come between us, so I decided not to send her the letter. I went to get her a card instead.

As I was in the store looking for cards, I heard a voice behind me. "Hey, who do we have here? The French Man himself; how are you? Looking for some nice sweet cards for your lady?"

It was Ben. "Hey! Someone is in love?"

"You scared me, man; you always appear like a cat. Ben, what's up? I am not in love. Don't tell anyone that you saw me, please. I'm looking for a card for Zola, but can't find the right one. I have checked almost all of the cards, but they're just the same old style."

"All of the cards?" Ben asked me. "That sounds like a man in love. Wow! It is about time; both of you deserve it. Let me see, this is what I would give my sweetheart," Ben said.

"Ben, for real, you have many sweethearts. Who are you talking about?"

"All of them. Keep my secret, and I keep yours. One of the new teachers likes me; he has been giving me money and helping me study."

"What, 'he'? No Ben, it is wrong. I can't keep it. A teacher and a 'he,' not even 'her'?"

"Forget about this conversation, François." Ben shook his head, singing and walking in the store.

"Well Ben, I am a one-woman man and I don't do teachers; not guys, Ben."

As soon as I said that, he kissed me. I was shocked, and very angry. "You should cut it off; what are you doing, man? You crazy man."

"I am sorry, I was trying to show you how to kiss your lady."

"No Ben, you crossed the line."

He agreed to stop whatever was developing between himself and the teacher, but kissing me was out of place.

"You don't have to practice on me. Ben, look, man, please help me find a nice card for my lady."

"I have an idea," Ben said. Why don't you come over to my house and practise a speech for your lady? I am a professional when it comes to dating you know."

"No, Man, I will pass. With all you told me today and what happened, you don't look professional at all," I told him and walked away.

I was thrilled to see Ben taking his education seriously, but what he said about the teacher…I had a big problem with that. He was one of the victims of the massive drug-abuse problem in our school. Ben was smuggled into the country as a child-porn victim from Eastern Europe. The godfathers used him as a gateway to reach the kids at Mandela High, and this affected his learning capacity. He had been with them since age nine, and he was nineteen when I left Mandela High. With his help, they recruited more students from our school.

Ben had a very handsome face, and natural blond hair. He was not a laid-back person; he went around making jokes and teasing. His silly jokes helped bring us together, but he was always in to our affair. Though he has that six-foot-two height, he did not touch a basketball at school, not once. Ben was often seen with the ladies on the cheering squad, so it surprises me that he would even listen to whomever that teacher was.

I did not express my heart's desire to my beautiful Zola, so I went home empty-handed with disappointment. "Oh, how has she stolen my heart, Aunt May. I just don't know what to say to her; I went this close, but I did not say anything. I just don't want to mess up."

"If that is the case, my son, you are not ready. You have your whole life ahead of you. Why don't you take it one day at a time?" Aunt May said. She told me not to beat myself up. The good Lord was going to keep us together, if it was his will, at the right time.

"Aunt May, please, is God going to determine who I love? What happened to our free will?"

But she got angry and spoke in a high tone: "I don't think that God appreciates you using his name the way you do. Don't forget, He is listening. I am not going to be a part of your sin."

I walked into her bedroom and there I saw on the wall a poem that took my breath away. I wanted to know where it came from, so I screamed her name from the room. "Aunt May!"

"Yes, Son, yes, Son?" she answered.

"*This* is how I feel about her..."

"Where are you and what are you talking about, Son?" She had to shout.

"Your poem, the one hanging in your room, the 'fire' thing."

"Oh dear." She came into the bedroom and sat down next to me on the bed. "King Solomon wrote this for his lover."

I asked her to read it for me. "I want to feel love."

"Well, Son, I don't know about the love part."

"Please... Aunt May."

"Okay, Son."

"Oh – and will you personalize it, pretend that you are Zola and I am François?"

"But you are François," she said.

"I'm confused, Aunt May. Do it the other way around."

"You are in love, Son, it is a natural reaction, and don't be scared. Do you want me to begin reading?"

"Yes, Aunt May, please."

"Zola...place me like a seal over your heart, like a seal on your arm; for your love is as strong as death, its jealousy unyielding as the grave. Your love burns like a blazing fire, and a mighty flame. Much water cannot quench my love for you. No river will be able to wash it away. If I was to give all my wealth of my home, it would be utterly scorned. You have nothing, and you live with me. You will have to sell me first." She stopped reading.

"Is that part of the poetry or are you spoiling my moment with Zola?"

"Zola is not here," Aunt May said. "And you are in my bed." She ended the reading.

"It is beautiful, Aunt May; will I ever be ready to tell her that to her face?"

"When the time comes, you will, Son, you will."

I never saw Aunt May in love with anyone, so I asked her about it, but she told me that she was in love with her maker. "It is God who is expressing His desire for me."

"How can you not fall in love, when God created love? This has nothing to do with Christianity; you decided not to fall in love. I am eighteen, and up to now, I can't understand your language."

"Yes, Child, it is not your place to understand me."

Chapter Five

I did not express myself and my love for her, but I still got to spend the evening with Zola. We also had two occasions in February to attend. Our school decided to celebrate Black History Month. Zola and Mr. Kamazulu were the guest speakers for the night. Zola knew about the party at school, but she did not know that she was a speaker. She was in total shock when we entered. She was given a certificate of excellence, as was Mr. Kamazulu. She was now a part of Black History month because she became one of the history makers; Mandela High will always remember her.

It was our last year of high school and Zola was going to be my prom queen. It was April and we were way ahead of schedule. Zola was elected as our valedictorian, and she was working hard to prepare a speech. I knew it meant a great deal to her and for the school. She inspired and motivated us, showed us that anything is possible. She taught us that we had to step out in order to step in. Mandela High was transformed forever. She did some amazing things for our school, and the community.

The prom was also around the corner so we were busy looking for the best dresses and suits. One of the ex-Fever Girls was planning an after-prom party in her parents' home. Vanity controlled her parents and their finances. Zola and I planned to go in matching white, but she later refused.

Aunt May said she would arrange for a limousine to pick us up. It was prom night and Zola looked more beautiful than ever. Her eyes were like rich jewels, she stood erect with her tall neck, very attractive. Her hair looked like the finest of silk, but soft and curly. Her lips were naturally glowing, with just a little shea butter. She smiled at me as the limousine driver let her in. I was surprised at her beauty and I could not say a word except "You look lovely, Zola." She was a true star, my star. I imagined her standing on the red carpet.

A light just shone upon her and she glowed, she looked like a princess, an exotic Cinderella princess. She wore an African traditional dress called a *Kenti*, with a combination of three colours, very striking.

The limousine arrived an hour early, so we went driving around the city. What a moment; it was like the Wind of Silence had just blown in my face and became instantly visible. It was the best day of my life. In reliving that moment, I can never get tired watching her beauty.

"I love it, and I love everything about tonight and I love you, François."

"I love you too, Zola. Wait – did you just say that you…love me?" I asked.

"Yes, I did. Do you want me to take it back?"

"Noooooooo! Not a chance! You are so beautiful, you are an angel."

"I will always be here for you. You are my best friend, and the closest thing to my heart."

"Today, I vow to never leave you or forsake you. I will always be the shoulder you cry on, Zola."

"You are getting too emotional on me, French Man. What happens when we go to university?"

"I will also be there."

"And when Africa decides to look for me?"

"Don't worry; we will all go with Mr. Kamazulu to Africa," I told her.

"François, yes, okay, stop daydreaming. We have to go to the prom."

"Yes, of course."

We laughed and chatted for a little while, then we left for the prom. Our friends had gotten tired of waiting, so they had decided to go ahead with the program. It was difficult for them, choosing the prom queen and king without Zola and me but as we opened the door, they were calling the winner:

"And this year the Mandela High prom King and Queen are…François and Zola!"

It was far beyond my imagination.

"Wow, we made it!" Zola said.

"You are the best, Zola."

"Thanks, Love, you are the greatest."

"What is going to happen after graduation, Zola?"

"It is not yet graduation, François. Enjoy the prom."

The prom was wonderful. The day before graduation we went to help Mr. Kamazulu prepare to leave.

"We will miss you, come back and visit us soon," Zola told him.

"No, I am not coming back! Why don't you all come to South Africa for a visit? This is a special invitation now that your Papa is running for presidency. You get to stay at the executive suite," Mr. Kamazulu told us.

"Do you think that he will win?" I asked him.

"He won twenty-seven years ago, but they cheated. Now we are going for the recount," Zola said boldly. "In developing or Third-World countries, they don't honour free and fair elections; whoever has the power always wins. Except, of course, if the United Nations keeps a close eye on the election, but even at that, they have their limits. I have said enough, but this time around, it is time for black South Africans to taste leadership, govern their own people, and assure the world that we are human and we are capable of leadership." Zola was talking looking right into Mr. Kamazulu's eyes, with tears rolling down her cheeks.

"You've been away from home for a long time; do you have a job waiting there for you?" one of the students asked him.

"Yes girls and boys. Do not worry; I am going to be fine. Besides, Africa is my home, and the rats there are more disciplined then you guys. When I say stop, they stop. Over here, when I say stop, you move. You have managed to reverse the definition of many words but I enjoy working with you all," Mr. Kamazulu said. "I am very proud of you all for your commitment to changing Mandela High. You all have made a difference in the world. Keep it up, and remember, there is much work for you ahead. I helped you get this far so push yourselves and move forward. Remember, success is in you, it is your heart's desire. Never stop fighting fear. I am feeling good about myself, and you all should try it as well."

He was really leaving us. We could not convince him to stay.

"We will not say good bye, but we will say thank you, African Power." Zola gave him a hug and she could not let go of him. She suddenly became emotional, and cried.

"Hey child, what is the matter?" he said. "Whenever you want to come to Africa, give me a call." Mr. Kamazulu told us that most Africans came to the West for political reasons. They would love to go back to Africa if all these lions could get their act together.

"The problem about Africa is this: when you speak your mind or the truth, you become a threat to the government. If you don't go to a safe place to stay, your family will find you killed," Zola said as she wiped her face.

"Hey, young lady, I don't have time to talk politics, but you are very right. There should be freedom of speech," Mr. Kamazulu said as he helped wipe the tears from Zola's face.

"I miss…I miss…I will miss you," she said.

"I am not leaving today," he said, "I will leave right after graduation tomorrow. So you have the next twenty-four hours to take the best out of me." He reminded Zola that they might have met somewhere before.

"If you feel this strong about knowing me, why don't you take me with you? Africa will be delighted to see me."

"Africa wants you, and Africa needs more of you. Okay boys and girls, that's enough, the movie will begin soon."

"Yes, Zola, we have to go," I told her.

"Wait! I have something to give you," Zola said.

"What is it, another quote?" Mr. Kamazulu asked.

"No!" she answered. "I can't send Papa a quote; he is the master of quotes. Every word from his mouth is meaningful. This is for you and for President Madiba of South Africa." She gave him the souvenir.

"Amen! He will be president." Mr. Kamazulu examined the object. "Zola, where did you get this?" he asked very anxiously.

"Yes, Zola, where did you get it? I said, laughing at her.

"I bought it at a garage sale."

"Whose garage sale? Wait a minute, what garage sale?" Mr. Kamazulu said. "Do you know what this is? It cost a fortune!"

"Yes, Zola," I said. "Where did you get that thing? You need the money for books, stationary, etc. I heard that college is very expensive; we need to save every penny," I explained to her.

"Money is not everything. Besides, I have a godfather who is going to be the next President of South Africa. If my grandmother runs out, he will run in."

I laughed at the sound of that and said, "Very funny. The president will drop everything he has to do and run to Canada to rescue you," I told her.

"It is called love, and I am his favourite," Zola said.

"Do you mean *one* of his favourites?" I asked her.

Mr. Kamazulu was standing over her.

Then she said, "It is antique and it is very beautiful; I could not resist it."

"Antique is not the right word for it; it is a real treasure," said Mr. Kamazulu. "I have read about it but I saw it only in a book. Now I have the honour to touch it. In the whole world only three of these were made. One is in the Pan-African headquarters, one is in Ghana, and the other is missing, now in my hand from the home of a garage. According to history – " he said, but Zola cut him off.

"No, please! We have to go, no more history. We are late for the movie," Zola quickly interrupted me, so he was not able to begin the story behind the treasure. We arrived at the movie theater, and the movie had started half an hour before we got there. So I suggested we go back. I wanted to hear the rest of the story he was about to tell us, so we headed back home.

If the treasure was as important as our teacher said it was, how did it end up in Canada? Even Mr. Kamazulu did not have an answer. When we got back to his place that night, I asked him to continue the story, but Zola was too tired to sit, so she decided to take a nap on the sofa.

"Okay, young man," said Mr. Kamazulu. "I will be very quick. There is a graduation tomorrow and you need plenty of rest."

"Yes, Sir!" I told him. The other students had left, so it was just the three of us.

He started by warning me that it was a very long story, but also assured me he would get to the point. "Many years ago, a man called Dr. Kwame Nkrumah started a freedom movement to free all of Africa from the hands of the Europeans. South Africa is still crying and dying to be free. Thank God our cries have reached Heaven and we have been sent help. The land of South Africa needs healing and Madiba is the only remedy we have.

"The Sudanese have been fighting since the beginning of the struggle for freedom in Africa, and they are still fighting. They need to come to one understanding and unite. So do the people of Angola. Colonialism dominated the entire African continent and every black man in the world became a slave. According to my father, the Europeans had all gone to

Africa and forcefully took their possessions and refused to go home. They exported the Africans as slaves, and some made Africa their home."

"I know that part, Mr. Kamazulu, but what is it about that treasure?"

"Patience, boy, you will not understand the story behind the treasure without the root of the story and the people. Call me Zulu," he said.

"What — after three years of Mr. Kamazulu, now you tell me to call you Mr. Zulu?"

"Yes, Zulu is easy," he said. "The young Kwame Nkrumah was very educated, and full of ambition. He saw a vision for the Africans in the world; not just Africa, but all nations who were under colonial rules. And he thought the only way he could achieve this was through education himself.

"During his study, he came in contact with many politicians like George Panmore and many others. He later formed his own political party and an organization of over 90,000 people. He freed his people from the hands of British government. In 1957, he became the first African Prime Minister in Ghana. Dr. Nkrumah led the Gold Coast, now Ghana, to their freedom, in 1957, on March 6. He worked together with two other great leaders, President Ahmed Sekou Toure of Guinea, and Prime Minister Patrice Lumumba of Congo. It wasn't long before Jomo Kenyataa from Kenya and others joined them to rise up for Africa.

"With these three people working together, it was the beginning of a new Africa in the world. Soon, all of Africa looked up to him for direction for their freedom. Among his supporters and advisers was the late President John F. Kennedy of the United States of America. My father had a picture with JFK, Dr. Kwame and himself in 1961, just before JFK was assassinated. Those were precious moments of his life. You can see President Kennedy standing next to my father with hope in his eyes, and full of joy and hope for the future of the black people. Every day I look at that photograph, I cry and pray to see all of Africa united. My father went back home to South Africa and he later got killed protesting against the apartheid.

Mr. Zulu paused, "It is going to take a little longer than I expected, so call your mother and let her know that I will drop you home."

"My Aunt May has no problem with me being here, she admires you greatly. Just continue the story." (I was lying, Aunt May wanted Mr. Zulu to sound like a Canadian. 'I never hear a word from that man; can't he go to the ESL class.' she would say.)

He continued: "He later renames the country after the ancient African kingdom, from Gold Cost to Ghana. Many activists went to Ghana from the United States and the Caribbean, crying out for knowledge to be free. Dr. Kwame Nkrumah organized the All-African Revolutionary Party. In 1958, all of Africa came together and discussed an important issue: 'Africa Must Unite.'"

When he said those words, Zola woke up, and she asked him to end the story. "You are leaving my favourite part out of the story, and I am impatient waiting."

"Hey, young lady, he said "Why are you not sleeping?"

"I love this story, and I love him. I can remember my mother telling me this story. I listened to all of his speeches, and I have read all of his books. I love Dr. Nkrumah; he was a good friend of my…mother. He is dead, but alive in me."

"Yes, young lady, when did your mother go to Africa? Dr. Nkrumah is a part of all black people and the father of Africa."

We laughed at Zola and Mr. Zulu told her to end the story. "Go ahead, my Jamaican sister."

"Why do you all think that I came from Jamaica? I am not a Jamaican. If I came from Jamaica, then where did you come from, Mr. Zulu? You taught us that every black man came from Africa so why will you not believe that I am an African?" She changed the tone of her voice and we became quiet.

"He saw a vision of a New Africa in the world ready to stand and face their own battle, he told his friends. Here, I will quote some of his words, so you know what a great man he was. I recorded his speeches in my head: 'This mid-20th century is for Africa; this decade is for African independence. It is going to be The United States of Africa. We have come to the end of segregation, which is a new beginning of a new Africa in the world. Tomorrow, all Africa will be united under one single flag with each star for each country. Africa is for African, black power.'

"From 1957 to 1966, Dr. Nkrumah led twenty-six African countries to their freedom. He said that all Africa will be one. It is the dream of all black man, whether Caribbeans, Africans in Africa, African-Americans, we all are one. But this seems impossible now, because greed has cost man his soul, and given birth to corruption; it will never happen."

"Zola, are you crying?"

"You are also crying, French Man."

"We are all crying. We should stop and get some sleep, for tomorrow is going to be busy," Mr. Zulu said in a sad voice.

She continued, "'We have to wake up, and we are not going back to sleep any more. Our independence is meaningless unless it reaches to the rest of the African continent. Let us unite, let us unite and keep hope alive.' These are words from Dr. Nkrumah."

After the three hours of history lesson, I was not sure if I would ever find out about the treasure.

"This is the great Wind of Change," said Mr. Zulu, holding up the object. "It was made in Angola in the early 1960's before they got their independence in the heat of the first war. Dr. Nkrumah travelled to Angola trying to end what seems to be an endless war that is still going on. The war was to liberate them, but it ended in civil war which led to death road. His thoughts behind the treasure were that one day Africa will unite and become one; there will be no need for any ethnicity. Black and white, we are all the same human race.

"This is our land and we are blessed with every natural resource; what Africa has is enough for the whole world. Dr. Nkrumah spent an awesome amount of money on the way to freedom. This treasure is never to leave the African soil. It belongs to the people of Africa. It should not have ended up in the West at a garage sale. We are still waiting for the Wind to blow and change the African continent. This symbolizes the love, peace and unity that Dr. Nkrumah and his associate extended to Africa. Unfortunately, there has not been a stronger leader to get closer to the vision. Greed and corruption has stolen their hearts. Every rising leader has been brutally assassinated with a bullet in the head, or a body totally damaged without a trace of how he died. You saw the example: twenty-seven years locked up for no reason. He got out only by the grace of God's divine intervention. No word of man was going to set him free.

"I guess the United States of Africa will never be. Did you see how many children died in Angola yesterday?" Zola said in tears.

"Hey, my little wise lady, stop crying. Angola, and Sudan, will rise up, and there will be complete peace in every valley, and on every mountain on earth. There is a season for everything. You know that even the cat eventually gets tired of chasing the mouse.

"The Africans once tried to come together as one, but there was a very strong antagonist among them who protested against the decision and the main brains behind the master plan died one at a time. At that time, the Nigerian president proposed that a plot of land be set aside in Cameroon as the headquarters. Up to today's date, the land is there."

For a second I thought that he forgot the main lesson. He continued:

"In the late 1980s, there was a young, brilliant and intelligent leader that was heading towards the vision of a united Africa…I really liked that guy. I was about to move to Burkina Faso because of him, but the usual thing happened to him. 'Sankara, Thomas Sankara'."

"Hey, I like that song, isn't that one of Alpha's songs?"

"Yes, Son! Sankara is the young leader that I am speaking about. Boys and girls, the rest is politics and history, my work here is done. I am in South Africa, and we are not yet a member of the Pan-African government, but very soon, very soon, it will happen. I am a Pan-African and most South Africans are; it is our root. Pertaining to the treasure, I will give it to Madiba. He will know what to do with it. One people, different colours, and different politics. Besides, I am not a politician."

"Zola, what are we to expect tomorrow? Did you hear the students? They can't wait for tomorrow to see you up there speaking. Are you envious?" I asked her, but she shook her head.

"Boy, I think you are more nervous than she is," said Mr. Zulu. "You should go and get some rest. Hey, my friend can you handle tomorrow? The crowd will be a little different from what you are used to. The principal has invited other distinguished guests. Do you want to practise your speech?" Mr. Zulu asked her, but saw she was only laughing at us.

"Mr. Teah was asking me how many pages you had written down."

"French Man, will you relax? I will be fine," she insisted.

Then Mr. Zulu stood up with his car keys in his hand. "Ooh, boys and girls," he said.

"Mr. Zulu, do you mean, boy and girl?" I corrected him.

"You are the brain, and I am only a substitute teacher," he said.

Zola jumped in: "Do you mean an undercover agent?"

"It works, doesn't it? Let us go now! It is very late. Very, very late."

He dropped us home. By the time I got home that night, it was almost 2:00 a.m. He told us to consider Thomas Sankara University, with its major in International Development. "You might like it."

I slept a little and woke up around 5:00, thinking about the black people and their struggles.

Thank God, all of that was over now. If only they could work together, Africa would be the greatest continent in the world managing their resources. I guess the people in charge couldn't allow that to happen. How could people have so much power over others and nothing could be done to stop them? With so much corruption and greed, would Africa ever come close to the vision of the United States?

I kept asking myself questions that I had no answers for, but I could not help it. "If they stop this ruthless conspiracy, the Africans will become one, and develop their beautiful continent. Could it really be true that there were secret rumours, but no secret was revealed? Aunt May would say "Rulers in high places." Since I couldn't make up my mind what to do in college, maybe I should consider studying International Development so I could be a real helping hand to people.

We all met on the campus just around 2:00 p.m., and Zola looked great as usual. We got in to the hall together, and it was time for the big moment. Our friends called me into the class to ask about Zola's capability of delivering the speech. It did not take long when she walked in the classroom.

"There you are. Why are you all in here, and why are you having a meeting without me?"

"We were wondering about what you're going to talk about. Whatever you do, don't say my name," Ben said.

Then another student said, "It is okay if you call my name in your speech, but nothing about the ugly things that we did in the past. Yes, my lady, something positive, because your grandmother is here to hear you speak. I know it will be great – and peaceful, right?"

The way he said it, I thought that he might have been Peace who Zola fed for the longest time. However, I was not going to play any detective. It was a happy day, and the atmosphere truly was alive, as we all gathered together sharing fun.

Zola laughed her eyes out, saying, "I can't believe you are all in here wondering and worrying about my speech. You will have to kidnap me, but

The Wind of Change

I am not telling any of you what is on my paper! You really have nothing to worry about. I can assure you that you will like it. Let's go out there and say good-bye to our wonderful teachers. By the way, you all look very suspicious…try to relax a bit. I should be the one worrying."

In the auditorium: "Our guest speaker today is a young lady who helped build this school on a rock. We do not have any words to describe her, but put your hands together and welcome our one and only, Zola, the woman of noble character…"

That was our principal introducing her, and we all stood up and applauded. Zola walked up to the stage in complete silence, and stood there for over five minutes obviously trying to fight the tears. Then she finally said:

"You did it. You have laid down a ground flow for the next generations to come. Take this experience with you and help contribute to the world. You were ready for it. You saw a vision and you believed that it was possible. You had a chance and you went for a change.

"Because of your hard work, today we receive the wind of excellence. It is love that brought Mandela High this far. When you find yourself climbing a mountain or in the dumps feeling discouraged, remember that you are not alone. Don't give up hope. Climb with your head held high; you will realize that it took you less time. I must admit, it was not easy coming this far. With perseverance, we did it, together.

"As we leave from here to pursue our future, let us remember Mandela High, where we cried together, and laughed together, where we fought the fight of hope and change. There is much work ahead of us and for us; you have the foundation in your hand. We survived Mandela High, and we will survive anywhere with careful thoughts of love and sharing. Remember, it is not what happened here, but what you did, and how you did it matters. That's what you take with you. Remember, 'Failure is not a defect, but a stepping stone to keep trying.' The child will fall many times while learning to walk; he has to master falling before standing firm to run the race of life. When you fail, keep trying until you get it right.

"We had great teachers and of course a wonderful principal who refused to let go of Mandela High. You are all awesome. On behalf of all of my mates here, we salute you for your encouragement and inspiration. Without you we would have stayed down in the valley, and perished. You believed in us and did not give up on Mandela High. Thank you. A wise man once said that the best teacher is one who brings the best out of a student, not he who inputs. You brought the best out of us. You have sowed a seed in us and we have ripened it. It is now our turn to sow seeds as much as we can, to make this earth a safer place. God bless you, God bless Mandela High, and God bless Canada."

Chapter Six

Most people expected an extraordinary speech from Zola, but she had given us a short speech instead, and it was the best. We were all incredibly motivated. She told her fellow students that college or university was never to be compromised. With Zola, we never knew what to expect. I was always learning new and wonderful things from her.

"It was a lovely day," Zola said as she walked over to me.

"Yes it was!"

I guess this is it, hey?" she said.

"Well, not totally! We have all summer to catch up and then college," I told her.

"Yes, college. I almost forgot about college," she lied.

"No, you did not. You are Zola, you can't forget."

"One last picture!" The school principal came running up to us with her camera. It was time for a great group hug with Mr. Zulu.

"Mr. Zulu, I will miss you; we are all going to miss you. How will our school survive without you?" said our principal.

"Yes, you will, and you can," Mr. Zulu answered.

"We want you to stay; you are a part of Mandela High now, a part of a big happy family here," the principal appealed.

But Mr. Zulu refused. "Thanks for the offer, but I have overstayed already."

"If it is for immigration reasons that you have to go, for the great job you've done at Mandela High, the immigration department will definitely consider your request as a skilled worker." She kept insisting that he stay because she did not know that Mr. Zulu had chosen not to get his permanent resident permit.

"My work here is done; the people back home need me. Madiba will become the president next year and I have to be there."

"Zola needs you, and I'd…I'd like you to stay. Are you married, Mr. Zulu?"

"Oh my principal, please call me Zulu – and no, I am not married. My work did not allow me to. I am very committed to my country, and my work. They have another mission for me."

"Another mission?" asked the principal. "What do you mean by that? Are you here on a mission… Are you a secret agent?" she whispered.

Mr. Zulu said, "Look, the Canadian government plays a big role in the liberation of South Africa and before his release from jail, Canada was our first hope. The Canadian government is involved with 'End Apartheid'. Look around you; you have people of all nations living together. The South Africans have suffered, and the youth have died like ants.

"It was planned that right after his release from prison, he would come to meet with the parliament members to discuss how to move forward."

"Sorry to interrupt you," I said, "but I need to talk to Mr. Zulu for a minute,"

"François, don't you know when not to disturb?" said the principal.

"I'm sorry, but it's important."

"This is important as well. Whoever it is and whatever it is can wait. I need to be with him now. Let me enjoy his company for this one last time," the principal said, so I stopped asking.

My principal had her eyes on Mr. Zulu ever since she got to know the real 'him.' He was quiet and a kind humble gentleman, and in fact quite remarkable.

As I turned my back to leave, he began to talk to the principal again: "Your school reputation was not good and it worried me. It was setting us back with the 'Free Mandela' protest. Every time I turned the TV on, there was some negative news about Mandela High. Children involved in drug deals, pornography, illegal gun sales, and bullying…this is a school here, not a battle field.

"It is not just the name that brought me here. These kids did not do these things on their own. There were underground secrets that no one can speak of. People died when they came close. These kids were used; the conspiracy in the world is against children, and it is our responsibility to protect them. They are the future leaders.

"With Madiba spending almost three decades in a jail cell, the African people were not ready to lose another great leader. Your government had decided to shut down the school for its safety. If Madiba came out and heard about this school, he would never have come to Canada. For many other reasons which I can't tell you, we had to step in and change this school forever," he said.

"My mission was accomplished, and the school is doing well. Here is your most successful graduation in ten years. Congratulations, my lady."

"What about Zola, is she one of you?" the principal asked.

"No, she is not, she is just a student," he responded.

"Wow, quite a story! I guess you do have to go."

"Yes, my lovely lady. You should come for the inauguration in South Africa."

They turned and started for the door. "François, what are you still doing here! Oh my God, have you been listening all this while?" my principal asked.

"Yes."

"How much did you hear?" She was now panicking.

"Everything," I told her. She was looking at me as if I did something wrong. She had no idea that I was familiar with the story, but I allowed her to be a top KGB secret agent for a moment.

"I am very disappointed in you, François, this is top secret and it can't be revealed to anyone. Not even the Jamaican girl."

"Yes, Madam. But she is not a Jamaican." (Zola didn't like to be called a Jamaican girl. We laughed at how she was ashamed of her background.)

"Okay, my good friends," said Mr. Zulu, "I have to catch my flight."

We drove him to Pearson Airport that afternoon. He almost missed his flight, but thank God, we were able to get him there in time.

Zola and I spent all summer together in Hamilton, volunteering at the Family church. Zola was more like Aunt May at church. She had that wonderful relationship with her church family but I did not. I had never fit into a church, and it didn't ever seem to work out. One morning, I felt that I had to let her know how I felt about the church. She came in very excited that day, but I disappointed her:

"Zola, I can't go with you tomorrow."

"Okay, but why?"

I told her I had some important things to take care of. She was not convinced. "What is more important than working at the church?" she asked me.

"The church is not the building, you know. We are the church."

"François, my love, if you are going to church to please me, then I will ask you not to."

"What?" I asked her."

"Sorry, Sweetie, that came out wrongly. God is within you." She rubbed my shoulder. "You need to develop a personal relationship with your God. You can fool me, but you cannot fool the Big Guy up there. He is watching everyone down here. Besides, they usually say, 'you can fool some people sometimes, but you cannot fool all the people all the time'. I knew that you didn't like it for a while now… Just be yourself and pray that God will reveal Himself to you."

"Oh, Zola, I have tried."

"Don't worry, if it is your desire, He will help you 'believe your unbelief'." She looked into my eyes. "Hey François, don't turn me into a pastor. I'm not."

"You are perfect; everything about you is perfect, Zola."

"No, Love, only God is perfect. Pastors are human themselves, and they are also depending on the Big Guy up there for grace," she said, then picked up her bag to leave.

I followed her. "College is going to be great, Zola; at least I will not have to worry about church," I told her.

"I cannot believe you just said that to me, French Man."

"No! I did not, the wind said it."

The summer was great, and we were ready to go to school. Both Zola and I were going to Thomas Sankara University, and her tuition was paid for by a scholarship. Maa did not have to worry about tuition, only the cost of the books.

I was going for international development just like Mr. Zulu had suggested. I enjoyed the classes but eventually I decided that it was not my ideal direction. A year later, I dropped it and started a business program. I wanted to dress in suits and discuss business, not solve problems in third world countries.

It was nearly two years, and I kept thinking about Mr. Zulu, and all his encouraging words and inspirational stories. Those words have been healing to my soul, and very comforting. It was difficult to forget Mr. Zulu. "Boys, I see greatness in you, all of you. You will be fine young men in the not too distant future," he would say. In the middle of my imagination, I heard a voice. It was Zola standing over me. "Hi, François."

"What a pleasant surprise!" I said. "I was just thinking about Mr. Zulu."

"Yes," Zola said, "I miss him too. I have some time coming up next month. I want to go see him. Do you want to come?"

"I'd love to, but I am behind with school work."

"Hey, Boy, you've been a very bad boy."

"Yes, Zola, that is very funny."

"I am going to give a lecture at the Haile Selassie University tomorrow. I will be there for a week. Did you listen to the announcement that… You look distracted François. Is everything all right?"

"Yes, what announcement?"

"I will be graduating earlier than expected."

"I heard it, Love. I am very happy for you. This calls for a celebration. Wait! What will happen after that?" I asked her."

"I will be doing what I was doing now, teaching and doing my masters."

"What about me? I mean us?"

She did not hear me; she had walked away. "Just a second, François, I will be right back. I think this girl needs help." She approached the girl. "Hello there, you look lost. Can I help you?"

The young student looked appreciative. "I brought my transcript, but I don't know my way to the main office. I will be attending here next year," the girl said.

"Oh that is good. You are a beautiful girl," said Zola. "What is your name?"

"Natasha Chizyuka."

"You have a beautiful name," Zola told her.

"Yes! It means, 'Joy'."

"That's lovely," Zola replied.

"Are you an African?" Natasha asked Zola.

"Yes, we are all from Africa, my love."

Natasha stood looking at Zola. Even with her heels, she was still small. "My father came from Zambia and my mother is from Zimbabwe."

"I like you," Zola said to the girl. "Why don't you take my card and give me a call sometime if you need any other information."

"Thanks, Zola!" Natasha said then walked away.

"Goodbye, and watch your steps, Dear," Zola said. "Where were we?" she asked me. "You, my dear François, have made a vow to always be there for me as God is willing and to protect me from all these giant professors. Is that right?"

"Yes, very right."

"When you vowed to love me forever, we became one." Zola smiled. "We are fine, François. We are more than fine," she said. "We are going to be fine. Whatever happens, I want you to know that I am here for you, French Man."

I listened with enormous relief. I was trying to protect my relationship with her, and of course protect her from those professors and the entire faculty staff, especially from Mr. Short Matheson who thought that he had just found his lost daughter. I did not like the way he made her cover for him while he pretended to be busy marking papers, but I needed not to worry; she was the wise girl who could take care of herself. She had so much going on and I did not want to push her, so I tried to take things slowly.

She gave me a big hug. "I love you, French Man. We are together for life."

"I will take your word on that," I told her. "I will see you in a week."

Zola came back a week later. She went with one of the professors to Montreal to receive an award. It was only two years and some months, and she was getting her BA. T.S. University could not comprehend her knowledge. She was too quick to understand. Mr. Zulu often referred to her as "the shaker of the tree." He would tell her that one day, she was going to shake the nation if she kept the lamp burning. I did not see her shaking any trees but Zola was shaking school, and lives were being transformed. Mr. Zulu also told Zola that he had dreamed a dream about her living in a palace.

When she heard of the dream, she told him that "With God all things are possible."

I didn't want to hurt her in any way so I often prayed that God would help me be a real man, because she didn't look as if she was ready for a relationship.

"Hey, Lover Boy, how are you? Are you still in love?" Ben stormed up to me under the tree.

"Hey Ben, how are you? Glad to see you, Man." Ben told me that he was also in Sankara.

"I am proud of you, Man. Welcome." I gave him a hug and offered to help him in any way I could.

"How is your lady – did you two maintain your relationship?"

"Yes, Ben, we are doing very well, thanks for asking. As a matter of fact, she is on her way to South Africa on an academic trip."

"South Africa, without you? With whom, to whom?"

"Ben, Ben, relax. It's just school, and work, and Mr. Zulu."

"You need to be a man," Ben said. "Your woman is in the spotlight; keep your eyes open. You can't trust these brainy ones."

"Yes, Ben, thanks for the advice, and I will definitely see you around."

Zola was a blessing to everyone she met and she was no "ordinary" girl. She was always found with the professors, and Harvard University actually offered her a fulltime job, but she was already doing that at Sankara.

I was becoming distracted by her success. She had big dreams and I did not fit anywhere in them. I decided to back off; I was not going to deprive her of living a full life.

She was spectacular, though. Her presence would both calm the sea and change the direction of the wind at any time. How could I have stood between that? Fifty percent of her earnings was set aside for different charities and organizations to help refugees around the world. And every time she was less busy, she went to the Children's Hospital to volunteer.

Zola would travel and lecture, then return the following day and rush to the hospital when she had to. I hardly saw her, and she did not go home as often as she would have liked. In fact, a few times Maa brought her ginseng tea to drink, but since she was not there, unfortunately for me, I had to drink it. I never liked that drink, even though it is healthy.

It was almost the end of the school year, and Zola was graduating. She had huge preparations to make, and was undergoing great stress. Her smile was gradually vanishing. When she was asked what the problem was, she would shake her head and say, "They have all lost their minds. My heart is weeping for the women and children." She was deeply troubled as she watched the African continent crashing in agony, and the Angolans continuing the long-lasting fight.

She could not understand that over five countries were under fire, and the Europeans were negotiating between Bosnia and Yugoslavia. The world was in complete chaos. "They are tearing the whole world apart; they have all lost their heads. They are all drinking water through their noses, leaving the innocent thirsty. Did you see the Liberian president being cut in pieces as he pleaded for his life? That is craziness to the highest level. They have allowed the wind to blow their hearts away leaving them without any feelings." She was right, war was senseless, and how could children kill their own families and friends?

She complained that she was not helping enough, but I often convinced her that she was doing more than the best. "The Africans needed one voice to stop the bloodshed. Zola, your donation is the best you can do."

Later, I saw her in the library. "Hey, French Man, nice to see you, where have you been?" she said, trying to wipe the tears from her face.

"It is going to be all right, don't worry. The United Nations is on top of it." I tried to council her, but there was not much I could do.

She slowly put a smile on her face. "The United Nations has been in Angola since 1975, in fact 1961. Maybe the end time is near," she said bitterly.

"Okay, my queen, it is time for the camera. Now! That is my African Queen right there, smile for the camera."

"Ha, ha. Hey, I look awful, François, you *can't* print those pictures."

"You are as beautiful as the Queen of Sheba," I said.

I managed to cheer her up and she began laughing again. "I am more than the Queen of Sheba. I am the African Queen.

Chapter Seven

We were weeks away from graduation, and Zola was given a last-minute assignment, a "house rule". Everyone talked about it on campus, and she would walk past me unaware. I had to call to get her attention. "Hey, Zola, how are you? How is the Sankara house rule?"

"You mean the golden rule?" She was glad to have run in to me. We walked outdoors and sat under a tree. "I have to work on the golden rules."

"It is a big project, Zola. Whatever you write, it can't be religious. You don't want any politically-correct war at Sankara." I had to warn her about this because anything spiritual might cause a real commotion. People were always looking for opportunities to accomplish their evil desires and blame others for it.

"I know, and you can't hide the truth either," she said.

She explained that the world was speedily turning around, and the truth was being swept under the carpet. Those who speak the truth go to prison, and those who lie are set free…walking the streets.

"Have you started?"

"No, French Man," she said.

I offered to help work on it, but she told me not to make a big deal out of it. "I will begin next week."

"That's fine. If you need help, I am free all of next week."

"Of course," she said. She looked at me in a fascinating way that told me we were in it together. "François, the world can reject everything else, but do unto others as you will have them do unto you. If you love yourself, then you will love others. So easy, but it seems hard for many."

"Hey, Zola, there are two African refugees in my class. Would you like to meet them?"

"I'd love to meet them, François, you know that."

"I am pretty sure that Orlando Pereira is from Angola, and the girl, I'm not sure where she's from and I don't remember her name. She witnessed some disgusting stuff down there, and everyone is talking about her hearing voices in her head. Apparently she is not doing well. I play basketball with Orlando every evening. He never says much, but he takes all of his frustration out on the ball. He is six-foot-three, and he plays really well. I think that he is mixed, because he is very light in complexion. He has a beautiful smile, though he rarely smiles. He takes his studies very seriously—straight A's." I gave some other details.

"François," said Zola, "I can't believe you are describing a man like that. You know every detail about him. Black hair, green eyes, pointed nose. You must have been paying close attention to him. Are you his secret admirer?"

"Funny, Zola, you will pay for that."

"Okay, Sir, sorry, but I want to meet both of them right now."

"No," I said. "Knowing you, you will get all emotional, and you have this big project ahead of you. The girl is doing a course with me. She doesn't talk much and she is often very moody and easily distracted."

"And you want me to wait for next week? Impossible. Anything, can happen between now and then. The project is a piece of cake. That girl is dying to talk to someone, and that someone has got to be me."

"Yes, Doc. What about Orlando?" I asked. "He has been here for a couple of years now, but apparently, everything is still fresh in his mind. Come to the gym room later, he will be there."

"That's war... When you survive, you get to relive the war all your life. When you get out, there are only two things to do. Either you stay in that horrible traumatic experience, or you fight to defeat the past by staying in the present. It is how you handle it. Now and here – that's what Orlando is doing. Let him keep playing the ball."

"You have never been to war, Zola."

"But you can imagine or pretend that you have seen one, François."

Zola had to rush over to Selassie University for a quick lecture. She was a little distracted after the war conversation. Like she said, the project was a piece of cake – easy. "Do unto others as you would have them do unto you."

It was the end of the school year, and we were busy with last-minute work. I did not see the Liberian girl anymore; I began wondering and worrying that something might have happened to her. Maybe Zola was right, and the girl needed help, I told myself.

As I was still wondering about her, I remembered seeing her with an empty pill bottle; it had fallen from her bag and I'd picked it up from the ground, just like I did with my grade-six teacher's pen. If she didn't come back to school, Zola would not forgive me.

"Forgive you for what?" Zola said, laughing, as she stood over me. "I want you to meet my good friend Mohamed Ali."

"Did you say Mohamed Ali? Wow, is this the legendary Ali Bombaye?" I was overjoyed. "I just want to say that I love you. You are the King of the Ring, Man, and you rock."

They both stood there looking at me as if I did not know what I was talking about. "Just a second," I said to Zola, "This is another Ali, right?" Zola tried to correct me, but it was too late. I had disgraced myself. "The King in the Ring is black, but you are white. Oh my goodness, I punked myself, he is not the boxer."

"You really never saw him in the ring before, right?" Mr. Ali asked me as he stroked his mustache, smiling. He looked Arabic, but he did not sound Arabic at all. He sounded like Zola and me, and he spoke only English. I answered by shaking my head. He stood over me, as tall as a giraffe. "No!"

"I am sorry to disappoint you," he said in a bass voice.

"I was over-excited upon hearing the name Ali. I apologize."

"Not a problem," he said and tapped my shoulder.

Zola had shown me a black-and-white photograph of Ali in the ring in the Congo. I had never seen him before except in this picture.

"Here is my card," said Mr. Ali. "Your friend told me that you need a job. Well, come and see me Monday at 11:30 am."

"Thank you, Sir, I will be there."

"Nice to meet you, François."

I was hoping that he would leave quickly, but he did not leave right away. Finally he said goodbye and walked away.

"Couldn't you say something to stop me from embarrassing myself?" I asked Zola.

"Come on, I did not want to spoil your moment with your greatest boxing hero."

"Thanks for nothing."

"You are welcome." She still had that giggle in her voice. "So François, do we meet the Liberian girl tomorrow?"

"Unfortunately, we can't" I said.

"And why not? Is there any problem?" Zola suggested that we go looking for the girl. "She might be hurting. What is her name?" she asked me. Zola was now getting anxious. I had forgotten the girl's name, and Zola knew this. "How could you forget an important person like that in a flash?"

"Since when did she become important?"

"Do not play smart with me, French Man," she said angrily.

"Sorry Zola! I didn't mean to sound so negative."

"I apologize too, François. I just want to connect with her."

We went searching for her, but she had stopped coming to school.

Later in the afternoon, we asked Mr. Matheson, one of the girl's professors. Surprisingly, this girl had dropped out even though she was a very bright according to Mr. Matheson. "She has a lot of issues to take care of," he said. "It is a waste of money, and of her time." He sat on his desk, his feet not reaching the ground, and continued to look up into Zola's face. "I advised her to put her course on hold until she can put herself together," he said.

"Did she tell you anything about herself?" Zola asked.

"She is troubled about the war back in her country."

"Most people are," said Zola. "I will try to follow up on her. It is a pity that I did not get to meet her before she left. Thanks, Mr. Matheson."

"Any time, Girl," he responded.

Zola went into the administration office. A few minutes later she came out laughing. "Thank you, French Man. You've been very helpful. I just looked at her record. She is called 'Sayba Marly'."

Zola was ecstatic, and she seemed to amaze me every time we were together. I could feel everything becoming and ending as an adventure. "I love you, Zola. You are my best friend," I said softly. "Please don't hold anything against me; you are a part of my life now."

"Okay, I forgive you seventy times seventy, but why will I do that?" she asked.

The Wind of Change

"Okay, Pastor Zola!"

"Oh, that reminds me. I need to give Pastor Fred a call to invite him to the graduation."

"He will love that, he will really love that."

Zola worked hard on her education. I wanted to invite her family, but I knew nothing about them. Even though Maa and Pastor Fred were going to be there, having her own folks around would have been even better.

Zola's achievements were beyond even my expectations. Most people would have liked to be in her position, and all she talked about was being the friend of a troubled refugee girl.

I was looking forward to my new job with Ali, and I was not sure of my sexuality. Since Ben moved into my room, I was not able to concentrate on a female-oriented relationship. Since he kissed me in the store when we were still at Mandela High, it all started coming back to me. I was having trouble with myself. I was not ready for such a huge commitment right now. Zola would never understand. "I can't be gay," I told myself.

Zola looked over my shoulder. "Is that Ben?" she asked.

"Where? No, Ben will not be here."

"He is coming this way." Zola began waving at Ben.

"Let us pretend like we are very busy, and he will just go away," I said.

"Why would you want to do that, François? I am disappointed in you."

"You will not understand," I told her, but Ben was already standing over us.

"Hey, lovebirds, you remember me?"

"How do you do, Ben? I am very proud of you for finding your way up here," Zola said as she hugged him."

"It is all because of you, Princess. You are the wind that blows the great oak tree and tumbles it to the ground; you bomb, Princess."

"Oh, wow! Then the oak tree wasn't strong after all," said Zola.

Ben left, then someone else approached us. "Oh, hello, Sayba!" I exclaimed. I heard you dropped your subjects. Sorry for been so inquisitive. I'm François, how do you do?"

"I'm very well! Thanks for asking," Sayba replied softly.

"You have a secret admirer." When I told her that, she blushed.

"I do?" she said as she put her right hand to her hair and tried to fix it. She quickly turned around to look at her face in a little mirror.

"She is right here."

"Oh, 'she'?" She said in a surprised tone.

"Are you disappointed? Well, here she is. This is Zola."

She turned to Zola and her eyes lit up. "Oh, yes!" exclaimed Sayba. I know who you are! I have been dying to meet you for so long. Nice to finally meet you. I am a big fan. I like you," Sayba said nervously.

"Oh, a fan, really?" Zola sounded surprised. "Nice to meet you too, Love."

"Wow! The pleasure is all mine," Sayba said with anxiousness while still trying to fix her hair.

Zola smiled. "François tells me that you are a Liberian girl?"

"Yes, I am!"

Zola talked to the girl, trying to make her comfortable. "I have never met a Liberian since I came here. Are you the Liberian girl that Michael Jackson sang about?"

Sayba was still shy. "Yes I am. I am also the same Liberian girl that is crying for help."

(Okay, maybe she was not so shy after all.)

"I'm sorry if I ignored your feelings," said Zola. "I just did not want to focus on the ugly negative things that are on the news. There are good and beautiful things about Liberia to focus on. I love Liberia," Zola whispered sadly.

"Thanks." Sayba accepted the compliment as she looked towards the east, avoiding eye contact with Zola.

"Was Michael Jackson really in love with a Liberian girl?" I asked Sayba.

"I have no idea," she said.

"That makes two of us," said Zola. "I guess it is our assignment to find out."

Sayba stood there looking at Zola obviously wondering if she would be able to answer the next question from her mouth. I tried to interrupt Zola to make it short, but she was up to something. I could feel it. Whatever it was, I didn't want her to tell me. I wanted to hear it from her myself. She would not have listened to me anyway until her goal was accomplished. Zola then gave Sayba a business card.

"I will call you," Sayba said, and Zola did not say anything.

"Of course, not a problem, we will be waiting for your call," I said.

"Can I give you my number?" Sayba asked.

At the sound of the word "number," both of us answered "Yes." Sayba grabbed a piece of paper as her hands shook and sweated like a bird with phobias wanting to fly but who couldn't.

"I just wanted to say that you are my role model, Zola. I am very delighted to meet you today. I had nothing doing on campus; however, I came here hoping to see you."

"Wow, isn't that something?" Zola said gladly. "Well Sayba! This is my lucky day; I am glad that you came this way."

"I will definitely give you a call," Sayba said.

We said goodbye to Sayba and watched as she walked away.

Zola turned to me. "Oh, Maa left a message that it is important that I go home this weekend. Zola was reminding me to go home with her. "I miss home," Zola said.

"Did you mean to say, you missed the food?" I asked.

"Yes Mr. Smarter-than-the-average-bear. I will see you later – I have some things that I have to take care of."

Late that afternoon, according to Zola, she was at the gas station and she realized that Sayba lived just half a block away, so she drove by Sayba's house. She told knocked on her door. Sayba answered and Zola and I greeted her. Zola told her that she was in the neighbourhood. Sayba had quickly put things under her bed and put her dirty clothes on the balcony.

"Sorry, I wasn't expecting anyone to visit me this time of the day.

"I'm sorry. If it is not the right time, I can come back another day."

"No, it is okay, I am happy that you came," Sayba responded quickly.

"It seems to me that you need a friend," Zola told her. "Why don't we go out for dinner? Do you like Chinese food? My grandmother is Chinese and she is one of the best cooks!" Zola saw that she was shy, and didn't know what to say to her.

The girl turned down the invitation. "I was just about to cook something," she replied.

"Okay – next time... Nice place you have here." Zola was still standing looking around the house.

"Thank you." Sayba quickly pushed some things under the sofa.

"Do you have any family here?" Zola asked her.

"No, I am alone."

"Oh I see." Zola noticed that the girl seemed a bit more comfortable. "I can't help myself, said Zola. "I have been thinking about you ever since I heard that you were on campus. There is a very powerful wind that is drawing me close to you. If you don't mind me asking you this, why did you stop going to school?" Zola talked as if she was a big sister to the girl. "Remember, education is your right, and no one can ever fight and rip it from your hands."

"Yes, and thanks for reminding me. Well," Sayba said, "part of it is the tuition cost, and the rest is…personal."

"If I can be of any help, please let me know especially with the tuition," Zola offered. "I will take care of your tuition whenever you are ready to go back. Just inform me in time."

"Oh, no, I will get a student loan next year; I am qualified for it."

Sayba declined Zola's offer, but Zola insisted on helping Sayba anyway. "I am able to take care of your fees; don't be silly. In fact, if you do more than your best, you get a percentage off your tuition. And about the personal…"

"It is a long story; do you have time to listen?" Sayba asked us.

"Only if you are ready and comfortable sharing with us."

"It has to do with the Liberian war." Then Sayba asked Zola if she was an African.

"Yes, I am!" she answered in such a tone that said she was tired of being asked to identify herself. "My dear, we are all one people on the earth. Besides, the root of all black men is Africa. My mother could have come from somewhere in South Africa, and my father from Ghana and they settled in Guinea. If we later moved to Liberia, and I am now here, where will I be from?"

The girl nodded understanding.

"We need to know where we came from, but during the process, we forgot the main idea. If we all stopped spending so much time on knowing the background of our neighbours and investing that time in what we can do to contribute to making earth a safer place for the next generation, we would all live in peace. I am here not because we both have the same skin colour, but I am here for love."

When Zola ended her emotional words, the room was quiet for a moment, then Sayba began speaking:

"I have never told anyone this before, until a few months ago. It is not like I forgot, but there are just some things that are far too painful to talk about. Sometimes it is hard moving on in life if you don't deal with things. And sometimes, because of the agony you once go through, you try to hide it at the back of your head in a safe place…and you forget that experience. Then, something happens to make you remember where you kept it, and you bring it back and it changes your whole life. I have tried to get rid of my frustrations, because of the destruction. I can't. It has become a wound that cannot easily be healed. My frustration has become my nightmare that will not go away. I thought it was healed, but it has left me with large scars…scars that are no longer invisible.

"I am depressed, frustrated and moody, and I can't get any sleep at night. My wounds have been reopened by the same person who cut me in the first place," Sayba continued to speak. "It is as if someone took a knife and dug into me. I am a Christian and I expected Jesus to have fixed this for me, but I have not seen him or any of the angels. I go to church every week, but I cannot talk to anybody about what is burning inside of me. No, I won't. If I did, nobody would understand, and no one will feel my pain. No one except people who have gone through a similar situation will understand. This is why I asked you if you are an African.

"Even at that, people can be very judgmental at times. I talked to my pastor briefly; it was hard for him. I asked him questions that he had no answers for. I was able to learn one thing from my conversation with him. He said to me, 'You are not going to like this, and neither do I, but it is the only way out. Forgive him.' 'This has been eating me up for some time now, and I am not ready to forgive him,' I told the pastor.

"Then the pastor said, 'When you sit and cry, and hate yourself, even wish that you are better dead than alive, that person is living their life, and they are happy and moving about their business. He has long forgotten you, but you remember him. But God did not forget. God will put him on the judgment seat one day.'"

"The pastor is one-hundred-percent right," said Zola, "but you don't have to forgive if you are not ready."

I nodded but remained quiet.

"Maybe now that I am going to tell you the whole story, I will find a way to forgive him – not that he deserves it, but for my own healing."

Zola told her to take a sip of water.

"I'm just going to start in the middle of the story," said Sayba.

"Wherever you start is okay with us."

Chapter Eight

Sayba sat down on the bed and began her story: "One morning in Liberia we woke up and there was screaming and crying everywhere in the community. I was in my pyjamas and I was forced to leave my home. I was fifteen then. More than twenty members of my family became displaced; we all went different ways.

"Two years later, I saw my mother's at the displacement camp. She was very troubled; she had not seen any of her family members. A couple of months later, some travellers told us that one of my mother's brothers was in one of our cities where the rebels' headquarters were.

"My mother cried and begged me to go and bring her brother and the rest of the family, knowing very well that it was not safe for girls to be there. She looked up to me to save my uncle's life. I put on tights under a dirty pair of jeans and rubbed some mud on my skin and face. Then I went to rub some cow manure on me. I thought if I smelled really stinky, they would not touch me. Then I headed for the road. When I arrived, I saw my uncle and his daughters, and one of my sisters who had been living with my uncle since she was three years old. I rested for three days, then I started planning a strategy of how to escape from the area.

"There were uncountable dead bodies of mothers and children lying all over the place, with others in line waiting to be executed. A little girl's parents had just been killed in front of her. She was sitting and crying, 'Mama', then he said 'Let that baby close her mouth or she will follow her ma.' There were rotting corpses sprawled all around. The stench was overpowering, and flies stuck to the dead bodies. The sight was horrifying. We were in the line for a long time, and when we reached the check point, they said that we could not pass. They wanted to make sure we were not enemies. (Enemies included the Mandigo tribe.)

"It was almost midnight, and we spent the night in a dark little room. We were a family of five – my uncle, his two daughters, and my sister and of course me. At night, everybody in that room was raped except me, because I smelled terrible; everyone who got near me told me I smelled like shit. They even had to put me outside.

In the morning, we were told to report to the headquarters. The rebel commando in charge was meeting with us for an interview. He confirmed that we were Muslim and Mandigo as well. They put three charges on us: 'Muslims, Madigo, and spies'. These charges meant death. Upon hearing the word 'death', I told him that we did not belong to any of the groups. Though we were Muslims, we had to lie in order to live. Luckily for me, I was able to speak other Liberian dialects, but none of my family did. My uncle was a Muslim, so he had a dark mark on his forehead. I tried to deny that we were who they said we were. Then, I was asked to say the Lord's Prayer, as a test to determine whether we were Muslims, but I passed the test. 'Is this a tribal war or a religious one?' I said. 'You ga big moth', eh 'You have got a big mouth' the rebel said as he prepared to kill me.

"He was not satisfied with me, and demanded I say the 23rd Psalm. At that time, my uncle had already been shot with an AK47 gun. It is all very clear in my head. The rebel told his boys to give him the gun. 'Gimme my AK47, le me blow somebole hea off, day think tha I'm jokin' with them.' 'Give me my AK47, and let me blow somebody's head off; they think that I am joking with them.'

"'We are nat here to play, we will fini al lo your.' 'We are not here to play; we will finish all of you.' he said. When he killed my uncle, they inserted lemon in him and gave him a live caterpillar to eat. They allowed him to die slowly. Second in line were my cousins. They told him where we came from, and where we were going. The commando shot them. The fourth person in line was my sister. Then he turned to me and said, 'I wil kep you fo las, you thin you kno too plety, smart gal. We wil kil al lo your, you nat belon here." I will keep you for last, we think you know too much. We will kill all of you. You don't belong here.'

"Then he pulled the trigger and killed my sister, and then he turned to me saying 'Is your time.' I was prepared to die," Sayba said.

I was shaking as I listened to her.

"I said the Lord's Prayer, and then the 23rd Psalm. Then, I didn't know how to really pray to God, but I lifted my hand towards Heaven and said, 'Thank you God, thank you for my life. Where are you, why is this happening?' Then I wet my underwear. Suddenly, he got distracted by some newcomers that he knew and someone whose father was a government official. I thought that it was better for him to shoot me from the back, so I began to run with the thought that I could fall at any moment.

"I didn't stop running; I just kept on running and running. I thought that I was shot, because my body was very hot. But it was all in my head. I was running with an unconscious mind. By the time I realized that I was alive, it was night-time. I remembered passing through a little town, but I did not stop. I slept in a clearing under some banana trees.

"The journey continued as soon as I saw the daylight. I found myself in a little town near the Liberian and the Sierra Leone border. I had long passed my destination. When I stopped, the first person I saw, I asked them to help me remove the bullets from my body. They told me that there was no such thing as bullets in my body. 'Bu you smee stink' 'But you smell stink', he told me.

"It took me three months to make my way back to my mother. At that time, the Liberian rebels were going in to Sierra Leone back and forth killing and looting. During the Liberian war, they only killed the people, but they cut the president's body parts off while he was still alive, as he prayed to die. In Sierra Leone they did not only killed, but they cut off the hands and legs of many people. They did not have mercy on anyone including babies. I found a little baby sitting by her dead mother with both hands cut off. I took the child with me, but she was in too much pain to have survived.

"I made it to my mother after all. When she asked me about her family, I shook my head saying, 'No Dia, I did not see them.' And my mother said, maybe they were airlifted; she heard that the United Nations was helping by airlifting people out of the country. 'Thank God,' my mother said. 'We will see them when everything is over.'

"That will be really good, Dia," I told her. I was never able to tell my mother my story, until God brought me here. I found a little safe place and locked up this incident and experience. So far it has worked, until a couple of months ago. It has all come back to me; I remember every little detail in my head. It's because I met the commander that killed my family in front of me, here in Canada.

"It was on a Friday, I entered a church for a wedding rehearsal, and I recognized him. His face is still the same even though he is bigger than he used to be, which makes his body a bit different. I was talking to myself, but some lady sitting next to me heard me as I talked.

"'Oh God,' I said. 'He is the one. He killed four members of my family.' Then the lady took my hand and began praying for me. When I opened my eyes, they were all gone. I thought that my mind was playing tricks on me again. On the day of the wedding, I had to help to make the food, so I was in the kitchen the whole time. I left the kitchen by 10:30 pm, so I went and found a place to sit while the others danced. I saw him enter, and he began jumping and dancing in the room. Then I went to the washroom to cry. After some time there, I was ready to leave.

"As I got in my car, something told me not to go home. 'No! If anyone should leave, let him be the one,' I said. 'I am not going anywhere.' Then I walked up to him and greeted him very politely.

"He responded well. Then he asked me, 'Have we met before?'

"At the sound of the words 'met before,' I got angry. 'Oh yes, of course, we have met.'

"Then he said to me, 'But I don't remember you, I don't remember you at all.'

"'You will remember me all right. Wait until I am done talking about how we met.' Then I went on telling him about our meeting point.

"'There was a time that I begged you not to kill my family; you ordered your guards to rape us overnight. In the morning you killed them, as you were about to kill me, someone else came who also deserve the death penalty according to you. You left me and went to kill them. Then I ran.'

"Then he asked me. 'Are you sure it was me? I think you are mistaking me for somebody else.' Then he stated his name.

"Yes, that was the name I remembered. I will never forget his face, you have a sister. 'It is in my brain,' I told him. And he wanted me to walk with him outside, but I refused. I told him that I was not going anywhere with a murderer. 'Small world isn't it?' But he did not hear me; he was too confused and he walked away. Many of my people at that party know how many people he killed, but they don't care. They welcome the ex-rebel in their home, and when he leaves, they point their finger behind him. They are all hypocrites," Sayba said.

I heard the two ladies crying aloud; they could not control themselves. Zola could not handle this; she was broken for Sayba. They cried for half an hour then we went home.

The next day, I had the feeling that Zola wanted to visit Sayba again. Zola agreed and we traveled to her apartment. Sayba did not live far from Sankara. There were no secrets between Zola and me. If she needed privacy with Sayba, she would tell me.

We arrived at Sayba's door and she welcomed us in. Sayba said: "You see, I can't go to school, I am not focused. I have to take care of this first, then school. They are still killing each other out there, and now other African countries have joined them in rebelling against their own people. They sell their souls in exchange for weapons to kill their own family, then accept other work from the devil himself. Where is the Black Power that we learned about in school? Where is Africa for the Africans? Where is the United States of Africa? The Africans have turned against themselves, and the United States of Africa has vanished into the air without a trace," Sayba said angrily.

"It is a beautiful dream," Zola said.

"Yes, it was," Sayba responded. "But Africa is far from becoming a United States. God is going to bring someone into this world that will accomplish His plans for the African people. Slowly, but surely. South Africa is free and Madiba is in politics again; he led a war without a sword. The world needs to learn from him. He is so old, how long will he be here with us? I saw him recently, and he did not look well. Twenty-seven years in the cold... He is here because God wanted him to be."

Zola replied: "This whole war is stupid, and it doesn't make any sense."

Sayba nodded. "Nobody understands."

"I do, Sweetie. Sayba, believe me, I do," Zola said as she blew her nose.

"I don't know why I'm telling you all of this, but it feels good speaking to someone about it for the first time."

"Friends are useful in a period like this. Do you have any friends around?" Zola asked.

"Oh, yes I do!" Sayba responded. "But...they think that it is not necessary to talk about the past. 'It happened in Liberia, and leave it there and move on,' one of my friends said. And another said, "People are being killed every day anyway. Accept it and move on."

"No!" I interrupted. "Your friends did not witness anything, and we all handle things differently."

"You are an eye witness to the war and it affected you greatly," said Zola. "It affected everyone, including me. Your approach to this will be totally different, and your reaction now is normal based on what you told me. Most people would be broken in pieces. It is only by the grace of God that you are still alive. I imagine your pain, so I am prepared to help you through this. I will go through this with you as long as it takes if you don't mind. If you need to talk, or you need anything, please let me know. This is the city of refuge, not of murderers. God will deal with him according to His will.

"The ex-rebel is our least worry right now! We will not target him; rather, we will target what happened to you. You are important and God will take care of you. Somebody has to stop them; someone has to put an end to all of this madness. Just the other day I went to see Madiba and he told me these very words:

"'We are in this world to live in freedom, not in fear. God gave us free will. Man should live in freedom.' Will you be okay tonight by yourself, or do you want me to spend the night here with you?" Zola asked.

"Yes, I would love that, but the place is not too..." Sayba tried to explain.

"Not too what – clean?" Zola finished the sentence for her. "Don't worry about cleaning. You will recover from these horrible nightmares." Then Zola began praying. "Oh, God, please help me, tell me what to do, and when to do it."

"Wow!" Sayba said. People talk about you and hold you up as an example, but seeing you in person standing in my home is an honour. You really are 'wind.' Where you blow, you clean the dust."

"My dear, it is not my doing, but it is my duty," Zola said, sounding as if she had a stuffy nose. "We all have our places in this world, and this is mine."

"You are just what I imagined you to be," said Sayba. "I still feel like I know you from somewhere, I just can't remember..."

"You sound like Mr. Zulu who thought that he knew me from somewhere, but realized that I was in his dream."

I talked to Sayba as I shook her hand. "I am really sorry that you had to go through all of this alone," I said. "I promise that we will help you recover. You will not forget what happened but you will surely learn to put this behind you." I gave her a hug. "You are the strongest person I have ever met. You can't give up now on life. You will not give up. We must find the man and turn him over to the police," I told the girls. I was ready to go after the guy, but Zola said that no such thing was going to happen.

"We are here to focus on Sayba, not those evil people. Let him live with the guilt of thousands of people's blood on his hands," Zola said. "That is, if he has a heart."

We discussed that if anyone should go after him, it should be the authorities. One thing we all agreed on was that he did not deserve to be in this society with us. He was a monster.

"Find a place in your heart to forgive him; your healing is the most important," said Zola.

Chapter Nine

※

I promised the girls that I would not try to go after the ex-rebel that had caused Sayba so much pain. But I still needed to know more about what had initiated the hostility in Liberia. I asked several questions about it. I had to find a means to know the whole story from Sayba without offending her. I was already hearing a voice in my ears:

Zola shook her finger at me. "You should be ashamed of yourself asking her those questions, French Man. How many times have you heard me call the world Liberia? You don't know your world history at all."

I was not ready for any confrontation with her, so I walked over to Sayba and whispered in her ear and asked her what the commotion in Liberia was really all about.

For some reason, I felt as if Zola knew much about the history of Liberia, and was always learning about other nations. She knew all about the Bosnian and Yugoslavian conflicts. I knew for sure that once Sayba started talking, Zola was going to come in somehow and finish it like she did with Mr. Zulu. She took world history very seriously, and she always seemed to have the right answers for me.

"Oh, François, it is a long story," Sayba said. "It is politics. When they become too involved with politics, innocent people begin suffering the consequences."

As soon as Sayba ended, Zola added, "It is ironic how that works, the innocent are often vulnerable and helpless so they are left alone in the lion's den to save themselves when it becomes too political. It should be the other way around, but they have all lost the meaning of life," Zola said with a sad face, still trying to fight back her tears as she comforted Sayba.

"Can't the United States do something to help Liberia since they are the super-power?" I asked the girls.

Then Zola said, "You are following up on world issues after all. I am very impressed."

"The headline was pointing directly at the United States with having much interest in Liberia, but I did not read the whole thing," I told them.

I stood up and walked over to Zola, and suddenly she began laughing out loud. Then Sayba quickly responded, still bitter about the war and her disappointment: "A US interest in what? The iron, rubber plantations, or the people? Once Liberia has Firestone, America will be interested in them, all right." Then she said, "I wish you had read the whole article."

I was a little upset at her comment so I jumped into a discussion with her. "Hey Sayba, don't talk like that, that's blaspheming. It's politics and you know that. Even in the United States, there are problems and the people are in great need. The US cannot solve all of the problems in the world, we have to be realistic, Sayba."

"François, you don't know what you're talking about," said Zola. "You need to go back to school and study world issues if you have an interest in what is happening in the world."

"I'm sorry, but I am speaking my mind and I think that there is truth in what I just said."

"They could have stopped it from happening, but the US allowed it to happen," said Sayba. "They sent Taylor to turn the country in to a blood field."

"Who is Taylor, anyway," I asked her.

"Don't you know who he is?"

"No." I did not have a clue where she was heading.

The two ladies exchanged looks as if there was something obvious that I didn't know.

"François, my body feels like an empty bucket right now, and I do not have the strength to refill it," said Zola."

I had no idea what she was talking about, and I had had enough parables from Zola. "What bucket are you talking about?"

Then she said, "Don't worry, French Man; I will empty it for you."

That was all I wanted.

The Wind of Change

She said, "Liberia and the US have a relationship that has been unique. In fact up to the mid 1980's, the Liberians were still using the United States dollar. I still remember the history of how Liberia got her independence. Actually, they never did. On one Flag Day, my mother dressed me up to go salute the president since the US president was visiting Liberia that day with his wife. My mom and I had just arrived a couple of months earlier from Guinea. I was still struggling with English. According to history…"

"Okay, Zola!" I interrupted. "How do you come up with all these histories? You are sitting daydreaming holding a flag in front of the US president and his wife. Are you making this up?"

"That's enough, French Man. I am going to deprive you of the important history of the Americo-Liberian relationship, since you know it all," she said jokingly.

"Americo-Liberian? Come on, Zola, I was complimenting you. It is not everyone that takes the time to educate themselves about their histories. I am very proud of you."

"Yes," Sayba said, "He is right, Zola, you love the earth and its inhabitants, so please tell us a bedtime story."

"Okay, guys, I will tell you who the Americo-Liberians were, or still are, but don't get too emotional on me. Besides, I will be sleeping very soon; I have much to do tomorrow."

I was happy that we'd managed to find a way to cheer Sayba up and distract her from what would have been a night of grief. So far, it turned out to be a night of laughter. In fact, we had an awesome night.

"Liberia has a unique history among all African states and a special bond with the United States," said Zola. "The relationship between the two nations goes back to the 1800s. The American Colonization Society established Liberia as a place to send freed African-American slaves. They slowly migrated to the colony and became known as Americo-Liberians. Henceforth, the country was named Liberia, meaning 'liberty'. The United States has always had a great influence on Liberian culture, customs and celebrations.

"In the year 1847, the Americo-Liberian settlers declared their independent country. It became the Republic of Liberia, naming the capital Monrovia after the 5th American president, James Monroe."

Sayba quickly interrupted Zola. "Just like in Zambia. Our beautiful waterfall is named after the Queen of England."

Zola talked a little about the waterfall and then continued with the Liberian history. "During those days, a philosopher named John Locker said that black people did not know any good things, and did not deserve any better. This is the reason I cried sometimes when the Africans were slaughtering each other in pieces. If you watch the video of Samuel Doe, the late president of Liberia, it makes me wonder. But again, as long as the devil is on this planet, evil is on the planet. The waterfall could have been named after our heroes that died trying to liberate Africa," Zola said.

"What did Queen Victoria do for Africa that we all have to remember her?" Sayba asked.

"Her people discovered Zambia, her people loved her, and they loved what they saw in Zambia. When you love someone or something, you always want to think about them and you give them the best," Zola said. "But all of that is in the past now. We are going to focus on the future, and what lies ahead of us. If we continue to point fingers at the things that happened in the past, we will not move on. We can remember, but not regress. They did what they had to do in Africa, because it was their time, and power was in their hands. However, the Africans are in control now.

"Can they do it on their own without help from the outside world? Is Africa able to manage their affairs?" Sayba asked as she opened a bottle of water.

Zola continued: "They are managing very well. That is why we are scattered around the world, looking for a place to call home, losing our family and loved ones. The Africans are the captains of their own ships, the choice is up to the leaders to roll the ship to the harbour or hit the iceberg and sink. Apparently, this is what is happening; it is heading in that direction. Africans need to do everything in their power to unite, and live in peace."

I thought for a second that she had forgotten the main story, but then she went on: "As you can see the flag is the same as the US flag, but the difference is that the Liberian one has a blue square in the corner with one white star. The Americo-Liberians established a nation that in many ways represented the land they knew as home. But they forgot one important thing…and I am not here to criticize but they forgot to integrate with the people they met in Liberia and of course develop the country.

"Furthermore, the country's constitution and political structure is all based on the American pattern, and of course the famous bank note was given to the Liberians. The other African states called them, 'Little America,' or as the French Man would say, *'petit Amerique'*. Soon after the settlement by the American Colonization Society, the United States managed the economic and military ties with Liberia throughout the 20th century. Liberia was never colonized, unlike other African countries.

"Do you know who Marcus Garvey was?"

"No," Sayba and I both answered.

"Well, he found out about Liberia and wanted to lead all of the black people back to Liberia. It would have been the headquarters for all of Africa according to him, but that is another story in itself. How can you not know your history?" she asked us, and then she continued with the Americo-Liberian discussion. "From 1822 until 1980, the Liberian presidents came directly from the United States. Except William R. Tolbert who was born in Liberia, but his families came from North Carolina. From the time of settlement up to now the US companies were exploiting the Liberian resources with a clear conscience.

"You heard Sayba talking about the plantations and the iron. Liberia provided much of the needed rubber for the US automobile industry. Then the United States also used Liberia strategically as a staging point for supplying troops and weapons during World War II, since it is located on the west coast of Africa. The civil war started with an Americo-Liberian who wanted to take over the government from the natives.

Then Sayba interrupted Zola: "I remember many students protesting at the US embassy, pleading with them to intervene before the country became a war zone. But that was the early 1990's when the war had just began after the mass killing in Ganta city that morning. We heard that hundreds of children were buried alive. It was reported that a truck was coming from Nimba County with kids, but those kids never made it to the city. When the war broke out in Monrovia, my friends and I ran over to the American Embassy, but we were not allowed to enter – only those Americo-Liberians who were US citizens or those that had family in the US," Sayba said as she sat on the sofa, vividly envisioning the horrible war that destroyed her family. She looked scared and depressed. She squeezed herself into the corner of the sofa, sitting with her finger in her mouth like a pacifier.

"We should get some sleep," said Zola. "I have a meeting with the United Nations first thing in the morning, which could turn into a job interview."

"Another job interview?" I asked her. She did not need another job. But when she said it was about the people, you leave it as it is.

"I am needed somewhere in the world," she said.

"Is that the end of the African American in Liberia?" I asked her.

"They are called Americo-Liberians, and, yes, François, I am not your history teacher. It is pretty late, and we all should be sleeping now."

I pleaded with her to end the story.

"The Liberian war is a story all by itself," she kept saying, "And I can't get into it, but I will tell you important information about them. The Americo-Liberians highly regarded Africa as a 'Promised Land', but they did not integrate into an African society. In Africa, they referred to themselves as 'Americans' and up to today they are recognized by the local Africans as Americans. The symbols of their state – its flag, slogan, and seal – and the structure of government they chose mirrored their American background and Diaspora experience.

"Anyway, even though identity is power, integration is very important and powerful. They met others living in the land and failed to recognize them. The land was already inhabited by various indigenous ethnic groups who had occupied the region for centuries. The introduction of a new ethnic group resulted in ethnic tensions with the sixteen existing ethnicities. In 1980, the government was reversed in a military rebellion and from 1989, December 24th, the country began suffering a civil war that was caused by an Americo-Liberian which brought Sayba here, separating her from her family by murder, then claiming that he is a victim himself. God will catch up with him, as long as it takes.

"I still believe that there is a chance for the African people to live in peace," Zola said. "This war in Liberia, is affecting all of Africa. There is going to be total peace not just in Liberia, but within the entire African continent. Madiba is sitting smiling at the future of Africa and I also see the future with him."

"How can there be peace when the poverty rate is as high as the sky?" asked Sayba. "Poverty is a horrible disease and nobody wants a taste of it." Sayba turned to Zola and spoke directly to her as if Zola had the answer to her questions. "If the leaders come together and put the countries' best interest at heart, thinking about what brought them into leadership, they will make it to the promised land." Sayba stood up and passed a cup of tea to Zola.

"Yes the promised land, the Heart of Africa," Zola said sadly. She was hurting, not just for Sayba, but for herself as well. She had remembered something about her own life that was not pleasant. She seemed a little distant, with a pale face. "I still remember when…I…I am sorry guys; I can't talk about this subject any longer. It breaks my heart to know that people can be this heartless. We are not politicians, and I have to sleep; I have a protocol first thing in the morning."

"Zola, who are you, and what part of the planet did you come from?" I asked her. "You are just unbelievable. There is something new to learn from you each time we are together."

"Good night, François. I love you too."

I left Zola as she was spending the night with Sayba, and went home to my roommate, Ben.

Ben and I shared the room until my departure from Sankara. He was not a bad roommate after all, but he often put his mouth where it did not belong. I did not feel comfortable sharing the room with him.

We successfully graduated from Sankara, and Zola as usual graduated with honour and dignity. Maa was very happy and proud of Zola on her graduation night. We had a very festive day, and enjoyed every moment of it.

Zola had to teach at Haile Selassie University that summer. Meanwhile, she came home every weekend to be with Sayba. Zola was very busy with work and involving herself with community support, so we did not see much of each other. Whenever she was not around, I would go check on Sayba. She got herself back in school the next semester, and she was able to conquer her fears.

One day, I went to see Sayba, and she wrote a letter of appreciation to Zola. "François, could you give this to Zola when she gets back?"

"Sure, Sayba. I'll bring it for you with pleasure," I said. I wanted to know what was in the letter, so I opened the envelope as soon as I got home.

It read: "Hello Zola. You have no idea what you have done for me. You taught me to believe in myself and keep my eyes on what was important – me. People often say that seeing is believing, but you told me to first believe and then I would be able to see the result. I was stuck on a road that I could not soar over. Then I got in a boat that I could not row. I was exhausted and ready to withdraw. I needed answers as to why I could not rise above this. Then you helped me realize that if I give up, I would never have found out why it happened the way it did. My answers were closer at hand than I thought, but yet appeared distant to me.

"You came along one day, and held my hand. Your caring tender touch reached me like the day star. You are everything I hoped you would be. Thanks for touching my heart and helping me to reach the 'rope.' Now I know that if I fall, I will be able to stand again. Thanks, Sayba."

This girl was brave and strong. She found a supernatural courage to move on, and let go of those bitter nights. She did it all on her own. We were there to support her and show her that we care. I guess this is what the world needs as Zola always said, "Just a little hand." She always told me that "If you help someone reach their goal, it will make you feel good about yourself. Love is the answer for everything. The world was established on love and we will walk through it with love, and it will end in love. Without love, how can there be peace?"

"I hate to admit this, but Zola is right," I said with a smile.

It had been nearly a year since we graduated from the university, but she had been working on her PHD as well. One day I went over to her house and to my surprise, she was home. It was not like her. "Hello, Zola. What are you doing home at this time of the day?" I asked her.

"And why is that a surprise?" she said. "It is still my home, isn't it? I am expecting an important call from…well, never mind. How is your aunt doing?" she asked, but at the same time, the phone rang.

"Do you want me to get that?" I asked.

She quickly replied "No. I will pick it up from here." She picked up the phone, and she did not say who it was, but the person told her to call back later in the day. "Come on François, we have to go back to the office. The plan has just changed."

"What was so important that had to be secret?" I asked.

"I was hiding from you, François."

It was a beautiful windy day, and the sun was shining with a hint of rainbow in the blue sky when we got to her office. Upon arrival, she took the phone and called an old family friend of the late Marcus Garvey. "Hello,

Sir! My name is Zola, and I am a graduate of Thomas Sankara University in Toronto. May I speak with Professor William Tolbert, please?"

I went around the bookcase to the other end of the office and picked up the other line...

"Yes, my dear, Tolbert on the line," he said quickly with a sense that he was glad and he had been awaiting her call.

"Thank you for taking this time to talk to me, Professor. Did you receive my letter?"

"Yes, I did, my love. As a matter of fact, I have it in my hand."

"I am very honoured, Sir. I appreciate you wanting to see me under the circumstances," Zola said in a soft voice with that promptness of gratitude she always had.

"You are welcome, my child. It is always a pleasure to see young people like you wanting to follow in their fathers' footsteps, going around the world encouraging young black people that they have as much equal opportunity and potential as any other race on this planet. Unfortunately, the young people today doubt themselves. They are engaging in negative activity or believing the deception that they are not good enough for this society."

"Maybe some of the old politicians need to step down and give the young people a chance, rather than scare them away," Zola said.

"Why didn't you come to look for me years ago, child?" asked the professor. "You are a very intelligent young lady."

"Thank you, Sir. I found out about you a year ago, and since then, I have been trying to contact you. Many times, your lawyer told me that it was not possible, because you were on your deathbed," Zola told him.

"I have been on my deathbed since my birth," said the professor. "I am here by God's grace."

At the sound of his response, I burst out laughing.

When Zola realized I was on the other line, she wrote me a note asking me to hang up the phone. She did not want the professor to know that there was someone else on the line but there was nothing that she could do to make me hang up. The professor's call was too important to have been interrupted. I knew Zola; she never would have told me about this discussion.

"They all started at a young age like you. They were determined to fight for their rights," the professor explained to Zola as she stood there with the phone in her hand, smiling, feeling almost as if she was already in Jamaica with the old professor. "Up, you mighty race, accomplish what you will." The professor imitated his greatest hero and friend with joy under his voice. 'Indeed, we have to keep fighting for what we will accomplish until we have accomplished it. I am an old man heading for the grave, but I am still here waiting for equality. Freedom is the right for all races, so freedom must reign, and Africa must rise up and unite as once or soon, there will be no Africa. Division can never be an answer.'"

"Why don't you come and meet me? And all the information that you need I will provide you with. I still remember Marcus' and Kwame's and young Panmore's first meeting and I recall every discussion they had. They…did I tell you that I was in the room when Malcolm died? I will tell you all about it, but only when you are here with me," he said.

"Thank you, Professor. I will be there tomorrow by the grace of God."

"Yes, my child, and I will see you tomorrow."

"I was very confident that once I spoke to you, you would want to see me," Zola said, over-excited at going back to the late 30's.

"Child, people without knowledge of their past history, origin and culture are like trees without roots," said the professor.

"And without a root, there is no tree. Good-bye, Sir. I will be seeing you tomorrow."

Zola hung up the phone. "I'm going to Jamaica!"

"Jamaica? You said that you are not a Jamaican."

"Does it really matter right now where I came from? I have been trying to get in contact with this professor for a long while now, and this is my only chance. He is on his death bed, and he wants to see me. Going to Jamaica and meeting the professor will be like meeting all those Black Power revolutionaries and civil-rights freedom fighters.

"I'm going back to my roots! Wait a minute, that's a Luke Dube song. I need some Bob Marley soul food in my system before getting to Jamaica," she said as she danced around in the office. If you know your history, then you know where you're coming from."

"Hey, Zola, please continue. I love that song."

"Then buy it," she said.
She was still singing as she left the office, "I am out of here."

Chapter Ten

※

Zola was so excited, and could not wait to meet Professor Tolbert, one of the 20th-century Black Power leaders. I did not how I was going to make it there, but I wanted to go too. Knowing her, it was definitely a "No." I had never taken a vacation since I started work, so my boss was all right with my absence, but it was Zola who I was worried about.

"I will be gone for a week. Work hard and work smart," she said as she packed her suitcase to visit the home town of Marcus Garvey. Zola was fortunate to get a flight to Jamaica the next day. I tried to go with her, but time could not permit me to leave that day, and even at that, there was no extra seat on the plane.

Sayba and I dropped her off at the airport. "I know that she loves the black histories," I said, "but she never talks about any Marcus Garvey. It was just an interest that popped up in her head."

"Oh, no, François, don't let her hear you saying that," said Sayba. You know her better than anyone around her, so know how important this is to her. Say nothing at all and find your way to Jamaica and support her, or do what you do best," Sayba said as if she was reading my mind. As much as I wanted to be there with Zola, I wanted the story too.

I decided to take the next flight available. I packed a few things in my bag and headed to the airport thinking that once I was there, it would be easy to get a seat. Sayba was right about that. Getting myself to Jamaica was better than complaining. I got a flight three hours after Zola left.

Zola had arrived in Jamaica on a Saturday afternoon. The one-hundred-and-fifteen-year-old professor wanted her to stay in the house with him. She told me later that upon her arrival, they went through photographs and letters, rough-copy speeches, some letters from the Ku Klux Klan, and so many other well-preserved items that had belonged to Marcus Garvey, those that the federal government did not know about.

I arrived that evening and went to the professor's house. When the maid opened the door, I told her I was Zola's husband, so she let me in.

As I got to the bedroom, I heard the old man saying, "This is Nkrumah and I on the left, at the university in England when we first met."

Zola noticed me standing in the hallway. "François, what are you doing here!" she exclaimed as she hugged me. "I thought there was no seat for you!" She was very happy to see me.

Professor Tolbert was lying in bed, propped up with some pillows. He looked at me then asked Zola if I was her husband.

"No, Sir, he is my friend, my good friend who feels like I owe him my life. He wants to know even when I go to the washroom and how I do it; he has taken away my rights of privacy."

"Young man, nice to meet you," he said, "but she will trust you when you give her some privacy. You both are different individuals, and you have different goals. You are short-sighted and she is looking ahead of herself. In order to win this lady, you have to love the human race and the earth.

"We are not like that," Zola interrupted him.

"One day, the black man will rule the United States of America, and there will come a day that Africa will stand up and fight poverty," said the professor. "As you can see, the coin had flipped over in South Africa. I was angry when Mandela made the decision to shake hands with the devils, but he had to. It was the only way out.

"Besides, from the beginning of Mandela's walks, it was about equal rights for all. But, there will come a time when the world will know that Black is as powerful and strong as it looks, and that even when it fades, it is still black," he said as he prepared himself to talk about the founders of the Black Power. Let's talk about Dr. Kwame. He was only a high school graduate, ready to fly over the world wanting nothing more in life than to be called "the Father of Africa", a visionary and an idealist whose ideas will never die.

"Kwame traveled to England to further his education and while there, he created an idea Black Power and Pan-Africa. He soon began researching and reading books, and became interested in moving the Black Power further. On the university campus, news of this young African man named

Kwame started spreading, so I had to meet him. Marcus had just immigrated to England after his deportation from Jamaica and Marcus wanted to meet Kwame immediately.

"When we met Marcus, he was no longer the Marcus Garvey that shocked the world. He stood in front of the white man during the day when the black man was less respected than toilet paper, and challenged him. He told the African-American that they all should go back to Africa where their roots were, and where God had given them everything. He was disgraced and powerless; he stood there looking at us with tears rolling down his eyes. Back in Jamaica, parents had allowed their children to mug and hit him on the street, and the United States government took over all of his access including the one in Jamaica. He was humiliated and broken when we met him. I never forgot what he told me.

"He said, 'Tolbert, they own the world and they own us. They will do to us whatever they like. Has God forgotten his beloved people? The Black man in the world today is like the children of Jacob in Egypt. Why can't they allow us to live and be free? Today, they have made me powerless, but I know that we were created with much power.'

"Then the young Kwame said, 'We are human. God created one man and one woman and we all have our place in the world. You can't give up; the people need you to give them courage. Where is the place for the black man in the world?' We encouraged Marcus and then left for the campus.

"There was no doubt in our minds that young Kwame was the one who was going to help free Africa from the hand of the Europeans. Marcus remembered the suffering of the black people, and he knew that he was not going to sit and allow the Black Power to go down the drain. In England, he kept himself encouraged and kept praying for his faithful members and family. He was alone but nobody was going to take away his confidence.

"I remember that Marcus told the young Kwame: 'If I die today, I know that my work here is done, but we will fight for the black's rights; God has created you to complete this work of faith which is the right of all human races.'

"Unfortunately, Marcus died too soon; he was dead before the actual death occurred. Young Kwame moved to the United States five years later when Marcus died," Professor Tolbert said, looking right into Zola's eyes, puffing his pipe in his mouth in and out as he explained.

"The young man arrived in the US and continued his studies. He soon became known for his brain and what was important to him, the Black Power, of course. He and I met again at the University of Pennsylvania and exchanged contacts. Seeing the people he interacted with and how he was well-informed about the underground movement, I believed that it was time for Africa.

"The Black Power was going to go to the next level in Africa where the black man was a slave in his own country, and even outside his country. Young Kwame one day told me that the black will be jailed, hunted in the trees like hunting for birds in the forest, and shot down. The conspiracy among rulers in the world has not given the black man much choice, but God will keep creating more of us until our voices are heard and freedom is given to the black man which is the birth inheritance.

"After the conversation young Kwame and I had, it did not take long before Marcus was reported dead, his second death, the real one. There had been a mistaken and negative obituary of him, and it may have triggered a stroke. I remembered sending a radio message to Harlem telling our co-workers there about the young African man, from England, who was trustworthy. During those days, our fun we had was gathering in groups finding new strategies for our freedom. The prison was our next home." The professor smiled as he thought of his youthful days.

"Are you comfortable, Sir?" Zola asked him. She was concerned about his comfort, since he was so old. "I think that it is enough for today, and you should rest," she said as she put some pillows under his neck and gave him water to cool his taste. Even though he was old and fading, his brain was as sharp as those days he seemed to remember – everything from the time of the Black Power up to the present war in his family. We wanted to give the professor some time to rest so we went out to the living room.

Zola said: "You are my husband? For real, François, you have to stop intruding. What are you doing here anyway?"

"I came to pay the professor my respects before he leaves the planet."

"How nice!"

We went back into the room and the old man asked again who I was.

"He is the one who thinks that nothing should pass his ears, Sir," Zola said.

"Why don't you call me Grandpa? Everyone calls me Grandpa."

"Okay, Sir, I will," she said.

He could not even stand, but he knew what he wanted. "Come and sit; we are getting to know each other," he said to me. "I am telling this young black girl who is rocking the world about the people who rocked the world during my time. Old age is catching up with me, so I need to take a nap and we will continue the story later," Professor Tolbert said as he lay under his blanket keeping warm with Zola sitting on the bed holding his hands.

He woke up four hours later, and the nurses were afraid that he was leaving very soon, but he told them that he would let them know if it was time. "My children want me to go so they can declare a family fight for my properties. I am not dying right now…and not until they forget about my death."

Zola seemed to make him feel very comfortable and she had not left him for more than fifteen minutes since we got there.

"If I die now, I will die smiling. I have seen the future of the Black Power and I have seen the black man all over the world sitting on the throne making worldwide decisions. People not being judged by the colour of their skin, but by their brains.

"I am happy that you are here my child," he told Zola. He went on describing the communication between Marcus and young Kwame from 1935 to 1940. Marcus had just received a letter from young Kwame when the newspaper reported him dead since the day he was not allowed to enter the United States any longer. They knew that he was not doing well with his health, so they could not wait for his death. Marcus knew that Kwame was going to be a leader not just for the Black Power or Pan-Africa, but he was the one to take Africa from the darkness to the light. 'Black man was not born a slave,' he would often say.

"Marcus took his last breath; he died unexpectedly. They were relieved when he died. When Marcus died there was much celebration in the city. They thought that that was the end of the Black Power, but that was just the beginning of a new Black Power that gave the black people the assurance they were powerful and beautiful. The Buffalo Soldiers who were stolen from Africa and scattered all over the world now stood up and demanded their freedom.

"We deserve to be free. He who the Lord set free, is free indeed," the old man said. Then he showed us a letter that was last written by Marcus to the potential young African leader, Kwame. Zola stopped him and wanted him to rest, but he was not an easy man. He wanted his will at all times. When he slept, Zola took the letter and handed it to me. I began reading:

"Son, the struggle continues until the whirlwind is calmed and changed. Until the last black man is free to live in any part of this world and has control of his body, mind and soul, and has total independence of self. According to them, I am the most dangerous enemy of the Negro race in America and in the world, because of my obligation to promote my people, because of my need for unity and peace in the world, because of my quest for equality, because of my essential need for getting back to Africa, because of my commitment to UNIA, because of my right for freedom, because of the urgency that Pan-Africa must stand... Also because of my desire to keep the Black Star Line a life, because of my wish for the black enterprise, because of the fact that I believe that a nation should be set aside to serve as a central home for all Africans, because I encouraged the black man not to fear, because I have started a movement that is bigger than my body itself, because of my hunger for uniting the black man...and because I believe that Africa is for the Africans.

"They are right; I am dangerously created to match with my brothers on the streets of Harlem without fear. I am dangerously created to parade with all black men from slavery to freedom in Liberia. Indeed, I am dangerously created because I have said that Africa is the motherland of all Negroes, from where all Negroes in slavery were taken against their will. Africa is the natural home of the black race. One day all blacks hope to look to Africa as the land of their vines and fig trees. It is necessary, therefore, to help the tribes who live in Africa advance to a higher civilization rather than allow them to lose it all. Therefore, I am dangerously created to be on a mission of encouraging all black man to have pride in their race. They should think of their race in the highest terms of human lives. To think that God made the black race perfect, and blessed them richly, to think that there is no one better than the black man, to think that the black people have the elements of human perfection and as such they must love themselves... Love yourselves better than anyone else. All beauty is in you and not outside of you, for God made you beautiful. Confine your affection, therefore, to your own race and God will bless you and men will honour you.

"And at last, I am dangerously created; I have travelled extensively throughout the world, and studying the economic, commercial and industrial needs of our people and I found out that the quickest and easiest way to reach them was by steamship communication. So immediately after I succeeded in forming the Universal Negro Improvement Association in America, I launched the idea of floating ships under the direction of Negroes. It could have been successful, but again the conspiracy of this world says that a black man is unable to accomplish such a great task – but they forget, or do not know, that the black man himself is great and powerful. Some of my own people believe a lie, that I am not who I say I am, but I tell you the truth in this letter – that I am everything that God says I am.

"Some of them betrayed me, because they did not have confidence in themselves. The only conspiracy that I saw during my fight for revolution is that a black man is not capable of doing what he was created for. We heard a lie, and we believed it. But the struggle must continue until we can believe in ourselves again. Tell the women to walk upright with their high heels. You should always encourage our black women that they are beautiful and they are the natural black stars.

"I survived the grave alone, but on the way to freedom, you cannot travel alone. You need to take with you as many people as possible, even if you can't trust everybody (some will sell you out). We don't want any more trouble, but we will not rest until we are free at last."

As soon as I got through reading, the professor woke up: "What time is it?" he asked.

"It is almost 8:00 pm," Zola told him as she looked at the clock on the wall.

"We should go to bed," he said.

"But you just woke up," I told him.

"I am 115 years old; sleep is what I am supposed to be doing," he responded. "Who are you, the husband?" he asked me again.

"Oh no, Sir, he is only with me," Zola said. "I am too busy to marry a man; he would divorce me early in the morning if there was no breakfast on the table, or if I choose a speech over him. I do not have time to take care of myself, and had it not been for Maa I would not have the strength to stand up," Zola said as she helped make him comfortable.

"You are doing better than the nurses," he said. "All the nurses take care of me without passion. 'I am only doing my work,' they usually say. Those are the exact words Marcus said when his marriage failed. You have to find a man that has the same interests as you. You need to sow seeds. They will be the future generation. Had it not been for Marcus, the black man would have probably still kept looking directly towards the whirlwind, still afraid and not having the confidence to change the direction.

"And the Little family. They were able to plant a seed, a good seed and that seed turned into a giant tree that they had to quickly cut down. It became a thorn in the human flesh. It was powerful and strong to the extent that it started reading minds. I will continue the letter tomorrow and I will tell you about who the Little family was, and how their influence helped to move the Black Power movement further after Marcus was dead."

"Good night, Sir… Grandpa," said Zola.

"Good night, my dear child."

"If you don't mind, I am just going to sleep on the sofa in case you need me in the middle of the night," Zola said.

"Oh child, this world will be a much better place when we all look out for each other. My children think that I am an old grumpy man who complains about everything. I pray that they live long enough to be my age, then they will know whether I am complaining or if I really am uncomfortable and lonely." He squeezed Zola's hand. "I can see that this young man loves you very much!" the professor said to Zola.

"Is it that obvious? I love him, but not that way; we are just friends now," said Zola.

She was still talking when I walked out to find the guest bedroom. Zola still loved me, I could tell from her voice. I hoped she would understand when she found out why we couldn't be together.

From the hallway, I heard the professor say: "You need him, but you can't trust him until you know for sure that he is in love with you. You are on a mission of making a remarkable change in this world; I felt it when you called me. I have seen the future through you and it is very bright. You are going around making a difference in the community.

"I have seen the glory that is going to cover the black man in the near future. They all fought hard to make the black man's dream a reality. All of the freedom fighters are dead, but their worlds are alive and will be revealed in every one of you until the dream is fulfilled. When I look at you, I see a little bit of all the revolutionaries, from Garvey to Mandela."

"But I am just a community worker, I am not a politician, Sir," Zola said.

"Yes, my child. Like I said, keep moving forward and don't look back and blame anyone for the past. Look back and be motivated to look forward at the light."

"We should get some sleep," Zola said, as she still held his hand.

"Yes, we will sleep, but first things first. The Dream Speech by the Honorable King has gradually come to reality, and the biggest surprise is on the way, after a decade from now. It will all come in to view; Do not forget this – Africa needs to unite and put away the guns. Do all in your power to help them put their arms around each other.

"There are natural born leaders that people are always willing to listen to and follow. You are a leader. When a leader is created and sent, that person should be given all the support in order to rise up in leadership. Thank God you have chosen not to believe the conspiracy theory of the world, and those who actually believe that the DNA of a black man is hostile," he said in a very serious tone.

I was still standing eavesdropping when I heard Zola say:

"Canada is not a bad country at all. The Europeans that possessed the land many years ago have made it their home and they are taking good care of it, unlike Africa. We have a beautiful waterfall."

"Yes, the Niagara, I have been there," he quickly cut her off. "Well, he asked, "Why isn't the falls called Garvey's Falls or Mandela's Falls?"

"Well, Sir…Grandpa, there is a Mandela High, it is one of Canada's best high schools. As a matter of fact, I went to Mandela High School in Toronto," Zola said, sounding tired.

"Well, on my way to Liberia after Marcus' death, I went to the Victoria Falls in Zambia; it is beautiful," he said.

"Yes, it is," Zola added. "I heard that it used to be called the Mtonga's Falls, good night, Grandpa. You should really get some sleep. We will talk about the Mtonga's Falls in the morning."

"I sleep all day. That's all I do – sleep, sleep, and sleep." He did not want to sleep, but I could see that Zola had had enough of talk for one day. I was very exhausted as well. It was almost midnight, and the old man wanted to stay up.

Zola said, "Well, Sir, I am tired. Can we please continue in the morning?" But he did not respond. Then she called him, thinking that he was angry or maybe dead, but he was only sleeping.

I went to the spare bedroom and went to sleep.

In the morning Zola and I went to the professor. Zola gave him a cup of hot cereal.

"How did you sleep, Grandpa?" she asked.

"Great, ready to roll. I am ready to go. We have to finish the letter today. And please call my grandson and tell him to drop by later. Make it sound serious and urgent… He will not come if it is not urgent."

"Yes, Grandpa, I will," Zola said.

"Let me see…," said the old man. "It was the uniform. It was a brilliant idea that the Black people wear a uniform. It unified us and it reminded us that we were more than just farmers and house helpers. It represented something very powerful when we agree and come together as one – anything and everything is possible. Women are not just housing wives; they are the bone under the flesh. Otherwise, the body will not stand.

"It is your turn now, to fight until you can't fight any more. We were forced out of Africa and scattered all over the world. They stole us and brought us here and made us slaves, they have occupied the land of our fathers, yet they called us homeless and poor. The black man is not poor; he is lacking management. 'Where is my home and where is my government?' Marcus would say. The black man wanted to belong, and if they had not sacrificed their lives to fight for freedom, we would still be roaming the earth without a place to call home," he said as he took the letter, fighting to open it.

I took the letter from him and opened it.

"Dear Son, this is where you come in. Africa is the motherland of all black men, from where all slaves were taken against their will. If you look around, you will see that only the blacks were slaves. Have you ever heard about the white slaves, or the slaves from China?"

"No, but I heard about what happened to the Japanese people during the Second World War… 'Grandpa'," I quickly said.

"Since when did the black man become a grandfather to a white man like you?" he asked.

"Well, Grandpa," said Zola, "the times are changing and the dream is becoming a reality. You can see that. Enough is enough, there is a time to blame people and there is a time to not blame."

"Let me tell you one thing that I have seen: I have seen the black man sitting in the White House, a complete climax, hmmm? I am not angry at you my son, I am just a grumpy old man. I am sorry; honour me and call me whatever you want to call me. Africa is the natural home of the black race, there is our DNA and tomorrow every black will look to Africa as the land of their blood vessel. It is necessary."

Chapter Eleven

"Is that all?" I asked him.

Professor Tolbert shook his head. "There's more, and I am going to give you the rest of these letters and all that I have for Marcus. Use them and help take the young people from the streets. Zola, you choose whether to finish the letter in front of this…French boy, or not. The decision is yours. I am going to tell you one more thing about Marcus. He did not do any of it. It was a setup. The rest is confidential; my advice is to use it for your knowledge."

"What about the Little family's story and their contribution to the black people, please?" I asked him.

"Mandela went to jail during their time and he came out after twenty-seven years of torture – twenty-seven years of sleeping in the cold and in the dark, expecting death every day to knock at his jail cell. A twenty-seven-year-old man, twenty-seven good years wasted behind bars for man's selfish desire. How wicked is the heart of man? I have prayed for my life to be taken, but God kept me alive to experience all of this. I have lived to see it all, a hundred and fifteen years; it is now time to go home," the old professor said with tears streaming down his face, now crying out loud.

"Grandpa, please don't cry," urged Zola. "It is okay. It is over now. He is free, and see what he was able to achieve."

"No! It is not over," the professor said. "Poverty, greed and corruption must be dealt with, and lastly, Africa must stop the bloodshed and unite all of the brothers."

He was a bit angry and overwhelmed so we tried to stabilize his temper. He went into the Little family's story: "Earl Little was a fine young preacher who believed that God created the earth so that mankind would be able to live freely and multiply. Unfortunately for him, he was not allowed to preach the 'good news' according to his beliefs. He was warned several times to change his style of preaching. Just like now, a group of Christians would come together and decide that that part of the Bible should not be taught because it would offend people who are not living according to the word of God.

"As a result, they go around discrediting other preachers and they teach the wrong message. The family was almost burned while in their home. That plot failed, but whoever wanted them dead was going to find another means so it would look like an accident. One day he had come from preaching at another location, tired but excited about the good things that God was doing in his life. Earl Little sent a message to meet me halfway along a little quiet road where we often met. I left my house and traveled along the road. I had almost entered the town when I heard a sound that seemed to have been a struggle in the bush. At that time, if one heard such struggles, you ran. I quickly looked again. It was Earl. They had just cut through his neck and they were all standing over him.

"I screamed and ran. They ran after me, but they did not catch up with me or see my face. I slept in the bush for almost a week. I almost did not believe what had happened… I was hoping it was all just a dream and I could go home. Seven days later, I went to see him and I heard that he was killed by a streetcar. My own family thought that I was also killed. They were preparing a memorial service for me when I showed up. 'We have to move away from here and maybe to Harlem,'" my mother told me.

"Mama," I said, "Harlem is a part of the United States where black people are found dead every day on the street. Besides, we can't keep running away from the problem. Michigan is our home now; we will stay and fight for our freedom.

"'Anyone who decides to fight the wind will not stand,' my mother said.

They later took the preacher's wife to a mental institution. My mother went to work and she did not come home. She was a house cleaner and apparently, she hanged herself one day after work." The professor was lying on the bed, sobbing uncontrollably as he explained his life journey. Zola tried to stop him but he was unstoppable.

"You are burning with fever," she said. "Let me give you something to ease your pain."

"No, child, it is all right. I am ready to go home. You can't keep me here any longer. I am glad that I was able to take you two on some of my life journey. I am honoured that you two came to see me."

I believed he wanted to "kick the bucket" while we were still there. He seemed to be in peace, according to how he looked now.

"Let me call your family again and tell them about your current status," Zola said as she picked up the phone.

"No, my child, don't. They can't wait for me to go, so they can fight over my property. They have enough material wealth. I have shared almost everything among them, but they are still not satisfied. What can you do with greedy people? My great-grandson is a lawyer, but he wants this home, but he will not get it. It is for charity.

"They expected that I would die before my eightieth birthday, but I disappointed them. I want to go in peace. You have brought me peace. Please let me enjoy this moment with you… Just give me some water."

It was hard for me to be there in the room with him. He was grumpy, but I had begun to like him. It was difficult to describe him, expect that he was very tall and thin with a light skin. I left and went into the next room to rest for a while. It was sad to know that a man like him, filled with knowledge, was leaving without any family members to say good-bye. He should be buried with honour, I told myself.

I called his great-grandson after all. As I called him, the first thing he said was, "The crazy old man is not yet dead?"

"No, he is not; he wants to see you," I said.

"No, I am too busy. I am his lawyer, so as soon as he dies, call me first before any of the family members."

I was shocked by his cold response.

After I hung up the phone, I went back to the professor's bedroom. He told Zola that Malcolm Little had had a tough life: "He saw what was happening to the black people in the United States and not just that, he saw all that his parents went through and what became of them. He had to continue the struggle of the black revolution. How much can a little child take in? Malcolm was a confused and troubled little boy who found himself in Harlem fighting for survival. Eventually, he found himself doing ten years in prison for burglary. After ten years, he got out and followed in his father's footsteps, fighting for the black revolution.

"The only difference between him and his father was their religions. Malcolm was clever and very intelligent. He travelled around the world fighting for the black power. He became a threat to the government, so they quickly made up their minds to get rid of him." The professor remembered this one incident in which they went to buy him off so that he would betray his brotherhood: "They twisted his words many times, and pushed his buttons as well, but he was committed to his organization and his people. 'I do not have any information to give you,' Malcolm had told them. 'You are insulting my intelligence as well as yours.' They offered him a ransomed amount of money so he would give them the names of his members. But he sent them to the head office.

"'Bitterness makes you want to get back at the people that hurt you,' Malcolm had said. 'Especially when after being a leader for so long, they suddenly remove you. It hurts, but makes you stronger if you are suspended for something. It makes you realize your wrongdoing. The law applies to the law enforcer as well as those under the enforcement of the law enforcer.' Malcolm talked with them and it was all recorded, I believe. What he was trying to say was that no man is above the law.

"One winter night, I received a call from him telling me that he was in the house with his family and the house had been set on fire. Almost a week later, he was killed – shot multiple times at a conference. My godson, Malcolm, was dead. I witnessed his death, his father's, and I saw his mother in the mental home often until she passed away. The strange thing about his death was that there was a hospital just across the street from where he was shot, and they could not help save his life. We screamed and cried, and no one crossed the street to help us. By the time the police got on the scene, Malcolm was dead. I never recovered from his death.

"Do not believe all the negative things you read about him. He fought for the freedom of all black men. What he went through on the streets of Harlem was tough, and he did not wish it for anyone. He was carrying a whole nation in him, and leadership was in him. Keep following your father's footsteps and inspire others, my child. I will quote one last word from Malcolm, for I am very tired."

The weary old professor spoke: "The American black man should be focusing his every effort toward building his own businesses, and decent homes for himself. As other ethnic groups have done, let the black people, wherever possible, patronize their own kind, and start in those ways to build up the black race's ability to do for itself.

"'This is the only way the American black man is ever going to get respect,' Malcolm had said. 'One thing the white man never can give the black man is self-respect! The black man never can become independent and recognized as a human being who is truly equal with other human beings until he has what they have, and until he is doing for himself what others are doing for themselves. The black man in the ghettoes, for instance, has to start self-correcting his own material, moral and spiritual defects and then the evils will vanish. The black man needs to start his own program to get rid of drunkenness, drug addiction, prostitution, and everything that is keeping him, and your people, from rising. The black man in America has to lift up his own sense of values.' Malcolm taught this and he meant every word he said.

"The rest of the information is in that box. I would rather give it to you than to my lazy family – and they might burn it all." He handed Zola a business card. "And this is my secret lawyer, he is going to give you open access to Jamaica, and this will be your home from now on. These properties are yours and he is going to help you fight my relatives. I appreciate you coming down here to listen to me explain my struggle. I am very calm. I have not felt this way before, and my time is near."

Zola told him that it was all right, and she did not want any of it. She pleaded with him to turn it over to his relatives. "They need it more than I do," she said.

"No, child," said the professor. "They *want* it more than you do. You have much work ahead of you. You need all the support you can get. The past week has been great. Going back to the past was what I was waiting for before leaving this earth. They are all waiting on me some place, and you will do well. Remember me, child – fear is a deadly weapon. Make sure to destroy it from your system and you will achieve your goal. *Black Power forever.*"

He was still talking, while leaving the world but I could feel that his struggles were over. "Zola, one of the grandsons wants us to call him as soon as it happens," I told her.

"No," she said. "We will call no one. He is going to go in peace."

He and Zola were connected to the same black struggle, and Dr. Nkrumah himself. The two bonded, and he had become a part of Zola's life. It was more than just a history lesson for me. The nurses and his new lawyer witnessed his death. The major had dropped by to check on him that day, and he checked on him as often as he could in his spare time, happy to have been there.

With the help of the City Mayor of Morant Bay, we buried him with honour. He was a great man and his people were proud of him. We spent another week in Jamaica before leaving.

Back at home, we discussed the experience. "I think that the reason he stayed alive this long was to get over the struggle of the past," Zola said. "He did not forgive, so he had been living his life in grief. Life is for enjoyment, not for enduring. Pretty sad."

However, I couldn't help disagreeing with her.

"Hey, where have you guys been?" asked Natasha. "Orlando has been looking for you for the past week."

"It is a long story, but I was in Jamaica," Zola said, putting down her boxes. "I will give Orlando a call later."

"I thought that you are not a Jamaican, so why did you go there?" Natasha asked.

"You all have ears and you have refused to listen. I am an African."

I nodded. "

Chapter Twelve

Zola had started dating a guy. I was a little sceptical about him, but she told me I had nothing to worry about.

"Do you love him?" I asked her, but she did not give me an answer. Maybe it was time for her to move on with her life, as she realized that I was just not attracted to her.

Zola called me from the hospital one Friday afternoon telling me that she was not doing well. I rushed over at once to see her. She looked well, but she did not feel well. The only time I knew her to be in hospital was when she had been bullied at Mandela High. When I asked the doctor what the problem was, he was not sure. They still had to do some tests on her.

"Hey, Girl, how are you?" I asked.

"They want me to get enough sleep and eat more food," she said, laughing. She tried to stand up, but she shook like an old lady in her nineties. Her voice was low and it was easy to tell that she was worried.

"What happened to your sweet voice, Zola?"

"Ah…ah, they…want me to do some…tests…ah."

I teased her a little just to cheer her up. "They are right, I think that's all that's wrong with you, and I am going to make sure you do what they say. Eat, sleep and plenty of rest is all you need."

"Yes, Father François. Has Ben left for France?" she asked.

"We are not talking about Ben right now, but he sends his love," I said, a bit harshly.

"How is Aunt May?"

"We are not going to talk about Aunt May, Natasha, or Sayba, Sweetie," I told her. "It is time to take care of Zola for a change. You are not a radio, and even the radio needs a battery or electricity to function."

"I will be fine! The Big Man is watching over me, you know that." Zola talked and laughed at the sound of her own voice. But I could see that she was scared, and worried.

"He is going to, because we can't do life without you," I said.

"No! You can't do life without *Him*," she said, pointing her finger up.

"Okay."

"Oh, and Huan Yue is on her way."

"You shouldn't have called her. You will have the old lady running out of breath."

"She is here."

"You see her from the hospital room parking her car, right?" I asked her.

"She is my grandmother, isn't she? I can smell her and feel her," Zola said.

"Hey, what's cooking?" Maa said, coming in through the doorway.

"I'm hungry Maa," Zola told her with tears.

"You are not just hungry, my darling; you need a good rest and a cup of ginseng drink. What did the doctor say?"

"I met a sick girl in BC, and I might have gotten the virus from her."

"Maa Huan, it is not just a virus," I said. "Zola has been very worried about the war around the world, and Jamaica was not a vacation trip either."

Zola quickly changed the subject when Maa left to meet the doctor.

"You are very stressed, Girl. You need to stop worrying," I told her, but she turned her face towards the window. She did not really look cheerful, but Natasha was going to spend the weekend with her in hospital just to keep her company.

"Keep your eyes on Zola, not on the doctors' fingers," I teased. "They are all married, and there are sick people, so be mindful of them by keeping your voice down."

Natasha was a very active and funny girl; whenever she was in the room, she would keep us laughing all the time. She told us that she wanted a man who had it all, but Maa Huan told her to work for her own money. "Otherwise, he might call you a gold digger," Zola told her.

"The men do it, too. I will prove to you that men are gold diggers themselves," Natasha responded.

Maa Huan, and I left together that evening. I called my boss to let him in on what was happening. He was not so happy about Zola's condition, and rushed back to the hospital to see her.

Maa Huan called me early Monday morning to pick Zola up from the hospital. When I got there I met Nathan visiting her, observing as he always did.

"Hello Nathaniel, how are you?" I greeted him.

"My name is Nathan."

"But what's wrong with Nathaniel? Isn't it the same?"

"I am doing well, French Man, and how are you?" he replied.

"Why are you calling me French Man? Only my friends call me French Man."

"But what are you, French Man?" Nathan asked.

"I am François."

"What is the meaning of François?"

"Okay, guys, that's enough. You both behave like kids, one of whose fathers works at McDonald's and the other's at the bank."

She seemed to like the guy, but I did not like him. She was at the hospital for three days and he showed up when she was discharged.

"François, you are a businessman. Don't you travel?" he asked me.

But I kept quiet this time. Zola wanted me to get to know her boyfriend better, but I could not find myself in the same room with him. "I am here to bring you to my house, Zola," I said, looking directly in Nathan's eyes.

"Well! That will not be possible," Zola said. "Nathan wants me to go home with him and I may be with him until Friday," said Zola confidently.

"For a week with him? But I will not be able to see you... Besides, Huan Yue told me to take you home. Nathan, for Christ's sake, will you be home to take care of her? Please let her go home with the people that love her."

"What are you trying to imply, François? She is my girlfriend isn't she? I love her, too. Don't you have a girlfriend? Leave her to live her life."

Nathan held her hand as he talked to me. The nurses were standing watching us as we argued over the patient's head. "François, you need to stop this obsession with Nathan!" said Zola. "Could you please try to get along with him for my sake? Stop speaking *for* me and listen *to* me."

"I see that you want to protect me, but he is my boyfriend. Can you provide my needs? You have the same goal. You comfort me, because you love me, and he protects me, because he loves me. I am the luckiest woman on the planet right now, but I don't feel lucky right now! It has been a long week for all of us. I can't wait to leave this place, and you both are not helping me get well. Maybe I should get a private room and stay here for a while."

When Zola had finished, I felt myself pitying her and decided to let him have her. Still…

"He is too diplomatic, and I don't like the way he treats you," I told her. For some reason, I just couldn't stop defending myself. They both kept quiet and stared at me. It did not take long; I heard a familiar voice, and it was Natasha:

"Hello, Tom and Jerry. Are you still fighting? I heard you from afar and the nurses are all laughing at you two. Aunt Zola, you look better than two hours ago."

"You mean, twelve hours ago," Zola said. "I feel great, too. Thanks to my two handsome gentlemen here who can't see eye-to-eye with each other."

"Uncle François, how are you? Uncle Nathan, you look good as usual."

"Thanks, Sweetie," Nathan said. "How are your studies coming along?"

"Oh, great! Working and studying…couldn't be any better you know. My mother wants to go back home but she can't because she sold our property to get here," Natasha said, sounding unconcerned.

"Natasha, what are you talking about?" I asked her.

"Oh, didn't Aunt Zola tell you? Never mind, we give God thanks," she responded quickly, still standing by Nathan.

"Why don't you come to the office sometime?" he offered. "If it is the transportation, I don't mind helping you at all."

"Thank you, Uncle Nathan."

"Natasha, Hon, you really don't have to work. Since you entered this room, you have earned more money out of your uncle's pocket than the nurses' overtime pay," Zola said.

"I love you all so much," Natasha said.

It was almost mid-day, and even though I disagreed with Nathan, I allowed him to take her home.

"Uncle François, do we meet Tuesday at my house to go over the guest list?" asked Natasha.

"Yes, Love, I might even see you tomorrow," I said, then walked away.

Natasha had started planning a late graduation surprise party for Zola before her illness. Zola worked so hard that she had no time for herself, and getting her PhD was a great achievement that we had to celebrate. She did not want a party, though. Whenever we had suggested it to her, she had counted the costs and said "No. Can't you see, we can better give the money to the Red Cross, for Christ's sake, not a party? They are crazy." Then she said:

"Women and children are dying on the street.
The leaders are sitting being slaughtered with the butcher knife.
When did Africa become a place for bloodshed?
Mama Africa, where are you?
She wants to reach down and help her children,
But she is helpless, and hopeless.
Those that once had a burning passion for her now despise her.
Her first son is no more, and her second son is left without a voice.
She is sitting wondering in sadness and confusion.
"Oh, I was once honoured, but now I am a disgrace.
She sits as her heart breaks for her precious gifts.
Babies are fainting and dying in the street.
Mothers stand and watch them stumble without a hand.
She cries and shouts for her child, but her voice is not heard.
She cries with tears of blood.
Her tears are pouring down her cheeks like a mighty rain.
And it has refused to stop.
She is comforted by those that killed her children.
The world drinks from the cup of bitter root.
They sit and laugh saying, 'We've destroyed them.
We are getting rich from their resources,
While they get poorer each day.
We will give them rice, and guns in exchange for diamonds', they say.

But they have forgotten to know that they still need children,
They can't survive without them.
But my sweet children, be of good courage,
Forget not the past, because there are better days ahead.
On that day, you will be respected for your decision,
And honoured for your position.
So fill yourself with hopes, and less of fear.
Arise, Africa, arise, and stand together in faith
And believe that soon and very soon, it will be a new day for you;"

I understood her passion for the dying children, and how much she wanted to protect the earth, but realistically, it was impossible. I can't count how many times she told me that she was created for a special purpose. The people are her purpose and she is my purpose. Losing her for me would be like having no life. Yes, I would get upset whenever I heard her poems, but I tried to reason with her as well. Children should be protected from the evil of this world. I only told her that she was killing herself slowly, and her obsession with the war needed to stop.

"When you look at me, who or what do you see, François?" she asked me.

I saw a beautiful lady trying hard, so hard that she was forgetting herself in the process. Then she accused me of being one of the people who go for peace talks holding a cigar.

"If you are my friend, share my interest," she said sadly.

"I am sorry, Love. I just wanted to tell you to take good care of yourself." We made up, and she left for B.C.

I felt obligated to protect her from everyone with bad intentions, and I "smelled" it all around her lover boy. I allowed him to take her home anyway; she had been looking forward to spending some time with Nathan for so long. *Why can't I let her go?*, I wondered. A part of me had rejected her as my partner. I had moved on since Sankara. Maybe it was time to let her be, I said to myself. As I look back now, I realize that I was selfish. It was not only Nathan. I did want *anyone* getting close to her. At one time, I had told Orlando to think of her as a sister and not to take advantage of her.

I remember when she met him; she could not stop talking about him. "He is tall, black and handsome, and not talkative," she would say. Since I could not be with her, the least I could do was let Nathan have her, even though it was hard swallowing my pride. "It is just for a moment," I had whispered in Nathan's ear. "I don't trust you with her."

Meanwhile, on the way to Nathan's house, Zola called me to let me know that she was going to her house and I should meet her there. "I knew it, he was good-looking for nothing. He can't take care of you."

"It was not what you think, François," she said.

"Sure!" I told her, but I was glad that she was not going with him.

"Okay, Love. I will be home waiting for you."

She was very intelligent and beautiful and well-connected too, to be with that guy. I could not come up with any answers as to why she chose him.

He brought her home late that evening. I tried chatting with him, but he drove away.

"What is the sombre face about?" Zola asked.

"I am so sorry!"

"Why are you apologizing?" she asked.

"I know how much you were looking forward to spending this time with him, but I don't like that guy. He is not trustworthy, but don't worry, everything will be fine." I told her. I was trying to comfort her, but she did not want to be comforted.

"You are the one with the sad face, François. Don't worry, Nathan is a good fellow."

"But he is not right for you."

"Not right for me? Who is right for me, François – you? Nathan is a real, responsible gentleman. Most men today are little boys who clothe themselves in expensive suits while their children sleep without drinking milk. I don't want to pamper any such man. I am not looking for a son, I want a partner. Besides, a relationship is not want I need right now. I love Nathan, and he loves me, too."

"No Zola, you don't mean that. You *like* him."

"Anything to get you off my back, François."

I knew that she was giving me a lecture, so I had to play along with her.

She lifted her head up and looked in to my eyes. "I am tired," she said, obviously trying to sort out her feelings.

"Maa called. She was here earlier; she brought the drink and some food."

"Thanks, Maa, I love you too. Life would be easy if everyone in the world were like Maa…she never worries about anything."

Chapter Thirteen

It was a beautiful day and the sun was shining, the air fragrant with spring. There was a fresh breeze blowing, but it was hot when I decided to go over to Natasha's place to touch base with her.

She had not invited Uncle Lover Boy yet.

"Oh no!" she said. "I forgot to invite Nathan. I'm going to give him a call right now." She ran to pick up the phone. "Hello, Uncle Nathan, it's Natasha.

"How are you, Natasha?"

"I'm very well, thanks be to the Big Guy up there," she said.

"What can I do for you?"

"It's Aunt Zola."

"What is it with her, is she okay?" Nathan asked.

"Oh, I'm sorry! It is nothing like that. We are giving Aunt Zola a surprise dinner party this weekend, and we want you to be there. She has been through much lately and your presence in her life has brightened up her face," said Natasha.

"Is that right?" he said, obviously feeling good about himself.

"It is true. She is usually a cheerful person, but the whole African war thing has been taking its toll on her. Giving her a party without you is like not having it at all. It is going to be her graduation party. Besides, my mother can't wait to meet you. She always tells me that whatever makes my heart smile is good for me. I guess you made her heart smile."

"Okay, Natasha, I will be there, but I will be a little late."

"Not a problem, Uncle Nathan. Love you."

"Love you too, Sweetie." He hung up the phone.

"Natasha, it was not necessary putting the phone on speaker," I said.

"Oh, okay, Uncle François."

"I will see you later this evening."

So Nathan would be at the party after all. I guess I just needed to accept the fact that I was sharing Zola with somebody else.

Later that day, Zola went over to Natasha's – in fact, in the afternoon as soon as I left. When I returned late that evening, to my surprise, Zola was still there with Natasha. Natasha's mother was there also.

"Hey, Beautiful," I said to Zola, "you look good for a woman who just got out of the hospital."

"Thanks, French Man," Zola said with a laugh, then emptied the last of the milk into her tea, probably thinking about the conversation that I had had with Nathan: that he did not really care about her. "Natasha, you don't have milk or cream in here; try to put some food in here. Don't tell me that President Mugabe has anything to do with your fridge being empty."

"No, but Mama is always saving the extra money to send to her friends and some family members she left behind. She often says that we don't need extra food – yogurt is for babies, she says. All the sweet and unnecessary food is not important for the body. I get to buy for myself and she keeps her money. She will someday go back and take over the Zimbabwe government," Natasha said, looking into her mother's eyes.

"If this was Zimbabwe, I would...put you in your place. It is not everything that is said behind closed doors you bring in to the open air. You are now a Canadian with a big mouth." Natasha's mother said. She was always ready to defend herself.

"You should have called me to pick you up. Did you take the taxi?" I asked Zola.

"Nathan brought me here," she replied.

"Oh! I see." I wasn't too happy that he had driven her, but I had to at least pretend to be. I volunteered to drive her home but Nathan was taking her to the theatre.

As we were sitting by the fire place talking, sharing jokes, and laughing, Zola began explaining to us how good it was to depend on God for everything: "Don't allow the situation to change who you are. The situation does not own you. You take full control of the situation. Besides, we are all God's children, you know."

Zola ended her lecture. Natasha kept asking her more questions, and I wanted her to stop. Life with Aunt May had never been easy. All I heard about was the power of the highest God and the power of the blood of Jesus. My Aunt May wanted me to be with only church friends. Apparently, she thought others might lead me to hell. It is ironic that Zola and I ended up being friends. Zola was a Christian, but she respected others around her and she kept an open mind to things. To many, she was Zola the smart girl from Mandela High. She was my everything. It felt good listening to her explain the Bible in a better way than many people I knew.

Zola spoke directly to Natasha: "If you desire greatness in this world, think about it and work hard towards it. It will attract you – but if you constantly think about negative things, that's what you will get."

Aunt May had tried over the years to keep me in the church, but I could not get that "life" in me. Nevertheless, though I had lost interest in going to church, I still believed in God. I just wanted to feel Him in my heart, and wanted to reach out to Him, but it seemed to be that every time I got a little closer, something pulled me back.

My Aunt May did not understand that. Even Zola did not. If there really was a God and He lived in me, He was going to help me get closer to Him. In the meantime, I was the Christian who heard the word and neglected it like many people.

"God is right in your heart, François; you will find Him the day you begin searching for Him," Natasha's mother said.

"We are not here to preach today," said Natasha.

"Has anyone heard from Sayba lately? I tried giving her a call, but she did not pick up," Zola said.

"I spoke to her not too long ago," answered Natasha. "She is writing her exams, but she said not to worry, she will be coming to the party." Natasha obviously did not realize that she had just blown the lid off the surprise.

"Which party?" Zola asked in surprise.

"My next-door neighbour is having her graduation party next week, and she invited Sayba, and you, too," Natasha quickly explained.

The doorbell rang, and I thought it was Nathan, but when I opened the door, I saw that it was Orlando, James, and James' sister.

"Hello, James, Orlando. Nice to see you guys.

"I wish that I could say the same to you," James said as he walked past me at the door.

"Orlando, nice to see you again," I said.

"You work for a company that has wanted me since last year," Orlando said.

"Yes, and we still want you."

"I am good with my job now, thanks anyway," Orlando said as he gave me a handshake.

"How long have you known James?" I asked Orlando.

"I met him downstairs. It was the first time meeting him," Orlando said.

James was a friend of Natasha's, and he had also graduated from Mandela High during our days there. He was lucky to have found a fulltime job right after graduation. When James entered the room, it seemed to become cloudy, murky. Nobody wanted him there, and apparently nobody dared to say a word. As he spoke to me, he smelled of beer and wine…and trouble. Under no circumstances would I allow Natasha to get involved with him. James was a smart boy who did not give any thought to his ways, and as a result he behaved foolishly. In fact, he never got enough of beer and wine, and he never stopped provoking his relatives. Now when he saw Zola, he walked to her and gave her a handshake, and began telling her how sorry he was to hear that she had been ill.

"In Africa, I am a king, and kings drink palm wine. Where is my palm wine?" he asked.

Then I turned to him and said, "Didn't your mother tell you that it is not good for a king to get drunk on wine or beer?"

"I don't know my Bible, but one thing I know is this, 'Give beer to those who are perishing, wine to those who are in anguish; let them drink and forget their poverty and remember their misery no more."

I told him, "No we don't have any beer or wine for you, because we don't want you to continue to oppress your family."

His sister sat down quietly.

"You sit here and act like you are perfect and you are all ready to go to heaven," he complained. He swore at his sister and called Zola a snake, then took a bottle of beer from his pocket to drink. Zola asked him to leave.

Before doing so, he turned to me and said, "So you think you got game? You sit with the ladies and act like you are one of them. I have nothing to say to you, I do not like men. I like women, a real beautiful woman like your precious Zola. Didn't your mother tell you to give her grandchildren, you homosexual."

"Homo what?" everyone repeated.

James left. The room was quiet for a minute or two, but it seemed like ten minutes or more. The neighbour had called the police, because her daughter who was visiting Natasha had ran home and told her that she heard James saying that he was going to blow someone's head off. No one said a word to me. We were all still sitting looking around, then we heard the sound of police cars and firefighters outside. I remember looking outside and seeing the police, but it did not occur to me that they were there for our protection.

The doorbell rang. We thought it might have been James again, and Zola went to the door to tell him that he was not welcome. But it was the police. "Ma'am, put your hands on your head and walk outside, please," said one of the officers.

Based on Zola's reputation in the community, one of the officers recognized her and began asking her questions. "Miss Zola, are you okay? Are you hurt, what kind of weapon do they have? How many people are in there? Are they black or white?" They asked ten questions at once.

"I am alright, thank God. Now may I put my hands down?" Zola said. "There are four people in there, two gentlemen and two ladies. It is not what you think. There is a very handsome black man who would not kill a fly. Neither would François."

"Did you see the weapon?" The officer kept asking questions.

"The French Man is in there and he is white…and a black girl who happens to be my goddaughter is in there with her mother."

"How dangerous are they?" the officer asked again.

"You are not listening. There are no weapons in here, and we are all family spending the evening together," Zola explained, her frustration mounting against the questions.

It was all a big misunderstanding. The officers entered and took statements from everyone in the house. For one of the officers, seeing Zola was like seeing the Queen of England. She had wanted to give Zola a hug, but she had to obey the police protocol. It was against the rules to allow your emotion to overtake you. Still, she got a signature for her mother and with a little note that said: "It is your prayer that keeps me standing… Keep praying for the children. With all my love, Zola."

It was nearly 10:30 pm and Nathan had not come. It had been a long day, and we were all very tired.

"What is taking Nathan so long?" asked Zola.

As soon as I suggested taking her home, he called, saying that he was just leaving the office. I did not want him taking her home, because we had to address the statement that had muted the mouth of everyone. I wanted to talk to her, but did she want to talk to me? If I had to explain myself, where was I going to start? *Zola, I'm sorry, but Ben kissed me first at Mandela, then at Sankara.*

I just let her be. She had drunk over five cups of tea that night. I looked in her eyes and began feeling her frustration. Zola and I were friends for half my life that she should be the last to find out such important information about me.

Nathan got there in one piece. "I don't think you should go out there by yourself…let him come and get you," I said. But she did not hear me, or maybe she pretended not to have heard me.

She did not want to hear any advice from me that night. We walked with her to the car, and Natasha hugged me and whispered in my ear saying: "No, Uncle François, no. You're going to break her heart, and she might go back to the hospital. She cannot find out that you left her to be with Ben."

I said good night to everyone and took my leave. I left my car at Natasha's, because I was not in a condition to drive. Was my being gay going to separate Zola and me for good? As for the party, we were on top of everything, but I knew there was trouble.

Zola was not just a friend. She was a part of my family since high school. Everyone knew that. I was now about to lose another member of my family. Knowing Zola, I felt she was going to forgive me if she was really who she claimed to be. I just needed to make her understand.

I began thinking about my job. I was the CEO of Ali & Ngo incorporated. If the news got to the press, I was not sure if his partners in Arabia would stay. I had not once met the 50% shareholder of the company. It was the mid 1990's and they were still fighting for gay rights, and some potential partners were definitely going to withdraw, I told myself. "*What if he doesn't want a homosexual to represent his company?*"

I got this job because of Zola. Would she be willing to talk to me after this betrayal? Zola was a believer, not just a Christian. She would ask me about the Bible's interpretation of homosexuality. Zola would never compromise on the Bible for me. That was it for my career. I saw the way she looked at me in the car; she was very disappointed in me. Under no circumstances was she ever going to trust me, based on my conduct.

Zola had not called me since the incident, but I was dying to talk to her, so I phoned her. The only thing she talked about was her life with Mr. Lover Boy.

"Oh, François, Nathan is really a nice man. I wish you would get to know him."

"Zola we need to talk, please talk to me."

She did not want to listen to anything I had to say to her. It was dinner with Nathan, a movie with Nathan; I had to cut her off. "Okay Zola, I've got to go. I will see you at the party then."

"Party! Which party?" she asked quickly.

"I am not sure I'll make it; I have to be at some place with Ali.

"Oh – Nathan is on the other line! Can we talk later, please, Sweetie?" And she hung up the phone.

I didn't like that guy for many reasons. Zola had always looked for a sign from up above in order to date a man and I don't believe that she got the sign here. He was the first person I saw her to be involved with in her life, but I knew he was wrong for her. She usually told me that her life had a purpose, so she could not just misuse her body and life.

"When people hear about me, let them see me and respect me," she said many times. I did not want her to regret what people would say if they saw her with Nathan. I remember a couple of months earlier, he wrote her telling how much he was in love with her unconditionally.

Nathan called her and asked her out for dinner. She was very happy, and called me on short notice to help her plan. She suggested that he should come to her house instead since he had never been there since they had met – and they had been dating for nearly six months. I agreed to help her. She called a cleaning service to give her home a total makeover. Second, she bought candles of spice mixed with fragrance of all kinds. Third, in the washroom she put incense of cinnamon and vanilla with a little mixture of caramel and spice. "The combination of all these scents is very relaxing, François."

Then she put around fresh roses of Sharon, with ocean and Ambi freshener sprayed around to give her home an outdoor scent. She went in to the bedroom and had the bedding changed to red and cream, her favourite colours. At the end of the preparation the house smelled like King Solomon's love garden, just like the Bible described it. It was left with the smell of spring flowers when they have just begun to bosom. French and Swiss food was the menu for the night.

Earlier that morning, she had ordered a set of lingerie, precious stuff; only three of its kind was manufactured. When I went to pick it up, I was told that a prince of one of the Middle East countries had ordered one, and the other was in Europe. The set that was in Canada was the one Zola got. Even though she planned for that evening with excitement, she was also afraid that it was not going to happen. She was distracted all day.

"God helped me prepare like this for your coming. I will be a part of everything, François. What a beautiful day it will be." She looked in my eyes and said, "It will also be a happy day when they decide to receive me as their queen; there is nothing compared to how beautiful that day will be."

She was scaring me. I wondered about her mental state of mind sometimes. I knew that the night was not going to happen; she was not ready for it.

"Search your heart, French Man, you will find answers. Don't be scared, reach out. I want nieces and nephews. When are you planning on getting married, François?" she asked.

Before leaving, I dimmed the lights, and put on the candles. She had dreamt of this day all her life and it was time. This was the big moment I had planned so hard for, but things were no longer the same. It was not my night, but Nathan's. I put on her favourite song; I practised dancing with her just before leaving. As much as I hated the whole idea, I had to help Zola plan her big night with Nathan. It was difficult going along with it, but it was my decision to break it off, so I had no one to blame.

She wore a red silk dress. As I stepped out, I rushed back in to use the washroom. I suddenly felt the sickness of stomach flu. I was vomiting, and using the toilet at the same time.

"What is the matter with you? Are you okay?" she asked me.

"Yes! I must have eaten something bad. Don't worry, I will be fine," I told her. No, I wasn't fine, but I had to lie in order not to spoil her night. I hugged her once more and left before she received her guest. I did not drive away, but continued to sit in my car with the hope that he didn't show up. I remember that before I left, she had put red wine on the table.

"François, if I did not know any better, I'd say there is alcohol in this wine." "Impossible, it is alcohol-free, Zola. I will see you tomorrow."

I sat in my car until 1:00 am and there was no sign of him. I figured she might have slept, so I entered and turned off the candles, for she had fallen asleep. I didn't go home in case she needed my help, but she did not call. So I drove away from the parking lot at 6:30 am. I talked to her later that day, but according to her, she was okay. She was hurting once again but, she never showed it or told anyone.

Nathan did not call her to apologize, so she called to see if he was all right, but he later told her, without any apparent guilt, that he had had a late business meeting. She did not allow the incident to take away her joy, so she went to church on Sunday evening, thinking, she could get some answers. The message that evening was about keeping your body pure, and waiting on God to choose your life partner. "There are always regrets if you don't choose your partners wisely," the pastor said. "If you are here, and are recently divorced, then I am talking to you. If you are here, and you are a youth, then I am talking to you, and of course the young adults. Today, God is telling you to wait on Him. Your time has not yet come."

The message was for her. She could not stop weeping. The pastor knew nothing about what had transpired on that Friday night. How did he put his hands on this message?

Life is not fair, I told myself. I went to the church searching for answers to my many questions, and could not find them, but instantly, it seemed, Zola got an answer to her question. She was happy that the night did not go according to plan, and whether it was out of guilt or shyness, she did not really talk about that night.

It was now Saturday, and I went to help Natasha with the party arrangements. There were dignitaries coming, so I had to make sure that there was enough security and police. One of her business partners had brought in a rare book of poetry costing $20,000 to be bid upon for charity. The total amount earned that night was at least $150,000. I spent nearly three hours at the hall getting things together. It was 5:30, and I had to leave and get ready before the guests arrived. On my way home, I made the decision not to show up for the party. After what happened, I was not ready to show my face in public.

A billion-dollar company's reputation was on the line and I was afraid that if my private life got on the news, some of his partners might withdraw – even though Canada is a free society. Pastor Fred would just tell the church that he could not wait to tell the world that he saw through me. The least that I could do was to end my job at Ali & Ngo. I went to my office that evening to clear up my desk.

While doing so, I left a note for Zola and my boss. Until now, Zola had not said a word to me. She had been my friend for the longest time and now I was going to lose her. My heart was grieving and breaking. But it was better this way. She was a part of my life now, maybe the only living family member. She was always thinking about what was right for me and what was not. My only living family had rejected me when she found out about me being who I was.

After our graduation from Sankara, Aunt May sent word that she wanted to talk to me. "François, this can't wait, it is urgent. You need to come at once." When I arrived that morning, she told me that it was time to get married to Zola. I told her that I was not ready. "Zola has been waiting all her life for you to propose. I want grandchildren, and she is preparing to give me grandkids. She loves you very dearly. I see the way she looks at you," Aunt May said.

"I would not make a good husband," I told her.

"She will make you a better man," said Aunt May. She told me that my father would have wanted me to marry Zola, and it was her prayer that Zola and I get married. "You told me to keep praying for the two of you, and that's what I have done all these years. You and that girl are soul mates. I know it and I can feel it in my heart. It is unique and it is powerful. Most people pray for an opportunity like this, and can't get it. A love like this will last forever, Son."

"Oh, Aunt May, you don't understand."

"Zola is a beautiful Christian girl who has the fear of God in her heart." She kept on talking and repeating herself. And then we got into an argument.

I spoke to her in a harsh voice. Then suddenly the words came out of my mouth: "I don't want to hurt you, Mama."

"No! Don't call me Mama. I am your aunt. Whenever you say that word, then you are about to hurt me."

"I don't think that I am attracted to her, not to any woman." It finally came out. "I am a homosexual."

"You are what? No you are not," she said. "You think you are, you imagine you are, but you are not. It is those people that you hang around with, making you think that way. That boy, Ben, is no longer welcome in my home."

"I am sorry, Aunt May, I am not attracted to women. I have tried but it is not working."

Zola was with me since high school. I was very fascinated by her, and later all of that changed. Aunt May still felt that it was possible for me to marry her, so she would not listen. "I want my grandchildren; you are my only living family. If you don't plant a seed in this world, that will be the end of you. Your father…your father…"

"My father is dead," I finished the sentence for her.

She began hitting me. She first put a slap in my left ear, and then she took the rod to me. When I told her she was hurting me, then she said. "I am beating Sodom and Gomorrah out of you. I spared the wrong in you for so long; now I realize that I have spoiled you. You are rotten, François."

Since that day, Aunt May decided we were no longer family, and a few days later, she had a stroke. Up to the time of Zola's party, she was in the nursing home. The doctors gave up on her. In fact, two weeks before Zola went to the hospital, the nurse called Pastor Fred to begin making other arrangements. They did not call me, because I believed that she was going to come through. God was not giving up on her so I did not either.

"In the midst of it all, God will come in when He is least expected, and show His strength." My Aunt May always told me this.

She was suffering because of me. I was not going to allow that wind to blow Zola away from all the people that needed her. She had her whole life ahead of her. It was better that the wind blew me instead.

Zola saw Aunt May twice a week, and read the Bible to her. Aunt May always said that encouraging words were healing and very pleasing to the soul. It always revived her soul. "Aunt May needed every word to wake her up," Zola said.

I had to protect my sweet Zola. I wrote my resignation letter and left it on my desk and also wrote one for Zola with just a few words, "I have disappointed you. Please forgive me. I want you to know that I love you very much, and I did not mean to hurt you. P.S.: please take good care of my Aunt May. Love you forever, Old School."

Chapter Fourteen

According to Natasha, the guests arrived at the banquet hall for the surprise party except for Nathan and myself. For once, he and I had something in common. Natasha explained: "Zola entered the hall with Uncle Ali and was very surprised. She had no clue whatsoever…you should have seen the surprise on her face."

This was the very first time we were giving Zola a party. Even with all her achievements, she did not want any. She would tell her friends a nice little gathering was better than an extravagant party. "It is a waste of money," she would say.

After all of the handshakes and greeting of guests, Zola realized that her lover boy and I were not there. She later explained that Zola walked right up to Natasha and asked her why we were not there. She had no idea that I wasn't going to be there. It was a party of over a hundred people, so she figured that I was somewhere around. Everyone who received an invitation was there. It was Zola's party, the lady who moves according to the wind!

I received over ten calls from her in a short five minutes. I just ignored all the calls that night; I was still at the office during that time. I did not want to be anyone's joke box, so I stayed away.

Music was playing, people were dancing while others animatedly discussed business. But Zola was pretending to be going with the flow. Usually on a day like this, I would be right by her side until the very end.

She went back to Natasha asking her why I was not there. "You are surely responsible for his absence, Natasha." Natasha told her that I was there until 5:30 and I left to go get dressed. "I don't know why he is not here, he looked happy this afternoon. Doesn't it have something to do with the breaking news early this week?"

"Which news? Oh my goodness, it is," said Zola. He tried calling me this week, but I did not give him a chance to talk. I was busy with my own life. I was so busy telling him about my life with Nathan, and I forgot to listen to what he had to say, or follow up on him. I really had a busy week, Natasha. This whole relationship thing is new to me, As much as I am excited, I also don't think that it will work."

When Nathan entered, Zola seemed to feel a bit of relief, though probably thought that I could enter at any moment as well. She walked up and gave him a hug, and tried kissing him, but he turned his head away to the other side. "Are you trying to stay away from François" she asked him.

He said that he did not like people monitoring his affairs. "He needs to back off."

"Nathan, you sound just like François. In life you need to accept people for who they are. The two of you need to accept each other."

"Aunt Zola asked my Uncle Nathan to help find you, but he said that you are a pepper bird. If he is absent from this party then he really needs this time to be alone. Give him time, please," Natasha said.

According to Zola, she drove to Mandela High that night thinking that I might have gone there to reflect, but to her surprise, I was not there. She had no idea where to begin her search. "We have been friends for too long, and I know the girls he has dated over the years. Why would he hide this from me? He actually believed for sure that there was a mix up.

"No, he is not. If he was a homosexual, I would know. Why should I listen to James? Whenever James drinks alcohol, he drinks his head full and talks nonsense non-stop. This is why the Bible advises believers not to get drunk on wine. When James takes in alcohol, his mouth becomes naked, and he is unable to guard his mouth."

But Zola wondered: What was so much more important than the party he organized for me?

She called the hospital asking about me, in case there might have been an accident. She also called the police, but they told her that I was not missing, and that the police would not accept my situation as that of a missing person. "Has it been 72 hours?" the officer asked her. They told her to go home and rest, but if there was any reason she thought that I could have been kidnapped, it was better to go in with the information. "We will definitely look into it," the officer told her.

"No, officer, nothing like that." Zola also thought that I might have gone to Aunt May's, so she drove there, but unfortunately for her, I was not there.

"There is something going on with François. Since the day he helped me with my lock at Mandela High we have been together. The French Man I know would never change overnight, just like that…"

Zola was very confused, and disturbed. She found herself in front of Pearson Airport, so she parked her car and went in there to find a comfortable place to sit as she thought about what to do next. Before entering the terminal, she remembered our friend, Ben.

"Oh, let me call Ben… Wait a second, could it be true? It is true." She caught her breath, suddenly feeling empty. "Ben is always coming for a visit; François went to visit Ben last month. Ben could not even complete his program at Sankara… He moved to Paris." The entire puzzle seemed to fit together, "The tight clothing, the business trip overnight, not keeping to one girlfriend… Oh my God, it is true. François is really not truthful with me."

It all made terrible sense to her, and then she found a seat to sit on inside the terminal.

I had missed my flight so I was waiting to catch the next plane to Jerusalem. Why Jerusalem? I didn't know. As I sat there, I heard behind me, "Wow – François! Oh God, why did it have to be me? He had me fooled all this time. The evidence was right there, but I never had the slightest idea that François was living a double life right under my nose. How dare you lie to me." She started to worry about my Aunt May, "It will break her heart, and she might not recover. I had a dream about her some time ago. I know that it is going to come true. I am not giving up on her, François; you should not also give up on her. I have to keep this news from the media; Aunt May can't talk, if she sees it on TV, it will break her even more," Zola said.

She needed a shoulder to cry on and a friend to hold her hand. Then she said. "WWJD? What would Jesus do? Up to the present time, she had not told Nathan. Without any delay, she took the phone and called him, "Hey, Hon, I am at Terminal 4. What time is the guest arriving?"

"Which guest and what are you doing there?" Nathan asked her.

"I don't know, I just found myself here, so I came in just to organize my thoughts. I will tell you when you get here," she said. "Did I wake you up?"

"Yes, you did," he said. "What about your friend?"

"Which of my friends? Oh, yes! He rescheduled his trip for next week."

"Why don't you go home and we will talk later after church?"

She said good-bye and hung up the phone.

Zola then called Ben in Europe, and Ben told her that he had spoken to me earlier. "He said he just needs a break."

"How could you, Ben? You knew that I loved him. Why couldn't you go find somebody else? When did all of this start? Is this how you repay me, Ben, by taking my man. Had it not been for you, we would be married and having children."

"I don't know all that he told you, but I am sorry, Princess," said Ben. "I am sorry things turned out this way. I hope that this doesn't change who you are."

But Zola was crying so hard she could not keep the phone to her ear. "Ben, shut up and tell me where he is. So you are now a professor? Don't lecture me about who I am." She did not wait for Ben to respond, but turned the phone off.

We were sitting on the same bench, but facing in opposite directions. She did not see me there.

Zola talked to herself: "I love you, and I have forgiven you for lying to me, I who you will be running away from. I am disappointed in you, but the Lord still loves you. He is good and His love never ends, and I don't love you any less than yesterday. You want to be gay, it's your life.

"We all in life have our struggles. You have made a choice to be who you want to be – and you are not attracted to me. I am perfectly fine with it. The only thing is this: you should have told me. I should not have been the last person to have found out that you are gay.

"In spite of this, I want to go through this with you, be sure of this decision. You can count on me anytime, French Man, and that is what friends are for. I don't desert my friends when they need me the most, not anybody for that matter." Zola began crying bitterly.

I felt so sorry for her, and my eyes were wet with tears. I turned around to tap her shoulder but before I could touch her, she fainted. She had not seen my face.

Thank God we were at the airport. I rushed over to her, and in no time, the paramedics were taking her to the hospital. The doctors said it did not look good, so I called Pastor Fred and Natasha. I was afraid to call Zola's grandmother. But eventually, she would have to know. I was shaking; this girl was in the hospital two weeks earlier, and now she was lying there fighting for her life. If Zola didn't make it, it was going to be the end of life for me. So I cried out. "No God, she will make it, she must make it. If you want anybody, take me instead, but not Zola, please, God."

Exactly what I was afraid of was happening. It was Sunday and of course the pastor had to go to church before going to pray, I assume. But I went to the washroom and when I came out, he was standing over her with Natasha praying. I did not enter, because I remembered the letter, so I went over to the office to retrieve it. I could not leave Zola lying in there, and just leave. She was the only one who had been there for me and my Aunt May. Not Zola – she was too important to the people to have lain there.

I went to the office, but the letter was gone. Mr. Ali was at the office; he had gone there after Zola's party. He apparently slept at the office thinking about the future of the company. "Who might have come in here after I left and taken the letters?"

Mr. Ali appeared at the door. "It is still my company, so I can come in whenever I want. François, you are a fine young man, and a good employee. We will miss you around," Mr. Ali said.

"Boss, I am sorry. (I always called him Boss.) I tried to tell you, but I couldn't. I messed up pretty bad, right? Everyone expected more from me, and I could not live up to their expectations. Zola is too perfect; I don't want to hurt her."

"Much is expected from the one who is giving much," Mr. Ali said.

"I am gay, Boss."

So, when did she find out?" he asked.

"Last night, but technically last week. I think she was in denial. I got into an argument with James and he told the girls."

Mr. Ali told me that he knew all along. "What about your mother?"

"Aunt May could not handle it when she found out. She is in there because of me, Boss. Now Zola is also in the hospital because of me. Who am I, Boss? I hurt the people that care about me the most. I did not go to the party last night, so she went looking for me. Please can I get my job and my letters back?"

"Under one condition – if you stop living a double life. If you really are who you say you are, don't be ashamed of yourself. If you feel guilty about anything, stop doing it."

"Boss, thank you. I appreciate this conversation. I cried this morning for a father, and here you are talking to me as if I was your son."

"You are my son. I pray that God will open your heart to receive me," he said in a low voice.

"Can I call you Dad?"

"Yes, Old School, call me whatever you like."

"I like 'Boss' better," I told him. "Oh – we have to go check on the First Lady for life."

"Don't worry, Son, she is going to be fine."

"Yes, she will be, she has got to be." And we left. "I love her, Boss I am just afraid of disappointing her."

"I love her too, Son."

I spent the day at the hospital. Zola was still unconscious. Maa entered the hospital with the room full of seniors. Those women were amazing. They prayed, and some sat down telling her tales of long ago. They were the church prayer warriors.

One of them said, "But who is going to make us cake on Tuesday?" Then another said, "All week I was not feeling well. I think that old age is catching up with me. I am not as strong as I used to be." And Maa reminded her that she was 90 years old. She was walking with a cane, and she was worried about old age!

When they were leaving, one of them told me not to disturb her; she was resting. She was at the feet of her lover. They sounded like my Aunt May. Sister Lavender who was more like a sister came to see her. She was a teacher from Mandela High, but since then, the two ladies had bonded. She had her own challenges in life, but she was always happy.

I called her the "action lady". Zola had told me that wherever I found myself, the people I met there were my family. Sister Lavender often visited my Aunt May as well.

Zola had me calling her Sister just like she had Natasha call me Uncle. I remember when Natasha began calling me Uncle at first, I did not feel comfortable, but she told me that it was a part of her tradition, "It will be disrespectful if Natasha called you by your name," Zola said, with Natasha's mother backing her:

"Yes Tasha, do not disrespect your elders. Do not allow the Western wind to blow your brain away; you are still an African child. In Zimbabwe, I called all my neighbours Uncle and Auntie. My name was *Mwanyise* which means accept defeat, but I refused to accept defeat. That's why I am here. My father was disappointed that I was a woman, because I did not do what the other women did. I challenged all the men in my village when I had to, which gave me a bad name, but I am a good person, don't get me wrong.

"When Tasha was born and I lost all of my properties to her father's family, I changed my name to Hondo, which means 'warrior fighter'. It's a man's name, but I didn't care, because I was ready to fight all the lazy men in the village and I did. I caused much trouble for them. They chased me out of the town and took my husband's properties. I ran and came over here, otherwise, my daughter was going to become a motherless child.

"Besides, I am glad that Natasha has an uncle like you. If this was Zimbabwe or Zambia, I would beat the gay out of you. My name is Hondo Tshuma now; call me Aunty Hondo from now on, François…you young people have no respect for your elders," Natasha's mother said with seriousness. She was a handful. No wonder they had driven her out of Zimbabwe!

"Oh François," Sister Lavender said, "In a time like this you should depend totally on Him for strength. The Lord's eyes are on Zola. She is a daughter of Zion. She is a fighter, she will come through."

"Thanks sister, Sister La – "

"Lavender," she said. "The colour purple, François."

Chapter Fifteen

I did not tell Nathan about Zola being hospitalized; I thought about calling him several times, but for me it was meaningless. Zola received get-well cards from around the world. Every day I took a bag full of letters home. Maa was just out of words; she didn't say much, but prayed a lot. For the first time I felt unusual and I had no one to talk to about it. Zola would have told me exactly what it was. I missed her so much. Maa had called me for lunch; she was weeping as we finished our lunch.

"Thanks, Maa, I am going to see my Aunt May from here."

"Give her my love, will you." She was tapping my shoulder as I left her.

I drove to the hospital. I entered her room and gave Aunt May a kiss. "Hello Aunt May, how are you today? You look good, Aunt May. Why are you not looking out the window today? I have missed you so much, Aunt May. I love you, Aunt May."

I took the brush and began brushing her hair. "I can't take this anymore; I need you to come back to me. Oh God, the only family I have are living in the wind right now. You have cut them out of my life. It is because of me that this had happened to them, so please take me instead.

"Aunt May, I destroyed your life, and I destroyed Zola's. I wish we could trade places. I don't deserve to live. Aunt May, you have been my source of life, and my supernatural breakthrough. You told me that with God all things are possible, and I can depend on Him for anything. I have used His name, and nothing is working out for me. Please pray and tell God to move in His power. If God did not want me to be gay, why did he allow it to happen? God, please, I can't lose them both. Let those lights shine on me.

"I have stayed too long in the dark," Aunt May, "I need you to hold my hand. You are more than conqueror…through him who loves you, you can make it. Just believe, Aunt May. I am at the top of the mountain now, and am alone and cold, and it is very dark. Soon the wind will blow me away. Say anything to your God to bring the two of you back to me. Aunt May, It has been five years and I am tired of waiting. I can't lose you."

I became emotionally distressed and it had taken a huge toll on my mental state of mind, so much so, that I was talking by myself. I was so afraid that I would lose them that my heartbeat and breathing had changed. I thought that I had developed asthma, but the doctor told me it was a normal reaction to emotion. I cried out of frustration, so I began crying and talking to God. "Open the heavens and let that light shine on me. I need the angels to surround this place. My mom and dad are dead, and all my siblings are no more. Why don't you take me too? Take me now! Heaven hear me, and answer me, heaven hear me. If there is a heaven, hear me now. Enough is enough. Suddenly, the room became very bright. I could not see beyond the light. It all became a dream to me.

Up until then, I was confused as to whether it was reality or a dream… I couldn't tell. I slept for a little while and then I was up again. Aunt May awakened and walked to the washroom for the first time in five years. When I woke up, my Aunt May was brushing my head. I screamed and cried. I did not know how to express myself. I ran over to the nursing station and called them in. "It has happened, Aunt May. Your God is alive and breathing after all. He came through for us." She told me that it was all right, that God was not angry at me. The nursing staff told her not to talk, and then she asked them for water. I was ecstatic.

One of the doctors told me that I was lucky, but I told him that "lucky" was not the word. "This is called a 'miracle' to the highest degree."

I called my pastor for the first time to let him know that God was still in the miracle business. Aunt May always said, "God will come in when everyone thinks that it is too late."

"Oh, Aunt May, I love you very much, you did it. I thank God for bringing you back. Zola must hear about this from me. Aunt May, can I leave to give Zola the good news?"

On my way out, Aunt May said that God had given me the secret key to answering prayer, but I was too happy to ask her what the key was.

It was amazing how the wind quickly blew and flipped things over. I was drifting around like a lonely island without a coconut tree, and in a little moment, I had more than I could imagine. My Aunt May returning to me was super-wonderful.

On my way to see Zola, I felt hungry, and wanted to eat something. This was the first time since she went into the hospital that I realized I was hungry, even though I had just had lunch with Maa. There was a coffee shop down the street, so I decided to get myself a sandwich. When I got there, I saw Nathan getting coffee.

"Oh, hello, François, how are you? I tried to get Zola on the phone, but unfortunately, she did not pick up, and I have been in and out of the country. Could you tell her that I will pass by tomorrow after church?"

"Okay, Nathan, I will definitely give her your message. Have a great day."

I just did not know who this guy was. Even Mr. Zulu from Africa and the President had sent Zola get-well cards and flowers. I thought that I should at least give him the benefit of the doubt, since he seemed not to know about Zola being hospitalized. So I ran after him on the street.

"Hey, Nathan. You know, Zola's been in the hospital for over a month now, have you not heard?"

"Of course not," he said. "I was on a business trip, and I got back just last week. What is the matter with her? Where is she, so I can go see her?"

I was looking at him in amazement, but gave him the information he needed. I lost my appetite; I just wanted to see Zola. Before getting to the hospital, I called Boss and Natasha to let them know that my Aunt May was back. They were all overjoyed. When I entered Zola's room, I saw a couple of ladies chatting with Sister Lavender. I was filled with excitement.

I took Zola's hand in my hand and began to talk to her. "It has been too long…it is time to wake up," I told her. "Zola, wake up. Aunt May is back and she can talk again. It is a miracle. The mercy of God is really great, He is alive." A nurse came in the room trying to stop me, but I told her that Zola was only sleeping and it was time for her to wake up. They called a security guard to get me out of the room. Before they could reach me, I hurried to hold her tight. They tried to get me off her, but I was stronger than all of them.

"Please come wake up, I can't survive living without you. Forgive me, please. Zola, you are my life, please come back to me." I was lying over her and felt her stomach move, and she sneezed three times.

She opened her eyes and looked at me. Then she smiled and squeezed my hand. "Hi, French Man, you look like hell. How was your trip? Nice to see you," she said.

"Thank God you are back. I have been so scared. Don't try to talk, you have plenty of time to talk." I thought she was trying to say something to me, but it was Nathan standing behind me.

"How are you, my dear?" he asked her.

"Better than all of you," Zola said to him.

"You scared us. Praise God that you are back. I am sorry, I just h – "

"Nathan has been very worried about you," I interrupted him. It was neither the time nor the place for explanations.

"I love you, Sweetie," Nathan said as he looked at her. He had not seen her for over a month, and he was standing there holding her hand. He turned to the doctors and nurses, thanking them.

I was about to give him a kick for neglecting her. But I had to be there for her; it was about her, not me or Nathan. He was her boyfriend after all. I had promised Zola that I was not going to fight Nathan any longer.

"How is your mother doing? Please give her my love. God will surely come through for her," he told me.

"My mother is doing well, Nathan, and thanks for your thoughts."

Generally, Nathan was a good fellow, but I did not see him to be that ideal man for Zola. He showed very little interest in her. In any case, Zola woke up, and it was a miracle. A week later, she went home, and my Aunt May was also, after five-plus years, recovering well. The doctor kept monitoring her condition. When they released her, I hired a nurse to live in with us. I was not willing to take any chances with her, but she totally opposed the idea. That was the Aunt May that I remembered, and she was back! She called me in to have a word with her one afternoon.

"François, please find a place for me. We don't have to live together."

"Aunt May, it's been five years, and we have much to talk about. Besides, I have missed you." She was my only blood relative and the one who took care of me. I could not see her anywhere else, but with me. I am everything I am because of her, even though she still didn't agree with my lifestyle. Even up to the time she got out of the hospital she believed that same-sex loving was wrong and that God was coming after me. She told me that she was going to accept my decision, but I did not believe her. I had to walk on a line. I was well-off now, and my job was guaranteed. Besides, success for me was useless if I did not take care of my responsibility. Zola told me that success was how many lives are blessed because of one's life. Aunt May was my responsibility, and it was my turn to bless her with my success.

However, I agreed with Aunt May not to talk about that day when she beat Gomorrah out of me, even though I had the burning desire to talk about it. On the other hand, Zola was very anxious to talk. I told her to take it easy; there was no need for urgency. I went to her house late on a Tuesday afternoon. Nathan had just come in to check on her. When he left, she called me to her bedside and said to me, "François, how could you have hidden something as important as this from me? What were you thinking? Don't you think that I deserved to know? Don't you trust me anymore? When I really found out, I was filled with humiliation, and shame. So if James had not told us, we would not have found out. How could I have been so stupid?"

"No! Don't say that Zola," I interrupted.

"Maybe I am not as important to you as I think I am."

"No! It is not like that, Zola. I did not want to hurt you."

"If being who you are will hurt me, than why will you hurt me?" she asked.

"That's just the way it is when it comes to homosexual life…being who I am," I replied. "Aunt May had always hoped that I would get married to you. I love you with all my heart, but I am struggling with the idea of being a husband. Everyone looks at us and expects us to be a couple, but something came in and took that desire away. You loved me, but I was not prepared for marriage. I also don't want to disappoint you. I tried to tell you, but I was afraid of your reaction. I can't lose you. When you were in that hospital room, you made me realize how important you are to me."

"François…but…"

"No! Please don't talk, let me finish. When Aunt May found out –

"Aunt May knew?" Zola asked me.

"Yes! This is the reason she left us for all those years. She had a dream and she saw us getting married. She wanted her grandchildren to come from you, because of who you were…your reputation, I guess. She said that God spoke to her before I even met you. She went on talking about my father's family tree, and you loving me the way you do. Then she said, "That girl has the fear of God, and I will not allow you to disappoint God."

"Then she said that we were destined to be together, and I was living in sin. We got into an argument and began exchanging words. Suddenly, she began trembling with frustration and a burning anger seemed to take over her entire being. She was out of control; I had never seen anything like that before. It was as if she was a different person. I wanted to leave the room, but she stood right before the door blocking me from leaving. She did not just think, she talked; she knew it all. Then she began flogging me. I later had pain all over my body. This is what she said: 'You are living in Sodom and Gomorrah, and I am taking that evil city out of you so you don't harm yourself.'" She then took a pause and asked me to walk out the door, and never to return."

"In Zambia, a boy was beaten to death just six months ago," Zola said.

I continued: "I tried to return but she did not accept me. Then I received the call from the hospital that she had been admitted. You remember when I told you I took a quick trip to Paris. When she beat me, I was really hurt, so I had to stay away until I was okay. You see, I had to protect you. You two mean the world to me. I did not want you to end up like Aunt May. But eventually, you did. You always told me that I am lost; yes I am. I love you, but I can't marry you. I am a chicken. Forgive me, my love."

"I don't hate you," she said. "I was just upset that you did not tell me, and I was worried about your mother as well. I found myself at the airport."

"I was at the airport sitting right behind you."

"But, how?" Zola asked.

"I heard you talking to Ben."

"Oh, you heard me?"

"Yes, I was on my way to Ngehima, and I missed my flight."

"Ben told me something else."

"I don't know how it happened, but we were on the same bench. I called the paramedics for you."

"Wow!" she said. "And you were right there to save me. How did a French man and a wise woman have this strong a bond?" Zola talked and laughed: "Life is hard sometimes, but these things happen for our good."

"As soon as I was about to tap your shoulder, then you fell over. I am sorry Zola, I am really sorry. I wanted you to finish talking so I could take your hand, but it was too late. You fell over and fainted."

She was just herself as she talked, looking as beautiful as always. "You see, my dear, that was a very dumb thing to have done," she said. You can't run away from people, and you can't run from your problems either. Whenever you find yourself in the middle of a problem, you should stand and face it. If you start to run away, you will keep running for the rest of your life. Do you know that the same people who praise Jesus were the same people that nailed him on the cross? All of this wasn't necessary. If only I knew, I would have made Aunt May understand.

"According to King Solomon, everything under the sun is meaningless. He had wisdom, knowledge and understanding at the end of his life. He became a fool, because he went against his own word. The only thing I will tell you is to fear God, not man."

"Let me tell you a story about my Uncle Kofi who had the calling to preach the good news. He did not want any problems and he did not like problems either. My beloved uncle is probably still looking for a church to pastor, because I told him to look for a church without people. Wherever there are people in the world, there will be problems. You just need to find a way to understand each other."

"Ha," I laughed. "Zola, you are very funny, and your poor uncle – he will never become a pastor."

"You got the message?" she said.

"Zola, you *are* back!" The lady who turns every negative into a positive was back for good. Here I had been feeling very guilty, and she found a way to make me feel better.

"Seriously, François, not everyone is going to accept you for what you are. Some will criticize you and some will provoke you, but you need to get used to it and move on. If you are still feeling guilty, then you know that you are doing wrong. If you are really proud of yourself, then stop hiding. If you are not comfortable with who you say you are, then stop. You hide things out of respect, but for how long will you be living in the dark? Your pastor does not hate you; he is praying for you that all goes well with you."

"If you are strongly feeling guilty and thinking about what the people around you are thinking of you, then you are not a gay. I suggest that you quickly go to Maa and ask for my hand in marriage, before it is too late for you. Do you see how Nathan and I are getting closer lately? I can't imagine what this whole hospital thing did to him."

Whenever that guy's name was mentioned I got upset, and I think she knew it. I knew that she loved him, but if she started falling in love with him, it would have been hard for me to separate them. He was not good for her. As I was sitting trying to find a way to make her understand, the doorbell rang. I ran, hoping that it was Maa, but it was Nathan again.

"Who is it?" Zola called.

"Oh, nobody special, just Nathan again. Did you forget something Nathan?"

"How are you, François?" he greeted me.

"I will take my leave now." I told Zola. "Natasha is coming to stay with you as long as necessary since you have refused to come home with me."

"Give my love to Aunt May, will you?" said Nathan.

"Sure, Nathan. But if you really care, stop calling her Aunt May. She is not your aunt."

"Then why don't you stop calling Hondo 'Sister? She is not your sister."

"Then why is Natasha calling me Uncle François?" Upon saying that, Nathan got very angry.

"There is something about that guy that I can't put my hands on," I said, and before I finished the sentence, Natasha ended it for me. "And I know you can't stand him either," Natasha said.

"Uncle François, they are in love, so leave them alone. When are you going to give up?" Natasha said.

"Never. He is not good for her. He is a fake. Could you please keep your eyes on her? Make sure that that lover boy doesn't upset her. Through this dilemma, he did not come to see her. He wanted her to go and recover at his house, but I will not let her go anywhere with him. Besides, Maa wants her to stay home." I felt it in my soul that he did not really love her, but he was there somehow. For whatever reason, only God knew. My girls were all okay, and I was overjoyed.

A year came and went, and work was getting busy. My personal secretary got married and moved to Denver, Colorado. I got a new secretary, but we did not connect at all. She was all about work, work, and work-related, which I disagreed with. My previous secretary Patience would force me to have my dinner when I was working late, and make sure that I was healthy and even relaxed. Since she found out that I did not have breakfast at home, she always got some for me on her way to the office. I really missed her, but life had to go on. She had her husband and family to take care of. Natasha would have been good for the job, but unfortunately, she was not reliable.

Aunt May fully recovered. She and I had a talk and we were going to be fine. All she wanted for me was to be happy. "If being what you are makes you happy, then let it be," she said – even though she still thought Zola was the partner for me.

We also talked about Zola and her "rotten" relationship. "It sounds like she needs to be rescued by Robin Hood," Aunt May said.

Zola didn't want to be rescued. I had tried every trick I could think of, but it was not working. I had other people try to separate Zola and Nathan but still she would not listen.

"If you are so bitter about the situation, why don't you propose to her?" said Aunt May.

"I love you too, Aunt May. Don't wait up for me."

It was 1996, and the gay movement was growing in popularity in the West. People began coming forward with their stories. I remembered Ben wanting me to go public as well, but I was not ready to make such a great commitment. I had thoughts and questions I could not answer. Even though Aunt May supported my decision, I also was not willing to put her through any more stress. I tried to keep my private life from the public as much as possible. There were stories of many kinds on TV. Changes were not easy to make, especially when it would hurt the people you love. When making decisions it was also very important to be mindful of others around you. I knew what I wanted and how I could get it, but was the timing right? Would my decision destroy the lives around me? These were questions I would ask myself. I felt I had a lot on my plate to consider at the time, and time usually told itself. I was not sure of myself.

There was a story that came up on the air about a good friend of ours who was cheating on his wife for years with the same sex. "After 25 years of marriage, you could not tell me this at home?" she said. "You bring me on national television to disgrace me?"

These men were workmates and were together for nearly ten years. It all started on his first day on the job, when the one had to show the other guy his office. They later met on the job and expressed feelings for each other.

Then, every day, one of them offered the staff coffee, and since he did not want anyone to find out, he volunteered to get six coffees each day. They had to keep a low profile because they might have lost their job if anyone found out about them. Sooner or later, they began having lunch and dinner together. With both men living in fear of losing their jobs and thinking their wives might find out, they began spending more hours on the job. The boss was impressed, and began paying them for the extra time.

Meanwhile at home, my friend tried as much as he could to stay away from his wife. He refused his morning coffee, and his dinner was always done in the microwave. The family dinner was cancelled; she begged him to take a day off, and when he took it, he was busy most of the day. He always complained that he was tired – and that she was getting too fat, that she needed to lose some weight. Their family tried to intervene and help, but it was of no use.

"Whenever I get home she is always sleeping. If she was helping me with the bills, maybe things would not be as they are," he said, but one thing he forgot to tell people was that he got home every day at twelve, midnight. He found and used all of the excuses he could think of, such as: "The children are more important to her than I am." She worked from home and began helping with the bills. To everyone's surprise, he still did not want her.

As soon as the kids had left home, he wanted a divorce. He quickly drew up the papers, and a week later, put them on the kitchen counter. She was shocked, but not surprised. "I knew he was seeing someone, and maybe with a baby involved." She told him that it was not all right, but it was okay. "I am going to sign it under one condition; I want to meet your lover. You owe me that at least," she told him. She wanted to meet the lady who had stolen her husband's heart. "Let's go on the TV show."

"Do we have to?" he asked her.

"Give me a reason why we can't go. No show, no divorce," she said.

A month later, they were on the TV show, with a couple of their family members and friends. His secret lifestyle was about to be revealed in public. The host met with everyone backstage, and asked him if for any reason he

The Wind of Change

wanted to stop the show, it was totally okay. But this man about to appear on TV was ready to move on with his life. The host let the woman know it was going to be painful. "If you don't want to go on with this, we can stop," said the host.

"No," said the woman. "I just want to look her in the eye and thank her for destroying my family."

"Okay then, let the camera begin to roll," the host said. The show went on for fifteen minutes and she invited Sam to join them. She was anxious but at the same time very calm. She recognized the name, because he talked to Sam every day when he got home. She heard him say the name, she even read the number to know who Sam was, but he and his ex-wife's voice came on the recorder, so she did not get to talk to Sam.

They called Sam out. When he came out, she thought he was one of the camera crew going to whisper in his ear. It did not take long, and then she said, "I just want to ask her if she enjoys tearing my family apart."

Everyone sat there with stony faces. The audience noticed; all except her. A moment later, the host asked her to meet Sam. "Sam? But I thought you are…are you leaving me for him? If I knew about him, I would have given you the divorce ten years ago. I have no strength to fight the wind," she told them. All of their family and friends were watching, waiting to see who Sam was. She wished that she had not gone on national television to find out.

I could still recollect the surprise on her face, and her children's faces as well. When they got home, they had a dead body to bury, because of their decision. When it came to same-sex dating, people were always hurt, life was always destroyed. People were not ready for controversial changes. I remembered when my secret life was revealed, and how the room became as quiet as still water. I heard everyone breathing. I really could not be bothered with any publication, and drama. Besides, I was too busy with work, and Aunt May could not handle it. Forcing people to change was like telling the wind to blow the direction you wished it to go.

The life style that I chose was my affair, not hers. Anyway, I had to make her my priority since she was my only living relative. She told me on many occasions that I was good for nothing. "Always consider the people around you, François, especially when it comes to the people you love. Do not break my heart twice," Aunt May would tell me. It was my decision based on the circumstances surrounding me. I was far from making such a decision. I was what I was, but if it would cost my aunty her life, I was not ready to lose her. I asked Ben to understand, but it was much more complicated than "understanding." I was falling in love with Zola.

It did not take long until Ben called, very happy and practically screaming on the phone that it was time to do it. "Will you marry me?"

"Ben, I have not seen you in two years. Are you drunk? Of course you are!" Apparently, the Europeans were okay with gay marriage, so he figured out it was time to focus on getting married. He told me to turn the TV on. When I did, I could see Europeans were practically on fire in the street hosting a gay parade. I told Ben that I would call him later, because he had been drinking, and the noise was too loud for me. He did not even get a word that I said, so I hung up and went to the café across the street opposite the hotel in New York City.

I went to that café whenever I was in New York, so I was well-known there. As soon as I entered, a guy walked up to me telling me that Ben was not to be trusted. He saw him on TV kissing another man. This particular guy was always on my back. "Will you and Ben take it to the next level?" he asked.

When he told me that, I stormed out of the café. I couldn't marry Ben. Every night that I went to bed, I still heard my Aunt May praying, hoping to see a change in me. The least I could do for her was to leave things as they were. Besides, my relationship with Ben was not what I had expected it to be. If I did decide to marry Ben, then I would have to go to Europe, and Ben had nothing to offer me. Ben was never really there. I hoped that someday people would understand the truth. And Zola…Zola was becoming more silly every day with her lover boy, and her African obsession.

I did not hear from Zola before leaving, so when in the US, I called her. She sounded as if she had been sleeping. "Sweetie, wake up, I missed you," I said gently. "Are you with Nathan?"

"No, but he sends his love." As sleepy as she sounded, she was also being sarcastic. "He was on his way to China, but due to bad weather, his flight was cancelled. I spoke to him, but he sounded very down. I am going to check on him later. François, he and I are just friends."

Hmmmm… Zola was beautiful and intelligent, but I found it difficult to believe that she was done with Nathan. I just wanted to get home quickly and be with her. Zola's beauty wasn't only physical; she was truly a "super-woman", and every woman. And she was so very creative in her thinking, always creating new things for me and the people around her. She was even nominated every year, for the best garden in the community. Really, Zola was every man's dream. If she left that guy, she would be instantly taken, claimed by another. I sometimes thought about the conversation she had had with the old professor about her career and marriage… I could not tell what she really wanted in terms of marriage.

When we were in high school, she had talked about marrying and having kids. I was now becoming concerned about her, even though she often told me not to worry about her.

"François, I could meet a guy now and marry him and after two kids, he could tell me we are not compatible. The next guy comes, and after a couple of months together, he packs his stuff and runs away, saying that he cannot father another man's children," she would tell me.

"Listen to me, François: all the single men out there have children, but they are always looking for single women to settle down with, running away from their responsibilities. They will not father their children, but depend on the system to father their children for them. How can a 45 year old man boldly tell his friends that his children's mother is on social assistance so he will not give her his $10, and they walk around wearing the latest Prada. It's wrong, and they need to change that mindset. Besides, I do think…I…oh, never mind, you will never understand," she said.

I sensed that there was something else troubling her other than Nathan. I knew that Nathan wasn't going to marry her, and she knew it as well, but she was obviously holding on to him for a reason I didn't know about.

Chapter Sixteen

"For every man, there is a Rebecca. Until my Isaac sends for me, I will be pure." Zola still had not known a man I was pleased to understand. Nathan was a gentleman after all. And yet, there were many questions to be answered. She was almost thirty and still was not sure if she was ready. Whenever Nathan's name came up in conversation, she would tell me there was more to life than what I thought.

Ben had always been the kind of boy who got the girls and was always surrounded by guys. When Ben arrived on campus, he told the boys he was a specialist in making relationships work, meaning that he was a coach or a teacher who knew all the right words to say to the girls. He knew that I had a struggle finding the right words for Zola, and he was the perfect person to help me overcome my fears. When I saw him standing over me under the tree, something in me was calling out to him for help. At that moment, he became my guardian angel.

Ben helped me put together a dinner for Zola. We had it all planned and I was prepared to ask Zola to marry me. Then suddenly I got cold feet and told Ben I was unable to go along as planned. When Zola entered the room and saw the beautiful flowers and dinner table, she was very happy. But during dinner, I told her that I was seeing somebody on campus and I did not want to hurt her.

She took a pause and began laughing. "Why do you make such a big deal out of things? It is not as if you are breaking up with me. We still love each other," she said. "I am too busy with work and thinking about how I can make Africa unite. I want the leaders to remember Addis Ababa (the capital city of Ethiopia). If they remember that great speech, they will realize that unity is the only way to solve the African problems."

Zola was not ready for a relationship with me or anybody else. If the African people were still dying on the street, she was not going to commit to becoming a wife. "With most of the African countries in the river trying to swim, they are drowning every day. I can't be worried about a husband right now."

She later asked me if I wanted her to read a speech that was written by Dr. Nkrumah. I was worried that the news would have made her break down. She was telling me about the African histories and she was hurting and had to find a way to comfort herself or turn the conversation around. "You saw someone you think you like, but you want to make sure that I am okay with it before you make a move right?" I asked.

"Not really, but I will say 'yes'!" she said as I laughed. "Now, Boy, listen to me," she said. "This was a very important day for the people of Africa. Sadly, this speech did not take into consideration the things for which Africa is paying the penalty today.

She sounded like Mr. Zulu as she fought back the tears. "Mr Zulu thought this, but not everything. I have been doing some homework about this and I believe that when you read this, you will understand why Mr. Zulu loves his African continent, and he will do anything for his people. We should all be like him. This world is about passing it on. Do you remember the treasure that I sent for the president? Well! The story that is behind the treasure developed from this speech."

"Zola, seriously, since I met you…you have been doing homework, you can not go into any speech today?" But she did not answer.

Nobody could have enough of her. Here we were having a romantic "heartbreak" dinner, and Zola had turned it in to a political freedom speech. She knew how to turn the negative in to a positive, and for this reason she was clothed with dignity and respect. Actually, she managed also to put together a little group in the community teaching them how to clothe themselves with respect and dignity.

In this course, Zola taught black women how to be and feel comfortable with their natural bodies. "Some of my black sisters find themselves in a society like this and fear comes upon them, and they begin thinking they are inferior. When this happens, they begin to reject themselves. We all need to feel comfortable with the way we look. Even twins can be different.

"We are created the way we are for a reason, and we cannot change that. King Solomon wrote saying 'How right they are to adore you. Dark I am, yet lovely. Do not stare at me because I am dark, because I am darkened by the sun.' She told them that if you think that you are too black then you are too beautiful. She referred her students to the proverbs of King Solomon, and the noble character of a woman. This group was meant for black women, but all races took interest in it.

This course was also helpful to the youth who were trying to live up to the media's image and expectations. These were some reasons that put fear in me for not being with her. I was never going to live up to her standards. To me, Zola was perfect to the end. Instead of calling her the wise woman, I called her the African Queen. History talked about how beautiful and wise the Queen of Sheba was, but Zola's wisdom and character surpassed all queens, even that of the Queen of Sheba. Zola was not a crowned queen, but she was a queen for the people, and of the people. She was like a candle in the wind… Everywhere she went she lit up the dark.

Then, she started with the speech again. "It was 1963, May 24, in Addis Ababa, Ethiopia when 32 African countries came together to found a union, and Dr. Nkrumah of Africa gave this speech for which most Africa stands and lives by. You already know his connection with Garvey. This speech is a blueprint of the African continent, but unfortunately again they have forgotten this historic day. The leaders of Africa need to remind each other.

"I am happy to be here in Addis Ababa on this most historic occasion. I bring with me the hopes and fraternal greetings of the government and people of Ghana. Our objective is African union now. There is no time to waste. We must unite now or perish. I am confident that by our concerted effort and determination, we shall lay here the foundations for a continental Union of African States. A whole continent has imposed a mandate upon us to lay the foundation of our union at this conference. It is our responsibility to execute this mandate by creating here and now, the formula upon which the requisite superstructure may be created.

"On this continent, it has not taken us long to discover that the struggle against colonialism does not end with the attainment of national independence. Independence is only the prelude to a new and more involved struggle for the right to conduct our own economic and social affairs, to construct our society according to our aspirations, unhampered by crushing and humiliating neo-colonialist controls and interference.

"From the start we have been threatened with frustration where rapid change is imperative, and with instability where sustained effort and ordered rule are indispensable. Neither sporadic act nor pious resolution can resolve our present problems. Nothing will be of avail, except the united act of a united Africa. We have already reached the stage where we must unite or sink into that condition which has made Latin America the unwilling and distressed prey of imperialism after one-and-a-half centuries of political independence."

I gave her my undivided attention, and she was happy. "For real, Zola, I do understand. I just want you to not be hard on yourself."

Zola ended the talk with a promise to the African people. "Can you see that Africa is sinking? Colonialism is finished, but the Africans have hit their boat on the ice block, and only unity can bring them back on shore."

"Zola, you need help!" I said, but she did not listen to a word I said.

"I was predestined from my birth to be your servant," she said. "In the shadow of his hand, he had protected me over the past years. Can a mother forget the baby on her breast? I will not forget Africa until they unite; I will not forsake my people. I am the first daughter of Africa, and their queen. I will speak and they will listen to me, and they will know that I am the queen for the people."

Before she ended that statement, I interrupted her, "Are you the Queen of Sheba, or Queen Elizabeth?"

I am neither of them. I am Queen Zola of the People's Kingdom," she said.

"Zola..."

"Yes!"

"You have just passed the audition. You are on your way to Hollywood. I didn't know that you were this good in acting. Hollywood will make a lot of money with you."

"I am not going to Hollywood. I am going to Africa where I belong as queen."

"Yes! We should call Mr. Zulu and go visit him." This is how that evening ended.

I went to see her the next day and she asked for Orlando, but I could not tell her his whereabouts. "You know Orlando, it is almost three months. You will see him soon," I told her, but she urgently demanded that she wanted to see him.

Zola went once a week to Ottawa, which made her busier than usual. But she loved it. For her, the more time she spent out of the house, the better it was. When it came to Zola, there was just something I could not understand, but often she would tell me that it was not my place to understand.

I had stopped by Zola's office to drop off some papers a few days later after having that talk with her, and Orlando had just entered as well.

"Orlando, where have you been? How are you? Hmmm, you look great," Zola said.

"I'm well. How are you, my lady? You look lovely, as always," Orlando said as he walked to her and gave her a hug.

"I have a plan and I need your help. We are going to invite the entire African continent here, I mean, the students from all over the world to meet here in Canada for a conference. One student representing each country," Zola said.

"What are you talking about, my lady? I don't think it is going to be a good idea right now. We are still waiting on the United Nations to give us a green light for the trip," Orlando said.

"As we wait, we will get busy with something else," she said. "I am a professor and an inspirational speaker, right?"

"Right!" Orlando said.

"Now, I am going to use my influence to reach out to the African leaders. Why don't you do something you love doing the most and get others to participate for a good cause? It is a part of my job."

"Zola, this is not Mandela High or Sankara sending you to Haile Selasie for a lecture or to be a speaker," Orlando said.

"It is called awareness, and that's my point. Sankara is sending me to tell the Africans to put an end to this bloodshed and all the other problems."

"How can Sankara University put you in this huge position and you are okay with it?" I asked.

Then Orlando said: "It is politics, Zola; there is always a hidden agenda when something like this is planned."

"No, this is called standing up for your rights. Since they cannot freely speak their minds in Africa, they will come here and do it." Zola talked as she passed me and reached out to pick up a file.

"I think that it is a good idea, if this is going to help you stop your madness, behaviours and obsession about the African problem, then by all means go ahead," I told them. Zola and Orlando were on this project together. I was too busy with work. "Zola, have you opened the box from the professor?"

"Funny, François."

She was going too far. Community service was good, but not politics.

"What is your plan?" Orlando asked her.

"My plan is this: 'Rise up Africa, and unite, show the world what you are made off.' Or, 'We want peace in Africa…peace in every country in Africa.' Use this statement on every invitation, everywhere in the world. Like I said, one university student represents her people. Whoever has the time will make it. This conference is going to be like the one they had in December of 1958."

She was serious about it. She quickly took her bag and asked me to go with her to Sankara to show her co-worker the proposal while we left Orlando at the office.

Upon her arrival, there was a little issue that needed her attention, but she was able to take care of it. Then, she put her proposal on the table, and they liked it.

"It is a brilliant idea," Professor Matheson said standing by her, ready to go along with Zola.

He and Zola always got along more than the others. Quite a man, he was. "It is an urgent matter that needs to be addressed with the Africans students worldwide," she told them. They had to let the government know what the plans were, and how soon this conference was going to take place.

"December 21 will be a perfect day."

I will discuss this and inform the ministry about it. But those that will be coming will need visas to enter Canada, and these things take time," the professor said.

"This is why diplomats are there, for they will take care of everything. They can't keep on killing innocent people every second. No, it is not right," she said to her co-worker as he sat on the phone making calls and pouring rope behind the scent.

Professor Matheson hung up the phone. "The ministry is all right with the idea but we need to send in a written request. Oh, and they are all right with the 13th of December," he told her.

"No, she said, "We can't do the 13th of December."

"Listen to this incredible news – maybe you forgot this," he said. "On the 13th of December 1958, Africa had their first All-African People's Conference. This conference will be for all African future leaders to come together just like in the 1950's. I love you, and I love working with you." He walked over to give her a hug. "How do you come up with all these ideas?" Professor Matheson asked her.

"No, please, call the ministry and ask them for the 21st of December. It is his birthday. This year would have made Thomas Sankara 50 years old. He was young and full of love and care for his people. The people of Burkina Faso and the whole African continent have not recovered from his death. He is one of my heroes. According to Malcolm X, things will never get better until we make them better. I want to help and make things better. Please."

"Okay, "said the professor. "I will help you speed up things."

A week later, an organization was set to work on the project. She gave them her plan, and opened the floor for suggestions. "We will pay a special tribute to Thomas Sankara and set him as an example to the young African students. Leadership will not walk to you; you have to walk to it, he proved that," she said. "The good thing about it is this: we will be holding this conference right here in his school. The people who don't know about him will know who Sankara was and his contribution to his nation…and hopefully, they will get more involved in politics. Besides, we want more international students at Sankara. Dictatorship leaders should step down and give the young people a chance."

Zola explained that the leaders were exchanging the resources for weapons to kill the children, while they, the leaders, sat in luxury and sent their children to live the best lives abroad. And as the innocent and poor children suffered, the leaders' children were in the Western world living life to the fullest. "No it is not right!" she told Matheson. "You are a big brain. Thank you for all your help; I really appreciate it. Life would be easy if the world had more of you... Unfortunately we have to manage with just one of you," she told him.

I had to rush, so she gave him a hug and left. "We will talk tomorrow, Love," I said.

"You don't belong here, Zola." he whispered in her ear as he hugged her. "Call your godfather and ask him for a job. Thank you."

The Ministry of Education thought it was a very good idea for the conference to be held in Canada. It was the beginning of a new political road. They promised to be very flexible with the invitations in terms of the visas. There was a representative coming from every country. Every Canadian embassy was already busy since the invitations were sent out. This conference was for the young African students to come together and find a way to end the many conflicts in Africa.

Preparation went on according to plan, and Zola was getting ready for an idea that jumped into her head and that was becoming a reality. It was already the 5th of December and the students at Sankara were taking exams and getting ready for the conference. It was a good idea, but the timing was wrong. Nobody had considered that Christmas was the busiest time of the year. For the students, it was fun – and a few of them were chosen to speak on behalf of their country.

Zola has been going through the boxes from the late Professor Tolbert. I was afraid for her. She wrote poems and songs, but she hung them in her washroom, or put them in a box. She had never expressed her feelings publicly about the war and the economic situation in the third-world country. I was against it, but everyone thought it was a good idea. Could it be that she had a hidden agenda other than Al-l African Youth Unite?

"What about if should there be a rally, and the students were uncontrollable?" I asked myself many questions, but all I could really do at this moment was to support her.

Orlando was working hard together with Zola on the project. She was happy again. There was no crying, even though she was worried, but then, she had something else to concentrate on.

"Black is powerful only when there is unity. I can't refuse a gorgeous lady like you." He would smile at her when he was asked to do a task.

I just hoped that the trip we took to Jamaica didn't change her perception about the people around her. She was my friend and I did not want her doing anything she would regret.

"Hi François, what are you thinking about now?" she asked. "You remember the donor I told you about from Mexico? They were on their way but the heart gave up. We need a 'plan B', otherwise, we will lose him."

"We will not lose him. Boss's heart will only give up when he gives up on life," she said with confidence.

Boss had been sick for a while and we tried to keep it from her as much as we could, but keeping it as a secret was not going to help us.

Chapter Seventeen

It was the 19th of December, and the huge university auditorium was ready for use. Students were also ready for the big day ahead that was going to change the lives of the young African people. Other protestors took the opportunity to print signs and posters. The Paparazzi were there to help the people read all about it.

On the 21st of December, everyone gathered together in the auditorium. The five thousand seats they had were all occupied. Robert Sobukwe's grandson, who was a student at the Samora Machel University from Togo, was the Master of Ceremonies. He introduced the program, giving a brief explanation for why thousands of young people had gathered in the city of Toronto.

The national anthem "*Oh Canada*" was sung. Then the Minister of Education stood up and welcomed everyone again and thanked them for their presence and participation in the conference. "We are here to share and receive information that will help improve our world. This is true education."

Then Zola was called to the stage. She was good at it; she had been in front of the people since Mandela High. Of course this crowd was a little larger than usual, but she could handle it.

"Prime Minister Piers, my co-workers, members of the faculties, student body, distinguished guests... Thank you for coming here to this conference on short notice. You are all welcome at Sankara University! As some of you already know, today marks the 48th birthday of one of Africa's most upright men – and we just recently celebrated the ten year anniversary since he was brutally killed along with many others because of his commitment to his people. He had a goal and he had a mission.

"I have called you here to tell you some of his goals and see how we can work together to achieve them. Before I go any further I would like for us to take a minute of silence to remember Africa's young leader who inspired his people. Leadership demands complete self-alertness, honesty, integrity, trustworthiness and dignity of representation. And most of all, to pay serious attention to the people you are leading. This man had all of the above qualities. Ladies and gentlemen, please stand as we remember Africa's Upright leader Captain Thomas Sankara.

Zola waited for the applause to subside. "Thank you! I will tell you a little about who he was and why it is important that young people get themselves involved in politics. Thomas Sankara was born on the 21st of December 1949 and he died on the 15th of October 1987. He was one of Africa's revolutionaries, and later became a theorist for Pan-Africa and the President of the Republic of Burkina Faso which means 'the land of the upright men'. He renamed the country himself. If we see a man in a military uniform, we often will think that he is going to war. Yes, he went to war and fought for freedom. He freed his people from the hands of the French men and brought the country into the hands of the upright men.

"He freed his people from dependence, bringing an independent government. When Sankara got into power in 1983, he launched a program for social and economic change that would enable young people to have a voice in their government. Not stopping there, he began focusing on famine, and a self-sufficiency program for the entire country. His first priority was public health, and he vaccinated 2.5 million children against tropical diseases as he continued his education campaign in every part of Burkina Faso. He would say, 'It is my desire to not see a child sitting at home because the parents cannot afford the price of education.' Estimably, he was able to construct 40 schools within 350 communities."

"He disliked lazy people. He would say, 'Lazy people belong to the devil, their minds are corrupt; and strong and courageous people belong to the Almighty God. I am doing this for you. I want you to rely on your own ability tomorrow. The future is bright, but it is also full of conspiracy.' He also commanded his people to plant two million trees, to help the land to flourish.

"Ladies, listen to this," Zola said. "Sankara adored women, and called every woman he met 'sweet mother'. "He gave them jobs in high places in the government, and encouraged them to work while expecting, 'because being pregnant doesn't mean sitting at home'. In order to achieve his goal, Sankara worked and joined hands with the local people to make history. As the young people worked, the seniors were there to give them water to drink, and food. At the end of the day, he still had time to socialize with them, because he was a young man himself who associated with every age group. He came to the people's 'heart' and here saw their needs."

She paused in between, because she realized that it was too quiet. Then she said "You are sitting thinking that the introduction is taking too long, but I am almost there.

"He did not look at himself as a supreme leader or a scary leader," she went on. "He was simply an ordinary man who wanted to change what was not right and impact lives. Soon, other leaders became attracted to his leadership and admired him for the love he had for his country. Others envied him for his desire to bring change, and they began looking for an opportunity to get rid of him. And of course they succeeded. He had big ideas and great plans for the people of Africa. He is truly missed. One morning he woke up and said these words. 'While revolutionaries and individuals can be killed, you cannot kill their ideas.' One week later, he was killed. The power brokers and his own brothers conspired against Thomas and killed him.

Captain Thomas Sankara was the only president who died poor according to reporters, because he said "No" to corruption and greed. His salary was often used to take care of external affairs and for the development of his beloved country. Ladies and gentlemen, with the little we have heard about this great man, we know that he was a charismatic leader and Africa has truly lost one of her best sons. For how long will this go on?

"Why is it that when a good leader dies, that becomes the end of him, and there is never someone to continue from where he stopped? But there are rising leaders that are going to finish the fight that he started. Greed, corruption and poverty…it is warfare, and until it is dealt with, there is no freedom for Africa or any part of the world. Remember this is a three-in-one war. We will begin with greed, because it is greed that gives birth to corruption, leaving poverty as an inheritance for the nation. So use all the tools and weapons you have in your hand if necessary. If you do not have anything in your hand, seek it and you will find it. Whatever you want in this world, you have to go after it; it will never come after you. I will give you an example of one of my good friends:

"She went to the pastor for a message from God, and he told her that it was a year of financial breakthrough, and God was going to bless his people with money. She sat down at home all year round waiting for the breakthrough to take place, not having it in mind that she had to step out of her comfort zone to get it. You have to be able to step out before you step in. She was in her apartment still praying for the breakthrough to knock at the door.

"Some of you have prayed that someday, you would find yourselves in Canada, treating the cold. The moment this invitation arrived in your school, you took advantage of it. You are here experiencing the beautiful white snow; how is the cold treating you? How is the weather, by the way? It has just snowed eight centimetres. Let us impact our world with the example of those that came before us and stand in unity. We are going to fight the desire of greed, and once that is out of the way, we will conquer corruption and finally, we will be able to reach out to poverty together.

"Sankara's interest was to mitigate everything that was holding the nation from progressing. We have enough resources and the population is growing every day. It is time for us to develop the ideas of Sankara and rely on ourselves. We keep running to the West for help and they are running to us for our resources. No, it is not right. When you leave from here, get involved in your environmental issues and encourage your family and friends to join hands and rise up with you.

"When I think about our leaders that fought for the Black Power, I realize the majority of them were young people: leaders like Robert Sobukwe from South Africa, who is called the 'man of integrity'... Prime Minister Patrice Lumumba... Sa...Samora... Machel...."

I could see that Zola could not hold her tears any longer, that she had become emotional and beaten by the memory of all those young people who died for their rights. There were many names on the paper, but she was now speechless. They had to get her away from the microphone and give her some water to drink. She was not able to come back until later. And though she had written a song to be sung at the end of the program, this was not going to be possible under these circumstances.

The Wind of Change

Every representative from Africa and other parts of the world had their chance to talk. Then a young girl, 18 years old or so, who had just graduated from the University of Madagascar, stood up and took the paper from Zola and spoke out. From what I could see, she soon had almost everyone weeping.

"We have come to remind you of the agreement you made in Ghana and in Addis Abba. In this late 20th century, Africa has had much bloodshed, but today we are here in the City of Toronto to speak out our minds and say no to the bloodshed. The earth is crying and cannot contain any more blood of the children. No, it is wrong. Africa has believed a lie that she is unable to stand, or make it on her own. No, it is not right. We were once slaves in the world, but today, we are refugees in the world looking for survival. No, it is wrong. No one is free without food, and no one is free without water.

"No, it is wrong. Our country's products are enough to feed us. Africa has enough to feed the whole world, but unfortunately, we suffer lack of management. No, it is wrong. Africa is rich; the children should not go to bed hungry. No, it is wrong. We should not be refugees or fugitives. We are future leaders. No, it is wrong. Did AIDS come from Africa? No! Has AIDS spread in every village in Africa killing our 90-year-old grandparents? Yes! Do they have the means of medication? No, and that also is wrong. Every day the black man is killed by other races and it is wrong for the black man to contribute to his brother's death. No, it is wrong. Yes, we should fight to end this mass corruption."

The young girl asked this question: "How can a shepherd go to the creek and leave his sheep up the mountain? This generation is going to stand together in unity and harmony, and we will minimize the poverty rate in the world. We are going to war, but we will use no weapons. We don't want to create more bloodshed. Let us continue to fight for our rights and speak out through songs or any means possible, until we are able to send the message across and our objectives have come into view. Let us continue until we win the war of poverty. Let us fight to keep the dream alive." Today, I clearly stand before you and say, 'Pan-Africa forever'! Amandla awethu!" (Power to the people) was shouted couple of times, then we sang part of the South African national anthem.

"Nkosi sikelel' Afrika (God bless Africa)

Maluphakanyisw' uphondo lwayo, (Let its Africa's horn be raised)
Yizwa imithandazo yethu, (Listen also to our prayers,)
Nkosi sikelela, thina lusapho lwayo. (Lord bless us, we are the family of it Africa)
Morena boloka setjhaba sa heso, Lord bless our nations,
O fedise dintwa le matshwenyeho," Stop wars and sufferings,
O se boloke, O se boloke setjhaba sa heso, Save it, save our nations,
Setjhaba sa Afrika. (The nations of Africa)

We came to the end of the program after four hours, but the party continued through the night. And there that evening, Zola finally was able to sing the theme song she had written for the conference.

"Rise up Africa, Rise up and stand together, Rise up it's time for unity... Rise up, your name is power... United States of Africa..."

"It could not have been any better than this," Professor Matheson said.

"I agree with you," Zola said as they were going to drop off some of the students that had stayed for Christmas. "Orlando, you can't go far from Ontario please, and keep in touch."

"Yes, Madam," he answered as he closed the door behind him.

It was early February in 1996 when I called Zola from Calgary. She was crying, and seemingly devastated about something. I could not get her to calm down. It was hard for her to speak; she was nearly choking. I became confused. *I know it, it's that Nathan guy. I thought that it was over between the two of you...?* I knew I was jumping to conclusions.

I had one more business meeting to attend and it was very important for us to get this business to join us. However, I called the airline to put me on the flight back to Toronto after my meeting. What was Zola's problem? Why could she not control herself? She had always told me to get ready for trouble at any time, because, trouble would come in unannounced. Why was she not ready for this – and what had Nathan done this time?

I could not answer those questions. "A Christian without tribulation isn't a Christian at all. Sometimes the wind will blow with storm, and sometimes it blows and clears dirt that the storm might have gathered in your path. As the wind blows, no one can change direction, or have the power to stop it." She would say that this was her storm and she was powerless. But this was not

Sayba or Orlando. She was going to find a way to deal with it. On the other hand, I was going to make sure that Nathan kept away from her, this time.

I was afraid that she might leave to go walking. Walking was good, but she would walk more than 25 kilometres, and that was wrong in such a condition. I still remembered when the war extended to the neighbouring countries in West Africa, and only God can testify to what it did to her. She walked all night drinking coffee, then she came home. She would sit by the TV and get the latest from CNN News. I tried calling her to let her know that I would be home in the morning, but she did not pick up the phone. I called a couple of people from the church. Maa lived not far away, but she was nowhere to be found. I called Boss to see if he could come to her aid, but he was not feeling well since his wife's death.

Boss and Zola had a unique relationship in the early days before he had given me the job. I saw that he had great interest in Zola, but then he fell in love with Varnity, a cheerleader who was also a bully at Mandela High. She was very beautiful, and used her pretty face to get whatever her heart desired. Every guy wanted to be with her. Zola would say "Behind that beautiful exterior, there is not much else there to find."

From what I heard, her mother had a heart attack one night because of her stupidity. Her father decided to drive the mom to the hospital, and they both died in a car crash while she was somewhere in the Middle East. Her parents were very wealthy, but she did not use the money wisely. Boss and I were having a meeting at the hotel close to the Square One Mall in Mississauga when we saw her having a drink. She walked over to our table and asked me if I remembered her. Of course I did. Who would forget a girl like Varnity? We talked a little and then we exchanged numbers. I did remember calling her, but she did not pick up, and I realized a few weeks later that she was in Paris with Boss. Apparently, Boss lost interest in Zola and got married to Varnity on their first trip to Paris.

They got married but I never saw those two together. She was traveling a lot; in fact she died on a boat cruise in the Bahamas. Boss received a call from the Canadian authorities that his boat had sunk and that Varnity and all her friends died on that boat. Since Boss went into the hospital he never came out.

Orlando's job did not permit him to stay around as often as possible. Right after the conference, he left for the Alberta area. I could have left that night, but they had cancelled all flights to Toronto that evening, because of stormy weather. I said a prayer for Zola, begging God to take care of her. She had always told me that if I found myself in a confused situation, I should look up toward heaven because that was where my help was coming from.

Meanwhile, I was still at the airport trying to get back home. Aunt May had gone over to Zola's house, waiting on her to get home. When Aunt May arrived, it did not take any time before Zola opened the door. She was soaking wet with puffy eyes. Aunt May was doing what she did the most – praying – and Zola's grandmother was on her way with some won ton soup.

Aunt May helped her clean up and made her get some rest on the sofa, with extra blankets to keep her warm. I had gotten her some special pyjamas in Paris a couple of months before; I don't know how Aunt May put her hands on them. It was supposed to be her birthday present. Zola was crazy about lovely pyjamas and lingerie. Besides, I thought it was lovely and sexy on her.

I remembered having a fight with Ben, he did not want me to get it for her, but the decision was mine to make because Zola was now a part of me that nobody could take away. I opened the door now, and saw her lying on the sofa. Maa was right behind me. I rushed over and took her in my arms, holding her tightly. I could not let go of her.

She opened her eyes, which were puffy and red, but to me they were as beautiful as always. I kissed her head and the top of her nose gently. Again I held her tightly telling her how much I loved her, and that she should never say that she was alone.

"I am taking you with me until you are all right," I told her.

"You don't have to do this; Maa is taking me to the shelter," she said.

I was surprised. "Maa Huan Yue, you don't have to. We will take care of her."

"Yes!" Aunt May told Maa.

"François, call me Maa. You are always getting yourself confused.

"Okay Maa, I will. Nathan is going to pay for this."

As soon as I said the words, she got angry. "What did Nathan do this time to you that he is going to pay for?" she asked me.

The Wind of Change

"Maa, I saw her on TV yesterday," said Zola, "she was in the crowd running on the old bridge. I recognized her, Maa, she is the one."

And Zola began to cry. We were not getting anywhere with her. She refused to be comforted and she also refused to go with me to my place. She was not herself, because she was saying things that only she understood. We wanted her to tell us who the woman she saw was, but she was too bitter to talk. Something terrible had happened, something was really wrong, and she was not able to talk about it. She was hurting.

Maa decided to go with her to Oakville. Actually, Maa had two 90-year-old friends who had just passed away, so it was going to be busy for her. Whatever was going on with Zola was important.

"I hate that Nathan guy, Maa."

"No, François, this has nothing to do with Nathan, Besides, you can't hate people; no one is born with hate. Hate is learned, then practiced, and sooner or later, you will be doing unimaginable things to Nathan. Do you know what you have done? You have given power to Nathan to rule you. You should start loving him," Maa said.

Zola was not able to talk, but after crying for some time, she finally slept. For the first time since high school, I felt connected to Zola in that special way. I knew that we had been close over the years, but this was different. This felt very different. I felt the closeness to her heart and I could hear the sound of her heart beating. I wanted to leave the room, but Aunt May was right over my head telling me to keep Zola next to me. I lifted her up and sat next to her on the sofa, and allowed her to lie on me with my hand in her silky hair. Every time she tried to speak, I interrupted her. I just wanted her to sleep, for it was a long 24 hours for her... That was why she was talking out of her mind.

Aunt May was standing in complete astonishment with her hand over her lips. She had always prayed that Zola and I would get this close. I could almost hear the sound of her praising God, but only her lips were moving. She often said that Zola and I were destined to be together as husband and wife. This was the first time that I thought she might be right. As much as it felt great, I was very uncomfortable and shy. "I knew that there was a Jerusalem in you, so I had to beat Gomorrah out of you. Very soon Jerusalem will begin to shine, and my friends will know that I raised a fine boy."

Aunt May's whole life was all about the tea ladies. They would constantly gossip about whose child was doing better and whose not.

We got home that evening and Maa went home with Zola. All week she refused to talk about what troubled her, but she was greatly distressed. She came home after a week, and kept herself busy as usual.

Zola was invited to the African Planet Awards ceremony for "best achievement and humanitarian" award. I accompanied her there and we met Nathan standing there too. We greeted him and walked away, and he even gave Zola a hug as if nothing had happened between them. He wasn't surprised to have seen her there. According to him, he went to support her. He kept direct eye contact with her trying to get her attention, and I kept direct contact with her trying to distract her. She went to the washroom during the show, and he later disappeared, obviously hoping to see her in the hall.

I was determined to keep them apart whether married or not. The fact that Nathan had not taken advantage of Zola told me that he was a "good guy", but I still felt he was not the right man for her. If I can remember rightly, once in a casual conversation, Nathan tried to explain to us about the tradition and culture in his country. He came from a traditional African family that did not believe in outside marriage. In words, if a woman did not come from that region or province, it was not possible for him to marry her. So a tangible relationship between them was never going to happen. I realized that sometimes I went too far and it made me look stupid. I just did not want her wasting her time on him.

I went looking for Zola, and I saw her standing talking to him, "Hey Zola, where have you been?"

"I'm standing here talking to Nathan, as you can see," she said.

"You...don't you think he has done enough harm to you?"

I warned him to stay away from her, but she disagreed with me. "François, Nathan is not my enemy. If he is, I will still have a word with him. If you keep your enemies close to you, they will not harm you, or their plans will not work. You need to stop your obsession with Nathan. If not, I will have to make a decision that we all may regret later." She gave Nathan a handshake, and arranged to see him later that week for a business meeting.

Knowing that Zola would even plan to see Nathan crushed my spirit. It did not make sense, but with Zola, nothing made sense. Her life was not her own, it was about the people, and for the people. As much as I loved her and wanted to protect her, I had to find a way to let her be herself which was becoming difficult for me. Besides, she had warned me to back off, or there were going to be consequences.

In the spring of that year, I realized that she was really not seeing the Lover Boy, but I knew that they kept in touch. I was really glad for her. Silly me, I arranged for her to go out on a date with Orlando, since he had a unique relationship with her. I started wondering about her and who or what she was. Her Canadian family could not answer my questions, and I was just not bold enough to ask Zola any questions about her family. Everyone around us thought I knew who she was. For all I knew, she was a Jamaican girl who did not want to identify as a Jamaican. I do know that she had much to deal with, so she was not really motivated to date.

In high school, she would say that everybody in Canada had come from somewhere. She was a black girl with a Chinese family. I was interested in finding out so much about her, but time was not on my side. Boss got very sick and the company was in my hands, so it was difficult to play detective. Besides, as I think of it now, I was a little selfish. Zola had a purpose for her life, and I can't say the same for myself. At that point of my life, I was at my defining moment still trying to find what I was looking for. I did not know where I was going, because I was still figuring out who I was. I was a very blessed and lucky man, but I was lost. Or let me just say that I was a confused boy as she often reminded me about that.

"What is the meaning of my life?" I asked myself. I was never motivated to do things, not even my work. I had a good job that paid me well, but further than that, I didn't know what life was all about, which made it difficult for me to move forward. I remembered in one of Zola's sessions she talked about motivation being a master key to excellence.

"Everything a man does under the sun, whether work, raising children or hobbies, if there is no motivation, it is very difficult to carry through. If you create passion for a task, you will be motivated, and the end result will be successful. Napoleon Hill said that people suffer much because of ignorance. I am encouraging you to challenge yourselves and create passion for whatever your heart desires. The result may surprise you." She was right about one thing: I was never passionate about anything.

I went to Zola's office to talk to her about Boss. I walked in on Zola and Maa chatting over tea. "God created man in his image, with a unique structure. If he had 'unified' us, we would not be unique after all. As different as we are, so are our needs and characters," said Zola. She told someone that she had a huge responsibility, and they should not add more to what she had to deal with. I wondered what 'responsibilities.' I did not really see it that way. She loved what she did and she was good at it. Her joy was in the people, so I didn't understand why she was complaining.

Zola was not working extra hours because she needed the money, she worked to change lives and touch lives. At times, I proposed to take care of her mortgage, but she would refuse. I later found out that she had paid off her mortgage. She believed that one-percent effort of 100 people was better than 100% of her own effort. She had enough time doing the things she loved the most. "It is called 'leverage', François."

Boss had been in and out of the hospital since his wife's death. His heart was failing, and he needed a transplant. It did not look good so he decided to do what he could do while still alive. He went and secretly signed his will without our awareness. The lawyer was to tell us only if the doctors thought that Boss was about to die. Every time I saw Boss, he still had enough strength to talk and move around.

Chapter Eighteen

※

Things did not look good for Boss. He called Zola at the hospital and began to confide in her some family history. I was expecting her at my office, but she called to tell me she was on her way to see Boss instead. She sounded worried, so I decided to follow her. We got there almost at the same time. "Hey, Boss, how are you?" Zola walked into the hospital room and I pretended I was waiting on another person.

"I am very well," he said. "I am just waiting for the Big Man up there to call me home."

"No!" Zola said, "You are not going anywhere. We still need you around here. Don't you believe in God? Keep the faith and talk to him from your heart and he will hear you."

"I am going to die – you are not listening. What is there to keep the faith on?"

Zola said, "You see, faith is the complete opposite of doubt. Faith is being sure of what you hope for and certain of what you do not see. You are doing the complete opposite," Zola said as she poured him a cup of water.

"I'm sorry if I offended you," she said, "but you have to believe that God is going to heal you before you receive your healing. Stretch out your hands; He is here, Boss. Every time I come to see you, I feel His presence. Know that you are not alone; He is fighting for you and with you. Because you are alive, many children are living. Your time has not yet come, Boss."

"Zola, please can you spend the day with me?" asked Boss. "I have some stuff on my chest, and I don't want to take it with me to the grave."

"I will stay if you stop telling me about the grave. Life and death is in the mouth. Whatever you pronounce on yourself, whether good, or bad will surely come to pass."

"Well, my queen, I will stop," said Boss.

"Okay," said Zola. "Then tell me what's on your mind."

Boss took a deep breath. "My family came from the other side of Afghanistan many years ago from a little place called Asadabad. My sister and I were born in Canada, but unfortunately, she was killed before her 18th birthday. Fatima and I were very close friends. She was more like my mother. Most people who saw us together would ask if she was my mother. Not a day goes by that I don't think about my sister. You are a perfect reminder of her; she was so bright and full of energy. The day she was killed, she told me that love was millions strong in the blood vessels that control human beings and she could not wait to see my blood vessels being controlled by that special person.

"She wanted to become a doctor and save many lives, but her life was taken away by the same people who gave her life. I tried to go after her murderers and kill them, but I realized that I would become a murderer myself. Besides, killing them was like killing myself. I never let go of her memory. In fact I spoke to her every day in my quiet time.

"Fatima grew up as a traditional Afghan girl, wearing *hijab* every day. When she was 17, my Dad wanted to take her back to his country to get her to marry his friend, but this friend was already married according to him.

"When my dad was coming to Canada, he promised his friend that his first daughter would become his wife. My father was married to his friend's sister who was my mother. So as the wind blew them to Canada, the Canadian wind changed everything. Fatima totally opposed the idea of going to Afghanistan, and she would often tell him that he was being silly.

"She was a regular Canadian girl who could not wait to remove her hijab. She began uncovering her hair at 17 when she was in school. This went on for at least a year without Mom and Dad finding out. One afternoon, her friends picked her up to go do their prom shopping. She quickly picked up her purse and ran out without her hijab. My father works as a security guard at the mall. He saw his daughter, who was pledged to be married to an imam, in the mall without her hijab. He covered his face in shame, and ran after her. He called her a disgrace, a shameless child. 'Your body belongs only to your husband,' he said, and went home to tell my mother. He blamed my mother for Fatima's behaviour, because he felt she did not discipline her daughter well.

"I was sitting on the sofa hearing them planning a plot to send her home to her husband. They quickly arranged a trip to Afghanistan after the graduation. They told her that it was okay if she did not want to marry the guy, but we all should go see him and visit the family members. For some reason, my sister did not believe them. Then he told her that he would allow her to go to the prom if she went and signed for her passport. Fatima went and signed the passport early that morning with excitement, because it was also the day of the prom.

"Her date called to let her know that he would be at the door by 7:00 pm; it was 5:00 pm then. When he arrived at the door, he phoned, but my parents did not pick up. He wanted to go, so he rang the bell. My father went to the door and opened it.

"Oh, good evening, Mr. Ali," the boy greeted him.

"What is so good about the evening?" my father responded.

The boy said, "Could you please tell Fatima – "

My father interrupted him. "No she is sick; she is running with fever, high fever.

"But I just talked to her!" the boy said.

He was not allowed to enter the house, and on his way to the car, he heard my father still talking.

"Allah is great; he has saved Fatima from this sinful world, from all of you." My dad continued to speak, "Fatima had two options, which was life and death. She chooses to die." The door was still open, and I heard the boy saying to my father that he was crazy. "Crazy old fool!" he said.

Boss continued. "He sat down on the grass in front of our house crying. And then I saw him there for as long as I looked through the window holding his hands on his head. Groups of people had surrounded him looking at our house. Some minutes later, there were police all over our home. I did not really know what was going on at the time, when I saw so many people and police; in fact, I thought that my father was going to be famous.

"Before the police arrived, I saw a woman; I think she was the boy's mother. She called my father a heartless beast. When the police entered, they saw my sister lying on top of the bed. I heard the officer say, "We are too late, she is dead. Call the Children's Aid, and get the boy out of here."

I was now crying for my parents, but I was not allowed to go with them. My parents had killed my only sister, and they were now going to jail for the rest of their lives. My mother was right there, but she did not say anything to stop my father. I was just five years old, but I remember everything. It was not easy growing up going from one foster home to the next. When I was fourteen, I went to a little shelter in Caledon, and they allowed me to stay there until I was 18.

"I missed my sister, and up to now I love her. I can't believe that it was forty years ago, it seems like it just happened yesterday. I asked God to take my parents and give me back my sister. I was still hurting, with much pain. I grew up with the thought that I was going to kill them when I turned 18. In fact, I had planned to buy a gun with my first salary and kill my parents. I was going to kill them and say that God was great, as well. But a voice kept stopping me. I bought a Quran and read it over ten times from the first page to the last, and I tell the truth, there is nowhere in that book that says killing people is the will of God."

"Yes, God is great, but his greatness does not include murder," Zola said. "You see, Boss, Allah is indeed great, but his name should not be used in vain or while satisfying their own selfish desires. God means love. But he is used as a scapegoat every day to perform evil acts. It is not right. Any religions that encourage murder are not of God.

"I am sorry; you have been carrying this burden on your own but you have family now that love you. I love you, and the French Man loves you, too. Yes, Boss, we love you," she assured him again. "You are going to come out of this. I know that God is going to come to your rescue. You have been through just too much; don't give up now, please." Zola was weeping as she talked. "Let me get you some water."

"Don't cry for me," said Boss. "I...I just wanted you to know where I came from, and what got me lying here."

"Where are they now?" Zola asked.

"They are still living in jail, they are doing life there," Boss said.

"Good," said Zola. "Evil people like them do not belong in our midst."

"You see, Honey Bunch, love is amazing," said Boss. "I do believe that the earth was created for us to live in love, not in hatred. Even though I don't go to a church or mosque, I still believe in God. The different religions have made the world a complicated place to live in. I go down on my knees to ask Him to keep me in perfect peace; it is unfortunate that I am here fighting for my life, but I have found peace with this. If it is the will of God, I will go." Boss continued confiding in Zola that he believed in giving. "Love is beautiful, and life is beautiful; living life in love is what we all should be doing. Unfortunately, I have had no one to control my blood vessels."

(Yes he was a generous giver, I can attest to that. He spent a million a year on charities, and kept a low profile with it.)

"In life when God gives to you," he said, "it is not yours to keep. It is to be shared with those who he blesses the least. The fingers of the hands are not equal and it will never be equal. This is why they need each other to work together. God actually speaks to me in dreams, I saw this calamity coming upon me, and I am not going to…"

"No, you will not," Zola stopped him again.

"It is too late now," Boss said.

She interrupted him again. "No! It is not! Have you ever read the Bible?"

"Yes! I did," Boss answered quickly. "As a matter of fact, I have a Bible in my office as we speak.

I approached the bed. "Oh, hello, Boss…Zola. I have some important papers that need your signature." I interrupted knowing I had red eyes, and pretending as if I had something in them.

"François, can the papers wait?" Zola asked me.

"No, Sweetie, it can't; it has a deadline. Besides, I was coming here anyway."

"Not a problem, Son, come in. I am glad you are here. I want you to hear the rest of the story."

"Thanks, Boss!" I said. "I will someday write my life story, and I will put in a little bit of everyone's life stories."

"French Man, if you were to write it, it won't be a story, it will be many books. Since I met you at Mandela High until now, you have been investigating, researching, and eavesdropping."

Boss continued. "I was going to kill them for my sister. I was very happy on that day when I bought the gun. On my way going there, I tried to buy a Bible but it was out of stock. I said that if I had killed them, then I would read it. When I arrived at the prison, the guard called them, but they were not prepared to see me that day.

"When I got home that afternoon, I went across the street and got a Bible from a church that was just at the corner of Dixie and Burnhamthorpe Roads "Logos Church." I did not know where to begin in the Bible. So I remember my mother telling my sister that, in order to go ahead, she had to look behind. I started, from the beginning when the heaven and the earth was created, I read through to the very end. I saw love and forgiveness, one after another. The only way I was going to see your pretty faces was to forgive my parents, otherwise, I was going to end up in jail like them. It was a very hard thing for me at the time, but I did it anyway.

"I still wanted to see them, so I went over to the prison. This time around, they were more than happy to see me. I entered and gave them a hug, and my mother touched my head telling me that I reminded her of my father when he was my age. After the happy moment, I asked him why he did it, but he screamed at me, saying that I must not mention that dead sinner's name in his happy moment with me. 'She deserved to die, and I do not regret anything. I would do it all over again if she was alive.' Then my father gave me a number and name of an uncle of mine so I could marry his daughter.

"Having a child in this world was not going to be good for me. You guys are enough for me," Boss said. "When God created this world, it was good and beautiful. God created man in his likeness."

Zola tried to cheer Boss up. "Love is the likeness of God according to my father. If God was a murderer, he would have allowed Abraham to kill his son on that mountain. Falling in love with people and standing in the gap for them is what the world needs to teach. It is beautiful to fall in love, to feel love and be in love. My mother had a quote, hanging over her bed that said: 'Love is the key that opens the heart, and holds a people together, not destruction.' My father liberated his people and country from slavery, and he sacrificed much for them. But the same people hated the fact that he was wiser than them, and he had plans to move not just his country forward, but the whole of Africa. One day, he went on a diplomatic trip, and they ganged up against him…and that led to his death.

"He became an alien in a place which he thought was the safest place, but even at that, he was denied freedom. He was born to be a freedom fighter, but he died a refugee slave. Another took his place, because they were ignorant and they thought that he was going to destroy their land. His people betrayed him because of his brilliant ideas for the people he loves."

I wanted to interrupt her, but it was too late; Zola was in her own world. She had brought the African crisis into Boss's life story. She continued:

"'Today, your beloved country is free.' That's what my father said to the people of Ghana. He was one of the greatest African leaders that ever lived. He left a legacy, that all Africa must unite, and we all can learn from him and make the world a better place. We all have a part to play in it. We need to double our efforts to bring peace to this planet. We are all God's children. I tell you the truth, guys, love is the only way."

"Yes, Professor Zola Nkrumah, you should go into politics," I teased her.

Then she went on. "To care for a nation, and give hope to his people was a joy for him. Why must a child live in fear for its life? Children are a blessing, but the enemy has opened his mouth to drink their blood every second of every hour. No, this is wrong. It needs to stop." Zola began to cry.

"Boss, I want you to put the experience with your father in the garbage, and focus on what you have in your hand. My mother often told me that my father's definition for experience was different from what she thought experience was. 'Experience is not what happened to you, but what you did when it happened is what you take with you and tell your story with.' We have to forget about what they have to us, and focus on what we are capable of doing, changing lives. There are children out there like you and they need us to rescue them. When the job is done, we will have much experience to tell our children. It requires teamwork, and together we can do it.

"Looking back at this, you however have achieved greatly, Boss," Zola said. You are an experienced teacher that many children will love to learn from and hear your story. You are one of Ontario's wealthiest and most handsome gentlemen. You are generously providing for the kids around the world. He will not make them cry over you now.

"Because of you, they are living. You are going to make it through, I can feel it, but when you give up, your heart will give up. Those kids need you, and they are praying for you. You have to keep on listening to that inner voice of yours. We need you here. That same voice is reminding me not to lose purpose in the world. You have to hold on to me, and your stubborn son over here, who has totally refused to grow up. You need to teach him how to back off when necessary." Zola spoke while looking right in my face.

"Yes, First Lady!" Boss said.

We spent the night at the hospital chatting with him.

Boss needed a new heart, so we started making plans just in case he died. Before leaving the hospital that morning, he had called me. "Son!"

"Yes, Boss!"

"I want you to know that I love you; the two of you are all I have left. if I don't make it..."

"You will make it." Zola spoke quickly while crying.

"I will not tell you what to do," he said, "but don't live your life wondering about tomorrow when you have not seen it. Certain things in this world are worth fighting for, especially when it has to do with the people we love. Achieving greatness is the most difficult thing to do."

"Hey, I might take a quick trip to Angola with Orlando, but now I have to be at the office," said Zola.

"Zola, you can't go to Angola, it is a death zone," I said.

"Thanks for reminding me, François, I will remember that. But I really have to go. There is someone from Burundi at the office that urgently needs to see me. Love you two, and no gossip please." Zola walked away. "I will call you later, Old School."

"How is Zola doing?" asked Boss with a lonely face. "Do you think that she is going to marry Nathan?"

"Never! I will not allow her to. Frankly, Boss, I do not know; she is not telling me much. Natasha tells me that he travels, but they are not in love like a couple...but she goes there often to check on things for him."

"She has a key to the apartment?"

"Yes."

"He is a good guy. I like him," Boss said.

"But he doesn't love her, and she knows it."

"They are friends, Son."

"If she has the door key, maybe they will be moving in together, Boss."

"I don't think so, and I hope they don't."

"There is always something with him, they are not even intimate."

"What, son? Are you serious about that?" Boss asked.

"It is true, Boss."

"But why?"

"She wants to get married first, she said it is tradition."

"There is just something about this girl that amazes me all the time. Wow, Son! She is not in love with him. That is the truth. You, on the other hand, you are in love with her, and you are in denial."

Boss listened to me as I talked about Zola, and he told me everything that Aunt May and Maa had always said. "Could it be true that I can be a husband to her? Could Zola really be my soul mate? No… not possible. Was I running away from responsibility, and that's why I am gay? But I have been a gay for so long, Boss."

"Son, you can't fool me anymore, I know what you are up to. You are a gay, but you are not living like one."

"I could not even tell Zola that I loved her in high school, Ben had to teach me. Even though she was my prom queen and forever best friend…I did not have the courage to stand before her and really tell her what I felt for her. I was not attracted to any other girl before, and I did not even give anyone else a chance to enter into my life or my heart. Will I make a good husband? Boss, do you think that I am afraid of committing to her?"

"Look here, Son! I am going to tell you this just once. If you don't go and get your woman, somebody else is going to get her soon, and you will lose her for good. Then you will live with regrets for the rest of your life. You have known Zola since high school; I will not tell you what you don't already know." Then Boss said: "Let me ask you a personal question: why are you not with Ben? Almost two years or more you have not seen him."

I told Boss that I was not with Ben, because I did not want to leave Zola. "She needs me over here."

"Then why are you not getting married to her?"

"Because I am gay."

"Son, you know what I think? You are a coward and a confused little boy who refuses to grow up. You are a disgrace to all men," Boss said, as the nurses checked his heartbeat.

He also told me that I looked like a gentleman, but yet still like a little boy, too. He thought that I wasn't sure of myself and that I was using Ben as a gay partner, which was wrong. "You can't move on, and you don't want the people around you to move on," he said and smiled at me.

I wanted him to understand, but no one understood me. Maybe they were all right, but I did not see how it could be true. "Boss, it is not what you think, please understand me." When I said that, I hoped he would say just what I needed to hear.

"I hope you think things through for your own sake, before it is late."

"Boss, you need to talk to Zola about going to Africa. It is dangerous."

"You know the lady; once she puts her mind to some... somebody, or something, no one can easily convince her out of it. Besides, if they knew that it wasn't safe for her, they would not have accepted her proposal."

I left Boss early that morning and left for work. Zola and Orlando were to leave two days later, to Angola.

Chapter Nineteen

I was concerned about Zola, but at that point, there was nothing I could do to stop her. The trip was arranged and she and Orlando were on their way to Africa. It was nearly four weeks, and I did not hear anything from Zola. I believed that she was all right until my secretary rushed into the office telling me that Maa was on the line and it was urgent.

"Maa, what is it, is everything all right?" I asked her.

"No François, it is Zola. She is in trouble – " The words poured out. "There are two government officials here in my house telling me that Zola has been taken hostage."

Upon hearing that from Maa, I banged down the phone out of fear and frustration. "No this cannot be true," I told myself. I began sweating at once, and it did not take long before Sayba called my secretary again, telling her to turn the television on. It was information about Zola. It was true; they really had her. A general was giving us the latest information on Zola's status in Angola.

Sayba was still on the line. "Something happened to her there, François?"

"I told her but she would not listen to me… She is dead. Oh, no, Sayba; what am I going to do without her?" I began to cry.

Sayba had to stop me. If she was near me, she would have kicked me from the sound of it. "Stop talking and listen to the news, François! And people usually say men are strong. Be a man. Men have heart in making drastic decisions that they never reconsider or think about the consequences. François, be a man and pull yourself together. You are being a chicken right now." She had to scream in order to stop me.

Then I stopped talking and I focused on the TV. A man was standing holding a paper in his hand. They had just shown her when she was at the peace conference. Then he said, "My name is General Alfaso Abrau, and right now we don't have any news on where they might have taken the Canadian young girl. She has been with them for more than 24 hours now, we don't know yet why they took her. We are trying to negotiate with them to release her."

"François, stop the chicken act and pray. I am from a war zone, and I know what these people are capable of. We can't lose her," said Sayba.

It was like a dream to me, I slapped myself five times hoping to wake up. It was true; they took her with them. "Sayba, what do we do?"

"Pray. She is a Canadian citizen, and she went there on a peace mission. Once those guys have a gun in their hands, they are right and you are wrong."

A couple of days later, another General called to tell the Canadian government that the warring factions believed that she went to Angola under false pretences. They also claimed that she went there as an undercover agent.

"We don't have any information for now; we will let you know if we have anything on her," the general said. They could not really come up with one charge, and we were confused. Orlando did not call me, but he was in touch with Maa Huan Yue and her family at all times.

Three days later, they showed us that Zola was alive, but not well. She was on camera, but she was not allowed to talk, and even if she had been allowed to, she was not able to speak for she did not have a mouth to talk. They had beaten her several times, so her face was covered with heavily swollen flesh, and her left arm was in a cloth tied to her neck which gave me hope that they were still operating under the human nature of morality.

Zola later explained that she was hit with a gun. It appeared that she had bruises on her face and parts of her body. Her eyes were swollen so it was hard to see them, and her lips were three times their normal size. She was sitting on the floor in a room full of human skulls with two little boys holding guns in their hands pointing right over her head. To live life is to love life. I'm not sure if either of them valued life at that moment.

"No, that's not Zola," I said. I did not recognize her.

Maa called me several times crying. She wanted to go to Africa, but they advised her not to. "Zola does not deserve this," Maa said.

"What is going to happen to her now?" one of Maa's daughters asked. She went on air appealing to the rebels to release her. "There is a mistake... She is not who you think she is. Zola will not step on an ant under her feet. This is madness, and you people need to let that child go."

Back in South Africa, President Mandela sent a special message to the kidnappers to release her. He told them that she was definitely not a spy and that everything she was doing in Angola was for love, and gratitude to nature. She was not a spy, and she had no hidden agenda. She was simply a supplier of love.

"Here in my hand is a souvenir she sent me from Canada when I just got out of jail," said Mandela. "This is a treasure that was made in Angola in 1959 and has very important information in it. Zola is also a treasure. She loves the planet Earth and she wants to save the environment. Please let her go...she is harmless."

Right after President Mandela had got through speaking, Sister Lavender called the broadcasting network, telling them that she was a good friend of Zola's. "I have something she wrote back in high school and I would like to read it."

I was on my way from Ottawa to meet Sister Lavender, but before I got there, she was live on TV wearing a beautiful scarlet dress with crème stripes, looking very fashionable. "Well," she said, "This is not about Zola, but this is something she wrote pretending to be President Mandela when he just came out of jail. She wrote this speech for her school presentation. Zola wore a suit and stood in front of the class, very happy, reading this:"

"My people: thank you for your love, and thank you because you care. We must all care, we are here to care. Thank you for your contribution to free Nelson Mandela. You made it happen. Your eagerness for change, your hunger and thirst for equality, is what kept me alive in the dark cell for 27 years. You were sitting, but you stood up for me. You marched, you sang and you spoke in faith that no man is superior to the other. Had it not been for you, I could not have come out. I served 27 years, but I was not alone. When I was lying on the cold floor, you were under the rain, under the snow, under the sun protesting day and night.

"You shared my pain and said no to apartheid, and I will do it again if I have to. I will not rest until there is total equality in South Africa and every part of the world where there is oppression, suppression, segregation, separation, and discrimination. We say no to all of that because it is abomination. Unfortunately, I am not young any more, but you are the future leaders and I need you to start from wherever I am going, to stop this fight of inequality.

Sister Lavender said, "I hope that those people listen to this speech and they will realize that Zola is not who they think she is." And then she was off the line.

I had no idea that Sister Lavender had that paper all this while. It was lovely, but I did not want us paying tribute to Zola. I wanted her to come home alive.

The Canadian officials and other world leaders met in the Congo to negotiate her release. The Congo captors were not demanding anything in exchange for her. They just kept her there with them because they felt betrayed by her. The Canadian Prime Minister spoke out, still pleading with them to name a price and he would arrange something for them. "This is our citizen, and we will not rest until we have brought her home."

Canada turned to Cuba with a solemn heart asking them to please intervene. But the US president spoke strongly. "Tell your boys to turn the girl over to Canada where she belongs. When I put my hands on you, you will not be able to smoke any more cigars."

There were reports coming in about her being dead, but we were still praying and crying that she would come home alive. It was just a few months earlier when she organized the student conference to unite. Sankara campus was hosting projects for her each day demanding that she be released, and the Angolan embassy was overcrowded with people each day as well. From the way we saw her on camera, we hoped and prayed for the best. Mr. Zulu went to Angola to see what he could do to help. His intervention did help me especially since I was able to talk to him every day.

It was over two weeks, and they were not saying anything. Her family thought she was dead, but they still kept praying for a miracle. I went searching to see what Canada had in common with Angola and how Canada was involved in the Angolan war. Was there any company in Canada supplying weapons to Angola? Was Canada one of the powers? I was looking for answers, but I got none. "Why, Zola?"

The United Nations Secretary-General had always been fond of Zola, and he adored her. He did not leave the African soil until they heard from the kidnappers to arrange a meeting. For weeks there was solemnity in the world and among women. Mandela High had its flag at half-mast every day and they said a special prayer for her. The principal said in one of her interviews, "We are known as a school of integrity because of that young lady. They need to send her home, and they must put the guns down and find other work to do." After a month of trying to free her, we were beginning to think that the worst might have happened to her.

"No, not her. They will realize that it is a mistake and release her," I told myself. Her family had given up, because at the peace meeting to release her, the rebels were not specific as to whether she was alive or not. I was at the hospital visiting Boss when we heard that she was found at a hospital in Namibia.

They dropped her there in a small town and the authorities were notified. One week later, Zola was back in Canada, admitted at Trillium Hospital where she recovered.

She was home and alive, but she refused to talk about it. She never talked about her one-month experience with them, not even with her doctor. "It was a misunderstanding," she told everyone.

The rebels felt betrayed by her, because she was seen on several occasions with all the factions including the government. "She has a hidden agenda," the spokesman for the warring faction said.

I couldn't understand how Orlando had allowed it to happen. He went there to be able to protect her, but instead led her directly into the fire.

Thank God that the Canadian authorities did not sit and wait for them to respond, but acted as quickly as possible. With the cordial relationship between Canada and Angola, she was home with her people; there was someone among them who was thinking morally. The Ambassador later was on air telling us that it was all just a misunderstanding, like Zola said. They had nothing against the Canadians, the Canadians did not support the war in Angola and they were one of the countries that had been fighting for peace in Angola ever since.

I remembered many times Zola told me that when it became too political, or people came too close to certain information, they died. She had come too close, so maybe it was just an indication for her to back off. She had refused to listen, and there were many unanswered questions. I still remembered when she arrived at Pearson Airport. She was brave and still believed that if she was given another chance she would do it all over again. She would go back until there was total peace.

She was not able to talk about her experience when she returned. She brought pictures of malnourished children, diamond-trading, zone pictures of abused women, and little war soldiers, naked babies covered in flies sitting by their dead mothers. Some of the kids' heads were bigger than their bodies, so they could not even stand. Her heart was breaking for them, but there was only so much she could do and much she could not. As soon as she got back, she was looking for another means of aid. I needed answers, but I was not getting anywhere with her, so I went looking for Orlando, hoping that he would help me. I called him up and luckily for me, he was available to have a drink with me.

During our drink, I approached him to enlighten me about their African trip. He told me to let go. I had to force it on him, but I wished I didn't have to. "Orlando, what really happened in Angola? Zola will not talk about it and she is very distracted since you got back. I want to be able to help her, but I can't do that if I don't know where to begin. Amigo, I hold you responsible for the trauma she is undergoing."

"Wow that's good, my friend, very good. You amaze me always," Orlando said. "Everyone that goes to a war zone leaves from there traumatized, except for the people who like to see bloodshed or those exchanging the weapons for diamonds or transporting the oil." Orlando spoke with both sadness and anger in his voice.

I almost wished I had not asked him. "How did those rebels get hold of her?" My confidence was gone, but I was still curious to know. "She was almost killed, and you went there in order to stop what happened from happening."

"Look, François, it is a death zone – everyone who enters a war country prays to leave from there alive. War takes a negative toll on a person's life in a way that they never forget, especially when they are a living witness. Zola is a witness to the war in Angola now. She is here but her heart is with those vulnerable and helpless people who are trapped there, and her experiences are not easy ones either. The things that she saw there will never be forgotten," Orlando said.

"You could have gone with her that night, Orlando; you know how dangerous it was. You could have simply said no to the trip when she asked you to accompany her."

Orlando sat down looking right in my face searching for the right words, but he could not find any. When he did finally have the courage to speak out, I was sorry to have mentioned Angola. I later tried to withdraw my questions, but it was too late. He was unstoppable. He began speaking out of frustration and pain that only God could share with him. "Look French Man, we are not here for a question-and-answer session, so be content that we are back, and safe. I have told you to let go of this matter. Don't ask intrusive questions that you know nothing about. In fact…let me ask you a question, Amigo. If you knew what transpired in Saurimo, or Luanda or even in a Ugandan refugee camp, would you do something to end the bloodshed?

"Are you going to be one of the ten percent in the world to care, or the ninety percent that see and hear it, and then turn their eyes and ears away? Have you been to Liberia or Sierra Leone where the baby died in Sayba's arms? Life is about caring and changing lives, my friend. There is a reason why you are in our midst, hearing what others don't know. If I tell you what went down in Angola, what are you going to do?

"Zola is running after the earth, and her goal is to protect the earth. Her vision is that everyone should live together in peace and love; that's just the way it is with Zola. Did she ever tell you the meaning of her name?"

"No."

"You should have checked it out, man," said Orlando. "She represents her name, François. Zola means, 'piece of the earth'. She was born to be a peacemaker. She often tells me that, 'There can never be freedom without equality.' You should have gone with us to Angola, and felt what we felt. If you had seen how blood is exchanged for diamonds and oil, you would feel some empathy."

Orlando was very angry as he talked to me, and I knew that he was driven by something. He actually made sense, and I did agree with him, even if I was not as open to him as Sayba and Natasha were. I tried to ask Zola questions about him, but Zola refused to tell me anything about him. Whenever I asked her, she would tell me that, "François, you are going to die without Orlando's story or he will have to tell you himself. If not, I am sorry!"

Maybe this was my chance. I was now hoping that after our conversation, we could be more than just friends. Besides, Zola and I had decided to put the Angolan experience behind us, and focus on the project there.

"The future of the youth club she started there is very important to her. Those are children whose parents are dead and some are physically and mentally wounded from the war," said Orlando. "I know Zola, she will be denied and hated many times, but she is not stopping until her goal has come into view and has become reality. I am going to help her again if need be. I would do anything for her and with her…because the children today are our rising leaders. Their future will develop from the lives surrounding them. We have to keep them alive. When the vision is clear, their ears will be sharp and their minds will focus on what is necessary. It is not about what happened to me or Zola. It is about sharing your gift to inspire the world or transform lives. Do not go around talking about something you know nothing about. My friend Franklin Roosevelt once said that 'Selfishness is the only real atheism,' so be careful or you might catch it. I often hear that participation of all humanity makes a nation stand strong.

"Do you have any idea what is happening down there? It is no joke! Yes, my friend, money is not everything, you know. You have enough money, and you are living a million-dollar lifestyle without anyone to care for or think about. Yes, I am here in Canada, but I can never turn my back on my people. I had a chance to change my life. It is now my turn to change lives. As for Zola, she saw dead babies and mothers on the street, little boys with rifles and heavy machine guns."

"I am sorry, Amigo," I said, "Maybe the right questions did not come out. I was concerned about you guys when I heard the news."

"You saw her on TV. She looked awful, but she is a strong woman and that is why she did not die."

"I will let go," I told him.

"Oh, French Man, but before you go, I want to ask you these questions," Orlando said.

"Oh, sure. I just hope I will be able to answer them."

"I'm not expecting any answers from you."

"But I don't mind giving answers to your questions, if I can," I told him.

"Well, we will see," he said. "Do you know what it is for a five-year-old boy to wake up and see his parents lying sleeping covered in blood, only to realize later that they have been sleeping for a long time with hundreds of other people and they are not going to wake up? Then he sees his baby sister crying, trying to put her dead mother's breast in her mouth and in the process she is licking the blood. I want you to imagine that you are that little boy going through this journey and tell me later how you feel. I am now going to tell you what happened in Angola after the story, as if you are there.

"You and your two-year-old sister don't even know what death means, and you are still standing over your parents for days and nights, trying to drive the flies away from their bodies. The blood has dried up. Then finally, you hold your sister's hand and try walking with her elsewhere, but she is too young and weak to walk. She is hungry and you can't give her any food. She lies over the breast of your dead mother again, this time you watch her lie over the breast and cry her heart out until she cannot move. When you turn her over, you see she is not breathing, because she is dead.

"Fugitives are moving left and right, looking for a safer place to go," Orlando continued. "You see some people falling because of a bullet, right before your eyes. You manage to follow a crowd towards a camp, but you can't walk a long distance. Remember, you are only a five-year-old child, François, and you are not able to run. They leave you behind standing there crying, and all of them disappeared. It is raining with icicles. You try to run back to your mother and you trip over a dead body and fall. You did not wake up, because you are very weak and helpless now. Finally, days later they come to put all of the dead bodies into a mass grave and someone realizes that you are still alive. They would normally get rid of you even though you are alive, but luckily for you, they call the Red Cross to come and take you.

"You are taken to a place where there are thousands of children whose families have also been brutally killed without a reason. You have stopped thinking about your mama and your sister, and you start thinking about food. There is no food, no clothes, and even no water to drink. They find a well, but the first people that drank from it died… Those that took a shower with it got a skin disease…and others got seriously sick from what is called cholera. They tell you that you are going to a safer place where you will be until things are under control, then you can return to your place of birth. The safer place is a camp with many tents."

Orlando paused. "You are happy because it is better than sleeping with dead bodies. The tent becomes your new home and the people around you become your new family. You see new people every day. Some show you compassion and some do their job without emotions, because they see these things every day, every time. Some tell you that they will help take good care of you. After a couple of months, they leave and another worker arrives. Then another one gives you hope that tomorrow will be a better day, because you will be able to eat more food than the day before. Food becomes your future and your comfort."

I listened to Orlando's outpouring in stunned silence. It was true – I could never have envisioned what it was like, along with all these details.

"Every day," Orlando went on, "You look among the hundreds of people, hoping you will see your mother even though you left them lying soaked in blood and covered with flies. Most of the friends you knew in the camp have died from illness. At night when it rains, the wind blows the tent over, leaving you without a roof over your head. When it rains, it becomes cold at night. Every day, children when they don't die from starvation, die died from malaria, or are exposed to other illnesses on the camp. Your comprehensions become poor and you are traumatized. There are over twenty languages spoken in the camp.

"Then you ask yourself, "What is the meaning of war? Why aren't your parents waking up to come meet you? Why are the relief workers coming and going? Why are the people walking up and down the streets? Why are the adults and children crying, when the adults are the ones to comfort the children? They are the caretakers. You ask yourself again: What is that heavy sound that you constantly hear; you stand up on the hill and see the city on fire, and smoke in the air. When is it going to stop? Will there be enough food for the next day? Will the people stop dying, will the people stop travelling? Will there be peace, and will somebody come and take me in to a better place as they have all promised? Will anybody love me? Does anybody even care, and will the heavy sound from the machine gun stop, and will they stop burning those houses?

"You think about when they are going to stop destroying innocent lives like your sister's. Days have gone by, weeks have gone by, months have gone by, and years have gone by. Then you realize that you are twelve years old. Now the reality hits you: that your parents are dead, and you watched your sister die with them. You begin to dream about them. You think that if you were strong enough, you could have saved your sister. Every day and night when it is quiet, you hear her crying in your ears. You begin to think that she is alive and you search for her in the camp, but she cannot be found. At night the wind howls, like a fox; the sound is so scary you can't sleep, because it sounds like your sister.

"How is it possible to find your two-year-old sister among thousands of children, she should be about ten now, you say to yourself. Out of frustration, you refuse your only comfort zone. You decide to leave the camp and go to the city where you will be able to work and live a normal life like any other child. You are now fifteen. In the city, you sleep in the marketplace after the women have left. During the day, you go around shining shoes and cleaning yards. Even at that, you have to be lucky enough, because there are others like you searching for the same opportunities.

"One day, you see a boy your age dressed up in a blue-and-white uniform with black shoes going to school. You shine his shoes and he gives you a centime. That is a little under 10 cents. You fall in love with the school idea, and hope that someday you will be a student no matter what it takes. You have found a new hope, and now you are standing on faith to achieve your dreams. However, you still sleep in the street under the market table hoping and waiting for a miracle.

"One day a middle-aged, man short with a big stomach and looking very mean, walks up to you and tells you to work for him in his house and he wants you to live there with him. He promises to take good care of you. He smiles at you and he sounds very encouraging. You think about the uniformed school boy and embrace the idea, and go with him. You enter a house that you can only see in books, and from up the hill. You wonder and become confused, because you thought that it was never possible for you to be sleeping in a house like this. Since your parents died, you had not been able to eat a proper meal on a table with a spoon and having orange juice and all that... You become a housecleaner for him and his guest. After a week, he tells you that there is a price to pay in order to live in that beautiful house – and the price is not just the cleaning and cooking.

"'Boy, life is about favours. I do you a favour and you do me a favour.' The man is rubbing his big belly.

"'What about school?' you ask him.

"'School is not one of the favours that I am doing for you.'

"The only thing that brought you in that house any way was school, but you agreed to the favour without knowing what it was. Then the man tells you that it should be a secret, that if you tell anyone you will be kicked out or he will take you back to the battlefront to be killed, then your dream of school or leaving the country will never come true. The camp is just at the border of Rwanda.

"'Every activity you see and that has transpired in this house should stay in this house. These are the house rules,' he said.

"You begin to do whatever it is that you were asked to do and it displeases you....horrifies you. You cried but with no tears, you wish that you had died with your parents. In that house, you see all kinds of people entering and leaving. People you only hear about or see on TV, people of all colours working together, sharing one secret. You hear words like 'cool war,' 'weapon,' 'diamond,' 'oil,' 'cigar,' 'shipments,' 'betray.' 'we will show them that we are powerful,' we will finish them all.'.... 'We will kill them all.'

"You can't tell anyone about what you hear or see. You remain very humble with the hope that one day you will be rescued by somebody or anybody. Then you continue to do your task, and pray that somebody comes and promises to take you away from that horrible mansion, from those wicked and heartless people, those child abusers and murderers, and corrupt people who are supposed to work for the people, but are working against the people.

"One Sunday morning, your guardian angel comes and tells you to go purchase something. As you leave the house, he meets you and put some nice clothes on you and takes you away, and far away where nobody can hurt you anymore. Where you will sleep soundly at night without any interruptions. Where you eat and drink and put on good clothes and go to school without a special favour. You find yourself in Canada, a nation with all colours, the land of peace and equality as they say. Then you say to yourself, 'indeed, there will be no freedom without equality.'

"So, French Man, did you imagine well? Before you answer me, let me tell you one more thing. I am the five-year-old boy, and the woman was my mother, and the little girl was my sister. Now tell me, why shouldn't I go to my country Angola, with Zola, who is only doing her work to help my people? She is trying to help make the earth a beautiful place as it was when the Creator created it.

"And you stand here telling me about danger. Yes, Angola is dangerous, and very beautiful as well. You often hear that 'There is no place like home.' I am here, but that's my home. I will make Canada my home when the bloodshed stops. You've got my story; do whatever you want to do with it. They are my people, and they are in need of a protector or someone to stand in the gap for them. I am going to tell you about what happened to Zola and what she did when we were in Angola.

"You wanted a story, I am giving you much story; you don't have to eavesdrop on this. Zola was a phenomenon, she went to all of the displacement camps giving aid to the people… She went and buried mothers and children. Not only that, but babies died in her hands. She then crossed the border and visited all of the nearest refugee camps in the area. She came in contact with a guy called San Tornio in Burundi in the refugee camp, where I used to be. He is a good-looking fellow with a masculine body, tall like me. He looks kind and innocent, but he is a snake. He knows all that runs down at the diamond creek, and he knows the value of all the diamonds. That's all I know about him, but I did see that he never kept his eyes off Zola. Wherever we went, we saw him there. We had nothing to hide, so we were not afraid, but still, it was uncomfortable. According to her, she met San Tornio transacting business in my old house, and she also saw my abuser. She tried to have them reason and compromise. The war has been too long.

"When we got to Luanda from Canada, that afternoon we went to book a room at the Alvalade Hotel, just five minutes' drive away from the airport. But when we got there, strangely enough, they were overbooked and had given our suite away. They had given our suite to an important guest who we later learned was one of the power brokers behind the diamond deal. That was our first disappointment. We later got a place in the Skyna Hotel which is in the heart of Luanda city center. It was very busy; no wonder Zola preferred the previous one. We settled in and we were ready to meet and discuss. We had breakfast and went straight into the boardroom; surprisingly we were all in the same hotel with the opposing leaders.

"Zola stood up in front of those big men and talked to them with courage, and not one flicker of fear in her eyes. She knew that she could reach out to them. She pleaded with the factions involved to think about all the lives that had been destroyed since 1975. According to Roosevelt Franklin 'If civilization is to survive, we must cultivate the science of human relationships – the ability of all peoples, of all kinds, to live together, in the same world at peace.' Life without peace is destruction. You have destroyed your parents, the children are tired and you are also overburdened. The only people who are not tired are those who are supporting you to keep on fighting, supplying the weapons every day to destroy your land. Can you look at Europe and how well they have united, and the stronger continental government they have made themselves? We as Africans should be fighting to come together as one and build Africa; the option is ours. Either we unite or keep on perishing.

"The world is watching a non-fiction war movie between gorillas and elephants leaving behind no grass. Almost one hundred years ago, Henry Sylvester William was a lawyer who used his intelligence and skill and fought for the black liberation. July 23, 24, 25, of 1900, he founded the first Pan-African conference in the city of London. He stood in the midst of the Europeans and challenged racism, socio-economic status of the black people all over the world. And he was very specific as to what the blacks should do in order to win the war of enslavement and segregation.

"William also invited W. E. B. Du Bois to join him and fight for the liberty and justice for the black race. Unfortunately, William died in his early fifties, but Du Bois was left to continue the fight for the survival of every black man in the world, with the belief that all Africans should have a neutral ground to come together in one unity. Robert N. Sobukwe joined forces and fought a war without a sword. Dr. Martin Luther King also led a war without bloodshed. As you can see, Madiba, he compromised his love for peace. We are Pan-Africans, let us say no to bloodshed and say yes to embrace togetherness. Do you remember the 1961 war? Do you realize that this is 1998 and still there is war in Angola?

"I had no idea she spoke Portuguese, then I heard her say, '*parar o derramamento de sangue e vamos trabalhar juntos para construir África*. (Stop the bloodshed and let us work together to build Africa.) For how long will you allow others to profit themselves through your effort or take what is rightfully yours? As long as they are receiving the diamonds, they will help you kill your brothers, your own mothers' sons. They don't care about whether we lived, or died. They need somewhere to keep shipping those leftover cold war weapons. It is time for us to have one voice and save our beautiful land. It is time to lay the commotion aside and look forward. It is time for peace like a fountain to flow down the earth for all man. As we dismiss from here today, let us remember that it is time for change. The late JFK often said that change is the law of life, and those who look only to the past or present are certain to miss the future. Let us be wise not to miss out on the future.'

"Zola finished, and then they agreed to meet again in the Congo after a month. They saw her getting in the way of something. You might think that the conference back in December was just a group of students coming together to have fun, but it was no fun. The message behind it was enough to shake the African leaders. It time for unity and no more bloodshed. Zola is nothing like you. You should be happy that you are here in Canada, François. If you knew what I'm talking about, you would understand why we had to go to Angola."

"It is okay, I really do understand, Amigo." I was standing there confused, praying that he would stop talking. But he couldn't; he kept on talking. I promised myself that this was going to be my last story.

"Right after the meeting in Luanda City, we decided to go to the displacement camps and refugee centers. There are countless charitable organizations over there; it is not everyone who takes pleasure in seeing innocent people suffering. Zola visited all of them one at a time. She believed that we could reach out to them, and she could not wait to meet with them in Congo. Nearly everywhere we went, that diamond boy was there, the surveillance without border.

"Our time was up and we had to leave. When we arrived in Kinshasa, we all booked at the same hotel again. We were happy, because right after the meeting, we were leaving for Canada. We all met according to plan. They all spoke given different terms and conditions, then Zola concluded with a paragraph why they should end the war again:

"'From 1961 up to the present, this conflict has had consequences for all mankind in the world, which has left the people of Angola with post-traumatic disorder, when Innocent babies are still being killed. It is very horrible. We are all facing the consequences of this war; first of all, we are tired, and exhausted," she said. Secondly, the war has destroyed everyone, including you. The war has completely changed our lives and perspective of things. Is the way of life hate or is the way of life love? The war is going on, and it has left us all broken in pieces. For the past weeks, I saw things that I could not have imagined. It has damaged us physically, mentally and emotionally. You guys need to stop. Open your eyes, open your ears, and make a decision with your mind and heart. This is about our beautiful African earth that is being pulled down. I have spent a little over a month here and it has not been an easy challenge for me. Some of you grew up in this. We need to love each other, not kill each other. Only love can lead us to the way.'

"They talked and they all sounded positive, exchanging handshakes. Then later on that night after dinner, a general from the opposing faction wanted to talk to her, though she did not tell me. She was to be in the lobby, but when I went there looking for her, she was not to be found. I sat there waiting on her, but she did not return. In fact, no one saw her in the lobby that night. They must have taken her away. I never left the lobby. As I was sitting there worried, I got a call to contact her family in Canada.

I was shaking and speechless. "Thank God for the peacemakers, and everyone's prayers were answered. She is back and alive."

Orlando got through talking and he took his car keys to leave. He did not take even a sip of beer. As it was when the waitress brought it, so it was when they took it back. I tried to council him but he walked away. "Amigo, I am sorry for your loss. Please forgive me," I said.

"Hey, François, I am a survivor, and I am my brother's keeper. Every chance that will be given me, I will take it and run with it until change can happen. It is all right, we all need to work together and help the others," Orlando said. "How is Ali?" he asked.

"Not good," I told him. "I am on my way to see him."

"Give him my love; I will drop by tomorrow or so," Orlando said.

We departed and I went home feeling guilt and heartbreak.

Chapter Twenty

True to the spirit that seemed to give her strength, Zola was back at work sooner than expected. She kept herself busy to the extent that we hardly talked or saw each other.

Orlando had been working directly with her since the trip. This was a good idea, as it meant he could keep his eyes on her. Sayba asked me to keep close eyes on Zola as well, for she was quickly distracted. Zola was not being rational with many things, and she refused to see a psychiatrist or a psychologist. She had just come from a lecture when I gave her a call to ask her to check on Boss as his condition was getting worse. She did not answer the phone and she was in the office. I checked on him and felt the urge to go over and see her.

I called Ben many times, but he was not answering his phone. I left message after message for him but he wouldn't return my calls. He had wanted me to move to Europe two years earlier, which was not possible. I told him: "Aunt May, my company, and Zola are all here, Ben…why don't you come to Canada?" He told me that I was double-minded and greedy. I had never looked at it that way. Ben had nothing to offer me. I was on my way to Japan, thinking I should take a little break from work and go see Ben. But since I had not heard from him, I went to New York instead.

Business was great, and we had just opened an office in Japan with four big business partners so I was very excited. I thought about Boss, then I felt sad. He was not going to be around to enjoy the success unless we found an organ donor. It took two to toot a glass, and I had no one to toot with, so there went my celebration. I was unable to celebrate when I thought about Boss. Zola still believed that God was coming through, but since she got home, she was not as energetic as she used to be.

I spent two days in New York just to relax myself a little. As I was walking around the city, I came across a lady with twin baby boys. I didn't know what came over me, but I did a strange thing. I walked right up to her, and greeted the boys. In a way, I felt love for her babies, and I wished that they were mine. Then I thought of Zola. If she had not wasted her time on Nathan, she would have had children of her own.

"Hey, how are you, and those adorable babies?" I said to the woman. "My girlfriend and I are thinking about having kids soon." It felt good lying, but was that necessary? "They are cute, and you are very blessed."

"Their father did not want them," she said. "He was happy when I told him that I had an abortion. I am glad that I kept them. He really doesn't know that I had them."

"Can I touch them?"

"Sure you can."

"What are their names?"

"Nathaniel and Jonathan," she answered. "I'm here to open an account for them."

"Are you from around here?"

"No! I'm from Canada," she said.

"What a coincidence – I am from Canada as well."

"I am from Mississauga," she said. "I work in downtown Toronto. Nice to meet you."

"Here, take my card. If you ever need help with anything or with the kids, call us, and my girlfriend and I will gladly help you." I handed over a ten-thousand-dollar cheque.

"Glory!" she said, and then I saw her quickly put the cheque in her bag with joy. "Is this a mistake, Sir? Did you really mean to give me this? Thank you! Thank you, and may God richly bless you."

She did not stand around to chat. I had to run after her with Zola's card. "Feel free to stop by any time…" Even at that, she did not hear me.

Seeing those babies had changed me. Something had happened to me and I could not understand it. *Zola cannot know about this*, I told myself. Zola had just gone to see Boss when I spoke to the doctor. Could those kids be Nathan's? No! Not possible. Besides, I needed her to be there for Boss, so it was better leaving her out of it. I was not going to disturb her mind about Nathan anymore; he was history. And she had seriously warned me to back off, or she was moving out of Ontario. "No more bad news," I told myself.

On my way to the hotel, I met my "secret admirer" again. This time, he was telling me something more than just cute. "So, your guy is getting married today, hmmm?" he said as he gave me a bottle of beer.

Was that a question or was he telling me something that I did not know about? "Who is getting married?" I asked him.

"We all saw him on TV, with his partner, in the Europe parade."

I was lost, and had no clue what he was talking about.

"Ben, your partner, of course," he said.

I left for the hotel. I did not know what was happening to me, but I saw my whole life before me. And suddenly, I heard myself talking. I could not hold back my tears; I became very emotional and lost. "Oh God, help me... If you choose not to, I do understand. She had been there for me all the way and all I had done was to reject her. I had been a little boy all along whose brain had been blown away by the wind and who is left with an empty skull."

"I am lost. I don't know what I want. Help me find my way back home, please, God." I didn't know how to even pray. I knew that I was crying bitterly. Just when I entered the lobby, I saw a handsome gentleman sitting with one of the waitresses standing over him working. It appeared as if he was waiting for her to finish her job, so they could leave together. I did not understand a word from their conversation, but it seemed very intense. I went a little closer, but I still did not hear them. But as the girl worked, her boyfriend or fiancé sat there keeping her company.

Every time she talked, he would clap his hands with laughter. He gave her his total attention. One at a time, her workmates came out to introduce themselves. I saw her laughing as she talked. I saw chemistry between them, of a kind that made me think only God could make such a thing possible. Their blood vessels were being controlled by each other. It was obvious they were in love. Then I asked myself if it was possible for me to have fallen in love like that. Did God want me to fall in love with Him like that, before loving myself or anyone else? I did not have answers.

I had money of my own, and my parents had been successful business owners. All of that money was in the bank, but I was not happy. It had felt so good, though, giving to the mother and twin babies.

My parents were nice people as I had often heard, and they did not deserve to die that young. I was not sure about my Aunt May; she did nothing with her life except to take care of me. She did not want to get married. She had put her life on hold to take care of me. Was she angry that she had had to do that?

But that was not important now; it was the love of God that I was now longing for. I wanted to be in love just like those two couples. It was the cry of my heart. I fooled myself and everyone around me. "Was I really in love with Ben, or had I used him?"

On the plane back to Toronto, I thought about many things. My life was all a lie. I was living a lie, and Ben had been there at the right time to help me. Ben had not come to Canada for a long time and I was paying for his mortgage, but he was still working double, according to him. Before leaving for Japan, I sent him some money to take care of some personal things. With Ben, it was always the same. The more money I gave him, the more he wanted. But that was all over now. I was done with him. Nathan didn't want Zola, and I was in love with Zola. It felt great saying it: "Yes, I am in love with Zola!" I screamed to myself on the plane. I was just going to be bold with her, I told myself. I hoped she would accept me. When I got off the plane, I called Zola...but she told me to stay away from her.

She was still not handling things properly since she got back from Africa, and she was breaking down slowly. Something was eating her up, and she still refused to speak out. It was like somebody else had taken her over. With her experiences in Africa and the disunity among the black people, she was hurting, and I was hurting for her.

Zola would often go into the washroom either vomiting or crying. She wanted to talk to someone who understood her, and at that point, she thought less of me as a person. I did not understand. I could not understand. There was nothing that I could do for her at that point.

It was urgent that I go to New York for a day. I hated leaving, but I had to. Before leaving, she had called Mr. Zulu.

Zola said, "Dr. Kwame said that the people and the nation are the same. If they are, Mr. Zulu, then why are they destroying each other?

"He saw it coming from afar; that was why he wanted the African continent to unite, to come together under one flag, but they have allowed outsiders to bring division among them. They can't even reason with each other.

"We have the blessing with all the natural resources you can think of. How impossible it is for Africa which has so many resources and so much talented brain power, to miss out on the opportunities of surviving?" Zola asked Mr. Zulu to give her an answer.

I was not able to help her, and it killed my soul. At least she was able to turn to Mr. Zulu for help.

The hospital called to let us know that it was not good with Boss. It was time for us to say good bye and Zola was still not composed since she came back from Angola. So she was in her own world again. Going to Africa was not a good idea, but everyone looked at me as if I was heartless. The war in Angola, Liberia, Bosnia, was all the same. War was war and blood got mixed-up with dust from what man was created from.

If the ground could have, it would have spilled out every bit of blood that it had drunk. War was caused by greed and power, one man wanting everything for himself. For over thirty years the Angolans had been fed with heavy machine-guns leaving them with empty skulls. But for Zola, it was not about who to blame now. It was about peace and reconciliation. She thought that it was a wakeup call and there was someone ready to answer the call. She had contacted hidden hands to stop the weapons-distribution in Angola. She put herself in more danger than she needed to be.

"One of the warring factions made a statement that took her to Angola. He said that when elephants fight, it is the grass that suffers. And her reply to him was, "Even the elephants need the grass to survive."

When she told me that she was going to Angola, I thought that she had lost her mind. She pulled every string that she could and was on the next plane to Angola. She kept speaking against war and the aftermath. "They speak peace, they teach peace, they even show peace, but they don't practise peace," she said in one of her speeches.

The media began focusing on her, which worried me. But everyone told me to stop my childish behaviour: "François, life is short. Say and do what you want to before it is too late." It was nearly a year ago that she knew a lady that was blown up on the bridge…actually a little over a year.

I went to visit her and she was watching the news on CNN when the Somalis were burning the US flag out of frustration. I wanted to talk to her, but she was constantly watching the news. We got into an argument and Nathan's name came up:

"Somalia is swimming in blood and you are talking to me about what Nathan did?" she asked me. "That country is the most dangerous place to be today. Do you listen to the news at all? Do you see how many of them are dying and how many of them are living in refugee camps around the world?"

"Zola, I can't stop it, and you can't, either. Unfortunately, the world is becoming more interested in bad news than the good news, but there are still good things happening in the world, you know," I told her.

Zola seemed very offended by my statement. She slammed the door behind her as she hurried to give a speech at the Stephen Biko University in Oakville. Zola, the girl who was once cheerful and filled with life now gradually fading away; she had changed. She seemed unable to pull herself together.

I knew that I had huge responsibilities with Boss, Zola and the company. I was confused, and did not know what to do. I had once said that she was not a politician, but she had become one overnight. She had been a member of an organization and they had elected her their leader. Zola advised international students in North America to fertilize their roots. She encouraged them to keep their heads up, not diverting from their roots.

To the refugees she said, "Today, you have found yourself in a foreign country as refugees or immigrants. But remember, this is only a place of refugees and leisure. You are the future leaders; you are the keys to the heart of Africa. You are hope, and Africa needs you to rise up again. Africa needs you for reinforcement. Africa needs you to survive. You are the cornerstone and the pillar that hold our powerful and great continent together. The elephant destroys the grass, but the rain will fall and the grass will flourish again. The elephant needs the grass for food."

Right after that speech, I went to see her, but she would not see me. There were never secrets between Zola and me, but I guess there is a first time for everything. I walked in on her talking to the President, but as soon as she saw me, she quickly hung up the phone.

"Hey François, this is confidential—do you mind?" she said.

I had to leave. And she went on. Talking to people who understood the problem was the right thing to do, but I did not like feeling like an outsider.

I remember going over to her house to sign some papers, and I overheard Maa telling her that she couldn't hide forever, except if she did not care or love them. I assume that they were talking about me and my Aunt May, but when she saw me again, she told me to take the papers over to the office.

I remember her telling me that if they knew that she was alive, they would have looked for her and their prayers would be answered. Then she asked me to give my opinion on a quote that I had no knowledge of. Even if I had given her my opinion, it was never going to be enough. She was living her life on quotes now, mixing up work with speeches. She had papers lying around the house in the office. She became a very troubled girl. She seemed to be living in another world. Thank God she had Sayba who understood the problems and was there to cover for her.

Sayba had given me a call one afternoon, that Zola wanted me to look at something, but when I walked in the office, she began talking as if she was losing her mind. At least that's what I thought.

"This is what he was talking about, François; if they were united, they would have achieved an excellent greatness. It is not too late, they can still make it if they try. I believe in my heart that they can come together and make Africa a better continent. They can make it one of the strongest in the world; God has already blessed the African nation with everything. They need to make their decisions wisely and with full knowledge. They need to stand together – that's the only way."

Then she asked me to turn my cell phone off. I could not do that. Boss was lying on his deathbed, and I was waiting on the Arabian prince to give me the name of a potential heart donor. "Please turn your phone off and listen to me for one second," she said.

One second was not what she was asking for. Zola started with Africa again.

"Zola, for real, you need to stop this madness before you drag yourself back into the hospital." I had to pray to be interrupted by anybody, somebody.

Luckily for me, Sayba walked into the office and told me that she was cancelling all of her appointments for the day: "I am very concerned about her, François; it has been like that since she came back. If you are not on my side, I will advise the two of you to leave," she stormed in on us in the office talking about her.

"I am all yours, Sweetie," I told her. I had to listen to one of Dr. Nkrumah's speeches:

"'My countrymen, the task ahead is great indeed, and heavy is the responsibility. And yet it is a noble and glorious challenge, a challenge which calls for the courage to dream, the courage to believe, the courage to dare, the courage to do, the courage to envision, the courage to fight, the courage to work, the courage to achieve, to achieve the highest excellences and the fullest greatness of man.' These were Dr. Nkrumah's words. Unfortunately, Angola had not been able to test that dream," she said.

"Zola, my love, this is really something that he meant for the people at that time; it has nothing to do with you. You can't keep going on repeating yourself," I told her. It was not healthy for her. She was excessively offended by my response. I did understand that she wanted to connect to her African roots. I would do the same if I had to, but this girl was driving herself crazy. Her obsession with Africa was not ending anytime soon. She took it too hard and too far. In high school, it was about saving it and making it one of the best schools in the world. But now, I am not sure any more.

I arranged for her to see a doctor, because she needed professional help. Just as I thought, she did exactly what I was afraid of all along. Thank God that it later works together for good. She was giving a speech at Biko University, and she took with her the wrong paper. Instead of an inspirational speech, she gave them a lesson on conspiracy in the most secret place which is the mind. When she realized it, it was too late. For the occasion, it was wrong, but many people testified that they were blessed to have heard the speech. But it all made sense to me later.

The speech: "There are conspiracies that exist in the world and today I am going to warn you about some and how you can overcome them. The deception operates in your mind, and the mind of your brother. It is only found in secret high places, its goal is: 'Destruction'.

"It tells you that you are not superior enough, and you will never excel. You are not pretty and you will never be accepted in the class of beauty. You are awkward in the society, and you will never be profitable in anything you lay your hands on. It limits your ability to function as a human. It tells you that you didn't meet the requirements to hold a membership in one of your favourite clubs. It tells you that you lacked knowledge, wisdom and understanding which make you disabled. It takes control of your body and gives you low self-esteem. It plays with your emotions and damages your mind. Then it leaves you broken and isolated, and then you become your own enemy. It steals your mind and makes you accept all of the lies it has made you believe. You finally become an island without even a coconut.

"The next conspiracy takes hold of your brother and gives him power over you. This time, its intention is to destroy you completely. It gives him the power to rule over you, the power to take away your position, the power to control your life; you become inferior to your brother. Your brother pays the price by becoming greedy and corrupt leaving him in egoism. The more he sees, the more he will be in want. The only way for survival is through supernatural wisdom," Zola said to the students.

She said that the students were all looking at themselves, but she did not pay any attention to their body language. She continued, "The enemy is real, and he is on this beautiful planet. But I tell you the truth: you must be prepared and alert at all times, to fight the battle that we face in this world today. Prepare yourselves by educating yourselves, and not allowing the enemy to take the best of you. Remember, you are not alone.

"Search wisdom and you will find it. Search knowledge, and you will find it. Search understanding and you will find it. When you do, and if you do, then you are ready for change. Change will happen only when you are ready. Remember that change is the development of life. The only identity I have of myself is this: I belong to the almighty God, not the devil. Evil is in our midst, but do not be afraid of it, but stay away from evil. Be strong and do not lose focus. Be ready to run the race, because he is smart and very wise as well, but you are smarter. Even though he lies and cheats, do not quit, do not give up, and do not leave the finish line until you are finished.

"Do not worry, you have greater power in you, and you are as wise as anyone can be in this world. You will overcome the many conspiracies in this world. You have the power to change whatever you want to change within you. You have the power to change what the world thinks about you. You can change the negative things that they have fed your mind with. Remember – in math, subtracting a negative gives a positive, which is equal to change.

"Ladies and Gentlemen, call for help and get out of the valley before you get run over. Walk in the present through the problems, not in the past with the problems. No mountain is too high and no valley is too low. You have what it takes to win, and run with it. Remember, love is the only way."

Chapter Twenty-one

To hear the woman you love beating herself up and crying that I would not understand and that it was my fault...it does something terrible to a man, surely to any feeling human. When I called Zola that afternoon, I felt myself becoming more and more confused and panicked – and longing to drive the hurt and accusation from her soul.

I did not even ask her what she was talking about. For the first time in my life I thought that Nathan could be of good courage. But he was nowhere to be found. I was far away from home; there was nothing I could have done from my position but to return home immediately. Zola sounded very bitter and confused on the phone. She was in trouble, and I was afraid that she was going right back to the hospital. She called and left an urgent message for Maa, but unfortunately, Maa was not home. Zola left a message that it was urgent that Maa find her.

She decided to go to Aunt May's instead. Maa got her first cell phone, but she never took it anywhere with her. It was often left on her dressing-table; she said that it was too big for her to carry. Zola often complained about this.

The receptionist at the shelter recognized the sadness in her voice, she later told the press. Zola called Aunt May telling her that she was not feeling well. Aunt May volunteered to pick her up but Zola refused, telling her that she would be right over. Luckily for me, there were no delays; I got home earlier than expected.

I entered the house and ran to Aunt May, crying on her shoulders to help me to get Zola. "Aunt May, she doesn't love me anymore, and she is not even speaking to me. It hurts, Aunt May; you have to help me get her to love me."

"But, Sweetheart, I thought you are gay – what happened?"

"Yes, I am! No, I was; it really doesn't matter what I am. I want to be with Zola, because I've realized that I can't live without her."

"Son, you are going to have to fix this on your own," she told me.

"Zola is the only woman for me. You have been right all along, Aunt May, and it might be too late."

"I hate to say that I told you so."

"Then don't say it, but I don't mind if you tell me. I messed up bad; I hope and pray that she forgives me…and that God will forgive me too."

"Don't worry, Son," said Aunt May. "Zola is on her way over here. Tell her exactly how you feel."

We were sitting waiting for her arrival, when my phone rang. It was Mr. Zulu. He was on the next flight to Canada, but before I had the chance to talk to him, he hung up. He had sounded very urgent.

"That was Mr. Zulu, he will be arriving in Canada by morning."

"What for?" Aunt May asked.

"I am not sure, but he said that he felt it in his spirit all along." I was happy, because he was going to help me remind Zola of the great time we had in high school. Besides he always told us that he had a dream and saw us getting married. The timing was great, and I could not have been any happier.

As we were sitting there watching the evening news, some breaking news came on from Indonesia. A tsunami had taken over an island there, and we suddenly saw Ben… *Ben* being washed away in to the sea! My heart tore, and I screamed. "Is that Ben?"

We cried together. "No, it is someone that resembles him," I said. "I spoke to him, not too…not too long…thank God – I mean, no, God, no – let it be a dream."

Then Aunt May said, "I told Ben to stand far away from the wave so it wouldn't take him with it, but he did not listen to me. If he had, and even though it was heavy, it wouldn't have taken him."

I could not believe my ears. "Stop comments like that. Don't you care?" I took the phone and called his sister, just in case I was wrong. Eyes can be deceitful sometimes. She was bitterly crying, telling me that Ben went to get married. A couple of days earlier, I had sent him some money; he had told me nothing about marriage. I was in complete shock. I told his sister that I had not seen him for nearly two years – also that I had been telling him I was busy with work and that Aunt May needed me around.

"Will you be going to bury him?" asked Aunt May.

"How can you ask me such a question, Aunt May? Is there a body, to be buried? You saw him going into the sea, didn't you?" I screamed at her out of frustration. "I am sorry, Aunt May, but this is not right. I am just confused right now. Yes…if there should be any memorial service, I will go."

"No, you can't," she said firmly. "The dead will have to bury the dead; you have work to do."

"Aunt May, I wonder sometimes which of the planets you came from! Animals have no soul but Ben had a soul. Who are you, Aunt May? You knew him from Mandela High."

"All I am trying to say is that God is depending on you to make this right," she said. "You can't let him down any longer than you have done. It is time to let the world see that there is a Jerusalem in you."

"Stop using the Lord's name in vain, Aunt May. "You claim that you love the Bible, but you don't practise what it says. Ben is…was God's creation with a heart."

I didn't know what had come over her, and it was not funny.

It was nearly 10 pm and Zola had not yet reached home. I was beginning to worry, and then the doorbell rang – but it was Maa with some food for Zola. "Hey *Fei Zi* (Fat Boy), what's cooking?"

"Great, Maa, but I am not fat any longer."

"Where is she, and why is your face so sad?" she asked.

"I have not seen her, Maa, and Ben is dead, but I love Zola."

"What, how, what killed him?" Maa asked, horrified.

"We just saw the sea swallow him up," I told her.

"God rest his soul. He was a fine young man, and very respectful. He had his whole life ahead of him. It is truly sad." Maa's response to Ben's death was what I needed to hear. It was very comforting. I was glad to hear those words from Maa. Ben had had some tough times in his life, only to die overnight… Indeed, he was a fine young man.

I was still standing at the door talking with Maa, when the phone rang. It was Zola's neighbour; she was telling me that there were some strangers around the house. Since mid-day she was trying to get a hold of Zola, but there was no answer and Sayba said that Zola did not work. She did not drive by the office all day. "We are a lovely community, and we want to keep it this way."

"Okay Ms. Jackson, thanks for the information. I will be right over."

"Maa, Zola is not here and there are some strange men patrolling around her house. I am going over there to check on things. "Something is not right! It has been five hours since she called to say that she was on her way here, but she has not arrived."

My phone rang again. It was a friend of mine telling me about Ben's death. Then it could not stop ringing. Everyone saw that Ben had been swallowed by the ocean waves.

The night wasn't getting any better. I began thinking that Zola was missing. These thoughts alone made me feel extremely uncomfortable. I had to pull myself together but I did not know how. Natasha and Sayba had not seen her either.

"Look guys, no need to panic, she is fine, she will be here soon," said Maa. I left to check on her house; there was no evidence of a break-in, but definitely there were men wearing black in the community. I called her again, and she did not pick up. At that point, I began to feel really ill. I was also thinking about Ben and life in general.

"Something terribly wrong…this is what happens when the world turns?" It was my question, but I could not answer it. I had to pull myself together.

Maa was calm, but she was worried at the same time.

"If this is the time to call on God to come down, will he really listen to a sinner like me?" I wondered. "Ben is no more and Zola is missing…what is there to pray for? What words would God want me to use?" It was a long day and the day was not ending anytime soon.

I suddenly heard Pastor Fred's fatherly voice in my ears. "Son, always remember that before you make it to Sunday, you will have to struggle through the rest of the six days. Sunday is the day of delivery and rejoicing."

It came to me that I had struggled all my life and I was still struggling. "I'm going to give up now, or fight to Sunday? Oh, Ben, poor Ben. Oh, God, please rest his soul in peace, and cover Zola with your feathers of protection." Zola was alive and I could fight to make it up to her. It was 12:00 am and she was not home.

Maa was still home when I got there. She looked at me in anguish, but I suggested that she go home just in case Zola might show up there. I missed a couple of calls from the Government of Canada; I was not sure what it was about. Also, when I was in her house, I noticed many calls coming in from them.

"Was Zola in some kind of trouble or what?" Aunt May asked me.

"I believe so…" I said. I didn't want to jump to any conclusions, even though the evidence was right before me.

Zola had never been the kind of girl who would break the law. She was straight and clean. The Prime Minister was her friend – and I was not talking about the South African President. Zola's own life depended on it. She was a good citizen, and she devoted her time to the community as well. Everybody loved Zola. She was the one who gave me strength, but I never told her. She encouraged and promoted multiculturalism in Canadian society – and made a difference. Zola was not just anybody; she was everybody, and a phenomenal woman.

I drove her grandmother home and came back. It was 2:00 am eastern time. It was summer and the weather was beautiful. The moon was shining with many stars in the sky. It would get quite cold at night, and that was one of my worries if she was out there somewhere. I was still waiting for a word but we were kept in the dark. Pastor Fred did not see her at choir practice that night, so he had called earlier to check on her.

At 5:00 am that morning, Fred's wife called to tell me that she had had a dream and Zola was all right. She also told me that something big was about to happen. "But it is nothing to worry about. There is danger, but it will pass over her. I would tell you to read Psalm 91, but you stopped believing in the Bible a long time ago."

"Oh no, I meant yes! I will read it. I do believe; please pray for me," I begged.

"Oh François," she said. "We have never stopped praying for you. Get some sleep and we will talk in the morning."

Sleep was not what I needed. I needed my life back and Zola was my life. If she was around, she would have told me that I never knew the importance of the rain forest until I travelled to the Sahara Desert. She was nowhere to be found.

It was morning and the doorbell rang. I rushed and opened it thinking that she was the one. It was Mr. Zulu, along with what seemed like many secret agents and government officials. "Where is the princess?" he asked.

"She did not come home yesterday. Why are you here and what is going on?"

"Did she tell you where she was going? When did you last see her or speak to her? Give me the names of her friends and their phone numbers. Is there anywhere you think she might have gone? Do you know who might want to harm her? Has she been behaving strangely lately?"

"You are not making sense, Mr. Zulu," I told him.

No, he was not making sense; none of the questions made any sense. I had no idea what was going on, but he seemed to assume that I knew.

"Don't you know?" he asked.

"Know what?" Aunt May responded quickly.

"We show hope and pray that they have not gotten to her," said Mr. Zulu.

"They... The people followed her into Canada?" Aunt May asked.

"Before you tell us anything, Maa Huan Yue is on her way," I told them.

My house was surrounded by cops and secret agents. Zola's home was also taken over by the same people. Then I remembered my Pastor's wife telling me of the dream she had. "Oh, my God, she's been kidnapped, Aunt May...she was on her way over here when they took her away. She is very important to the African people. We have to find her!"

Mr. Zulu was on the phone with the Canadian Interpol agency. Their suspicions were right. "She should not have gone to Angola; I told my princess that," said Mr Zulu.

"Who is Angola?" Aunt May asked."

"Angola is in Africa, where she went last spring," I answered quietly, so she would stop asking silly questions.

"Where was Zola taken?" she asked again.

"Aunt May, "I said, "we need you to be still for a moment, please!"

Everyone talked together.

"What is the matter? We need to know what can of trouble she got herself into, and she sure knows how to pretend. The Bible says – "

"We don't want the Bible to talk now, please, Aunt May. This is serious."

She was still eager to talk. "What is in the dark will come to light."

Then Mr Zulu responded: "Not in this case, Mother. Please stop using the Bible in vain."

"She can be like that sometimes – please forgive her."

Aunt May was not giving them a chance to do their work. I had to stop her, or she was going to keep going. "The Prime Minister said that we should leave it as calm as possible until she is found.

"The media can't get on this story until she is found."

Mr. Zulu turned to talk to one of the agents. "It is too late; the BBC news is covering the story." The agent walked to the television to turn it on.

"Which story? Has Zola become a story again?" I asked Mr. Zulu.

"Yes! She is a big story; she is the story for the people."

He asked for the remote-control. Aunt May was sitting waiting for Christian author/speaker Joyce Meyer to come on. "No, I don't have BBC on my television, you have to go in his room; this TV has only TBN." Aunt May was holding onto the remote.

"Aunt May, we do not have time for TBN or any drama right now, so please turn the TV on." I took over the remote.

When we switched to the BBC channel, they were talking about Africa's lost treasure who was going to be the queen of the new continental government, and she was in Canada. The African Union president was on the news thanking the Canadians for the life of their Princess Zola. She was the headline news on every continent around the world. She was once the breaking news, but not like this. This was different. A whole continent's unity depended on her; she was the one who was going to lead the African people to the Heart of Africa.

"What?" asked Aunt May. The daughter of the Pan-Africans – who told them that? Will Africa come together and become one? It is impossible. The Africans are killing each other and they almost killed her. Why would Zola go back there and become their queen?" When Aunt May asked her questions, I looked at her then turned my face away.

The Secretary General of the United Nations was on the news telling the African Nations that Zola was fine, and she was indeed the treasure that the Africans had been looking for. "She is a bright, brave and courageous girl, as we are all aware of her recent experience in Angola, which she is still recovering from. Her contribution to the Canadian government has been great, and she is a very sweet young lady. Zola Elizabeth Fatima Ngomaloma is doing very well.

"I was just on the line with the Canadian government. This is incredible news for us all. They will get to the public as soon as possible. Today is a day of rejoicing for peacemakers. I had interacted with this young lady and I had no idea she was the one in question. We have done a complete background check and we know that she is the one for the throne. As the Secretary General for the United Nations, I am asking you to lay down your weapons and rejoice, for your princess has been found, and she is coming home."

When you think about home, you think about rest.
Peace and quietness,
When you hear laughter and joy
Is where you love and give
But you also see tears, and then you see unity to dry the tears.
Home is where the heart longs to be. People can help you get a home, but people can't give you a home. Home is where you put your heart.

"Wait a minute, is Zola an African?" Aunt May asked as if she was disappointed.

"Yes!" Mr. Zulu answered.

"But she...is a good girl...so why does she go and get herself in trouble?" Aunt May asked again.

"Please, Aunt May, for real, good people are always in trouble. It is not what she did, but who she is that put her in trouble," Mr. Zulu said.

Aunt May stood up and began walking around. "Africa is always in trouble."

"We need you to stop interrupting us or you will have to go up to your room," I warned. "Maybe you should go up to your room now; we don't need you to analyze the situation. We will call you if need comes to be. If we need a technician we will let you know," I told her.

"This is not good for Canada," said one of the agents. "The Canadians have had Zola for all her life, and when this incredible story comes up, now they lose her." He stared out the window. "Let us pray that she is all right. Every African country that is represented in Canada showed its concern and love for the princess.

The Afro Fest was just a week earlier, and most of the guests were still around. The city of Toronto was still jam-packed with visitors. As I was sitting thinking, Mr. Zulu asked if she was at the festival.

"Yes, she was a speaker there," I told them. Zola had again shocked the world. This time around she was called "hope"; she was going to be a real peacemaker, unlike in Angola. It reminded me of the time Mr. Zulu told us that he would call her a "shaker of the tree".

"Zola has never wronged a soul, so who would want to harm her?" I asked Mr. Zulu. "She is the daughter of Africa and a peacemaker. Many people, it seems, want to stop peace from happening. She is the Redeemer's child with a great brain like that of her forefathers."

Pan-Africa goes way back to the late 1800's. There have been many controversies among the leaders of Africa and philosophers, and they have come to the agreement that Africa will only make a stronger continent when they come together, as a continental government. This decision was not arrived at overnight, trust me. My princess will fight corruption and she will never trade lives for weapons. Corruption is a difficult subject to discuss, because even those that speak against it are corrupt. They will try to stop her from sitting on the throne."

"Which throne?" Aunt May asked. "Mr. Zulu, for real, who are they?"

"We need to find her, that's what we should worry about for now," said Mr. Zulu.

My comprehension of the whole story was poor, and my auntie was not making it any easier for me. We were waiting for Maa Huan Yue to hear what Mr. Zulu had to say. Mr. Zulu sat us down and began explaining the situation to us.

Chapter Twenty-two

Before Mr. Zulu had said very much, one of the agents rushed into the house. They had found Zola in the flower bush at the back of my house. She was unconscious. They used the back door to bring her into the house. She was cold and had developed a high fever. According to the agent, we had to keep things as calm as possible – and we had to keep pretending that she was safe at home.

The neighbour had called the TV station and told them that Zola might be missing. When we brought her into the house, we put her on the sofa and sent for the doctor. Zola was weak and helpless. I sat next to her and held her close to me until the doctor came. She held tight on to me and would not let go; she definitely was not the Zola I knew. We were about to call the paramedics, but the doctor arrived and said that he could treat her at home.

After two hours of our keeping her warm, she finally said her first words, "Nobody loves me, and *he* is after me."

The doctor told me to keep talking to her so she would come back. "Oh Zola, my first love, if only you could open your eyes… Let me pour my heart out to you. I am ready to take you as my wife and cherish you for the rest of our lives. I promise that you will never be alone… Forgive me for neglecting you."

"No!" everyone said together. "Do not remind her of the negatives."

"Okay, Doc, I will try," I told him. "Zola, I realize that I love you. People travel miles away to buy, when they can get better quality next door. That's like what I did…It might be too late for us, but please give me a chance, Zola…give me a chance to love you."

Maa arrived. Mr. Zulu said , "My beautiful Grandmother, how have you been?

Maa smiled. "Tǎ jiǎng bèi fákuǎn" (Do not worry, she will be fine).

Mr. Zulu hugged Maa and gave her his seat. She was confused by what she saw, and actually had seen some paparazzi at her house. Luckily for her, Ms. Lavender was on time to answer the questions. Dressed in crème and purple, she was prepared for the occasion as usual, even though she was very worried about Zola's safety.

Maa walked in just when Mr. Zulu was explaining the story. "So, tell me what's cooking?" she asked him.

"I have come to save the African Queen. That girl has not been composed since she got back, so please take care of her," Maa said.

Miss Lavender was worried, but she was also enjoying the moment of attention. She was always around, and we were blessed to have her with us.

"Okay! I will tell you about the present before going into the past. Do you guys remember the trip she took to Africa? Well, she made a great impact on the opposition... Indeed, they are tired and they are ready to lay down their weapons. As you know this, they said that she is too much of a trustworthy person. In today's world, when you are blameless, people don't seem to trust you. Apparently, they still think that she was there on a mission apart from volunteering. So far, she proved it by not remaining quiet.

"She has asked questions and stopped a lot of things from happening. They are monitoring every move she makes; she has become a threat and she must be stopped, otherwise they will go out of business. At one of the universities, one of the Rwandan refugees spotted someone there who they think should not be anywhere in Canada among refugees. She reported the matter to the police, and he is being watched as we speak. According to the girl, this guy was bad news. Because of him, many native Gbantu lost their lives. San Tornio is a friend to everybody, and nearly everyone knows who he is. The police did their background check and he is here on a visiting visa. He was seen two times this week around Zola's office during working hours.

"To cut matters short, they want Zola eliminated; she is making progress with the peace campaign. Last week at the African festival, it was confirmed that San Tornio was tailing her," the agent explained.

"But...is he dangerous to society?" asked Aunt May.

"Yes, he is."

We all talked together. "If the government finds him, he will be arrested and may be brought to trial, but if they find him, they will kill him," Mr Zulu said.

"If… Who are they?" Maa asked.

"The KGB, I'm afraid."

"The KGB wants Zola dead, and they want San Tornio dead as well."

"Thank you Aunt May, but we don't need you finishing the story for us," I told her. She had intruded enough, and there was nothing I could do to make her stop.

"This is the best part of the story."

"No Mr. Zulu, this is not the time for jokes. Please just be yourself, and talk normally."

"Do not worry," he said. "Princess is going to be fine. Do you remember the treasure, the one she sent to her godfather?"

"Yes."

"She did not buy it. It belonged to her. She sent it to him. There was a message in it from 1959 that even Zola did not know about. A couple of months ago, when he made a plea for the rebels to free Zola, Pan-Africans contacted him. I forgot to give him the treasure after the election; it was still in my possession until a few months ago.

"The first African black prime minister of Ghana created the treasure," continued Mr. Zulu. "He was the main motivating force behind this focus on Zola. His vision extended beyond Ghana to all colonized African states, and he became a very powerful force against the colonization of Africa. He died before the Angola war began in 1975… Well not quite. That is another story in itself. I taught you this from the history class." Mr. Zulu was obviously trying to refresh my mind.

"I don't think you should be giving us a history lesson now. Zola needs us!" I told him.

But he was not happy with my comment. He was ready for a history lesson. "Boy, you need to know why she is important, so just be patient and listen. Besides, if you don't know where she came from, how will you know where she is going," Mr. Zulu warned me.

"Besides, there is nothing we can do at this point but wait, and as we wait, I will talk. In 1958, they formed the Organization of African

Unity at the conference with the purpose of working together in Unity and Freedom for the African people. Five years later, the 32 independent African States met in Addis Ababa, Ethiopia, and had the most inspirational conference. It was a great day, but unfortunately, there will always be people to oppose great ideas.

"Soon after that, Dr. Nkrumah began writing books. One particular book described how foreign companies and governments were getting rich by the exploitation of the African people. Eventually, the book created for him many more antagonists in the world than he already had. His intention was that Africa would become one and say no to exploitation, which led to his death."

"Yes, I know part of the story," I said. Zola had tried over the years to get me interested in his speeches, but I did not know that she was connected to him. Mr. Zulu, you always told Zola that you knew her from somewhere."

"Yes I did, only I had never actually seen her anywhere. I had a dream about her, many times – of serving her. She was a queen in my dreams.

"On February 24th, 1966 his government was overthrown by a Ghana military coup while on a trip to Hanoi, North Vietnam, and China. He was in exile in the neighbouring country of Guinea, in its capital city Conakry. There, he spent the rest of his short life nearly imprisoned by his own friend. He suffered greatly before dying. And he died a lonely man in Romania. The Ghanaians went for his body and buried him.

"They usually say that, 'if your house doesn't sell you, the street will not buy you.' He freed Ghana out of the hands of the British… His people chased him out of Ghana; he died, and they got his body, and buried him. Years later, they remembered him, and realized that he was a great man. Today, he is remembered as one of the most honourable philosophers in the world.

"Boy, transformation will only come when you are well-informed, so listen to the whole story. You might want to explain it to someone someday, and somewhere. He wrote a letter before leaving for treatment outside of Guinea. In his letter he pleaded for the African people to unite, and that it was the only way to prosperity, and a free Africa. If Africa does not unite, they will become a red river, instead of a green field. And it is happening as we speak.

"Now, back to the treasure..." said Mr. Zulu. "The treasure I took with me to South Africa belongs to the People's palace: she is the queen for the people. Each of the treasures is worth over three billion dollars, as when they were first discovered in the late 1970's. Just like I told you, one is in the People's Republic of Ghana, and one is with the Pan-African Union, and whoever has the one is the crowned Queen of Africa. At least, if the leaders of Africa desire unity. There was a beautiful letter in the treasure that she sent to South Africa, matching the one in Ghana and the OAU. Whoever has the treasure, is the owner of the crown.

"As you all know that Africa has become a battle field of red grass, the members of the Union have decided to unite under one flag with a star for each country, just like he said. The only difference is, each country will still hold to her president, but they will be governed by the queen. Every decision about the continent of Africa will be brought before her majesty Zola for final notice. Her bloodline will rule forever. With so many divisions in Africa, she can put an end to the madness and worthless war among her beloved people. This is the answer.

"There are two countries in France and Italy as well, both governed by two leaders. Why can't France and Monaco fight, or Italy and Rome? Because they understand the power of unity and leadership. If Africa desires coming together, then they will do just fine. In fact, there is a big kingdom set aside in the heart of Africa, ready for her with an office from each country. The flag is prepared, and they have been working on this project for many years.

"So, Zola's trip to Angola was painful, but it was the end of the search for our secret redeemer. Going public with this information was going to put many people's lives in jeopardy. Like the story of the princess and the special shoe, every young woman wanted to be Cinderella. In Zola's case, many people would have even gone as far as making a duplicate of this treasure."

"How is she, doctor? Do you think they got to her before we did?" Maa sat praying and hoping that her Zola would survive her fever. She really did not care about the politics; all she wanted was for her precious Zola to wake up. "If she refuses go to Africa, can she stay? Can the Canadian government protect her from the kingdom thing?" Maa asked.

"Remember, they will protect her when it comes to that. But under no circumstances will she refuse – she loves her people," Maa said with a weary smile.

"Yes, I can testify to that," I added.

"Hey, Fei Zi, Fat Boy, do you see how much Canada loves Madiba? It is no coincidence that she came here… In all this, we thank God, this is her calling."

"Oh Aunt May, how could I have ever doubted the way I feel about Zola? I love her so much!"

"Well, Son, I am not sure about that now. I am confident of the security system in Canada, but if she has to go to Africa, then…I…" Her voice faltered for a moment. "She is a strong and sassy black woman who has been contributing to the world since high school. Of course, she is going to receive the maximum security. I am not afraid; the Canadians are going to protect her here. This has also explained her behaviour and interest in the African affairs, and her reaction to world issues.

"Yes, Boy," said Mr. Zulu. "Zola is a natural leader who was born to lead her people to the promised land…just like all the people before her."

"What is the next plan, Doc? The world is waiting for a speech from her, since the news about her has been spreading. We heard that it is soundless on the battle field, and even in Angola, rebels have neglected their weapons. The Africans are rejoicing, as if they are cheering for a soccer game."

One of the men in black said, "Hey, Boy, don't worry about a speech; the Foreign Minister will take care of it. When they know that it is safe for her to appear to the public, they will let us know. San Tornio is still out there. We don't know what he is capable of doing."

"Well, San Tornio might not be dangerous, but the KGB people are," Mr. Zulu said.

"Thank God she made it here safely," Maa said. "We will give her time. If she doesn't wake up by evening, we will take her away from here. People might notice that she is in here."

"But I can't believe that Zola knew all of this and she kept it as a secret from us!" I told Mr. Zulu.

"Hey, Son, some things are better kept a secret. She is a lady, and a real lady knows how to guard her mouth and watch her steps."

The doctor suddenly drew our attention to the TV. It was Zola's godfather the President (Nelson Mandela) who was holding a press conference even though he knew about her present condition.

"Canada indeed is a friend to Africa, and we are happy for this great exchange that is about to take place. Today, the African people have decided to seek first the political kingdom, united under one queen. Now we know that from now on, all other things will be added to the African wealth. Peace that passes all understanding is bestowed on Africa.

"The princess, soon to be the queen, is among my numerous godchildren. I have spoken to her on several occasions and she is in good hands, and has learned from the best politicians in the world. We saw what she went through and the legacy she has made for herself in her lifetime. With the Canadians implementing full support, we the Africans have nothing to worry about. She is young and full with wisdom, and such people think way ahead of time. Today, as the wind of time blows throughout Africa, the wind of peace will rest upon Africa and shower us with the wind of great power.

"Today, as the wind of time has fully matured and is ready to give birth to change, we will remember the pioneers and all the freedom fighters of Pan-Africa. The motive behind the Pan-African government has always been unity and prosperity for all, and always will be. Today, I remember my good friend for his great achievements, and his intention for his beloved continent. He paved the way for us all.

"This decision was not an easy one; it had to be done behind the scenes to be possible and successful. I am very proud of the Princess Zola and her contributions to the Canadian society and her love for mankind. You often hear 'Like father, like son.' Here, it is 'like father like daughter.' All her fathers are known to be stubborn, and they never take no for an answer when the right answer is yes. Indeed, today is a remarkable day for us all. I am very happy to live and see a United Continental Africa. As Canada, on behalf of South Africa and other sister states, we are saying, 'thank you'."

When he got through with his speech he lifted his right hand and said, "Power for the people."

Zola had no clue what was happening in the world yet; she was still sleeping in my arms. I had not gone to the office or been to work since I got back from New York, and I needed to sign some documents, so Sister Lavender brought them over to the house.

The Canadian Swat Team explained that they caught a white male who they believed was a suspect working against this faith of testimony from happening.

"Are these people more powerful than you guys?" I asked them.

"Why do you think that San Tornio is here?" the agent asked me. "San Tornio is in danger, wherever he is, and he is probably hiding to save his own life! Enough information for now. We have to find a way to get her out of here."

I tried to talk, but they wanted me to be quiet. "No more comments, it is political."

So we kept Zola away from the public. Eventually, she opened up her eyes. I could see she was still very weak and helpless.

"What a *relief*," said Maa, who had been standing over the doctor the whole time. She had kept telling them to take her to the hospital, but now Zola had woken up…had come through after all. Her eyes were open and here she was, right in my arms. This time around there was no Nathan to take the glory. I just wanted Zola to be safe and healthy again. Aunt May was staring right into my face, but I ignored her.

I looked into Zola's eyes and then I told her that I loved her. She looked at me and smiled! She wasn't talking yet, though.

Zola had not seen Mr. Zulu yet. So I held her hand and kissed her, then I told her that I loved her again and I wanted her to be my wife. Just before I finished the sentence, she saw Mr. Zulu and screamed…and actually jumped almost around his shoulders.

"I've missed you, I've missed you! What are you doing here? Have you come to marry my former school principal?" she asked him.

"Yes, my princess, I missed you, too! And I vowed to serve you for the rest of my life. Wherever you are, there I will be. When I am no more, my wife and children will be your servants."

The Wind of Change

"You are not married, Mr. Zulu, and you don't have children either!" I said.

"What are you talking about, Mr. Zulu?" Zola asked him.

"You see, my princess, in my dreams you are my queen, and I was serving you," he said. "You are the queen that I have been dreaming about all my life. It is no secret now; these men are here to protect you. Africa is ready to receive you as their queen. The People of Ghana had their first beauty contest in 1958, and a new queen was chosen. Today, Africa is honouring you as a queen forever.

"The palace is ready for you, and there are delegations from every part of Africa meeting right now as we speak, discussing your safety and future," continued Mr. Zulu. "You are on the news all over the world. When I met you at Mandela High, I knew that you were created to be a leader. Destiny cannot be ignored, or denied. From now on, my queen, I will call you Rolihlahla, 'The shaker of trees'. The King of Swaziland will be arriving tomorrow with many other leaders as members of the delegation to take you home. We have to get back in time for the FIFA final, but in the meantime, Cameron is playing today and let's see who is leading." Mr. Zulu quickly changed the channel.

It was not safe at my house, nor at her house, so the Prime Minister had arranged a secret place for her to be for the time being. And he was talking about the World Cup… I did not understand any of the language they were speaking.

The only language I knew was to express my desire for Zola before they took her away. I went back to her and asked her: "Will you be my wife?"

She laughed at me. "We will have as many children as you want, and we will spend the rest of our lives together. You are my forever thing, and I cannot live life without you," Zola said.

"I ran after the wind searching for an empty dream. It was a beautiful dream, I said to myself. I did not want to wake up from my sleep. I realized that it was just a dream, but the dream actually became a reality. My heart rejoiced, and melted away. As soon as I tried to put my hands on it, it became surreal…not real. The dream was empty. Zola, in an empty box, and in an empty space. But you are my reality."

She was looking at me as if she did not understand a word I had said. "Are you all right, François? Why are you tripping?" she asked me. "I wrote that poem when I realized that Nathan was a mistake... But how can you want me? You are gay; you are not attracted to women," she reminded me. "What about Ben? You love him. Don't worry! You are welcome in the palace, François, and Aunt May too. If all of this is true, Maa will be going with me...Aunt May will not be alone," Zola said.

"I am, I meant that I was. Can I live in Africa with you as your husband?" I said urgently.

"I know that you love me, but not enough to be my husband," she said. "Has Ben become an empty wind?"

"Oh, dear... Ben is dead, and it is a long story," said Aunt May.

"But how? What happened? Poor Ben! May his soul rest in peace."

"If he had a soul," Aunt May murmured.

I shook my head in frustration.

"I am confused," said Zola, "with too much information giving me more headache than I can handle! Wait a minute... Now that Ben is dead, you want me to take his place? Who do you think I am? I love you very much François, but I can't marry you. We are not in Mandela High anymore. We have all grown up. Besides, I have decided to go home. What happened to me in Angola, it is happening to many young girls in the world. I am going where I am needed.

"You can't go home," I told her."

"Why not?" she asked. The king will be here by morning."

"I do not trust that king, I have read about him – he has too many women," I told her.

"Who are you talking about, François?" she asked.

"The King of Swaziland! You are beautiful and he is taking all of the beautiful women for himself. As beautiful as you are, he will ask for your hand in marriage. The African kings are allowed to marry many wives."

"You know, French Man, Nathan was right about you. You don't want me, and you don't want anybody to have me. You should be worried about Cheick O Toure (in mining), not the king. If he is still alive, he will be coming as well."

"Who is he?" Aunt asked.

"My first love."

"You never talked about him!" I was furious. "So you had your boyfriend all along?"

"No, French Man, I wish I had. I was eight. It's all coming back to me now!"

"Hey, Sweetie, calm down. You are raising your voice. I don't know you to be like that."

"François, there is a first time for everything if necessary."

"You are not making sense right now," I said.

"Look – we were kids and he promised to marry me. But really, we should not be talking about marriage right now… You should be grieving for Ben."

But Mr. Zulu disagreed. "I strongly feel that marriage is a very important matter to be discussed," he said.

As soon as Zola was done speaking, my body became hot like fire. I rushed to the washroom, vomiting like a three-months-pregnant woman. When I came out, Zola was on the phone with the Mayor of Mississauga, and after that, with the African Union president, Mr. Tony Sankor.

My heart was melting like wax, and I was sweating as if someone had emptied a bucket of water over my head. "Aunt May, please say something." I turned to her.

Aunt May was trying to have a talk with Zola, but I interrupted her. "I mean…you should go and pray for me," I said. "Zola, please."

"Look, François, she said. "I am empty, and you can see the work that lies ahead of me now. I don't have time to play games. I have thought about this all my life, and I am ready if, they are ready for a queen…." Zola said and stood up, but she was still so weak she had to sit down.

I called Mr. Zulu, barely one step away, and asked him a few questions, since he seemed to think I was being silly. "What will happen if Libya and Egypt later stand against this decision of a united Africa?"

"Boy, I can see that you are very troubled about this, but this decision was not made unknown to Libya or Egypt."

"Look," I said, "What is going to happen when Africa begins to fight with greed as always, and my Zola will be in the midst of the sirocco? What about the ongoing religious fighting in Nigeria? And Zola – she is a Christian who believes in every word from the Bible. Mr. Zulu – what if they don't accept the fact that she is a Christian? She might go to bed and not wake up!"

"I taught you this, that we are all different in faith, beliefs, and skin colours, but there is only one love and that is the only way to peace," he said. "Even though the sun has not darkened their skins as much, Egypt and Algeria are still Africans and proud ones, too. The Sirocco of Zola will blow on them."

"But you heard what the spokesman of Nigeria said, due to the government—"

"Don't be silly, Boy," he cut me off. "It will not happen the way you are thinking." Mr. Zulu tapped my shoulder.

"I want Zola to think about this before she accepts this queen thing!" I said vehemently. "Just about a month ago, she told me about the conspiracy that took place in Nigeria. You know that President Sina Abacha was found dead in his villa after he had just come from the airport, receiving Yasser Arafat with Hosni Mubarak and Muhammad Al Gaddafi. It is deeper than we think, she told me herself. It is political. It is by the grace of God that…there is a possibility that those four leaders were going to be found dead together in Nigeria. According to one source, he was surrounded by close friends and loved ones until 2:30 in the morning. The question is not who killed Abacha, but what was the intention of whoever engineered it, and how many people wanted to kill him?"

Mr. Zulu was quiet, then said, "Boy, you have to be careful how you say certain things. This is why we need Zola, so these things will stop happening." He shook his head with shame.

I did not want to be selfish, but I did not understand anything either. I could not get Zola to accept my proposal. She did not even trust that I was serious. I had worked hard on my relationship with Zola over the years, but I guess not hard enough for her to know that I was speaking the truth. Zola was going to leave me and there was nothing I could do to make her accept me. It was certain. I had known her for nearly two decades.

As we were still trying to talk, the doorbell rang, and I felt myself freaking out. They were there to take my lover away, my friend, and my soul mate! Zola had always been my heart's desire, and I would take her with me to eternity. She was no longer (if she had ever been) an ordinary girl. Instead, she was the lost princess from Africa who was going back to her roots. I felt lost, speechless. Was this my defeating moment, or was there more to come? I asked myself. Who else could I have turned to?

My aunt looked at me as if she was hiding something. "God help me," I cried out. I felt I had no way out.

I called her in private to talk to her, but it was of no use.

"What really happened while I was gone?" asked Mr. Zulu. "How did the two of you meet, and why are you not married, and having children? I expected to have seen you as a couple by now."

"Oh, Mr. Zulu, it is a long story! I don't know where to start."

"Start from Mandela High before my arrival. We have enough time, Son. Oh no, I'm sorry…forget that thought. It is of no use, we have to leave now, and the limo is outside waiting. You had her, and now we need her."

"Please my wise lady, don't leave me," I begged. "I have prayed for the day that I would have the courage to stand in front of you and ask for your hand in marriage. You are my joy, Zola, and you know it. You made me who I am, and all that I have become. Ben is no more; even Ben knew that I was in love with you."

"I know that you love me," she said, "but it is too late, French Man, I am sorry."

"Three years ago," I burst out, "Ben told me that I wasn't gay enough for him. I love you too much and I was afraid of hurting you. I have always felt this strong connection between us, but I was too proud to come forward. I went to Ben to help me say the right words to you at Mandela High and he kissed me…so I was never able to say it. At Sankara, the same thing happened. And actually, Ben was helping me propose to marry you, the very night that I broke up with you.

"He later told me that he thought I was gay again, since I was unable to talk to you about my feelings. Marshall and I were never together. I was confused, just like now."

"No, François," Zola said, "You are greedy. You have held onto me for too long. It is time to let go. I can't sit and wait for you to decide whether you are a 'he' or a 'she'."

"Honey, everybody wanted to be with you at university, those whose shoes I could not fit. Ben told me that you were having secret meetings with Boss, so it was better if we did not get together.

"To be frank," she said, "the only reason I did not accept Nathan was that I was very much in love with you. It was so hard watching you with him. I figured you would leave him and be with me, but Ben was there and he became a distraction as well. No, François, you became greedy, and very selfish."

"Please hear me out," I said. Three years ago, Ben found my secret box and saw all my Valentine cards to you. I kept all the cards from high school up to the present. I usually bought two sets of cards; I would give you one, and keep the other. The one that I gave you was to my best friend, and the one that I kept was for my wife, my angel. Please let me go with you to Africa, my lady, and be one of your slaves—"

"No, you can't," Zola interrupted. "Boss is here and he needs you. What about your commitment to the company?"

"No, not just that," Mr. Zulu added. "We have a tradition in Africa, that if you are not married here, she will not marry you in Africa. She will be the Queen of Africa sitting on the throne in the people's palace, and you are a Canadian. If you were already married, no problem, but when she gets to Africa, her husband will be waiting to marry her."

"That is a man-made tradition and it is stupid!" I said. "She doesn't love him. She can't marry a stranger!"

"Yes, Son, I know, but traditions make Africa. Without tradition, there would be no Africa," Mr. Zulu said, and walked away from me.

He had talked as if it was no big deal. But now Zola told me that the many different traditions were causing the tribal wars in Africa, and how "tradition" could come and take my woman from me. "French man, I have always loved you and you know it, but it is not important now. I am a real princess from a real world, not Cinderella or Princess Fiona. Africa is real and so are the people. Besides, I still want kids. There are going to be children from all over the world living with me and you can't handle that, so please, my love, let go of me."

Upon hearing this, I ran to the washroom. When I got out, I saw the royal delegates on TV, and how good-looking the king was. I turned to my Aunt May for help, but she could not do anything to make Zola marry me. It was a complete disaster. The thought of me living without her, actually made me pass out. We did not need any more tragedy around! They quickly called the ambulance for me, and as it turned out, I was going to be fine. The hospital was trying for hours to call us but could not get us, so they finally got Aunt May on the phone to tell her that Boss needed to see us.

"It is time," the lady said. "Ali is going soon, so it is time to say good-bye."

Zola began weeping and cried "Oh no, Boss!" and jumped up from her chair. "We have to rush over there fast. I will get the lawyer. Let's take my car." Ready as she was to run over to see Boss, Zola had forgotten her title – and her safety was important now.

"No, my lady, I'm afraid that is impossible. You cannot be seen in public right now," Mr. Zulu said.

"You don't know what you are talking about. I am leaving whether you agree or not."

"They might try to harm you so that you will not sit on the throne." Mr. Zulu looked very worried for the Princess's safety.

Zola suddenly sat down and looked worried as well. "Then we will use the ambulance to get there. We can explain later to the authorities, but we have to go now – he is a family member."

We all, including the agents, headed over to see Boss.

Before we arrived at the hospital, I whispered in her ear telling her that I was a changed man. "I am ready for a future with you Zola." She did not say anything.

Chapter Twenty-three

When we got to the hospital that night, Boss was now on life support. He removed the mask from his face and grabbed my hand, squashing it. He called Zola closer. "Hey!" he said. "I have my family here with me. I love you guys very much, never forget that. I want you to know that we fought, but life has given up on me."

"No, Boss, said Zola in an anguished voice. "Don't give up on life. It will mean you have given up on me as well." He turned towards me.

"Hey, Son, I saw Ben going in to the ocean. I am so sorry. You have so many lovely people around you. Don't be troubled." He was dying, and yet he was encouraging me to be happy. How many people like him were there in this world?

I felt just broken in pieces, like a glass shattered into small particles. I was losing three people at once, and there was nothing I could do.

"Come on, Son!" he said. "You look like hell… What's going on? It's okay, don't weep for me. Let me go home and rest. It has been a long lonely road for me. I am so tired, fighting abnormality and humanity. The earth is to be a place of beauty, not a place for danger." He was looking right in my face. I could not tell him about the Princess's departure.

Then she jumped in and said, "Yes, the earth is beautiful, and I am a piece of the earth. Please hold on to me. You can't leave me…I need you with me," Zola said as she prayed over him.

I held his other hand in mine, and said, "Oh, Boss, please hold on just a little bit longer. We will get a donor, God please help us renew his heart." Indeed, I was still hoping for a donor, but time had run out.

The old man looked pitiful, and yet cheerful. I hesitated to tell him about the Princess's trip to Africa. He had nobody in this world, expect

Zola and me. Boss was intelligent, and obviously knew that Zola and I were not getting back together. I was not sure if the entire African Queen situation had something to do with his going too soon. As for myself, I had lost several pounds, and still counting, in just two days.

This was not about me or Zola; it was about Boss, who was dying. With all the money that we had, we could not save him from this. Zola had often told me that money was just temporary desire. It couldn't buy happiness or life. Even with five million dollars, we could not give Boss a new heart. He was dying, without a seed or heir in the world, and his own parents were long dead. "I messed up badly," I told myself.

The lawyer called to say he was almost at the hospital to read the will. I walked over to Zola and tried to hold her hand, but she pulled away from me. She was weeping, and she refused to be consoled, standing there seeming to feel like a failure. In all of Zola's life from high school to that hospital room, she had always found a solution to a problem. She could not help Boss, her own family. It wounded the heart to see this.

This was beyond her. Only God knew what was going to happen. "This is something for God to fix not me, Old School," she said. Boss was not saying much, but trying to tell us that life without love was meaningless. "Love will penetrate the heart and take away the bitterness..." he said. "And...and..." He could not find the words.

Zola came in finishing the sentence for him, not wanting him to talk. "Love will open the heart and fill in the empty holes, leaving it completely healed. Unfortunately, the hole in the broken heart could not be filled. You are going into the grave with it, but in heaven, it will all be made whole again." When she was finished talking, I pressed myself a little closer to her and spoke in a gentle voice asking her to give me a chance: "Do it for him. He wants us together, and I want us back together."

"We were... We can't get together as a couple," she said.

"But I am a changed man. Meanwhile, he is dying and he has given me his heart."

She looked at me as if she did not believe a word I said. I had felt love in my heart, the kind that I had always longed for. It was so different, and hard to express. It was difficult going to church not feeling the love of God in my heart. I looked around and felt that I did not belong there. "I wanted a relationship with God all along, not a religion, but all I saw in my church was religion. The kind that made me hate going to church. An hour later she told me that I was one of those who always look for a "scapegoat".

I do not deserve to be alive, I thought, *but how am I going to do it?* Boss needed a heart, and I was going to give him my heart. I went in to the nursing station and asked to talk to the doctor in charge. Pastor had traveled and his father was away as well. We were just unfortunate that day, because there was no priest available to see me. I implored the doctor to take my heart instead, and gave him many reasons why, and that I did not deserve to live.

He looked at me in astonishment. The only thing he said was, "You are crazy. Get out of my office."

I refused, so he called security. They began to drag me outside, but then he seemed to feel sorry for me and told them to leave me. As soon as they let go of me, I rushed behind the nursing station and grabbed a surgery kit with knives and scalpels and a bottle that seemed to be a deadly poison. The security would stop me as soon as possible, but I was going to drink all of this, and die, so Boss could have my heart. There was one security guard standing behind me, but I did not see him. They quickly distracted me and knocked me onto the floor. Then they yanked the kit away and kicked me out of the hospital. I stumbled around in a daze.

The lawyer had not yet come. I felt hopeless, powerless, and lost. They called the hospital social worker to try to put some sense in my head. It was not about who was right or wrong. My friend was dying, one had just died, and one was leaving me. I promised her that I would behave myself if they would allow me back. "There is nothing compared to the loss of a loved one, but you have to hang on to the good memory and let them go in peace," she told me.

When I got back in the room, Boss had just asked to talk to a man of God, but there was none around. Boss also tried to tell Aunt May to ensure that we didn't waste any more of our time, because, as he said, "time waits for no one."

Aunt May prayed for Boss in his final rest. "God forgive all his sins, he lived an unworthy life, a life of ignoring the fact that you assist. Now, Lord, please receive him home sinless."

"Aunt May, I can't believe you said that!" I exclaimed in a whisper. You don't pray like that for a man who is on his death bed. You are the sinner and heaven should hear you, and forgive your sins."

Then Boss struggled to speak. "I do trust in God, and I know that he has been watching over me all this while... There is a time to live and a time to die. It is my time. In fact, as we speak, His angels are sitting in here... They have come to take me home."

"Oh, Boss, please don't go, give us more time... We will surely find a heart for you!" Zola said.

"It is okay, my love," he said. "I am homesick. Besides, my sister Fatima is waiting on me, I have missed her. I have struggled much. Let me go and rest."

Boss was holding Zola's hand as he said his final words. It was happening; we were right there seeing Boss leaving the earth, and it was very emotional for us all. This was also one experience I didn't ever want to think about, as death was life's worst enemy.

The lawyer had just entered, and saw Boss trying to take his last breath in and out.

"It is about time you are here, my friend. I thought I was going without saying good-bye." Boss's words were slow and laborious.

The lawyer loosened his hand grip on Boss, and began reading aloud. In a sense, we were not really interested in the will and any final instructions. Whatever Boss wanted me to do, was all right for me. We were all very sad, but there was nothing we could have done to change the situation. The will was read and we were very surprised to hear its details.

Boss had named Zola as his business partner – whereas I had thought all along that it was the Arabian Prince who was his secret partner. I felt my body go numb with shock.

Further, we learned that Boss shared 50% of his assets among the things that mattered to him the most. Ten percent to the Children's Hospital in Toronto for cancer research, ten percent to the hospital where he was going to die, five percent to Natasha's mother (and if she was going back to Zimbabwe, she would receive it all in cash). As for the rest of it, he had given it to me, since he had no one else.

Boss was now slipping away slowly, and could hardly open his eyes. His last words were, "The angels are in this room, they want you all to make a wish and it will be granted to you. Make sure it is your heart's desire… I love you all… We will meet on that beautiful day."

"Wait," said Zola quickly. "You did not receive Jesus, before dying."

"If I did not, I would still be here suffering. It is all right. I am tired; the Lord is my strength." Those were his last words. The room was filled with sadness. Even the nurses were standing around, crying. They had cared for him for so long. Though it was their work, and patients came and went frequently, Boss was special and they were going to miss him.

Zola was sitting and I was standing over her next to the bed. I could smell the perfume in her hair. She often washed her hair with Indian myrrh, and conditioned it with lotion that gave it a fresh ocean scent, all this touched up with a little hair spray. I could not resist that sweet smell from her hair and the heat from her body. We did not know what to do with Boss lying trying to hold on to life, so I put my pinkie finger in her hand and she quickly grabbed it. She was still holding Boss's hand.

I went down on my knees and hugged her as we were all weeping out loud. I gently kissed her, and she kissed me back. I lifted her in my arms and said, "Thank you, God, this is my life now. This cleans me and gives me worthwhile responsibility. Give me the ability and the courage to be a man." When I said all of this, we both moved towards Boss and embraced him as we cried. The lawyer had dropped the papers on the floor, the monitors were down, and all of the lights were off. And it suddenly became silent. The doctors and nurses monitoring his heart from the nursing station rushed into the room a few minutes later, sounding like a huge rain pounding and falling. I was crushed, and beaten. It did not take long. Then they wanted to take him away.

We were still huddled over him. Then I heard, "Son, dreams will come true and take a path that will lead you to a beautiful tomorrow. Appreciate all of the wonderful things that go around you and allow yourself to be loved. People come and go, but love will come to stay. To love is to live and to live is to love. Life is love."

My eyes opened. He was still lying there with his eyes closed. Peace and quiet filled the room. It was amazing…and even though we had not wanted him to go, I was pleased that he did not have to suffer anymore. The room was filled with doctors and nurses. They checked him. Zola refused to let go of him, though, so they left her hugging him and left the room.

He was gone to be with the dead, not with the living. I held onto her. In a way, Boss dead had given me new hope. "Well, Boss, you are in another place now."

Zola opened her eyes. "Angels will wrap you in glory...you are now healed." she said.

I prayed that my wish would come through. I had lost two people in a week, and I was not prepared to lose another.

The beginning of the week, I was a man without a soul, but with a breathing body. It was a long week for me. I really thought my time had come, and I was ready to kick the bucket and leave this earth, but then I had other funeral arrangements to make, and I had to consider Zola's departure as well. I was in hell, but love was worth fighting for. I was going to fight for Zola. I was among the living so I had a chance.

Boss was wealthy, but he always said that his money was not for him to keep, it was to help others and heal the world. Whoever needed his money for survival...the money was for them. I was going to continue Boss's legacy of life, so taking my own life was not the solution. I had not been thinking clearly. Ben had died an uncertain death with a soul, but if I had killed myself, I would have gone straight to hell without a judgment seat for me.

"Aunt May, you are the one God sent to bring me out of Gomorrah and lead me to Jerusalem."

"I am proud of you, Son," she said. "I have the capacity to love others like myself."

"I have some decisions to make, Aunt May."

"Yes, Son, we all do."

Zola was sad as soon as she walked out of the room. She realized that she was soon to be the queen of Africa.

It was almost morning. Mr. Zulu reminded her of the present situation, and that some African diplomats had arrived. Zola bent her head over Boss, and then lay down for a nap. I wanted to surprise her, so I quickly ran to the house to get her favourite song. I really did not have to go, but something pushed me to do it. I made an incredible discovery at Zola's house. There was a letter for her from the Children's Village in Monrovia. I sat down and looked at it for ten minutes wondering if I should open it or not. I finally decided to put it with the other mail. The letter could have been for Sayba, I thought. But there was a question popping in my head that I could not answer. Why would a letter from Monrovia come to Zola's house? I was very tempted to read it, but I walked away leaving it there. I practically heard her telling me to put the letter away.

Zola was truly a remarkable person. She had written a complete response for the song called *"It has always been you"*. But if she did not love me, who was she in love with?

I was back at the hospital, and I met her eyes, still close. It was not easy getting in, because the paparazzi had set up their cameras around to get her on TV.

I remember the letter, and I regretted not reading it. I wanted to go back to get it. But we had to find a way to get Zola out of the hospital safe and sound. They called for reinforcements, and in less than ten minutes, there were more officers to help guard the princess.

I was sitting looking at her, like she did to me when I went to help her open her lock. When she opened her eyes, I was there, smiling and she smiled back at me. It was a good sign.

"Hey, Sunshine, some coffee?" I asked, but she suggested tea instead. Her grandmother was all right at the hospital with her tea. But even though we had made up, I was still confused about how things were going to be.

Chapter Twenty-four

※

"How do you feel about going back to Africa as the people's queen?" That was what they wanted to know. They managed to get Zola out of the hospital without any notice or comments. The news had spread around the world, even if she had not actually appeared on TV. And now, with her recent experiences in Angola, how was she going to handle the coronation and her new life? Only Zola was going to answer those questions. I guessed they would have to wait on her, until she was ready.

I was told not to go with them to the hotel because of political reasons. Zola was now a Pan-African diplomat who needed maximum protection. I knew Zola had always been in the spotlight, but never in my wildest dreams had I imagined such a situation. This explained her actions and thoughts about Africa and world issues, especially her response to the World Bank when they offered her a job. She said it as if she knew more than I knew about them: "I can never see myself working for the World Bank," she said. "It is the last thing I will do before death. They don't need me; they want me but I go where I am needed."

I needed to go to the office and inform our partners that Boss did not make it, and start funeral arrangements as soon as possible. I had much to do, and Zola had to help me over the phone. We decided to give him a quiet memorial service.

I wondered, how could Zola be my boss and I knew nothing about it? Why could she not just tell me? If I ever asked her, she would give me an answer that would turn out to be an assignment, like, "Life is a mystery, François; those who desire it, will find it. You can't discover all at once. Up to today, the mysteries behind the Bible are still being revealed to pastors who search them. Her life has been nothing but a surprise rollercoaster. I opened the letter I had found and began to read:

"Dear Fatima,

This is Kula Ngamor from the children's village in Monrovia. Sorry for the delay. I received all of your letters, but I was waiting on my pastor to give me some more information. I will tell you the little that I know about your mother. Indeed, she was a lovely woman, and it was our pleasure to work with her all these years. Though there was a break in between, we always managed to meet in the centre and look after the children.

"After the first war in 1992, the city was filled with homeless children. Had it not been for your mother, we could have lost all of them through illnesses and hunger. Before the international relief workers came to our aid, your mother often went to the bush looking for meals and herbals for the children. Life in Liberia was counted as worthless at the time. People died every day to the extent that they began losing heart for life. They said that it was war, and people would keep dying until they had seen the end result. They called that heartless murderer the Old Man, but I called him CT. As far as I am concerned, he is a rebel leader.

"He trained boys not to have any respect for life other than their own. Women and men were disgraced every day by CT's little boys on the street. The UN is here, but CT runs the show. As I write you this letter, I hear the children running outside to see the president passing, but in my eyes, he is still a rebel leader who is still killing innocent people. Four of the girls were taken by his son, last week. When he was tired with them, he passed them over to his friends. The ECOWAS (Economic Community of West African States) soldiers and other peace organizations are telling us to fear not, that there is peace. But as long as CT is in this country, there will be no peace for the people.

"One day back in '92 around October, your mother went to the bush with a couple of the youth to get us food. On that day, another warring faction attacked CT and his boys. They started to fight heavily in the city. The whole city was on fire, and we became displaced.

"After months of fighting, they ceased fire for a little bit. We did not see your mother, until a couple of years later when she came back with the five of them that went to the bush in Sierra Leone. They were arrested and taken across the line against their will. I was happy to have seen them, but their hands were cut off. I am so sorry to tell you this.

"I was happy when we received the letter from you. Because of the war, we have not had a stable address. She hated seeing herself like that. Many days and nights before October, she cried that you would come and rescue her. But when they came back, she stopped talking about you.

"When the Red Cross message came for her from your foster parents, she was missing then. I heard her name on the radio, but she was nowhere to be found. What you saw months back is true. Heavy gun fighting had started between CT's government and another group from the former President Samuel Doe tribe. They call themselves 'Butt naked.' They removed their clothes and killed human beings like chickens, just like they were when their mother gave birth to them. They explained that it was easy smelling the enemy when naked. Every street in Monrovia up to now is crying blood. Our area was not safe, so we decided to go to a safer place. It was like a ghost town that has been set on fire to finish the ghost. In the smoke we managed to get out; when we got over the old bridge, those shameless good-for-nothing empty-skull murderers bombed the bridge.

"Your mother was among the people walking on the bridge with hundreds of others. Those who could swim survived, and those that were very much wounded died on the spot. Unfortunately your mother was not safe from this tragedy. She was unable to swim as I told you about both her hands being cut off. I am sorry, love. I was very fond of her, she told me much about you and her family back in Guinea Conakry. When it became quiet, and they went to clean the street, a body was found on Providence Island just a five to ten minute walk from the Old Bridge. Of course it was your mother. I recognized her clothes and she had no hands. We found a place near the Children's Center and buried her there.

"Like I said, I was not sure if I should reply to your letter, but the pastor told me that you deserve to know about your mother's last days and struggles. I have the information about your mother's family. If you have any questions, please feel free to write me. I am going to manage the center; your mother would want me to keep the children smiling. Doing the happy thing with the children brought her joy.

"Yours truly,

"Kula."

"No," I screamed. "It is wrong...not Zola's mother." It was not Sayba explaining this time around, nor Orlando or Boss who was gone and ready to be buried. It was Zola's own story that she knew nothing about. I was going to tell the story. I felt sick to my stomach and began to imagine the pain she went through living without both hands, how she struggled to swim or she allowed herself to drown. Who knows, maybe the bomb killed her first. This was not Zola's story; it was my story that I had to tell her. I instantly felt a connection between the woman and myself. This was different than the other stories I had heard. I was living in agony.

"Zola can never find this letter," I told myself. I quickly took it and left. But it seemed I could feel her presence in the room. *"French Man, what are you hiding?"* I could not have kept it from her, but at least just for a moment. I felt crazy, and how my day was going to be, I had no idea. I had Boss who was waiting to be buried, and Zola who was going to govern the people who thought that they could not survive without the help of other nations. They believed every lie they had ever been told. The greed, corruption and power took her mother away from her.

When we were still at university, she would tell me that Africa was free from colonization, but was to be free from greed and poverty. She never lost a debate. She would argue that "Although the majority of the African continent appears to be poor, it is extremely worthy." The political issue and greed in Africa is the one that has held them in prison and it is heartbreaking for the children of Africa. From high school up to the present, her focus has been on Africa. She researched and travelled afar to meet leaders and elders from Africa to tell them the source of the African problems. Zola had been trying all along to continue the vision and dreams of her forefathers, but I was too busy to see it. No one believed she was not a Jamaican, until we made a joke out of it.

Zola lived a very careful life with the thought that it was one day coming to this. Did she know the whole story about becoming a queen? Part of it, yes! From the day I met her until now, she has been honoured and respected by great people. Look at her relationship with the South African president; she worked hard for it. She was also in Ottawa helping to promote multiculturalism. With this experience, her work would become even easier as a queen. She had prepared herself for this in the past years doing what she loved the most.

Zola said that destiny was very important in the early earthly journey. I can't imagine how many times she told me that I didn't know who I was. "In order to move forward, you need to know your previous position," she would say. She often corrected people when she was referred to as a Jamaican girl. "I am not a Jamaican," she would say. "You look at the colour of my skin and call me a Jamaican girl, but what colour of people live in Africa? Do all black people come from Jamaica?" She once made an appearance at the local Afro and Carassauga multicultural festival, encouraging and supporting participants and attendees, stating that their identity was who they were.

"There is power in identity. Your identity is your confidence and it will give you strength when you find yourself away from home. Is identity a paper or is identity *who you are*? Identity is where you want to be and who you are," she told me.

Zola had the audacity to stand up for what was right. I knew the Africans had not made a mistake by putting her on the throne. Loss of identity was the erosion of destiny, and Zola was never going to compromise her identity.

"Never compromise your identity; otherwise you will water down your destiny. Protection of your identity is the key to preservation of your destiny."

Was I going to hide who Zola was, or where she came from? If this was a conversation, she would have said that her identity was who she was. However, I had to snap out of this kind of issue and get back to business. It was already three days past now, and we were going to bury Boss.

I saw Zola the night before the funeral, but I did not tell her about her letter. She was too devastated that Boss had died. She was beating herself up, but there was nothing I could do. As much as I wanted to talk to her about the partnership at Ali and Ngo, it was not the right moment. Had she hid from me, or did she just not want me to know that she was my boss? It was summer and Natasha was away, so she did not make it for the funeral. It was truly a solemn time for the family. She did not want to speak at the burial but she did it anyway. We left and planned to meet at the hotel.

I went over to the hotel later that day to check on her, and surprisingly there were many more diplomats who came to accompany her than I had thought. I saw a couple of people at the funeral, but I thought they were friends of Boss. Among the delegates to Canada were Mawete Lumumba from Congo, the family of Thomas Sankara, the First Family from Ghana, and many other diplomats. Also, and very important to Zola, Cheick Toure and even Kwame Ture's son were all part of the diplomatic delegation.

Losing Boss was like losing my father, and I received a letter telling me that my mother had been killed in the Monrovia bombing. It felt as if the end of the world had come, and as soon as Zola left for Africa without me, my time would have come to follow my parents. Zola needed me to be there for her. No matter what was going to happen, I planned to be there. Since I read the letter about her mother's death, I was not able to look in her eyes. She understood that I was hurting, so she could not have asked me. It was a happy time and a sad time for all of us.

Cheick, Toure and Zola were born practically at the same time, according to his explanation. I got to the hotel, and her friend Toure, who I knew nothing about, was giving her more of a history lesson than Mr. Zulu ever had. When I got there, I heard him say, "Uncle Nkrumah was the Guinea co-president. His interest was to bridge all of Africa together."

Cheick spoke out, just like Zola always said: "It is only possible through a continental government. This is the only way Africa is going to control her economic and natural resources. "My father loved Uncle Nkrumah, but with so much happening among the African leaders, trust was gone, and my father believed that his co-worker was going to join hands with the power brokers and assassinate him and take over Guinea. By then, their good friend Lumumba had already been killed long before they pushed him away from Ghana. During that period, black leaders and activists were being assassinated almost every day. In a period of five years, several top leaders had died, including the late President Kennedy, because he had shown to the world that he cared about equality."

I was sitting looking at him getting acquainted with Zola. I thought to myself that he was the right man, and that they would make a great team.

I couldn't compete with him; he was into politics more than I was. He could represent Zola anywhere and anytime. "Seeing the disasters and tragedy, the death that was happening, my father became afraid and kept a close eye on his friend and the co-president of Guinea. Soon after that, the co-president was isolated; no freedom of peace was given to him. His health was failing, and he was given less care and attention. One day, he woke up from bed and found out his cook was dead! He felt helpless, betrayed and confused.

He thought that they might have killed the cook in order to get to him, he told Uncle Ture. Dr. Nkrumah knew that his life was very much in danger; it was just a matter of time before they got to him. The doctors gave him six months to live. Confused, broken and disappointed, he left Guinea for Europe, trying to fight the cancer in his body. But it was impossible, because Dr. Nkrumah's life was already "cancelled" by the Ghanaian people, since 1966, in spirit; it was now happening in the physical. In Europe, the final work was done, and the founding member, former president of Ghana and co-president of Guinea, died April 27, 1972.

And Zola was born April 27 1972. When the news escalated, that's when her mother went into labour. "Zola and I are the godchildren of the late Kwame Ture. All of what I am telling you is documented." Cheick looked at Zola, smiling. "Uncle Ture was right there when it all took place, and may his soul rest in peace. Our godfather wanted me to search for you; it was his dying wish that one day Zola would be found," Cheick said.

This was information I had learned in history class, but now this was reality. I had heard about these people, but to actually come close to meeting them was now an incredible moment for me. Since I had met Zola, it had been nothing but adventure!

Now Cheick was telling us about the great Stokely Carmichael AKA Kwame Ture, and the former president of Guinea Conakry. "Uncle Ture confided much in me, with the reason why Dr. Nkrumah died a lonely man. I will tell you much about Guinea later. First things first," said Cheick.

"Those days were just like now, where you never know who is pulling the wire. The wire was pulled behind the scene, and our fathers were separated just like that. When Dr. Nkrumah died, my father grieved for a long time then he woke up and believed that everyone was out to kill him. He was still a trustworthy man, during the founding of the Organization of Africa Union. As time went by, he lost trust in people around him. The Republic of Guinea became his private property. He turned to divinations for help. Whatever they told him is what he believed. As the result, whenever he noticed any funny behaviour from his government officials, he would jail them, or they would disappear without a trace.

"It was difficult forgiving my father for the disappearance of Zola and her mother. When Zola left the president's compound, we were just seven. I was furious and frustrated with my father, but Uncle Ture helped me understand that if my father had not made himself as dangerous as he was, his own brothers would have killed him and succeeded him like the late president Thomas Sankara. It is almost impossible to see an ex-African president."

I could not believe that Zola was a real politician's daughter. It was in her blood. She had told me once that her father's name was also Francis.

It was difficult getting into the hotel; they checked me from head to toe. They actually searched me, in case I had a weapon.

Cheick explained that his father's traditional spiritual man had told him that the survival of united Africa lay in the hands of Zola.

"I overheard my father saying that he was going to jail Zola and her mother for conspiracy. Zola could not have done any wrong," Cheick said. "Everyone who entered that prison did not come out alive. I knew that I had to do something to help them escape. In 1980, I was eight years old. I helped Uncle Ture arrange for Zola and her mother to escape from Guinea. Do you remember me handing the treasure to you at the bus station in Madina?" Cheick asked Zola, still holding her hand as he fought to help Zola remember.

Cheick continued to explain that he had taken them to the bus station to give them a chance to live. He didn't want to know where they were going, because he might have told his father if asked or pressed. Cheick worked with the African Interpol, and later became the secretary-general of the Organization of the African Union. And he had never stopped searching for Zola. "Uncle…Uncle Ture made me promise him that I was going to look for you and find you," Cheick said with tears running down his face.

They were sitting in the lobby, Zola holding hands with her old friend, as he explained their great escape. "But what was going to happen now, and what was going to be the next thing on the agenda?" I asked myself. They couldn't take her back to Africa just like that; she was in the care of the Canadian government until she reached the palace. I was now hoping that this government had some kind of tradition or regulation that would hold her back, allowing me to spend some time with her.

Such an incredible decision for the African continent was also very important for my own country. "Can the Canadians say that the Africans are not being fair?" my Aunt May would say. "Zola's trip to Canada was all planned by God. Canada was the right country for her, Zola was the right person, and it all happened at the right time. The timing was right for everyone except me. I loved Zola and I wanted her to marry me, but I also needed to prove to all those people that I was in love with her.

Cheick had been waiting all his life to wed her; he called her "Fatima." The idea was that she was going to get married to Cheick for the love of

Africa, in keeping with the tradition of their fathers. I could not fight such traditions and politics, and Mr. Zulu could not help me. The only person who could help me was me. Zola, it seemed, had nothing to say, but she was ready for the throne.

That afternoon, I met up with the African diplomats and expressed my desire for Zola, making them understand that I loved her, and I was asking for her hand in marriage.

"Boy, who is here with you?" asked the President of Gabon. "In Africa, your parents are the ones to ask for the orange in the tree; it is disrespectful to us that you come with empty hands to look for your bride."

They asked me questions I could not answer, and my past was now haunting me. I could not stand in front of all those great leaders and tell them that I was not sure if I loved her or was attracted to females. They already knew that Cheick was going to marry her before the crowning if necessary. Zola would do anything for her people to unite. If I really did love her as I claimed, we should have been a couple after university.

"Son, you should have married her when you had the chance, but we will take over from here now." It was the president from the Jomo Kenyatta library and museum whispering in my ear.

But just before I left the hotel, Cheick walked up to me expressing his feelings for Zola. Then he said, "Zola's happiness is as important as the continent of Africa. The tears you are shedding are not enough. If you demonstrate love, love will find you." He tapped my shoulder, and told me to be a man. But what did being a man have to do with my love for Zola? He was asking me to deny my feelings for her?

She was in tears that afternoon when I saw her, and was not saying much. It was a complicated situation, but I had to think like a man now. The freedom of a whole continent depended on the decision I was going to make. Was I going to be selfish enough to confuse her, or love her enough to let go? (and let Africa's power for the people step in). Besides, since I met Zola, I realized how her heart had been in Africa while her body lived in Canada.

She hated the war in Africa. I saw how broken she was when we met Natasha's mother, and Sayba, and then what happened with Orlando, and then the trip that almost took her life away. I was also worried what this might do to her if she ever found out about her own mother. Zola had invested all her life getting ready for this day, so I had to make a wise decision and be the man that the Africans wanted me to be. Everybody around the world was getting ready for these big eventful days. The Afrofest visitors were still in the city, and the Caribbeans were preparing for the Caribana festival. The great princess Zola's wedding was also coming up, to be followed by the coronation in Cameroon a few months later. Zola was the news of the century and Canada was the place to be. All eyes were on this country!

In fact, since it was announced that Zola had been found, there was celebration in the streets, with joy and laughter everywhere in Africa. I was not happy that my princess was leaving, but I was happy that all of this was happening in Canada where equality is an objective. She was finally going to be happy; it was just so sad and unfortunate that we had lost Boss around the same time. This had helped put Canada on the world map again. There was a woman on CNN shouting, "The princess is alive and she is coming home! It was their intention to turn Africa in to a battle field, for the love of money. But we are going to show the world that we can do this, and we will do this together."

There were festivities in the city among the Africans and well-wishers. "It was just like when the colonial rule ended in Ghana, only this time it was different," said the lady on the news. "It was the entire continent fulfilling a destiny, a decision that goes way back to S. William and W.E.B. Du Bois, the fathers and founding members of Pan-Africa. All the brain powers have come together and empowered a young woman to control the Sirocco. One at a time, they are reliving it in her. In fact, it was in July of 1900 when William arranged the first meeting that has brought Africa to this historic day. We don't want to push this, but could this be what we think it is?"

Just like this woman on the news, the media was on top of it, and seemed to know it all. "During the sixties, it seemed like just a dream, but forty years later, the dream has become a reality. The African leaders have realized they were misguided, but they are now ready to live life in a new prosperous Africa."

How marvellous! I was walking under the rain with thoughts in my head, but I did not feel a drop on my body. The press were thinking about it all. I had called Papa in South Africa to help me, but there was nothing he could do for me, even though he was Zola's godfather and had great influence in politics. He could not change the situation. It had nothing to do with having a chair in the Organization or not. All the political analysts were giving their opinions about what was to be expected of her, and what not to expect. In a situation like this, they would get on TV and talk about what the people wanted, but not what they could do to help.

I am not a politician, but I knew what the people of Africa needed, and wanted. I decided to take a long walk and think about my life, and suddenly, I heard her telling me that I was a little boy clothed in a man's skin. I did not know the meaning of that since I had heard her say it after high school, but I figured it out as I sat there listening to Cheick speak about Zola. I saw a real man in him, a man who was not afraid of standing up for what was right. Cheick was full of integrity, and proud and responsible as well. He and Zola could make a perfect couple.

When Zola and I had been at university, there was a poem in her room. Now a woman was reading that very poem, on the Breakfast News. "How did she put her hands on it?" I was talking to myself, but a woman next to me in the bar, quickly answered, saying that she was a good friend. "Good friend? I never saw that lady in my life before," I told her.

"Well! If you lift up your head, maybe you will know who she is."

Of course I knew her. It was Sister Lavender. This poem was written for a drama play at one of the universities in the North, but she used her thoughts and feelings for Africa to demonstrate it. Sister Lavender was always affected by Zola's smile, not forgetting how much she loved the people around her. Among our friends, she was the only one brave enough to face a television station.

> "The father of Africa is grieving in the grave and has refused to accept any comfort.
> He left enough for his children to live in comfort, yet they are living in distress.
> He hears about their suffering, and he feels the pain of their wounds,
> He hears their cries, but he cannot wipe their tears.
> He hears the sound of the gun that has buried them in the mass grave.
> They are begging from their own resources, but they will beg no more,
> They are homeless on their own farms, when their land is endless.

They are hungry on their own plantation, and it is flourishing with fruit of all kinds.
They are gloating while others died, but he gives them a word of faith. He binds up their wounds with a word of hope that one sweet day Africa will rise up and unite.
On that day, there will be a stronger and united Africa."

"Well, this was something I saw in the washroom, so I took it. Zola has the heart of gold," Sister Lavender said on air. "Whenever Zola was alone she would devote her time to poems about the people, so this is a very good decision. The Africans are not making a mistake. I am going with her to Africa, right, Hon? Well, my husband has already agreed; he is very shy. I had to practically force him here. I have always wanted to go to Africa and find my DNA; our DNA is now with the princess. I have loved that child since I first saw her, right, Hon? My husband will not talk, but he loves Africa too.

Chapter Twenty-five

I was world-famous in a way I had never wanted to be. The media knew more about me than I knew about myself. It was a surreal experience, and getting to that point did not take very long; there were photos of me on every television station you could think of. They knew everything about Ben and me, and how he had died just a few days ago.

But one thing they did not know about me was how much I have loved Zola all my life. When Zola did not hear from me, she would not go to sleep. They did not know that I sent her a cup of coffee every morning, up to now, for the past ten years. But of course, the media would not be interested in that. There was a man who made his way from the *Mississauga News* to come and see me. He wanted to know how I felt about Zola returning to Africa, and my relationship with her. I was not in the mood to talk to anyone, but I still made an appointment for the following day.

At this point, Zola was my strength and my courage. She always told me that "Being deeply loved by someone gives you strength, while loving someone deeply gives you courage." The thought of her calmed my spirit.

As for me, I told my Aunt May that it was not what she was going to be that developed my desire for her, it was about who she was that mattered. But Aunt May knew that she was my queen before she became the people's queen, even if Africa decided that I was not going to marry her because of who I was, so let it be. I went home and got into my bed still wearing my shoes.

Aunt May asked me about my plans, but I had no plans. So much had happened in a short time, so I was out of breath and energy. I was given a day to tell the Pan African leaders how much I loved her and how far I was willing to go. "Well, Son! Are you going to allow them to take her away to the jungle? We love her too."

"How can you say that? I'm glad there is nobody around to hear that word coming from you. She belongs to the people. She was *born* for this purpose, as if you don't know.

"By the way Aunt May, you embarrassed me with all the many questions you asked, and it was not funny. Was it on purpose?" I asked her.

But she did not comment. She also could not take her eyes off me. I did not sleep that night; I needed a kind of supernatural wisdom to take care of the situation. This time around, the wise women could not help me. They wanted me to think "beyond" and be creative. "Think outside the box, Son."

But the truth was, I had no "thinking cap" to use. "I can't fix this, I am sorry. Oh, God, I need You to strengthen me, please!" I cried out.

"Yes, Son, go right ahead and talk to Him. He is waiting to hear from you. With all your sins, make heaven angry and let them come to punish you. Let's see if He will come through for you, after all the disgrace you have brought upon God. You have lived your life in sin and you are now asking for mercy... You will soon follow Ben. The curse is on you all, and may God deal with you according to His will."

"What are you talking about, Aunt May? You are scaring me."

"Nothing, Son," she said.

With all the circumstances surrounding me, although I knew it was impossible, I wanted her back. Zola was a beautiful girl; it was her or nobody. It had always been this way. I went to bed that night hoping not to wake up from sleep. Aunt May kept coming in and out of my room with apparently the thought that I might harm myself. I was trying to make sense of what she was saying but I did not understand her.

Before going home that night, I went to Nathan asking him to help me get Zola. I told myself he could actually help me, but it was no use. When I called him up, he told me he had to finish watching the soccer game, that the FIFA game was on that year in France.

Then I called him up the next day. He had just finished an interview, and was on his way to see Zola. He and I had not gotten along over the years because of Zola. I just could not allow him to have her – she was a much better person than him. They say that identity is power and Nathan had more power over me. He gave himself power, and he and Zola had different meanings for identity. Zola was never going to marry him.

In her world, there was no such thing as discrimination, and she accepted everyone as they were. Once you had a red blood cell, you were a member of mankind. But Nathan – he seemed of no use, except as a show-off. Even though I did not sleep much that night, and pounded and pummelled my pillow until it was limp, I actually woke up feeling refreshed, though was still worried about Aunt May's judgmental behaviours.

A friend of my aunt stopped by early that morning and told her that I wanted to marry Zola because of the new information about who she was. "It is wrong, May. You know your boy doesn't like women. You have to stop him!"

In the morning, I asked Aunt May to go with me over to see Zola, but she looked at me with a concerned face. "God, I can't lose my boy. Please, help him realize that he belongs here."

"Aunt May, what are you talking about?"

"Yes, Son! A philosopher once described black Africa as inhumane. Son, listen to me. I am going to get real with you. He said that the black Africans are not human, that they are only good for four things: war, destitution, debt and crime. Look at what they are doing to their own people. If you go to Africa, you will become like them, or they will kill you before you have a chance to run."

"Aunt May, what has come over you? I am going to pretend that I did not hear you again."

"Son, when you look around, what do you see? There is war everywhere in Africa. Your life will be in great danger there. Your mother was born in Uganda, and they chased her out of there. They will not accept any white man to rule over them again. Those people are very angry for what we did to them. They don't know how to love."

"Oh, Aunt May, please stop," I said. "You should have been the one in line for a new heart. You never told me anything about my mother, and…I have been living with the enemy all my life. And you call yourself a child of God? Where is your morality, and tell me where in that Bible does it say black people are not human?

"You have always prayed for Zola and me to get married and start a family – and today you stand in front of me and judge her by a statement that was said hundreds of years ago? What happened to the wise woman, the one you so much desired for me? She is the daughter you never had, and everything that you can never be. People like you have helped to destroy the world rather than heal…you are an enemy of progress. Do yourself a favour and don't go to church any more, otherwise, the fire will burn you. As we sit here talking, there are people judging me as well. What are you going to say when you hear all the ugly names I am being called? What did you say to your friend when she called me 'gold digger'?"

"Well…I…" Aunt May could not even talk.

"Well my beloved mother – "

"I am not your mother."

"I just lost you. Good-bye, Mother."

"You are my brother's son."

I walked away with a decision never to see her face. Obviously, I did not believe what I heard from my only relative. I prayed that it was all just a joke, and a dream. It was not getting any better for me. It seemed to be as if there was a challenge for each day. If Aunt May of all people would reject Zola, then anything under the sun was possible. If she meant everything she said, then people like her did not belong anywhere in the community. I did not tell Zola. I just let go, and considered Aunt May to be ignorant of the truth.

I walked away confused, sat down and cried over Aunt May's behaviour, and then I suddenly imagined Zola's mother drowning, without a hand to help her back on shore. I imagined Sayba's family being shot right before her eyes, and imagined Orlando's baby sister lying over her dead mother struggling to get the breast to her mouth. How much pain was she in when they had to cut off the second hand? How much pain did Orlando feel when he had to watch his sister die over his mother? What was war? Must they kill before they made up? Did they think about what came after war? Who were they fighting for and fighting against? Was war really the solution for the revolution? Just a slap in the face can kill a man, so why would they make such a heavy machine gun to kill people? I guessed we would never know.

For a second, I had forgotten about Zola and the throne. Who was going to help me get Zola? I was on my own. I was just a baby when my family was killed in a car accident, according to Aunt May, leaving me behind to fight the struggle of life. Aunt May raised me in the church and taught me the principles of life. She protected me so much from the outside world, but had neglected to prepare me for it. "Take down God's telephone number; whenever you are in trouble, call Him and He will be there on the double. Whenever you are in trouble, call Jer 33:3," she had often told me.

"But I have called You all my life and I have not seen You, nor heard from You," I thought. Who am I and what am I? Why have You forgotten me, God? *I am no different from Orlando and the rest of my friends. I am 33 years old and I am still calling your number. Are You going to sit and watch the Africans take the one thing that matters to me away from me?*

People often said that personality cannot be changed, but I have said it can be upgraded. I, François became a new man after hearing all of the different stories that seem so much alike. And I had made the decision – to support Zola all the way to the throne, so I wiped my tears and headed to the hotel to have my last dance with her.

The sooner she was on the throne, the better it would be for everyone, so the crowning was going to be as soon as possible. But when I got to the hotel, she gave me and others some news. I was not sure if she had started working on a speech, but just to be on the safe side, I began putting ideas together to make it a bit easier. We made a vow to always stand by each other, and I was going to stand by her. The government of Canada was one-hundred-percent supportive of what was about to happen, and after all, Zola was one of us, and a goodwill ambassador to the United Nations. The Canadian government wanted to stand by Zola until she was on the throne, but before this, they agreed to give her a wedding in Canada, so her flight was postponed.

When I arrived at the hotel later that day, it was getting busier; there were more politicians and paparazzi than the day before. Cheick came well-equipped with the intention of getting married to Zola, if necessary. He had a ring that cost over $2 million dollars. He also had a political background and was already working for Pan-Africa.

As well, Cheick loved Zola. They wanted to know if I truly loved her, because the survival of Pan Africa and the rest of the African states' futures depended on her. The question I asked myself was, "How could I ever have proven myself to be the right man for her?" It was a question that I had asked myself since Mandela High, and it had cost me my life with Zola. I was done with proving myself to people and convincing myself about Zola, though I knew I was being judged by my previous life style. Ben had just died, so it was enough to disqualify me. "Will they even believe me if I told them that I am a changed man?" I thought. I had had my confiding moment, and he alone knew where I had been.

I was glad to have been alive to celebrate with Zola. It was only by chance that I was standing among those people, and able to be a part of Zola's life. She was going to be the first Queen of the new Africa, and for such a position, anybody and everybody would want to marry her!

Cheick was a smart man and with a history with Zola. There seemed no question about it that he was going to marry her. With beauty beyond measure (perhaps I was biased), a high sense of fashion whether North American or African, smart, loving, loyal and sassy…and educated and ambitious enough to make a good political mate with heart…it would be a privilege for any man to have her as his wife. Of course I wanted to be that man; who wouldn't want a wise woman as a wife? I always knew she was a special girl who deserved the world, but she did not want the world. She was in love with her people and her identity, which was her calling. Chosen for greatness, she was the people's heart – though had a humble heart with a meek spirit. She was a true servant and a queen.

With my past that was just yesterday for which I was being prosecuted by the media, I had to think about Zola and what the people of Africa wanted. I had to think about their expectations, and think about how this decision would affect them and their new political government.

When I entered the suite, she ran over to give me a warm welcome, as I stared at the people within. Then she kissed me on my forehead. It was our usual routine, and I was pleased. She introduced me to the rest of her family. As Africa was gaining momentum, so were the Canadians getting ready to give Zola, soon to be the African queen, an extravagant wedding. The Canadians were going to miss her, but they were also overjoyed that finally the Africans were taking this big step of change. It was the great wind of change that was usually only possible in dreams, but this was becoming a reality. It was all working out at the right time – and at a time when the world still thought that Africans belonged to the last, lowest class of mankind and humanity.

Libya and Egypt together were one of the "bones" behind "Africa Must Unite". Since the Nigerian incident, they had not been able to appear in public. Gaddafi's two sons would make it for the wedding. Within a short

The Wind of Change

while, the media was showing a complete documentary of the queen's palace. The construction had begun years earlier, when the OAU made the verdict that it was time for the member states to come together as one. In the Tanzania summit, it was voted upon that the palace be built in Cameroon since geography had located this place to be the central point of Africa. This region, I knew, was incredibly diverse, with its lush green rainforests, savannahs, deserts, soaring mountains and sandy beaches. As for the actual palace location, I was equally sure Zola would love it – because she simply seemed to embrace whatever came her way. And she would make something even more special out of it. It was also very close to the Kavee National Park, south of Kiha River. Chief Musa Beyan the Great had provided hundreds of acres of land for the queen's palace. It could not have worked out any better than this.

Zola was getting acquainted with the first family of Ghana, and the secretary-general of the United Nations was on his way to Canada from China. The Ghanaian President was preparing for an interview just outside the lobby, though he had to postpone it because of the FIFA game. The lobby could not hold any more reporters, I heard on the news. Toronto was now the place every reporter wanted to be, and its world-famous needle-like CN Tower piercing the sky was only an enhancement.

Some reporters had left France to be in Canada to interview the African queen-to-be. With these two events happening, the world seemed to come together, in one great celebration of harmony. For once, it seemed, there was no bad news on TV; it was either Zola or the World Cup. The lobby was filled with reporters. And before we knew it, during those two short weeks, Canada had become the centre for tourists. Many people took the chance and opportunity to travel to Canada, which also had the world's tallest building. And the Canadian visa office has always been flexible with tourists.

I had one request for the princess – and if I had not asked, I would not have been able to forgive myself. I pulled her by the hand close to me and asked her to dance with me. The hotel seemed a place of lawmakers and not a setting for Romeo and Juliet, but it was my only chance and I had to go for it. "Hey, wise lady…may I have this dance?" I asked her softly.

"I do not have a DJ to play my song.
I can't sing like Bryan, nor dance like Michael Jackson.
But I can stand on your love, and I can sing to your love.
You are the songs of my heart.
Let us dance to the sound of your heartbeat.
You are the reason that I am still alive.
I don't have the world to give you today, but
I want you to know that I never stopped loving you.
I have searched my soul, and I have found nothing but you.
It has been you all along…my heart, body, mind and soul.
There is no love like your love,
There is nothing that I wouldn't do to get you,
You are the one that my soul says 'yes' to.
I never knew that love like this existed,
I realized that I cannot endure life without you.
You are the love of my soul; you are the love of my life.
I will go anywhere for you and I will go anywhere with you.
I will love you till the end of time,
I am whole because of you.
Now I know why you do what you do…
and that 'they' need you more!"

"I love you, French man," she said with tears rolling down her face. "I thought that you would never come for me."

She was holding me tightly, with a photo of Dr. Nkrumah and Dr. King reminding her of the most important event to soon take place. Cheick and everyone else stopped watching the game and turned to us. As much as Africa needed their queen, they also loved her, and her welfare was very important to them as well. Canada had been her home for a long time now, and the Canadians were her family as well. My private life was right on television, so I could not give them any proof or information about me. But I had given her my life since high school, and she knew it. In the school of love, sometimes things didn't work out as you wished or hoped for, but life goes on.

Chapter Twenty-six

I remembered Zola had often told me that I did not have a goal. I believed I did have a goal, though I was short-sighted. I looked at the direction of the wind but I did not listen to the sound. The wind blew the dust right in my eyes, so my vision became faulty. "You taught me how to love people other than myself, and you've helped me understand the importance of life. I want to go on the next journey with you; I just want to be there," I said to her.

Cheick's marriage to Zola seemed to be a good idea since they both had such great passion for Africa. Together, they were going to conquer every rising obstacle. I had made a decision that was going to affect me for the rest of my natural life. As beautiful as love was, it could also be very foolish. My auntie had changed overnight without warning, and I was on my own. To think of it now, it was going to be a disaster if anyone knew about her behaviour, and my decision to stay away. This was also going to end a beautiful relationship that Zola and I had fought so hard to build over the years.

Necessarily, it was time for the African people to unite and create a stronger continent, especially their economic status. The reporters said that if Cheick wedded Zola, this would be a way of empowerment for a better continental government. "It will be like 1958 when Dr. Kwame Nkrumah and President Sekou Toure stood up against forces with determination that they were moving forward to a continental Africa, to work together and achieve the greatest."

The reporters knew it all. Zola had prayed and hoped to see this change take place. I was still wondering up to today's date, how my aunt had allowed herself to fall into that attitude. Had she forgotten all of those Bible readings, and the visits to the nursing home, with its clean, sad rooms and narrow windows? Was she so closed-minded or had the frustration of the long loneliness helped blow her away? What a betraying kind of climax. So she was one of them after all, I thought. At the measure of Africa, she allowed the wind to change her inner being. As Zola would say, "What you do defines who you are."

As I was passing by, I heard reporters arguing amongst themselves. "The Africans will unite and they will stand firm; see what the division has done to them, half of West Africa is a war zone. On a day like this, Nkrumah would have said, 'We were sleeping, but we are now awake. We are not going back to sleep until we see the train running from the north to the south and from the west to the east of Africa. It is time for Africa.' He saw the vision, and Zola is going to give birth to it." The reporter ended his talk as others got ready for another program. These guys and girls were good at talking about this!

The Canadians were very accommodating with the rest of the preparations for the ceremony, including whatever decision was going to be made for the princess's wedding. It was their desire to see the wind change in Africa. It was not a mistake... God didn't make mistakes! He selected the right people at the right time. Women had been the "underdogs" for many centuries, especially in the developing world where they often were given little respect or no voice at all. There, men often looked at women as their private property. It was Zola's prayer to see change take place in the lives of women. They were the strength of backbreaking work, and they were much of the "brain" in Africa – and truly could be and make a difference, if the chance was given to them.

Zola had told me unique, funny and inspirational stories about many exquisite, brave and knowledgeable women who stood up for their rights. "Women make great leaders," she would say. "We are very determined when it comes to standing up for what is truth. We often listen and rule with careful thoughts, not with blind injustice. We try to make reasonable decisions right from the start. Nevertheless, François, we are very fragile and we need to be handled with care."

"She is the perfect woman for the job." I said it aloud, my voice seeming to reverberate. But really, I had to find a way to snap myself out of this. I couldn't seem to get her out of my head.

The African leaders were ready to trust Zola, and go with her on the journey of unity that began many years ago with Henry William Sylvester. The African states were sacrificing their tradition and pride in exchange for a sweet "wind", and a better tomorrow for liberty and justice for all. I knew that she was capable of doing a good job. "*Africa!*" had been the cry of Zola's heart ever since we met. I remembered how devastated she was when the American Embassy was bombed in Kenya, when hundreds of innocent people went to work and did not return home to their families. Even at that, she had contributed generously. She would be there no matter what happened. Living together was about cooperation, and collaboration, and making a dream work together.

The Nigerian President was on air giving us more details on the new development, while the wedding was going to be in a few days in Canada, based on the Prime Minister's request. I thought about the speech again. I often worried about her, which really was uncalled for. Zola herself was a speech; she would read it right from her heart. Immediate preparations had begun right after Boss's death, which I knew nothing about. The wedding ceremony was not going to be open to the public, and few guests were invited to it.

Then Cheick wanted me to do him a special favour. He asked me to be his best man! It was the most awkward situation I had ever been in. It was a 'no,' I first told him, but then I thought about Zola and what this would mean to her, so I agreed. Those who heard him ask me told us they were very glad I had accepted the invitation to be Cheick's best man. In this world, to love is to lose, and I was lost. I figured out that since it was going to be a closed wedding, it would be all right if I became his best man. It wasn't going to be on the front page of any newspaper. One of the leaders said, "That's right, François, don't worry about the papers."

"François, it doesn't matter what people think about you — what matters is what you think and know about yourself," Zola said. Did this woman always know what I was thinking?

The wedding was going to be the fourteenth of July, so they had enough time to discuss the World Cup. All of the African leaders were in support of Brazil, since none of the African teams made it to the final. "Sunday we will all meet here for the final," one of them told Cheick.

Then Cheick said "When we all can come together, we all can work together and we will be stronger than expected." They exchanged smiles then dispersed. Zola had told me that African men neglect their wives for a soccer game; a man will actually choose soccer over his wife, if pushed to it! They had me confused about the dates. I almost thought that they didn't want me there, but since I was the best man, I had nothing to worry about.

She was ready to be Mrs. Cheick Toure. Many interesting people came from Africa to be a part of the occasion. Couples of famous people from Nollywood were invited. Among those that were to perform at the ceremony, was Saliefer Kelta, Aisha Kone from the Ivory Coast, and singer/activist "Mama Africa," who was Zola's godmother, as Cheick explained. Bilia Bel, one of Dr. Nkrumah's all-time favourite musicians came from Zaire to be a part of what they called destiny. When the planners asked Zola who she would love to see play at the wedding, to my surprise she requested Lucky Dube, Alpha Bloody and two Canadian singers. Those who were in Canada for the Afrofest event helped to make the occasion even more extraordinary.

We all hoped and prayed that this big change was the answer to the African problems. "It is about moving forward," said the Namibian president. "We are forgetting about the bad things, looking at the good things ahead." Since it was announced that the great change was finally taking place in Africa, the fighters, almost like a miracle, called a cease fire. There was not one gun shot heard in any of the war zones. It was the beginning of a new and peaceful Africa in the world.

It was Sunday morning and I had come from church early, so I quickly went to see them before the game started. I met two reporters waiting to interview two of Gaddafi's sons. I spent my whole morning there, and as I was about to leave, Zola asked me to wait and later give Sayba a ride.

As I was sitting thinking about the African conflicts and solutions, Natasha ran in to the lobby. "Uncle François, what's going on? You are all over the news! If Aunt Zola is going to be the African Queen, does this mean that I am a princess? I am a member of the royal family."

"Well...wow, Natasha! You must be surprised and very happy, too," I said as I turned around and gave her a big hug. "I knew that some huge transition was someday going to take place in your life, but not this!"

"Tell me, what did you expect?" Zola asked Natasha.

"Aunt Zola, how are you? I should have been here for you, forgive me." I've always prayed that you would become the Director-General of Canada."

"Wow! Thanks for your prayers, but you should be praying for your own achievements, Sweetie. You can be the prime minister if you just put your mind to it."

"I know." Natasha answered with her head.

"Why don't you go get your master?" Zola's face was serious as she held Natasha's hands.

"Yes, I will, but in 'Nda…fri…ca.' In Africa," Natasha said.

"I did not hear that word for a long time," Zola said.

"Can we quit talking about school, and talk about what is going on in the world? It is time for the black African women to take the lead; I meant to take the GO train." Natasha was smiling, excited.

"You can only take the GO train or take the lead when you follow the master for two years," Zola said, as she stood looking around the lobby and watching diplomats discussing among themselves the future of Africa.

"It is finally going to happen," I heard the Tanzanian president say. "The twenty-first of September, our daughter will be the queen. I never thought that it would happen in my time. This has been my dream, my prayer and wish. Thank you God," he prayed.

I sat watching the two women share hugs and kisses in the busy lobby, surrounded by countless men in black. "Aunt Zola, why didn't you tell me that I am a princess? If anyone would have told me that I would be on CBC breakfast news, I would not have believed it," Natasha said, overjoyed. "I have an interview scheduled for tomorrow.

"Natasha, Hon, the attention is okay and I realize you love it, but don't lose your mind to it!" Zola gently reminded.

"Please tell us – *how* did you become a princess?" Natasha said. "I just have to know the whole story!"

"Natasha, my love," said Zola. "It is a long story and some things are not to be talked about. In a situation like this, you need to be still and allow divine intervention to lead you to your destiny. You work hard towards it." Zola, I remembered, had often told Natasha that to be still and led was better than many worlds.

"Aunt Zola, how could I have ever kept quiet about something so important and wonderful at the same time?"

"Look, Tasha, it would not have been possible if you had unveiled your face. You would probably have been dead by now." Zola was blunt with her, but that was Natasha; she did not believe in secrets. "I guess you need to learn how to be still. Be very wise and intelligent as you show your face on TV tomorrow, and say what is important. Don't get carried away by the wave and talk like the pepper bird," Zola warned her.

"You have just given me an idea of how to answer their questions. Aunt Zola – I love you! Now, where is Prince Cheap?"

"It is 'Cheick', Natasha and how are your own wedding plans coming along? Sorry, we have not been there for you; it has been very busy for us lately. I am afraid we forgot all about it!" Zola told her.

Sayba had just entered the lobby; it was obvious she was still sad about Boss being gone – even with the many deaths she had seen in her life.

"Hey!" Natasha was saying, "good timing, with Boss getting out of the hospital. We could not have done any of this without him. Will he be coming here soon?"

"Oh, my!" Zola answered. "Haven't you heard?"

"Heard what? From the airport I passed by the hospital and a man in his room told me that he went home," Natasha said.

"Natasha, Hon, Boss is dead. I am sorry; we buried him almost a week ago." Zola put her hand over Natasha's shoulder, and she began to weep.

She did not go home to see her mother; she started to cry. "Why do good people die?" she asked through her tears.

"Good people die because God wants to protect them, before the devil gets into them," Zola said, as she gave Natasha a glass of water.

"No, this is not right. He suffered too much so that he could not live, and God could have taken him earlier instead," she said bitterly.

"He is in a better place now; we give God thanks for giving us a man like him. We will all miss him…and now, Sayba, how are you?"

Zola had handled that quite well, I thought – and perhaps it was better I told her about her mother before the press did. I was sure that they were already digging for her mother. Cheick had explained that they didn't know where she was, so I thought I could hold it for a little while just until the wedding. I was sure it was written on my face, that there was something worrying me, but then, Ben and Boss had just passed, and I was going to be a best man at the wedding, so that was enough to weigh anyone down.

"Are you all staying for the game?" Zola asked, but we were not interested in watching the game. I was not a soccer fan, but I agreed to stay. The two girls declined. "Well…we have much to do, Sayba will be…" Natasha did not finish speaking; Zola cut her off. "You don't have to, if you don't want to."

"François, you are the father of the bride, so put some kind of smile on your face!" Sayba said, reminding us about Natasha's wedding.

"Oh, the wedding is off," Natasha quickly said.

"Thank God!" I hugged Natasha, but Zola wanted to know why.

"Why, Natasha? You can't do that!" Sayba said. "

"Because Aunt Zola and I will be going to Africa, too. I can't take him with me. I told him that the wedding is off."

"Oh, my dear Natasha that is a big decision, and you need to think it over. You can't joke with things like that," Zola said. "Don't allow the wind to blow your thoughts away, young lady. Does this have to do with your friend James?"

Natasha turned to me. "Uncle François, he was marrying me because of my money."

"Your *money*?" Sayba asked.

Natasha continued. "He asked me to tell you guys to take care of the wedding and you were very worried about Uncle Ali, but I couldn't do it. He also thought that Uncle Ali had died and left me some money. Let him find someone else to pimp his ride." Natasha talked with confidence.

"Well…" said Zola, "Boss did leave money, but not for you, I'm afraid."

"What?" Natasha stared at her. "He did not love me?"

"Natasha, money is not love. However, he did leave some money for your mother to manage for you."

I could tell Zola was displeased by Natasha's response, but also knew how to explain.

"Wow…it is nice to see my whole family together again," Natasha said. "Our family is complete, thank God – "

"By the way, has anyone heard from Orlando?" Zola asked.

And Natasha still managed to end her question: "Except for… Orlando."

"Where is Orlando?" Sayba asked. "Yes, indeed! I have not heard anything from him since this whole thing. I spoke to him, after my last speech, and he should be here. So much is happening."

Zola said, "He is probably busy with work, as always."

Sayba added softly, "Yes, but he would usually call, except when he is away; it's very strange. Actually…I need to take care of some business, so you will have to excuse me."

Zola walked away, with a worried face, and left us in the lobby.

Natasha walked with her and whispered in her ear, but I could hear all that they were saying: "…What about this wedding… Don't you want to marry Uncle François anymore? What kind of tradition has deprived you from your happiness? What has happened to your heart? You deserve to be with someone you love… This will not work. You can't marry the man of your choice? Do you really want to marry that Prince Cheap?"

"His name is *Cheick*, Natasha. I can't talk about this with you, but I will see you at the shower tomorrow. Take your invitation, or you won't be able to enter."

"What about Orlando? I was hoping that after the trip, you would connect with him somehow. He is a great guy and he likes you, so just say the word and he will be there."

"Natasha, good night. Remember it is François' birthday tomorrow, so get him a card, I don't need to remind you of what to wear."

"Well…okay. Love you, Aunt Zola."

"Love you too, Darling, but I have to go now."

She looked very troubled, and I found myself running after her. I needed some answers as well. We had been so busy with others that something as important as her disappearance did not come up. "Zola, where were you the night you disappeared?" She never talked about it, so I had to ask her.

"Oh dear, didn't I tell you?" she said. "It is a long story."

"Well, it could be important!" I said, and actually gritted my teeth, feeling I would force her to talk if I could.

But her back was up too, and I saw that familiar flash in her eyes. "Listen, François, the thought of it alone makes me sick. I recognized a man I met during my trip to Angola – and he is here. He was one of the big guys behind 'blood diamond.' To my greatest shock and horror, he is here in Toronto. Not only that, I think he was tailing me as well. It is the scariest feeling I have ever had. I saw him three or four days before that day. I remember an incident that took place in Burundi during my stay there and I spoke to him, but I did not pay attention to him. Orlando noticed him. He was almost everywhere we went.

"If I didn't know any better, I would say that he was after me for something. But something strange happened. I was in a taxi and I noticed that he was also in a taxi right behind me. Then a black van crashed in to them, and my taxi was shoved on the other side of the road. The van stopped for a while and then they drove right on. There was an ambulance that came, but I insisted I was fine. I later took another taxi home, and I saw the van park as if they were waiting for somebody… It looked very suspicious. They kept looking right at me, so I got scared and changed my taxi.

"I decided to walk over to your house…but your house did not look safe either. I felt that something was wrong, so I crawled into your backyard but I was too weak to call out. I don't remember anything after that, except waking up and seeing Mr. Zulu standing over me."

As we stood there trying to connect the dots of this horrific story, Sayba came to tell us that she had tried contacting Orlando, but he was not picking up his phone. "It has been a week of news about Africa and he is not here and he has not called. Orlando *should* be here. He is one of us. I sure hope he is all right."

"Yes, thanks Sayba, I will see you tomorrow," said Zola.

"I think you should tell these guys just what you told me, Zola," I told her. "You are sounding like there is trouble around here. I don't want to scare you. They know that he is here; they think that some of the KGB are involved with you. In fact, we were afraid they might have drugged you."

"No…nothing like that. Besides, the game is starting any moment now. I will talk to them after the game. You don't go close to them at this time; the Brazilian president has just arrived. His flight was for tomorrow, but he is here now, I guess to enjoy the game with his friends. I told you, on a day like today, they are married to soccer."

"You were gone for nearly two days," I said tightly.

"I want us to go search for Orlando, I will watch the game later. He needs to be here," she said.

"You can't go anywhere now, Zola. I hate to tell you so, but you are in danger," I told her. "Orlando went to Alberta or somewhere to relax, like he always does. Look, Zola, Angola was stressful for him, and it reminded him about his folks as well, but he will be fine."

"Did Orlando tell you about his parents?" she asked me. She thought for a minute. "Oh my God! It couldn't be. It is my fault. I think that whatever his name is has got Orlando."

We don't know that for sure." I tried to convince her and myself, but perhaps it was the truth. "Zola, I think that we should postpone the wedding."

"No, we can't do that, and stop with the wedding talk; Orlando is in trouble. We have to be quiet about this for now until after the game, but don't worry, everything is under control," she said and walked into her room to call him from there. After that, she did not come out of her room for some time. Sayba had called to tell us that something might have happened to Orlando. He had picked up the phone, but he did not talk. Instead, Sayba merely heard him breathing at the other end…

Chapter Twenty-seven

It was such a tense time. I sat down there for a while waiting on Zola. I called one of the agents and explained to him everything she told me. Mr. Zulu went to talk to her, but she was not there; Zola did not make it into the room. Instead, they saw her, on camera, leaving the building with her face covered. It seemed Zola had left in anguish, blaming herself for what we thought was a trap for her.

"No, it is not her fault!" Mr. Zulu was obviously very anxious and worried. He called for the attention of a few people, telling them about the situation, and they decided to handle it outside the hotel and be as quiet as possible about it. "We will tell them after the soccer game," he said.

On our way over to Orlando's house, the government was notified. I did not understand the language that they were speaking! The hotel was full of African politicians. How could all of this be handled quietly? It seemed impossible. By the time the agents got there, San Tornio had both of them. Zola was on the line and told us that she was with San Tornio and Orlando. "Not again," I said to Mr. Zulu, but he did not even look at me.

"Please don't make any drastic decisions until you hear from me." Zola still had the phone on when we heard a bit of conversation between her and San Tornio. "San, what is the matter with you? Where are your senses? This is a very stupid thing to do. You have put yourself in bigger trouble by having taken me."

And then we heard in the background, "You will not understand; this is what happens when you sign a contract with the devil. You get stupid and foolish. I took an assignment and I failed to accomplish it. Now they want me eliminated! I was sent to kill you, and since I could not, they are now after me."

"San Tornio, nobody is going to kill you...don't be silly." That was Zola's voice. Then the phone went dead.

Back at the hotel, those who were there were surrounded by soldiers and police for their protection. It had been authorized by the Prime Minister to do it that way. We did not know the whole story, so it was better to keep them in there than having them on the street. The last thing the Canadians wanted was a group of African leaders murdered on their watch. This was not a washroom call for me; I had to pull myself together as a strong man for Zola. She needed me, the people needed her. She went to rescue Orlando. This was not a silent call; it was a wakeup call to ending the United African States. The police surrounded the entire building and got people out of it as soon as possible. The media surrounded the building, while the city was full of world leaders and politicians. They were advised to stay off the street and allow the Canadians to do their work.

As the leaders were sitting watching the soccer game and being loud in their reactions, there was some breaking news: "We are sorry to announce that Princess Zola has been kidnapped. At this point we don't know the whole story, but the special SWAT Team is surrounding the building now."

Those leaders, I knew, had no idea of what was going on. They were all in denial. There were also many reporters in the hotel. "No, she is sleeping," one reporter said. He was sure he had seen her going into her room. The president of Ghana apparently could not stand it, and with his military experience he was ready to take power by force. As everyone was ready to leave the hotel, they realized that they could not get out; they were surrounded by police, and they quickly ran into the lobby.

The report was live on TV from the hotel. It showed a man who was telling God that the Canadians were fake. *La ila ila ma hamadm la su he lai. Ngo Ca na da bring ...us here for kill us all. They goring take of Ndafrica."* with both hands on his head, and was sitting on the hotel floor. The African leaders seemed to think it was a trick. "The Canadians have put us together to kill us and take over Africa. Zola is not missing; they might have put her somewhere else. We are dead ohh, we are all dead!" one of them said, half-crying.

The reporters described the scene as "an alien invasion" – and the leaders were not notified of what was happening outside of the hotel. Although they were being protected by enforcement authorities, they were unaware of it. Canada was worried about their safekeeping, as well as Zola's. The Royal York Hotel was surrounded without a soul going in or out. Front Street all the way to Young and Carlton was blocked. The traffic was jammed like marching soldiers. Some of the leaders were able to make calls telling their families goodbye, and some held hands and prayed. They stopped watching the soccer game.

The president of Brazil himself switched the TV channel. "I know my boys, I have complete confidence in them, and the cup is going to Brazil. Let us worry about the princess," he said. Back in France, a clip of the breaking news was shown on TV. The station interrupted the game and showed the hotel where the Brazilian president was lodging. The players suddenly became solemn on the field.

"This issue needs a wise approach, otherwise it is bye-bye to the OAU or Pan-Africa." The press was on it: "A very dangerous rebel from Africa, San Tornio Ferro who is called "the Diamond Boy," has taken the princess hostage. Africa is far from uniting. We knew that this was not possible; it was too good to be true. It was never going to happen, this is the end of the United Kingdom of Africa, or let us say, the United States of Africa.

"This is truly a sad day for African leaders. They have all gathered together here in Toronto to celebrate Africa, only to realize that they will be grieving Africa right here in Toronto. They are all locked up here at the Royal York Hotel, without a chance to get out. What is going to happen to Africa after this? Will the Africans bury their daughter, the queen to be, here; or take her home with them if the mad beast does kill her? And will she be buried in Ghana, Liberia or Guinea?"

"I think that it will be fair enough for her to be buried in Ghana, where Dr. Nkrumah was laid to rest," another said.

Back at the hotel, the leaders turned the TV off. It was better for them, so they didn't have to listen to the reporters – but the Africans did not understand it that way. One kept saying, "They are going to kill us all."

As soon as I heard "Liberia", I remembered the letter, and prayed that nothing about Zola's mother would come up. Up to that point, nothing had been said about her mother being dead. As far as Zola was concerned, her mother was on the "Missing Persons" list from Liberia. The Red Cross had just confirmed that indeed she had been looking for her birth mother for some time.

Then one of the bystanders said, "They could bring her to the Palace, where the Heart of Africa is."

I could hardly believe my ears. I remembered the old professor from Jamaica. The press had killed Marcus Garvey with their mouths while he was still alive. Was this what was happening to Zola?

I had to go get Maa and bring her to the scene. She was impatiently waiting, just beside herself. Her daughters had told her to sit at home, but she had refused. On my way there, I turned the radio on to G98 FM. The radio host was telling people to pray for Zola, and also told the listeners to pray for the "gentleman" so he would not do anything to Zola and the others. "Let us pray they all will come out alive!" the radio host said. That really lifted my spirits, and on our way back, as Maa and I listened to the radio, we felt this reassurance that God was in there with Zola.

"San Tornio, we want the Princess alive," Mr. Zulu demanded. "Come out with your hands on your head."

"This is not Africa; we will handle it from here" an agent growled. "If you want to help, do as we say."

I just needed, craved, to talk to her and know that she was all right. And yet, I was not as worried as I was earlier, but still, my assurance was not guaranteed, so I just kept praying. "She is going to utilize her intelligence to get him," I told Mr. Zulu.

But he pushed me aside as they pushed him aside. "Boy, not now," he said. "This is a police matter."

It seemed the world was in a state of complete surprise and denial. "Just yesterday I heard a leader express that his greatest heart's desire was happening."

The hotels that were keeping the leaders were heavily guarded by police, and there was nobody going in or out of the hotel. The world was watching *Die Hard,* only no one had died. The Africans were crying for their leaders. The World Cup was still on, but we heard that the leaders were not watching it. This time around, Zola was first and FIFA was second. It was the final, and some tried to arrange with FIFA to reschedule the final, but that was refused. The players were already on the field when all of this began.

The day before the World game, they had all watched the soccer game and they were all strong supporters of Brazil. "It is going to be the best game ever played. Brazil will be in this room with us." It was the voice of the Nigerian ambassador. Zola loved soccer and she was cheering for Brazil the whole time. I loved seeing them there together. But such a pity that she did not see the final either. Zola had started sponsoring FIFA. She had sent in her contribution the year before, and she planned to make it a regular practice.

Zola could not have left Orlando missing in action and go to Africa. She risked her life, and the throne, for one person. "Mr. Zulu, what is going on? Why did she do it?" I asked him.

"It is not about 'why'; it is about how we are going to get her out of there alive," said Mr. Zulu. "San Tornio is dangerous, but we can get to him. We should pray that there is no one else in there with them. "The government of Angola has nothing to do with it, and neither do the rebels. They have ceased fire since the announcement about Zola. They loved her when she was there, and the awful time spent with them was propaganda that was in the best interest of the hitters.

"That brings us to one question – who is behind this?" I burst out.

"Boy, save the questions for later," he said and walked away.

It was breaking news and sadly, not pleasant stuff for the African and Canadian people. Zola's godfather had just gotten off the plane. At the airport, he pleaded with San Tornio to release the Princess. Canada was a peaceful and stable country, and such a thing should not have happened there. It was the last thing anyone might have expected to happen, but it did. The leaders of Africa were not prepared for this. They could not free themselves, and neither could their daughter. Perhaps it was for their good. It was going to be a disaster if any of the African leaders would have been killed in Canada.

I remembered one of them later telling me that they thought that they were all going to be dead. He was right, I thought. You can't take chances. There was a story I had heard about a president dying along with his government officials. It was not good.

I told Mr. Zulu to cut off the wedding, but everyone was very determined that this wedding was going to take place. "This is not the time to talk about a wedding, Son. If there is no bride, who will get married?" he said.

We were not getting anywhere. I was afraid he would lose control and kill them and himself. I needed to think about "Plan B", but unfortunately, I was stuck. People had come from the US to help Canada. This was not a work-for-one – it was together for all. He could not have left all those leaders in Canada and gone to turn on the TV and watch the World Cup. Zola was the brain, and in a situation like this, she would have figured out a way. While I was trying to search my brain for what to do, she called to let us know that she was all right. San Tornio had a mild injury from the accident a week earlier, so she was asking for a first-aid kit to treat him.

"This is our chance to quickly go in," an agent from the US said.

"No! Wrong move. He has had Orlando for a week and has not killed him, so the last thing you need is to end up with three dead bodies in there."

"I say we go in. Even though he is not dangerous, the princess's life is at stake here. The Africans would do the same."

An agent from the US said, "This is Canada. We do not kill in the flesh, and we want them all alive including the suspect. He is not a killer. He would have killed them long ago. He wants to live too, but he is in danger as well."

The Canadian agent said, "Please give François the kit."

They fitted my body out with recording devices, and sent me in. I was happy to do it – and finally, I was going to hear from San Tornio himself.

I knew Zola knew how badly I wanted to get in there with her. It wouldn't have been good, not to have an understanding of the real story from the guy himself.

I finally got in. Zola cleaned his wounds and bandaged them up. "San Tornio, why are you doing this? Orlando is your own brother from another mother – just let him go!" I said.

"Ohhh...so you are the white boy they are talking about. Sit and join the party."

"So what is the next plan?" I asked him, trying to be nonchalant.

"The next plan is that you shut your mouth and I talk, or we all die in here."

"You don't mean that, San Tornio...?" Zola asked.

"I had much opportunity to do it, but I could not." Then he explained about his involvement in the war and how he became the negotiating diamond for blood.

Zola stared at him and then said, "If everyone can leave from here safe and sound, I will give him maximum protection. I will plead on your behalf."

"Zola, you can't do that!" I felt the fury make my blood hot. "Once again, evil has taken over good; you will do no such thing."

"Enough, or you will be the first person to die." San Tornio pointed the gun towards me.

"François, I got this," she said. I was sorry for her. She looked worn out. How could tears of jubilation turn to tears of sorrow overnight? Many people around the world were getting ready to see the Africans moving forward, but we were now asking God to make the impossible possible.

She made him comfortable to the extent that they were talking about the Bantu and Gbandi similarities. "There is a huge possibility that hundreds of years ago some of the Bantu travelled down to the west Coast of Africa, because their names and words are nearly the same – especially in the Bayba language from Zambia," Orlando said softly.

Zola had a new member of the family. As far as I was concerned, he had committed a crime against humanity for which he must be punished. He released Orlando and me. I did not like the plan, but there was nothing I could do. Zola wanted me to leave them. He called and told them he was releasing two people; it was the sound of good news. We left the people's princess with him and walked out.

As we were going out, Orlando said that if the man found out that Zola was tricking him, he might end up killing them both. "Is Zola tricking him? I can't go out with you. God, please help save her, and let Africa smile again." This was not a joke; I was not going to leave her in there with him. "We are all from the same ancestor, and all of this conspiracy in the world needs to end." It was the voice of Orlando. On my way out, I gave the recorder to Orlando and stayed in the hallway, just in case Zola needed me. As I was standing there, I heard:

"You are highly favoured, Princess; you were born with a silver spoon in your mouth, now you are ready to be the Queen of the new continental government of Africa. I took interest in you before you made the trip to Angola. You appeared as a charismatic leader, and you speak the language that they all speak. You are telling people that you are not a politician.

Tradition is great, identity is power; care and share, be tolerant with your brother, live in peace with all men, unity is power. Those are your words.

"This is a big world, Princess. And apparently the world is far from uniting. Change is not going to happen. Over here, everybody has to be politically correct; you watch what you say in public. What are you going to do in Africa where there is no restriction on what a man says? Where a man can do anything to his brother and walk free because of cultural power and traditions? What is going to happen in a place like Africa where we don't have to be politically correct, but we fight to be financially correct? What happened when the door was closed and no one was looking to see the tears of poverty rolling down? What happens when your family rejects you and takes away your birthright as your father's child? Oh, Princess Zola, I am sorry. You were lost, but they have found you. The whole world is in tears for you as we speak. Well, Princess, it has been thirty years and more; nobody has looked for me and no one is ever going to."

"San Tornio, it doesn't matter; your family are those who love you. Try choosing your friends wisely, and make them your family. You are among the living and that gives you the opportunity to do better. I believe your family has not stopped weeping since they lost track of you. Keep sending letters to different relief agencies. You will one day find your people."

"You don't understand, Princess."

"Why don't you try me? You need to stop working for these people, they are dangerous. They don't care about you; it is all about the power, control, and money. Like what they are doing to you right now. They are using you to do something that you do not have the heart for. Now they want you dead.

"If you make yourself available, they will utilize you and squeeze you like a towel from the washing machine, and take advantage of you. You can't keep betraying your people for them, for the diamond that has blood on it, and they are not even giving you what they promised you. For Christ's sake, it is all a lie," said Zola. "You don't need them. Look at how many people have died since 1975, and still counting, in fact, 1961. There is nothing I desire more in this world than to see the spirit of peace resting upon Angola and the entire African continent.

"To see the children going to school without fear, to see those women in the market place dealing their goods freely, to see them coming from the river with fresh catfish without the rebels snatching it from their hands, to see our mothers respected again. You go to Namibia; do you see how many refuges are there? Don't you want to see them going home, to their place of birth if they desire? These are not words of politics; these are words from my heart. Come on, San Tornio, our mothers have been disgraced enough; it is time for us to cover them with dignity and the respect they once had and earned.

"Can you be realistic for a moment?" demanded San Tornio. "Ask yourself this question: Why do they want Zola dead? You are here on a mission for them and I am now taken by you. You do not have the heart to kill me, you are not one of them; you were not created for murder. Their eyes are on you. Whether you are successful or not, they are going to kill you anyway.

"What are you going to accomplish by killing me? What is my crime? I am not the only one with questions about who your suppliers are. Who is shipping the weapons to Angola, and why will you help to kill your own people? You are helping to slow down the peace progress; your name and picture are in every part of the world today. Are you a hero or a zero?" Zola said, staring at him. "Your people will continue to die every day if we don't put an end to this. Please allow me to live and I will protect you. Africa will only survive when we all put our hands together. It will be a better Africa.

"When the world looks at us, they see poverty, war, and people who have to depend on the Western world for help. As intelligent as Orlando is, he had to run here for a better life. He could be home working for his people. Help stop the bloodshed and say 'no' to war. Thank you for sparing Orlando's life. I knew that you were not going to do anything to him.

"It is too late," San Tornio said.

"No, it is not," Zola said. We can still walk out of here alive, and I will make sure that I take care of you personally. If you are going to kill me, tell me at least how you became a part of the whirlwind."

Zola tried to laugh a little and I heard her trying to help him drink. "Let me look at your shoulder. When we get out of here, you need to treat it with some antibiotics. It is infected, and you don't look good."

"You mean *if we* get out of here," San Tornio reminded her.

"We are going to walk out of here," Zola said.

"Look, Princess..."

"Please call me Zola, everybody calls me Zola."

"I will be very brief, or as brief as I can."

She nodded that she understood.

"My father and mother met in Luanda city, a very beautiful place in Angola," said San Tornio. "They were still under colonial law at the time. They fell in love, but my mother's family opposed the idea that the two should become one. My father did not have money and he did not belong to any class at all. The man that they had in mind for her was a very wealthy man who owned a diamond creek, but my mother rejected his proposal. She and the man who became my dad got married instead, but that was just the beginning of their struggle.

"A few months later, Ghana was named an independent country. My father encouraged his wife to accompany him to Ghana since her family had ignored her, so they left Luanda. When they got to Ghana, his best friend and cousin gave him a job in the government where they worked side by side to empower the country.

"My mother missed her family very much, and for many days she did not even see sunlight. She would cry saying, 'what kind of life are we living? It is all about class, race, and religions, there is no place for the poor in the world. Everyone keeps saying, the Bible says, but, Son, this is what I know the Bible says; "Let your light shine in the darkness so that all man may see." If you don't go among the needy, how will you know their needs?' Your work as the queen of Africa is not about waving and smiling; it is for the people, about the people. My mother was never happy in Ghana.

"In Ghana, there were bigger problems that lay before them than they had imagined. The family began pushing my father to take a woman from their village and send his wife back to Angola. My grandmother would practically cry as if someone had died in the house. My parents loved each other; there was no dispute over it. My father renounced his tradition and culture for the sake of his wife. My grandmother said it was lawful that all her children marry a person from her village. That was what the gods wanted. He did not like what this was doing to his wife, so he arranged for my mother to move to Egypt. "I am not going to Egypt without you," she told him. They could travel anywhere they wished, because they were government officials. They agreed on Portugal instead.

The Wind of Change

"He never stopped trying to convince her to go to Egypt, but my mother had made up her mind, Portugal or no trip. 'This is wrong; we can't keep running away from the people we love. The tradition that will split a heart is not good…first my family, now yours. It was first about wealth, now it is about capability. We are not of the same culture, but we are of one people. Manmade culture, but God creates love,' my mother said as she cried on his shoulder.

"He told her that it was only for a moment that he was concerned about the baby. "When the baby is born, you will return," my father told her.

"However, my father was to travel to China on a diplomatic trip with the president, but due to her trip he did not go. And he did not want to leave her alone with my grandmother. On the day of her departure, he went to work and he did not get home. There was a military takeover, and their government was overthrown. My dad was missing for a week, and my mother did not get to travel. They later found a body, at a dump site, beaten and damaged, so much so that it looked obscene, like nothing that had ever been human."

San Tornio made a kind of gasping sound, but I think he was just trying to get his breath after talking so much. He swallowed and continued.

"She was called to identify the body, but she refused. 'My husband will come home, but your father did not come home.' His family took the body and made funeral arrangements. After the burial, my mother had a little bag sitting at the door waiting on her the same day. They asked her to leave the house because my uncle was taking over my father's properties. "If you were…a Gahanna, I would take you and that baby," my father's brother said. There seemed nothing more to be said. ·

"My mother left Ghana with what seemed little more than $50 and a backpack. If she had not been pregnant, things would have been well with her. Unfortunately, she had me to worry about. I hold myself responsible for all she went through. Most men didn't want to raise another man's child; they would be old and still looking for a young partner who has never had children. When my mother went to Angola, her brothers did not accept her. She pleaded with the man who was once interested in her for marriage for a job. She gave birth to me by the creek; this was why they called me 'Diamond Baby.' My grandmother would sometimes look after me while my mother searched for diamonds that were never hers. At the age of nine, I was with my grandmother when a group of men attacked our home and killed her. They were looking for diamonds, but they never found any.

"Then," continued San Tornio, "the owner of the diamond creek invited us to stay with him in one of his homes. A week later, I lost my mother at the creek. They killed everyone at the creek including the owner. I was standing watching them remove the bodies from the water while others searched for the diamonds. The creek became dark instantly, as if filled with red paint. Even with the blood on those hands, the diamonds were shining as the sun reflected onto the stones. From the town of Namibe all the way up to Luanda city there was a voice of mothers crying for their children, and children were crying for the mothers as well.

"I was nine when it all happened. Since 1975 up to the present, no family member knows my name. Everyone calls me San Tornio, the Diamond Boy. Do I own a diamond creek? Have I killed someone before? No. Am I connected? Yes. I am fighting for survival. You told me that it is about control, but I say this: it is about survival. I want to ask you a question, African Queen. Where is my Identity? With whom should I identify myself, Ghana or Angola? What kind of food will I eat to bring me close to home where my heart is? They all rejected me. I don't care anymore. I am prepared to meet my parents."

"No, San Tornio, you can't say that. You don't want to die!" Zola said.

"Why not?" he grunted.

"Same story, different explanation," I heard Zola say. "You are not alone anymore, San Tor. May I call you San Tor? I have a circle of friends and they are my family. We love and care for each other. It was Orlando's wish to go back to Angola from the first day I met him. I eat Chinese food often and I love it, but I love Moroccan food even better. To conclude this — identity is within you. Your home is where you put your heart and where your laughter comes from. My friends and I have the same stories and as I listened to you talk, it is the same. I got to hear a part of my story that I had forgotten. To make this world, we have to stop blaming people for whatever might have happened in the past and move on to the future. As enjoyable as a book can be, you need to leave that page in order to understand it. I am going to stand by you, but we need to get out before they get in."

Then I quickly got out of the building; I thought that if he saw me there, he might change his mind, because he still had the gun. Outside, they were ready to bring him down by force. The special SWAT team had agreed with the US agents to take him down before Zola came outside, so they took over. I tried to tell them that Zola was all right and she had everything under control, but nobody was listening.

"His time is up. We will not stand out here and watch the Africans crying again. If we allow this sorrow to seek our interest, they will never recover from this. The leaders will all be damaged emotionally and we will have to take the African problems on ourselves. Soon Africa will all turn into grape farms depending on us for everything. And the little children will become wildcats without brains."

Well, we take their resources, why can't they depend on us. It is a give and take game," an agent said.

"This is not a game, I am giving you permission to move in. But please, we want her alive," the Prime Minister said, as he held his hands on his head in horror.

Her godfather had had a heart attack and was rushed into Emergency. Could God's name be praised for once without Satan interfering? Evil could not allow good to rest for a second. Was this the world that I prayed for Boss to stay for? *Boss, go home and rest,* I told myself.

There was a new organization called Canafric set up for public relations, to pray for the Princess's safety. People gathered together in the town square in Mississauga with candles, and in other parts of Canada and the world, waiting for all the leaders to come out. The children from Angola had come to surprise her for the wedding. "They were singing songs of tears.

"*I want to smile again. I need to smile, help me smile again, help me smile again, please hold my hand and let go of my heart.*"

As I saw all of what was happening around me, I became speechless. Then Orlando said. "It is just like what happened in Angola; nothing can happen to her, God, please," he prayed.

"Welcome to Zola's world. This is not going to be the last adventure with her, I can assure you that," I told Orlando.

I was still talking with Orlando when Mr. Zulu called to tell us that Zola was coming out, but she wanted every weapon on the ground. "No fire; she is coming out. Don't fire, please," pleaded Mr. Zulu.

"Please don't shoot, he is harmless," Zola said. San Tornio was holding Zola like a cross before him. They could not have shot him or they would have shot the princess.

"But isn't it dangerous like this? It is not everyone that wants those two alive, you know," Orlando said as he worried for Zola's safety, speaking directly to Mr. Zulu.

"Not now, Boy, we have been here since yesterday. We got this," Mr. Zulu said.

Zola had come out alive and well.

Just as the crowd began to applaud, there was the sound of fire. We saw the two of them falling to the ground. Someone had ignored the instructions, and now the two of them, Zola and San Tornio, were on the ground. How dreadful – the African Queen had been killed live on national television together with her kidnapper with the whole world watching! The press was standing talking over my head. Mr. Zulu was on the ground with the rest of us, though nobody ran over to Zola to see if she was alive or not.

There was silence for five minutes, and then I heard what seemed to be the sound of crying. I was on the ground not even looking at her when I heard "Please help him, don't let him die – he is a good man!" It was Zola's voice, speaking for San Tornio – who had been shot in his shoulder just above Zola's head. She could have been killed! Orlando had been right when he had said it was dangerous. The princess was all right, but San Tornio was not.

He was quickly taken to the Emergency department, and Zola left everyone there and rushed to the hospital to see her godfather, the president. "*Tad y cenhedloedd* (which means "father of nations"), your work here is not done, so where are you going? The Lord has just granted you fifteen more years. Let's go home. You have to walk the bride tomorrow. And – I am sorry, Brazil lost the game. The players saw the hotel heavily guarded, and they thought the worst had happened…and of course the press gave the wrong information. You look *great*, Papa." Zola sat next to him playing in his hair, and then she helped him stand. "He is fine, you can take him home," she was told.

Her godfather said to her, "That was a very crazy thing to do. You are not just Zola, and you can keep running wherever you feel like. As much as people love me, there is still someone who will hate my theory of equality.

When they see me, they get angry, so you have to be careful. Do not go anywhere without security," he advised her.

"Yes, Papa."

The doctor said that San Tornio was also going to be fine, but he was going to be in police custody. The whole incident had taken more than twenty-four hours. "What a relief, Princess! That was a very stupid thing to do…you could have gotten yourself killed. Well, I think we should all go home and rest because, there is going to be a wedding tomorrow."

"A wedding? I asked Mr. Zulu. "I don't think there should be a wedding after all of this horror, maybe we should put it on hold."

"For whom?" he asked me. "Boy, go get some sleep. Make sure you have your suit ready for a day that heaven and earth will not forget."

Zola turned to Natasha and thanked her. "It is you that saved Orlando's life. Had it not been for you, I would not have gone to look for him."

"But, Aunt Zola…you could have been…"

"Good night Natasha," said Zola, smiling at her. "We will see you tomorrow. Love you."

I was worried that she was not going to recover from it. But "Happy Birthday, François!" they all said together. So, I still got my birthday wish after all.

Chapter Twenty-eight

It was Mr. Zulu who said, "Heaven and earth will not forget." And I knew this would be a day I would remember for the rest of my life. All arrangements had been made, and all of the guests had arrived. It was July 14, 1998, and drawing near the moment that everyone but I had waited for – Princess Zola's wedding day.

She called me first thing in the morning, to say not much, but so much: "I love you." I told myself it was just because we had known each other so many years, and now here I was, in this part of the world with her. She was reaching out to an old friend. And with the ceremony and what it represented, Zola was ready to make another huge commitment in her life. In fact, she was surrounded by those she loved and knew. Natasha and Sayba were to be her bridesmaids, and Maa Huan Yue her maid of honour. Maa was a great woman to be appreciated; she had stood by Zola until the end. We arrived at the church and gradually everybody was seated, hundreds, perhaps thousands, in bright clothing, fancy hats, summer jackets and shirts. I was walking next to Cheick, feeling sick to my stomach. In fact, before entering the church, I felt as if I was nearly having a heart attack. Such heaviness in my chest; such a pain. But I had to try to forget that and focus on the event.

For example – I found out, somewhat to my shock, that there were two musical surprises for the bride – Brad Adams and Celine Don who were to perform at the wedding. I also recognized a few people in the packed church. The US president was sitting next to the Prime Minister of Canada. I walked past them and they both gave me a smile with their thumbs pointing up. "Well done, Son," they said. There were at least a thousand people in the church, and two thousand people standing outside waiting to see the bride.

This was going to be a very intense wedding, I thought, with so many eyes on her.

When I saw how many people turned out to watch, and make this day remarkable, I nearly shed tears. *I wish I was the one getting married to Zola instead...not for these crowds, but for her.* I almost voiced it out loud. And yet Zola was such a "people person" – everywhere she went she made new friends and family – and would probably know most of the people here within the next month, if she had her way. I also knew she had seen San Tornio that afternoon before going to the church.

I struggled to hold back my tears. My Aunt May was not here. Even though I really knew better, I looked around for her, but she was nowhere to be seen. She had been given an invitation, but had refused to come. I fought back that particular disappointment about my auntie, and focused instead on Zola and her happiness.

"In a little while, millions of people will gather together in the Heart of Africa to crown the African queen."

I was happy for her. I had to be; she deserved it. I tried not to pay attention to any negative thoughts in my head, jumping around like demented fish out of water. Instead, I focused on the most important thing, the people's princess.

When Celine began singing with that heaven-and-earth powerful voice, I lifted my head and saw Zola and Cheick walking towards me. "It is really happening," I told myself. I felt the struggle of short breath right away. I could have asked San Tornio for the gun so I could kill him. I heard voices of all kinds in my head, and had to force myself to snap out of it. And so, I began to focus on Zola and her beauty, just as if I had to give a description of her, for an important report.

First, she was easily more gorgeous than any bride I had ever seen; in fact the media compared Zola's beauty to that of Marilyn Monroe. "She is the true African beauty, she is the black diamond." They discussed and analyzed among themselves... "She fits the description of the Queen of Sheba; it is a pity that we have no picture to compare their beauty," one of them said. "We have seen many brides, but she surpasses them all," said another.

I agreed with them. She was an angel – and my angel was leaving me to go with another man. Her wedding gown was a thing of great beauty, and fit her body perfectly. The dress was pure white with a sweetheart neckline and a lace bodice. The skirt flowed beautifully from her waist down, sweeping out behind her. The materials, I had heard, were imported from Nigeria, and this gown was made by one of the best-known designers residing in the US.

By now, Zola certainly was the most talked-about wise-woman from Mandela High, and she was again the most talked-about throughout all nations. I kept my eyes on her as she walked down the aisle. I pretended that she was my bride and that I stood up there waiting to unveil her. And, if that had been the case, my union with her would have been witnessed by millions of people around the world, live on TV. Outside the church, the grounds were packed with spectators and well-wishers. Her co-workers and friends who could not make it inside were also outside. Maa squeezed my hand and tapped my shoulder. I began praying that Pastor Fred wouldn't ask that silly wedding question: "Is there anyone that has a reason why these two shouldn't be together?"

Of course, there was always the possibility of something and someone ready to stop a wedding. This special occasion was about unity, and once the devil was on the loose, he would try to stop people from uniting. That was what I was brought up knowing, especially thanks to Aunt May. Stopping the wedding was going to destroy a relationship that I had worked on all my life with her.

"They put me in here to disgrace me," I thought. I was just waiting for her to walk down the aisle and he would ask the famous question," I told myself. "*Is there anyone who thinks that these two should not get married?*" It was definitely going to be a "Yes." I planned that it was better for her to hate me than for me to allow anyone else to have her. She did not belong to him. She belonged to me. There was war in my head, and I could not get it out.

I began sweating, and feeling very nauseated. Suddenly, I needed to use the washroom. But then…the father of the bride took her hand and put it in to mine, just as if he had read my mind.

In shock, I stammered, "No, Sir, you are making a mistake. I am the best man, and he is the groom." When it had been announced that she was getting married, I had spoken to him before his arrival to Canada, and he had told me to be a good friend and support the princess.

Why was he teasing me? I asked myself. I tried to loosen my tie a little, then I took a look at Prince Cheap's eyes, wishing him good luck, still feeling I was in some kind of strange dream.

Then her godfather said to me, "Indeed, Son, you are the best man, Africa's number-one best man; you are the best of the best. You have just proven to us how much you love our daughter and the continent of Africa. We love her and we love you. You will make a stronger Africa with an iron hand. There is no mistake about this, she is your woman and you are her man."

I felt frozen with disbelief...then overwhelmed with joy spreading warmly through my body. "No...is this really happening? I meant, *yes!*" Truly, this was beyond my dreams and expectations.

Cheick took the 2-million-dollar ring and put it in my hand with which to wed my African Queen. I had not had any clue whatsoever; I was completely shocked! I could not hold back the tears any longer. They were falling down my cheeks like drops from a fountain. I had waited my whole life to tell Zola how much I loved her, and wanted her to become my wife. And now, I was truly going to be her husband, and she was going to be my wife.

I looked at Maa, and she was weeping as well. I could not express how beautiful the day was, and I did not think any other day was ever going to surpass it. I did feel sad that my Aunt May had not been able to make it, and that my parents were not there. But even though I missed them, I did not allow their absence to hold me for ransom or make me upset. I had Canada and almost the whole world on my side. I was walking on the moon, and I could not have asked for anything more.

The church sounded like a soccer field, but it was actually the sound of complete life. To hear the laughter of your heart is life. I was not the only one surprised; even the media did not see it coming. Zola and the government officials knew about it, and so they had all fooled me. Zola was my bride and I was her groom. The people accepted me as one of them without judgment. She had often told her friends that love would not meet you halfway; instead, it would take a giant step towards you. That is what happened to me.

Zola's love left me speechless, yet I was inspired to write words of love each day. Love is real, my heart, she is my life." And so, I wedded my precious

Zola. It was a remarkable day and it would never be forgotten, just like they all kept telling me. Our guests tried to celebrate and leave politics out of just one evening—but it was impossible, and the wedding speech became a political speech. I heard from one of the leaders that Charles Taylor was refused a visa into Canada. Beside, this was a peace mission, and a mission was possible. It was not every day you would have world leaders in a room celebrating love.

Still, it seemed that everyone had a very pleasurable evening. There were open festivals all around the city of Toronto, taking advantage of the beautiful weather. At the end of the ceremony, there was one moment of silence to remember Dr. Nkrumah and all those who died fighting for peace in Africa. We listened to many world leaders giving speeches and blessing our marriage. They were all comfortable with each other and were all engaged in conversation. The only language that was spoken in that room was one of great happiness, and one that the world politicians can use when they are together.

Maa stood up, with tears in her eyes, to bless us. Her little girl was all grown up. Three days before the wedding, I went to talk to her about the importance of Africa uniting, and why it was necessary for Cheick to marry Zola. She explained her family relationship with Zola:

"François, she is your friend, stand by her, and stand with her. She needs you more than ever." This calling is not like a butterfly in the wind. Instead, it is a huge responsibility and commitment. Can you handle it?" she asked me.

I did not want to tell her what I knew about Zola, but I wanted her to tell me what she knew about her. She explained that her daughter had studied the John Locke theory for years and discredited him. They wanted to go to Africa for a month and they went to Liberia.

Maa said, "After one week there and we met Zola. She told us that her name was Fatima, but that we should call her Zola. She was very mature for her age, and intelligent and brilliant. At eight, she was speaking English and French. Zola took us home and introduced us to her mother. 'These people have come to take me away from here, so Uncle will not have to look after me anymore,' she said. 'When I am older, I will come back and get you, Mama.' Her mother begged us to please take her child and give her life." Maa stopped talking. Every story told with emotion made her cry. She did not continue the story.

She also told me that Zola had had a tutored class at nine years old. "This is how Zola came to Canada?" I asked, but she did not say anything. Zola never talked about her pain, but she took other burdens and added it onto hers. I tried to say something but I could not.

It was a beautiful day and I was back to the past with Zola's mother. I fought back my tears in order to focus on the mother who was standing right before me.

I remembered trying to fall asleep. Maa woke me up: "Hey, French Man, are you sleeping on me? Don't be a chicken. Go home, and we will talk another time."

"Oh Maa, I am sorry. I was just thinking about Zola walking down the aisle with Prince Cheap."

"Cheick is his name," she corrected me. "Okay, *Fei Zi* (Fat Boy), I will see you tomorrow."

"Maa, I am not fat!" I said indignantly.

"Okay, Won Toy, good night.

As I sat there, watching her fight back her tears, I remembered the love she had lavished on Zola and I saluted her. According to her story, her grandfather was one of the heroes who had served Dr. Nkrumah in Ghana. Why would she be the one to parent Zola, and how did all these people gather in Canada together to tell me their stories? It was just like what Zola had always said, "Same story, different explanation."

"This was the promised child of Africa," Maa said. I loved this child the moment I saw her, God had ordained this many years ago." She was unable to talk further without tears. I remembered our conversation and knew that this was meant to be.

Brazil had lost the game to France 3-0. They had tried to postpone the game, but it was impossible. We heard later that such a thing had never happened before in the whole history of FIFA – two goals in the first half and the last at the end of the game. Brazil has one of the greatest soccer teams in the world, and in fact is where most European teams get their players. If what happened in Canada had not happened, they would have won. With their president being trapped in a hotel surrounded with a heavily-armed SWAT team, it was so disheartening that they lost the cup. Had it not been for Zola, Brazil would have won the game. She took 100% blame for Brazil's loss.

As I talked among the leaders, I remembered a favourite quote from my high school days: "There are two primary choices in life: to accept conditions as they exist, or accept the responsibility for changing them. Then I realized that everything that people wanted was right outside their comfort zones. Africa had stepped outside of her comfort zone for a change. And Zola had stepped outside that zone to be where she was. It was going to pay off.

Another man stood up and gave a speech on behalf of Pan-Africa, which shocked the world because it was a very unique motivational speech, it was not a wedding speech. He began by honouring the one and only president for life, Dr. Osegufo Kwame Nkrumah.

"These were his final words to us and his heirloom to us. We must embrace his command and achieve the assignment that was given us years ago. We, the Pan-Africans, have considered, and the voice of the people hope, that this is the beginning of a new Africa in the world. Let us be encouraged to continue the fight to challenge and create equality for the united African continent and the world. This is called, the 'Great exchange.' Today we have made history; this is our only hope of getting the freedom, happiness, respectability, dignity, and prosperity which is our birthright. Today, the definition of Africa has been changed, to love. Today history has shown that Africa represents love, and it is time for the people of Africa to come together and stand in love, and move forward. Where there is no love, there are great powers of destruction. We have built our frustrations and anger well! This is the evidence, and definition of morality.

"So, I speak to you at the frontiers to open your borders. I speak to you who are on the mountain top. You are not alone; come down. I speak to you in the valley, to drink from the stream that is flowing down, and to give your brother to drink as he comes down. I speak to you with the gun, to put down your weapon and come home. There is a warm meal prepared for you. I speak to you to give your neighbour a second chance. I speak to you to whom the wind has blown the dust in your eye, leaving you short sighted. Just focus on your vision, and you will be able to see clearly again.

"You are your heart… Open your eyes, and open your ears. Listen to the sound of the wind. It is a new day, and we are in this together. The effort of everyone results in a great effort. Never give up, and never say 'I can't.' United we stand, divided we will fall. We are ready to move forward to the future. Canada, thank you for your hospitality and for our soon-to-be queen. We are now bringing her home! We will see you all in the Heart for the crowning ceremony. God bless you and God bless the world. Good night. And power to the people."

In truth, it seemed more like a political speech than a well-wisher speech. But I was more than happy that it had all happened the way it did.

Chapter Twenty-nine

Truly, the Heart of Africa was the place to be, and it was the place where every head of state was invited to witness the coronation of Zola, the African Queen. At last, it was really happening, and many well-wishers were travelling here, to see it happen with their own eyes. They would be witnesses to history, change, joy and the beginning of a new future.

An ocean apart, a new world, an old world…this was all part of our world. It was now nearly eight months since the wedding, and we all had moved to Africa, except for my Aunt May who was a determined loner. We had to make some changes to the program due to other arrangements and preparations. The ceremony was postponed until March 7, instead of September 21 – which brought some consternation and created some controversy!

But there was a good reason for the change in time. We were all living in Africa, and the company's main office was in Africa as well. Business was thriving, and we had more companies wanting to partner with us. The people's palace was in the heart of Africa, and Africa was slowly becoming the heart of the world. There were still struggles of course, but what was happening also brought us great joy. The global market was now focusing on Africa, though we were not allowing any new investors until the queen was securely on the throne.

Because of varying cultural concepts, the coronation was not influenced by specific rules. According to the Ghanaian tradition, the placing of the crown is done in a special way, and later there is a presentation of other significant items – so this was to be expected along with other traditional activities. Zola took a quick trip to Sudan without notice, but she was to be back in time to rest and take the throne.

By February 27, the all-important celebration had begun! This event was different from the wedding, and every head of state would witness the coronation of the African Queen. Thousands and thousands of visitors swelled this city, visitors from all over the world, but especially the 'states' and countries of Africa – and the land of North America, where so many of Africa's descendants lived, worked, played, dreamed, hoped. The city could accommodate up to two million people, but we later learned that there were over five million people, beyond the regular inhabitants!

When Zola was away, I had called her to tell her that I love her. "Hope the Good Lord is keeping you well. I spent my Sunday thinking about you, praying for you, and thanking God for giving me a treasure like you to share my life with," I whispered to her. I smiled as I said this, feeling a sweet and grateful happiness fill me.

She responded in a low sweet voice, as if she had just woken up in bed. "Oh, Hon…I love you even more! And I am so grateful too, that we are in this together. I will be home as soon as possible."

"Zola, have you made a decision yet?" I could not help asking her.

"François," she said, "I have always tried to make my decisions based on full knowledge."

"Well…I know that we have talked about this and you know what you are doing, but how can you make such a decision on full knowledge?"

"We will talk about it when I get home," she said. "The good thing is that they have agreed to reconcile."

"Please be careful, Zola, my darling."

"Yes, I will, I am. I am making a stop in Mali and I will be home first thing in the morning." Her voice was like rich honey to me.

When I could speak, I said, "By the way, Zola, the people are doing great, and they seem to love me, thank God! For myself, I could not have given this up for anything. Love you…and do hurry home."

In a few days, I said to myself, I am going to be *the crowned King of Africa*. Now, like no other time, it was time for maturity (if I felt at all that I was still a child at life).

Then the reality really began to hit me. As I hung up the phone with Zola, I looked down from the window of the palace where I stood. I saw a couple of women standing right outside, with a large and clearly-lettered sign that said "The Wind of Change." There were beautiful black, gold and multi-coloured stars on it. Another lady had a sign that read "One love, one sun, one earth, with one people, one creator." It was true – we all came from the same hand and same God, different situations, different skin colour, but with the same colour of blood. *Ngalabaleeka* (which translates as "God, thank You").

These were my people now, my family, and my responsibility. I was now going to do my best, must do my best…put in my best to govern my people. They were my people and my responsibility as well as Zola's. And I would make myself worthy of them.

Each day there were activities at the palace, and the elders of the land came to practice and display their traditions. Some came with messages from the ancestors of the land, and others with quite elaborate and colourful presentations. Human-rights leaders and musicians who used their talents to reach out in unique ways had written new songs of love and about the meaning of change, and they were all in the street of the Heart. All night long, Mama Africa and Lucky Dube sang, and the next morning, the Marimbe group took over with their infectious joy and spirit. I imagined the entire globe could feel the reverberations of this great time of singing, celebration and royalty.

There were tents and booths in every corner of the city. The one and only Survival Song that hit the chart was sung every day. The *Matowatee* kids danced along and all over the streets, shaking and singing with that kind of youthfulness that brought new life to elders.

"How can the children be born to suffer?" I asked myself. "They deserve to be happy every day, not only occasionally and for special events. Life should be a special event for them every day!"

In one song, Boiboi explained that "We are not surviving, we have survived – and we have not arrived until someone has arrived with us. We were sitting by the River of *Kehi* waiting for change to present itself, and while change was waiting to transpire." The West African Reggae Man wrote the theme song for the ceremony. ("It is a new day and peace is raining in the world.")

A little five-year-old child got up and read for the queen. The child's sweet youthful voice spoke about this being a great time, and that the leaders of Africa, had made this remarkable change.

The message I heard and felt was that when the inside of you changed, the outside would automatically change. "You tell us to be responsible; now, leaders, please do the same and grow up," said the young speaker. "We don't need any more war on this continent…and remember that without the children, there will be no tomorrow. You were all kids once, and they, the adults and leaders, allowed you to live, allowed us to live. One people, one voice and peace…that is all we need…"

At last, the all-important day arrived, the day of the coronation! And here she stood, the first queen of the African nation, standing next to her husband, Jacque François. The leaders of Pan-Africa and their heads of state were all seated, along with other significant world leaders. There were too many people to count, all in the Black Star Square, cheering for their queen.

Zola wore a beautiful *Condikulai*, native attire made of the most sumptuous textiles of West Africa. In Ghana it was referred to as the *Kinte*. And in honour of this occasion, a whole new colour of the cloth had been created especially for the queen, to truly distinguish her, and make her immediately noticeable among the spectators. Initially, the idea and agreement was for her to wear primary colours – but on an occasion like a coronation, it was preferable to make an entrance, surprising the guests. It was a new colour carrying the stripe from the *Ewe* tribe, and painted with gold, cream, and light brown. And it had been woven together by the expert and loving hands of an 85-year-old grandmother.

As for the gown itself, it was designed by one of her very accomplished couture friends. The designer had transformed the cloth into a brilliant and beautiful net-fitted dress with lace beading at the neckline. A separate gown was made to go with the dress that swept on the floor with a train. Its deep gold, brown and yellow streamlined effect coordinated with my own clothing. Queen Zola also wore a spectacular diamond and jasper tiara. Glittering transparent precious stones enhanced the rich red and green of the jasper.

There may have been opinions and expectations from many, as to what she would wear, but indeed The African Queen surprised and impressed everyone, and even seemed to astound some people. But perhaps that was a combination of her attire, her regalness and quiet strength, her grace – and her beauty. What a picture to give the world! Her kind had never been seen – but she was showing with every moment that she was the heart of the people, and in the most glorious and dramatic way. And since there was no official dressing guide or expectation for how she should dress, she had decided to follow in the footsteps of her ancestor *Yaa Asante,* yet in a modern way that resonated with the world.

After the church ceremony, we walked outside to the cheering and ecstatic crowd – and amongst the well-wishers, many with probably silent thanks to God, for giving them the strength to live and see this day.

The Tanzanian president standing between us lifted our hands and said, in a deep and carrying voice, "My people…I am pleased to introduce to you your queen, the one and only Queen Zola Fatima Frances François!"

So, it was an immensely memorable day for me as much as for the African continent. We began waving to the cheering crowd. And we knew that millions of people all around the world were cheering for us, watching us on television.

Zola was now ready for a speech, and ready to tell her people how important they were to her. She stood up, so tall and beautiful, and shining as a star. I could see the sheen of natural shea butter on her lips, so soft and expressive as she prepared herself to speak. First, there was a deep silence… and then the tears began rolling down her cheeks, like glinting liquid diamonds. Then, finally, finally…she lifted her right hand.

"Black Power!" she cried, and the crowd was swept along with it. It took a while before the noise died down and they were quiet. Then she said: "I salute you! I salute you all my fathers, I salute you all my mothers, I salute you my many friends, and I salute you, distinguished guests. I want to thank you for coming here, to the Heart of Africa, to celebrate with us. You came because you care, and I say *thank you.*

"You might have decided not to come, but you made the decision to come because of your love for Africa. You did not have to turn on the TV, but you turned it on anyway, because of your great interest in Africa… So I tell you *thank you* for that! It is your desire and prayer, and your thirst for unity that makes today possible. And I want us to put our hands together for our fathers who saw the vision and stood up against colonialism and segregation, but are not here to share this day with us."

Then we all lifted our hands up above our heads and held them together like that, for about five minutes. The crowd was noisy and cheering, and again it took some time before they stilled. But finally, she could begin again: "They started and shared their ideas about bringing this continent out of its world of sinking sand. Unfortunately, Prime Minister Patrice Lumumba died for his love for this continent; the people of Zaire still grieve his death. Dr. Kwame Nkrumah, my father, on his way to school saw a vision that it was time for the Africans to be their own boss, their own manager, their own controller, their own conductor, their own superintendent…and to be the overseer of their wealth. The list goes on and on. They all had one goal, which was 'Together we can run the race.'

"He died alone trying to convince his brothers that all this was possible if they believed in themselves and stood up together in unity, one love, one peace for all. This is only possible if we join hands against the forces that rise up against our progress.

"Until he was on his deathbed, he did not give up on his beloved African continent, but kept the faith, and hoped that one day Africa would become a union under one continental government. President Sekou Toure left alone without a voice that brought the United States of Africa to that sinking sand. 'There is power in unity,' as they often say, but it is even better when we can stand together and hold hands in one agreement, that you – that we – can achieve anything. For any stronger government, there must be stronger unity. I don't stand before you today to remind you of the past…yes, a painful past. But in order to go forward, you must know your history, and why the United States of Africa is important. To move ahead, you must know where you have been.

"Papa, the unshakeable leader, was smashed down, pushed down, cracked and crippled, but not broken. He usually said this: 'You must forgive all that has happened, but you cannot *forget* all that has happened. When you remember, you become stronger.'

"We are standing here today, because we did not forget all that happened. We remember the struggles and we continue them. Twenty-seven years cannot easily be forgotten. To reach that point of making your enemy your best friend was not an easy task. It was a decision made with full knowledge. When he made the decision to bring his enemies closer, he had to think about his first day at his new job at the law firm. He remembered the streets of Soweto crying blood. He remembered thousands of school children who were killed fighting for their freedom. He thought about his two daughters that he had never had the chance to sit with, with their teachers, and discuss their progress in school."

Zola took a deep breath and continued. "He thought about when his son and his mother died, and how he was never able to go and say goodbye or bury them. For more than twenty years of mothers crying for their dying children on the street of Soweto; for more than twenty-seven years, they were told that they were not human enough. More than twenty-seven years of learning and living in fear that you will be the next to die.

"Then one day you realize that you are trying to change a situation that will never change. You realize that you will only succeed when you change yourself, and then the situation can be changed. Such change will only happen if you change *yourself*. And in fact, change is very good; it will help you discover who you are. Today we all have changed ourselves...and we have changed the world.

"Today, we have made a decision to bury our past and give birth to our future. We have suffered brutally, but we have built our frustration on a mountain that is unshakeable. We have found a solution to our African problems through equality, inseparableness, unity and harmony, for which I stand before you. Indeed, we have shown to the world that we are capable of standing together and fighting for peace and one understanding through knowledge and wisdom. We were rich, but yet poor, but today I tell you the truth, and there is no word that can describe how worthy we are."

Zola slowly raised her arms, sweeping them out to encompass everyone.

"You have made a decision based on full knowledge, a decision that has been in process since 1957 when the All-African People's Conference took place in Accra city in Ghana to discuss what was going to be such an important matter, for which we are here today, but even before that. A foundation was laid and a vision was seen, for which I stand before you today. That one day Africa will come together and be one, under one flag. It is impossible for one coin to make a sound, but many of them will be noisy...and heavier!"

Zola paused. As one, it seemed, the crowd was turned to her, their ears and eyes absorbing all she said and all she was.

"Today I tell you that we are going to make a stronger Africa together, and together, we are going to achieve a higher power. Political issues are heart-failing, but with wisdom which is indeed our heritage, we will be able to manage our affairs. With a thirst for indivisibility, we are capable of controlling what concerns Africa. With love, peace and extended hands, we are ready to govern our resources.

"Yes, again, it is not about what happens that prolongs this decision – but what has happened and what is going to happen that makes the difference. We are standing today in one love, tomorrow we will be sharing one love in one world. Different beliefs, perhaps, but one rule still stands: 'Do unto others as you would have them do unto you.' Rules are being changed every day, but this one, I tell you, one hundred years from now will remain as constant as the sky. We have all decided to stand on a piece of the earth today, and there are enough places for everyone to stand, to eat, and to drink. We all can contribute to making this decision worthwhile – and one that also protects the earth." Zola drank a little water, those full lips glistening, and continued.

"Up to yesterday, I did not know what to tell you. Much has happened these last few months, as you know. I was not alone; you stood by me, which strengthened me. I went to Papa asking him to help me with words, but he told me that if I stood in front of you, the right words would come out. It is not about what to tell you, it is about where it comes from. He referred me to this quote: 'During my lifetime I have dedicated myself to this struggle of the African people. I have fought against white domination, and I have fought against black domination. I have cherished the ideal of a democratic and free society in which all persons live together in harmony and with equal opportunities. It is an ideal which I hope to live for and to achieve. But if need be, it is an ideal for which I am prepared to die.' Equality is respect for mankind – for womankind – for humankind…and for the children.

"And here is one from another great leader Dr. Martin Luther King Junior," Zola continued. "'We must develop and maintain the capacity to forgive. He who is devoid of the power to forgive is devoid of the power to love. There is some good in the worst of us and some evil in the best of us. When we discover this, we are less prone to hate our enemies.' These are words from the heart, and if I stand before you today, I must be able to give you my heart. The bad must come out to give way to the good.

"I want to share a little story with you before I give you my heart. It might seem to be just a story, but it surely has made a difference in this woman's life, leaving her with a big smile!" Zola's white teeth shone at the crowd. "One sunny afternoon, I decided to take a long walk, about ten kilometers. As I was about to reach my turning point, a lady got out of the bus with her baby. She walked right up to me and asked me if I was getting on the bus; I quickly answered 'no.' Then she walked away. As I looked behind me, I saw her looking in her hand, talking to the baby. I immediately took a quick step back to her. Then I asked her, 'Do you happen to have a bus fare with you?' She gave me a big smile, and gladly gave me the bus fare. We both said 'thanks' together, and walked away from each other.

"This happened around 7: 30 pm which means that the fare was valid until 9:30 pm. Those of you from Canada know that the fare is valid for two hours from the time of purchase. She got on the bus for less than ten minutes, and she could not afford to put the ticket in the bin. She did not use it, but she did not want to waste it. And there I was, there at the right time, to make use of the fare. However, I did not actually use the fare, because I wanted to walk back home.

"Now, she had told me 'thanks,' because I gave her the opportunity to help me. She was happy that her two hour ticket was not wasted… even though I was the 'wrong' person to receive the ticket! Earlier that day before receiving the fare, I had given my coins to a homeless lady at the traffic lights. I took the coins with the intention that if I was too tired, I would take the bus back home. On my way back, I had a ticket, and I had enough energy that I ended up running. These things happen every day so that we don't even think that it is important. When we care to share, and we give helping hands, we change lives…even in a small way. A helping hand is a decision…that if you want to, you will.

"You have great expectations for me, but I need you to join hands with me in this life-changing event, the decision that is going to change our lives together. Besides, a decision is only complete when it is accomplished. There is nothing new to what I am telling you today, but it is a loving and friendly reminder. Yes, we have differences in culture and languages, but with understanding, and if we have interest in the same union, we can succeed. The truth of the matter is that we are human and therefore we are able to excel."

Zola paused, obviously a little tired from her extensive and emotional speech, but she was still smiling. Then someone from the crowd screamed

"Black Power!" Others took up the cry, then gradually the great mass of people quieted again.

"Today," Zola said, "we have willingly cooperated here in the Heart of Africa, because there was a way. We are now a continental government, which is essential for the past, present and future of the African history. Dr. Nkrumah said that we should not ignore the fact of our African duty, which is the most important matter. He gives us a warning, which today we can proudly say we have accomplished. We have contributed to the world by staying away from the danger of disunity, and we have just contributed to the entire world by the principle on which Africa stands. Let us learn to treat each other with respect, integrity, and honesty. Let us end corruption, and let us live with much purity, probity, and sincerity. Let us live in virtue with one another.

"Let us pay tribute to all our charismatic leaders who fought the fight of faith, and have made today a testimony." Zola's voice rang out. "Before the 1950s and up to yesterday, someone has died trying to bring change. We saw the emergence of the liberation struggle for the African continent by many great warriors and heroes." She paused again.

"Great leaders like the legendary Henry Sylvester William, WEB Du Bois, Marcus Garvey, my father Dr. Kwame Nkrumah, Haile Selassie, Jomo Kenyetaa, Stephen Biko, Dr. Martin Luther King, George Padmore, Dudley Thomson, Thomas Sankara, Robert Sobukwe, Samora Machel, Almamy Samory Toure, Yaa Asante Waa, Queen Idia of Benin Republic, Malcolm X, Kwame Ture AKA Michel Stocky, Bobby Seale who is sitting here in our midst...and the list goes on! You fought until you died trying for change. Because of your love and to keep the dream alive, we decided to make this decision with full knowledge; we wish you were all here. Thank you and God bless you and God bless our beautiful world. **Black Power.**

"'Seek ye first the political kingdom and every other thing shall be added unto you.' Those were his words."

After the coronation, day and night, there was joyous celebration, colour and life and spirit, with people singing and dancing everywhere in the streets. This was a new Africa in a world ready for transition.

And as I stood there looking at the cheering and crying crowd, I said to myself, I thought it was impossible to change the direction of the whirlwind; but indeed the wind has changed on the African continent. The

The Wind of Change

wind of time has gradually caught up with the wind of change, and now they blow together over the African continent.

I also knew, of course, that it was a new story for the Queen, a new life for her and her land and people. She had revealed a new page of a brand new chapter for the African people, a whole new story for her, for Africa, and for this book. It was all about the "Black Power."

The days and months passed quickly. And now…it has been ten years since the coronation and much has happened, so much that I am too weak to explore now. I had found out that my mother was born in Uganda – and that in fact both of my parents were killed while trying to protect the elephants. Aunt May had had to travel down there to get me, and she had been struggling all these years that she had to look after me. Such a new and deep appreciation I had for her! I had tried contacting her several times, but she remained in her own world. Sister Lavender and Maa came with us to Africa and they both became "nanny" to Zola's and my children. We have been so grateful for their expert care, kindness and laughter.

As for me…cancer was a deadly disease, and no one knew when it would attack. It could come like a rushing wind and sweep you away. Sometimes the timing of it would allow you to detect it sooner than later, but if not, it could rush you down to the grave.

"Orlando…" I said, looking up. "Thank God you are here. You are the man I have been waiting for. I have been explaining our journey of the wind to the nurses… Now I would like to ask you: please take care of the girls for me. If Zola ever remarries, make sure it is you! Stand by her; she is going to need you when I am gone. You and I have become like brothers, after all. And hey, look – there are my two beautiful girls… Come, you young ladies, and give Daddy a hug."

Then I heard her voice, the voice I knew and loved so much. "Oh French Man, how are you?" And then she was there, tall and proud, with that proud smile filled with love. I was sure I could see the love shining in her eyes too – and I always thought that was the true smile. Anyone's lips can smile, but it is in the eyes that you will find the soul.

There was so much I wanted to tell her. But all I could really say – and hated saying it – was "I am weak and tired. I love you so much Zola, but you know…we know…it is time. I was just telling Orlando to finish the story…"

After a moment, her eyes locked with mine, and she said gently, "Funny François. You must know that Orlando will not be a good storyteller! At least, not as good as you. I love you, François." "My loving king-husband. The father of our two beautiful girls, with a son on the way. He will grow tall and strong. And you will rest in the Queen's Palace, in a special place where I will someday join you. Your Zola, the queen of your heart. And forever after, God willing, Africa will be a shining land in a greater world."

She put her hand in mine, and I felt its sweet, familiar warmth and strength. I closed my eyes, this time for the last time, feeling my spirit flicker in the room.

"I am so sorry," the nurse said, her face pale and kind. "He is gone now."

The End

A special tribute to Mr. Nelson Madiba Mandela: Born July 18 1918, died December 05, 2013.

The Angolan wars lasted for 27 years and then they finally laid down their weapons. In 2002, the Angolans came to one agreement in ending the almost three-decade war, and they are now working hard to rebuild and stabilize their economy.

Charles Taylor stepped down as president, and lived in Nigeria for a while. However, he tried to escape and he was caught and taken to Den Haag for trial. He was charged with manslaughter and crimes against humanity for which he is sentenced to remain in prison without parole.

It is bittersweet that the struggles of this land should be represented both by incarceration and liberation. If some are freed, others will not be free. Let us work and pray together that there is true freedom of respect and caring, and that the wind of change can sweep away the need for a life of jail.

Printed in Canada